SHAFTER

SEEDS AMONG THE STARS
BOOK I

MARGARET MCGAFFEY FISK

TTO
PUBLISHING

Cover Design by Deranged Doctor Design
www.derangeddoctordesign.com

TTO Publishing logo design by Blue Harvest Creative
www.blueharvestcreative.com

Custom scene break by ddb Design
i-ddb.com

Shafter

Published by
TTO Publishing

ISBN-10: 1-63139-001-5
ISBN-13: 978-1-63139-001-2

First Print Edition, Second Printing

Visit the author at:
Website: www.margaretmcgaffeyfisk.com
Twitter: @Marfisk
Google Plus: +MargaretMcGaffeyFiskAuthor
Facebook: MargaretMcGaffeyFisk

PRAISE FOR THE BOOKS OF
MARGARET MCGAFFEY FISK

SHAFTER

"Trina's life revolves around protecting her family and as a shafter, the lowest of Ceric society, her choices are limited to what she can steal. However, a chance at a new life aboard a colony-bound ship teaches her a new way of life and the price of unquestioned loyalty in this exciting tale, rich with cultural world building and science fiction adventure. This is a story you'll love, with a tale you won't want to see end!"
— Lazette Gifford, author of *Glory* —

"While the heroine yearns for another world, you'll crave any universe, any tale, created by this exciting new speculative fiction author. In Shafter, McGaffey Fisk delivers an inter-planetary colony system and populates it with complex and sympathetic characters. Travel from the tunnels of Ceric to the stars beyond with a master thief and her master storyteller."
— Valerie Comer, author of *Majai's Fury* —

SECRETS

"Through her young heroine and hero, the author breathes life into a curious, exciting and often dangerous world of steam, sail, sentient machines, loyal friendships and deeds of quiet bravery undertaken in the face of widespread fear and bigotry, to deliver a clever, entertaining and unique new take on Victorian Steampunk."
— David Bridger, author of *A Flight of Thieves* (*Sky Ships*) —

OTHER WORKS BY
MARGARET MCGAFFEY FISK

SEEDS AMONG THE STARS
(science fiction adventure)

Trainee

Apprentice

The Captain's Chair (Indie Traders short story)

THE STEAMSHIP CHRONICLES
(steampunk adventure)

Safe Haven

Secrets

Threats

Gifts

Box Set 1 (Books 1-3)

UNCOMMON LORDS AND LADIES
(sweet regency romances)

Beneath the Mask

A Country Masquerade

An Innocent Secret

SHORT STORIES (eBook only)

Forged

War Child

Curve of Her Claw (illustrated by Star Olsen)

Visit margaretmcgaffeyfisk.com for more information about these and other titles

C oins sounded faintly as Trina dropped the purse on the metal table, their noise dampened by a scarf she'd twisted between them. Fence, the shafter big man, paid a good sum for what she could steal from the polit houses up in the sun, enough to feed them and pay for Mother's medicine.

Trina turned to smile at her sister, but her expression faded when she met Katie's gaze.

Her sister's round face bore lines from fatigue. Even her curls, carrot-red to Trina's blond, hung lank. Dark shadows gave her translucent skin an almost haunted cast. For a moment, Trina saw a reflection of Big Man Fence in her sister's pale features. Neither he nor Katie ever left the tunnels below First City.

Without smiling, her sister took the pouch and spilled its contents on the table, shaking the coins free of the scarf. "Twelve silvers, a half silver and three copper?" If anything, her haunted look deepened. "What did you do? How did you get the money?"

Trina felt her jaw tighten but forced the muscles to relax under her sister's pleading look. "It's from the find I told you about. I got the necklace and some earrings. Bargained well for them too." She could not keep the pride from her voice after beating Fence at his own game.

"Nothing more?"

Trina pulled Katie into a tight hug. "Nothing more. The necklace held pure gems. Almost had to walk away from Fence to get a good deal." She launched into the tale of her latest encounter with the trader, trying her best to make it amusing.

Katie didn't need another excuse to worry. Trina could manage Fence as long as Katie watched over their mother.

"I could work. Like Mother did. I already bring in some when I sell my patchwork blankets."

Trina choked on the next part of her story, but her sister ignored the sound as she continued, "Then you wouldn't have to go out on the surface, and especially not into polit houses. It's too dangerous. You could stay with Mother, and I'd go do nursing in one of the shafter hostels. They'd never know Mother was part of the experiments."

"Mother needs you."

Trina left no room for argument, but Katie argued anyway. "You can watch her as well as I can. We'd do okay. Like before Mother fell sick. You wouldn't have to take chances. You'd be safe."

Trina jerked away. She walked to the back wall, tracing her fingers along the embedded tunnel map that hung beneath their timekeeper as she often did. "Mother kept us on the remains of what our father left her and you know it. No shafter would work with a victim of the experiments. Besides, shafter jobs don't pay enough to cover her meds." She looked away, unable to face her sister when she'd deliberately kept the costs hidden.

"How much?" The strangled words sounded forced as they passed Katie's lips.

Trina gave her head a mute shake.

"I need to know. You tell me everything or I'll go seek a job. You'll have to choose between abandoning Mother and thieving. Maybe you enjoy it too much."

Trina stared at the wall as she answered, "Nine silvers."

Her sister sank to the floor as if shock removed the ability to support her limbs. "Nine silvers," she repeated blindly. "So much."

Trina wrapped thin arms around Katie's stout form, rocking her sister back and forth. "Hush. It'll be okay. I'll make it okay."

Their mother had called Trina "My Protector" and she swore to live up to the name.

Katie swiveled and pulled Trina into her arms, as though she were the one needing comfort. "It *will* be okay," she promised, tears tightening her voice. "We'll make it work somehow. We always do."

TRINA KNEW KATIE HADN'T wanted her to leave so quickly, but Mother needed the medicine and that meant a trip back to the surface.

She peered through the tiny opening and blinked against the bright sunlight before she could check for anyone in the alleyway. Though going to a surface apothecary was dangerous, shafters believed any who were foolish enough to be trapped by polits deserved what they got. Shafter doctors wouldn't treat those who escaped the experiments because the scientists poisoned their subjects with fatal viruses, and no shafter wanted to risk infection.

The apothecary Trina went to charged a steep price, but she didn't hide behind fancy lies. She was honest about their mother's state.

If their polit father had stayed true to his promise, their mother would have been treated by the best of doctors with no thought to the cost. Instead, the tales about him had no more substance than the fairy dust in the books he'd left behind. His money ran out, and their mother bartered as many of the books as she could with Fence, who liked to collect polit treasures even though he couldn't read. Then, when all but the most battered books were gone, Trina took up stealing to feed her family and keep their mother alive.

She wriggled free, stopping long enough to dust her clothes and rub the fabric over her face so she could pretend to come from one of the buildings. Once metal worms raced between the cities, carrying the polits and laborers. Now only shafters came from below, a world nestled in the bones of ancient times.

When reasonably clean, Trina could still pass for a child thanks to her slight build instead of being marked a shafter.

She glanced at the sun, surprised to see it hanging so low in the sky. She'd lost more time to arguing with Katie than she'd expected. If enforcers caught her, the extra coin would not keep Katie for long.

Trina could speak like a surface dweller and so might be able to convince the patrol they had the wrong person, but she didn't want to test that theory. Her father taught Mother to read and use proper speech before leaving on a colony ship with the promise to send for her. The twins would have been born into the protected life of a polit had he claimed her from the start. As it was, he didn't even know his daughters existed, but their mother had spent every moment she could spare preparing them for when their father's courier arrived. She'd believed that he would send for them until she became too sick to care.

Trina crossed the path and entered a side street, weaving in and out of the crowd without brushing or bumping anyone. Her smallest knife remained stowed despite the tempting items dangling a quick swipe away from her hands. She needed the medicine. Anything else just distracted from her purpose, thoughts of her father worst of all.

The deep blue doors of the shop rose before her. A traditional mortar and pestle symbol hung above the window, the sign that brought fear to her mother's eyes when pressed on medicine bottles. The experiments may have ended years ago, but the disease kept those memories fresh.

Trina knocked once, twice, then waited three breaths before rapping her knuckles three times in quick succession. Their secret signal. The apothecary would only open the door to her if no one else stood within. Though Trina felt exposed out on the street, it held many opportunities for escape. Inside the store, she'd be an easier target.

The door swung open, its well-oiled hinges whispering against each other.

"I wondered when you'd get here. You are leaving it quite late, aren't you?"

She followed the older woman into the darkened shop, happy when the door closed and its bulk protected her from prying eyes. "I came when I could. Last batch's almost gone."

"You're lucky I put the ingredients aside for you. My polit customers like that medication, but you deserve it more." The apothecary grimaced, pushing dark brown curls away from her face and revealing features better suited for joy than the mixture of guilt and pity they held.

"I came when I could," Trina repeated stubbornly, placing her empty bottle on the counter. She tried not to give anything away, but the apothecary made it hard with her kind interest. Trina had already revealed her name even though she didn't know what the apothecary was called. Laborers, like polits, had nonsense names. Shafters—real shafters at least—earned their names like her friend Piper whose metal pipe proved so effective as a weapon.

"Go have some crackers. I'm afraid I already ate the cheese, but it's something. It will take me a little time to mix the potion. Go." She made a shooing gesture, waving Trina toward the table.

Trina nibbled cracker after cracker, waiting until they softened in her mouth before sending them down her dry throat. She tried to make the treat last, but her stomach pressed against her spine.

The rhythmic sound of the pestle grinding the ingredients for her mother's potion lulled Trina into a thoughtful state. She'd long grown used to the apothecary's muttering, the subject always the same.

"Some cully root and betline. Not much to offer as penance for what they did."

The noise stopped for a moment, and Trina looked up.

"She'd better not miss a day. A body can't fight when overwhelmed, enhanced immune system or not. You're much too young to be on your own. Keep her strong. It's all you can do."

Trina nodded, not bothering to reveal her true age of almost fifteen, or that her mother had been bedridden for more than three years now. The medicine kept some of the pain away, but it offered no cure. Maybe it would have if she'd found the apothecary in the beginning, but Piper hadn't taught her how to navigate the surface back then.

She slipped another cracker into her mouth as the pounding started up again, but coughed when it dusted her throat.

"Get yourself a drink from the flask over there. It's berry juice. The one you like so much." The woman spoke without pausing as she ground the powders and herbs filling her mortar.

Trina found the flask with ease. She reached for a cup, a rare item down in the shafts, and watched the purple liquid splash into kiln-hardened clay.

The sweet-tart juice woke her senses, delighting them. Trina wished she could provide such treats for her sister even as she reminded herself to be grateful they had running water, something available to few shafters. The copper-stained liquid they drank at home had a strong flavor, but not a good one.

"There. That should hold for four weeks, more than usual, but I don't want you running out if you come late again." The woman's face stretched into a pained smile as she held two bottles where Trina had expected only one. "If I can't change what's been done to your people in the past, the least I can do is suffer whining from polits to give you this much."

A blush heated Trina's cheeks as she stared at the bottles. "I don't have enough," she muttered. Something about the woman's expression made her embarrassed to offer even the coin she could, but she paid her debts.

"You'll bring extra next time. Two weeks. Don't waste this gift unless you have to. Keep your mother comfortable." The last made Trina wonder how much the apothecary suspected.

The woman brushed a hand against Trina's straight hair but Trina jerked away from the touch. "Thanks. Nine silvers for the one?"

A frown crossed the apothecary's face before she nodded. "Nine silvers." She waited for Trina to pull out the coins from her hidden purse before handing over the bottles. "You take care of your family and keep safe."

As soon as the silver rested in the woman's hand and Trina had tucked the bottles into a hidden pocket under her tunic, she nodded, her smile more of a grimace. "As safe as I can."

She pulled at the door without waiting for a reply, and with a quick glance up and down the street, Trina set off on a different path than she'd used to come here, a path that took her by the chain-link fence surrounding Ceric's only spaceport.

Her feet slowed as if of their own will. She ran her fingers along the metal links. The faint tick made her smile, but the spaceship in the distance held her attention as it roared to life. A flash of light followed by a roll of thunder louder than the strongest summer storms transformed the ship into a backwards shooting star in the daytime sky.

She rose on tiptoe as though she could ride its tail, her fingers clenched around the metal links barring her from dreams of stars and joining the Spacer Guild.

No shafter ever crossed this fence. Trade with spacers was in polit hands, and the colony leaders pretended shafters didn't exist.

The medicine said just what polits thought of those who lived in the shafts beneath the aging colony. She'd never live on the surface much less leave Ceric altogether.

CHAPTER 2

T he cool glass bottle pressed against Trina's skin, absorbing the chill air of the shafts. Here, she found reality. A shafter dying from an engineered disease. The disease should have ensured the genetic changes tested on Trina's mother couldn't be passed to the next generation. Instead, the enhanced immune system they'd given Mother had fought off the virus for years, long enough to bear and raise the twins. Neither Trina nor Katie ever got sick. And they showed no sign of the deadly infection.

A fresh cry echoed from the back room as Trina relocked the door, their only defense should someone see the powered light that shined through the thick plastic covering the top of their raised front wall. Their mother wouldn't let them hide the light. She wanted to be sure it could guide a messenger who never came.

"Hard day?" Trina said as she caught sight of her sister once she mounted the short flight of stairs. The protector was back in full force, even down to the staccato language common among shafters. She reminded herself to gentle it.

"Mother's breaking through the medicine again. She's in so much pain."

"Increase it."

"At nine silvers? How will we pay?" Katie pushed up off the ground where she'd been sewing and headed for their mother's door, clearly regretting the question.

Trina trailed after her, pausing at the head of their mother's cot. She struggled to connect the withered form with their vibrant mother, an image almost faded into a fairy tale.

"Pour her what remains. The apothecary gave us extra. If you don't, it won't matter anymore. She says pain kills Mother faster."

"Sometimes I wonder if she'd find that a blessing."

Trina grabbed her sister's arm and pulled her out of the room. "How can you say something like that? And right in front of Mother?"

Katie sank into one of the salvaged desk chairs, letting the chair spin around once before dropping her foot to stop it. "Have you never thought it? I'm here every day and all she feels is pain. She barely eats, sleeps only fitfully, and the pain gets stronger. We've increased the dose four times already, far past what your surface apothecary said would kill her."

Trina stalked toward Katie. "She didn't know our mother then. This medicine's as pure as polits take. If Mother wanted to go, she'd go. She's fighting too hard for us to give up on her."

Katie lowered her face into both hands, a sigh whispering between her lips. "I know. It's just that you're not here every day, all day. You don't hear her. On days like today, well, I don't know if it's worth it."

Trina crouched in front of the chair and peered up at her sister. "It *is* worth it. It has to be. Mother's in there somewhere. It might not seem like it, but her spirit's fighting to survive. If you look deep, you'll see her hiding."

Katie responded with a shaky smile. "Maybe I will."

Trina bounced up. "What you need is a break. You take the extra ha'silver and coppers." She shoved the pouch of what little remained into her sister's hands. "Go down to the market. Get some supplies. I'll stay with Mother."

Glancing at the purse then at her mother's door, Katie nodded. "Maybe just for a little while. We do need some things. You'll be all right?"

"I'll be fine. Mother will sleep. You be careful though. It's getting late."

"I know. Stay to the lit paths in the market and don't come straight back. It's like you don't know who gets the groceries around here." Katie said the last with a laugh.

Ignoring the humor, Trina gave her sister a grim nod. "Better to wait than lead someone here. I can leave Mother sleeping if you don't get back soon enough. I'll come get you."

"Maybe you should give me one of your knives," Katie said in a clear attempt to lighten the air.

Trina barked a single laugh. "You'd be more likely to slice your own wrist. Just watch yourself."

"Better than you do up there." Katie pointed to the ceiling.

Before Trina could protest, her sister gathered up the coins, twisted them through the scarf to silence them once again, and stepped out into the darkness.

CHAPTER 3

T rina stayed locked in their apartment for five days, trying to keep busy. She cooked for Katie and her mother, and tried not to track how quickly the medicine bottle emptied. She even patched some clothing they could wear in the shafts. Her ugly needlework would mark her up on the surface.

She let her sister think worry kept her there, and Katie's exhaustion did make her nervous, but Katie didn't recognize, in the fanciful tale Trina had told, just how angry Big Man Fence would be that she'd bested him. Better to let his temper cool than chance turning him against them.

She had many rules to keep them safe. No one knew where they lived, not even Piper who'd been a good friend to her. No one knew they had the power and water their father arranged before leaving.

The apartment's remote location and strong lock wouldn't stand against a determined search and assault. She didn't hold on to what she stole longer than it took to exchange it, and Fence didn't reveal how much he paid. He couldn't thieve it back, either, because word would spread. Honoring the deals kept everyone where they wanted to be, and kept secret things secret.

She still owed on the second bottle, though, and the heavy purses celebrants carried during the Festival that had just started proved too much of a temptation. Fence would have to break any large coin, but she could gather enough smaller to pay her debts.

Despite all those good reasons, the confinement drove her from the apartment as much as any need, that and knowing the Festival had begun.

She'd grown too antsy to stay in their apartment another day.

Trina pressed into a wedge of shadow made by the building's ornate facade and surveyed the square. The shade did little to protect against Ceric's muggy heat, but here she could survey all the polits, laborers, and even those responsible for what little tech had survived the early days. This square stood between most of the city and the fairgrounds, so Trina would have her pick of targets.

She shifted slightly until a cool wind blew over her face as she scanned the crowd for a good mark. Two young ladies on a bench next to the central fountain caught her eye for a moment. From the smiles on their faces, they enjoyed the occasional splashes of water blown by the same breeze.

Trina took a step toward them then noticed how their hems were frayed and grimy, not with the dirt of one day, but with steady, ground-in mud from working outside. Even if those two had any coin, they needed it. They would have bought, or made, new Festival clothes otherwise.

The sun rose higher and wind brought dust clouds with it, adding grit to the humid air.

Trina pulled back into her corner and yawned. As much as she preferred it up here under the sun where they belonged, she needed to snag a few sizable purses and get back home. Katie seemed more irritable and tired lately. The dark patches under her sister's eyes could signal something much more frightening than exhaustion. Just because they hadn't caught their mother's sickness yet didn't mean they never would.

At least trips to the shafter market seemed to help. Katie looked happier when she came back in, enjoying the time away without any pressure to rush home, happier even than when she sewed complicated patterns into their blankets with scraps of cloth. Mother had taught Katie the practice, and as their mother worsened, Katie sewed more often, living up to the first Ceric doctrine of performing manual labor to ease the spirit.

Still, Trina wished the doctrine had not been necessary. It came into being when tech failed the early colony. If more tech had survived, or she could gain access to the spacers past the fence, maybe they'd have a cure for her mother.

She muffled a sour laugh at the impossible thought. Even here at Festival where all types of people rubbed shoulders and enjoyed the annual celebration, shafters weren't welcome. Most surface dwellers thought shafters were barely human, as if they'd recognize a true shafter from a great distance. Trina hadn't revealed where she came from to the apothecary at first out of fear, but her mother's illness gave them away. Luckily, the woman hadn't been like most of her kind.

In those early days when cryo losses took the work animals and disease struck down many who could run the technology, the cool darkness of the abandoned transit tunnels offered a better hope than found in the doctrine's promises. Shafters had little interest in a good afterlife, not when it meant hard manual labor for the local polits in a harsh climate. Shafter life might be difficult, but at least they weren't owned, or so shafters liked to tell themselves.

She saw them as trapped. Even the lowest of laborers seemed to have enough to eat while most shafters had skin stretched tight over their bones. A shafter couldn't hide the truth well enough to work on the surface for more than a few days, and few from the surface were willing to trade extra foodstuffs.

Trina came alert, her gaze watchful even as her thoughts wandered.

Three men staggered into the square, held upright only by their linked arms and rhythmic sway. They'd started revelry early this morning from the look of them. Her lip curled in disgust. Most likely polits who'd forgotten the value of working with their own hands. They failed to follow the doctrine even in spirit. While laborers made the final changes to their Festival gear or caught up on other tasks, polits had servants who worked long into the night to prepare them. Bright and early on Festival days, the polits spilled into taverns, especially the young ones.

She turned away to look for others. Drunken marks might seem easy to a new thief, but she found them unpredictable, making it hard to judge the snatch and grab. They tended to be more aggressive and harder to escape if they caught her, while any injury to a polit came with a death sentence if the enforcers captured her.

A better chance would come.

Her gaze drifted back over the thick purse that dangled from the shorter one's belt by a thin leather strap. It called out to her knife. Would he notice a simple toss? She sighed in regret, knowing better than to try for it.

What wasted lives. They did nothing of value. Her talents gave her freedom to work with finesse while her knife skills kept her safe from other shafters. It might not be what the doctrine intended, but Trina wasn't afraid of hard work. She fed and protected her family with the labor of her own hands.

"How do you do, fine ladies?"

The slurred words drew Trina's gaze back to the polits, their progress having stopped in front of the laborers she'd noticed earlier. The men's shaky attempts at elegant bows almost made her laugh until she saw the women shudder.

The polit with the big purse leaned in, bracing his arm against the back of the bench.

Trina flinched, imagining his hot, liquor-laden breath stroking her cheek as the woman shifted away.

"What? The young ladies won't speak with me? I'm a polit, you hear. The grand polit!"

The nearer woman moved then, smothering her giggles behind a hand.

"You don't believe me?" He shifted his gaze to the second woman, almost toppling onto her friend's lap.

Clearly unfamiliar with drunken men, the laborer looked him up and down. "You're much too young for such a position. And I'd like to think our grand polit could handle his drink." She turned away.

"Let them be, Paul. They meant no harm. What lady would acknowledge you in this state anyway?"

Trina realized she'd been so involved in the pageant in front of her, she'd forgotten about his friends. From the words, at least one wasn't as drunk as this Paul. She saw the other eyeing the shadows and pulled in as far as she could to escape detection.

"It's not safe here. Let's go to the tavern. We'll find some real women to dally with there." The third man spoke this time, pulling on Paul's arm.

"Let go. Now you insult me." Paul pushed against his friend, the movement more of a lurch than a shove. "I don't need to find some tavern girl from the lowest of laborers. These ladies will do just as well. What's your name?" He grabbed the second woman's arm and pulled, jerking her tight against his side.

Before she thought through her actions, Trina thrust free of her hiding spot and swaggered over to them, tossing her four-inch blade from hand to hand. "You're looking for a real woman, are you? No mere tavern wench?" She threw the knife into the sky so it tumbled over and over until she caught the sharp edge on the down curve. She'd practiced hard, knowing intimidation often made a better weapon than force.

Paul shouldered the woman aside, leaving her to drop back onto the bench. He seemed more sober and dangerous than moments before.

His friends flanked him, turning to face this new threat. They were smart enough to watch the knife instead of dismissing her slight form or apparent youth. Though her head barely reached their chests, Paul's friends were not fools.

"You should show courtesy to one who is surely greater than you'll ever be, Grand Polit." She emphasized the title with a sarcastic bite, showing off her sophisticated speech in another attempt to throw them and mask her shafter blood.

Trina stopped just out of their reach, gesturing for the women to leave with a movement of her head. "I'd think your thin blood would teach you some manners, if only to keep that flesh clear of scars."

Paul jerked forward at her words, but his friends held him tight. His movement startled the women out of their frozen terror and they rose. Paul grabbed the nearest, his grip firm enough that the woman gasped in pain.

An image of Katie in the same position flashed before Trina. "Let her go." The words came out fast and furious, though quiet.

"Who're you to school me, shafter brat?" Despite his friends restraining his body, nothing controlled the man's tongue.

She laughed at a truth he'd thought to use as an insult. If they'd known her to be a shafter, these men wouldn't hesitate to call the enforcers.

The woman trapped under his hand whimpered. Her friend stood by, too far to be touched, but ready to grab the other woman and run if given an opening.

Trina swore she'd offer them that chance.

"You think you can stop me? Are you really willing to risk death for these ladies?" He emphasized ladies until it sounded dirty, and even his friends looked surprised.

Trina wished they had called the enforcers. She had the skills to evade security forces, and they wouldn't tolerate such rude behavior even in a polit. Not at Festival when all the surface folk were equals.

Taking a deep breath, she adjusted her stance and half raised one arm. "You willing to risk a scar on that pretty face?"

He paused, catching the meaning behind her words, but he didn't consider long.

Trina lost the time to weigh the risks as he grabbed the woman's dress, her bodice separating with a sharp tear.

She was hardly aware of the knife as it left her hand, or the swift movement replacing the blade with two others. Time seemed to slow, allowing her to understand just what she'd done too late to change it.

Steel flashed in the light as it flew true.

A bright red line appeared across the polit's wrist, and he dropped his hold on the woman.

The knife hit cobblestones with a clatter that echoed through the stunned silence.

Paul grabbed his wrist with a shout, blood appearing between his fingers.

The women slipped away.

She hadn't cut him deep enough to scar, but it bled enough to scare. His friends took a step toward her but stopped when they saw her new weapons.

The three polits glared at her as Paul wrapped his wrist with a handkerchief. She looked each of them in the eye, hefting the knives in her hands. They stepped away together, but Paul gained enough arrogance with the distance to call back, "You may be grinning now, little thief, but my father will have a say in this matter. He'll treat you like a shafter for what you've done."

His words reminded Trina why she'd come, and another knife left her hands.

She waited until the polits disappeared around a corner before moving forward to collect the two knives and the heavy purse her second toss had brought to the ground. The polit hadn't even noticed his loss.

A touch on her shoulder sent Trina into a defensive stance. She bounced away, her third knife at the ready and the purse thrust down her neckline where it made a solid lump against her waist.

The woman jerked when faced with the blade, a small squeak emitting from her lips.

Trina relaxed her defensive pose as she identified one of the two laborers. They must have waited just out of sight. The woman had patched her torn dress with a handkerchief covering the exposed skin.

"Thank you so much. I don't know what we would have done without you. How can we repay this aid?"

Trina half turned, reaching for her first knife. She glanced at it, happy to see she'd made a clean cut with blood only welling up after the blade had gone. "I needed a diversion anyway. You served well. There's money enough in his purse." She kept her voice gruff and ran a finger along the knife, testing the edge. A frown creased her forehead when she felt new nicks. She'd have to sharpen it again, weakening the blade.

"But at such risk."

Trina ducked under the woman's hand, wishing she hadn't heard the last as she snatched the knife she'd used to gain the purse. Without another word, she slipped away then jammed the dangling end of her scarf into the polit's coins as soon as she was hidden from view. Her fingers twisted the fabric around until it muffled their noise. She'd had no choice, but avoiding capture was even more urgent now.

CHAPTER 4

T rina still hadn't figured out what to tell her sister when she made the last turn to get home. She wouldn't be able to keep this from Katie, but what could she say?

Katie thought the streets held fewer risks than stealing from houses only because she'd never been within arm's reach of an enforcer patrol. Again, Trina wondered why she hadn't ignored the situation.

Her sigh echoed down the tunnel, the sound blending into the wealth of small noises always present in the shafts. She couldn't have left those women any more than Katie would ever walk away from their mother. If Mother asked for release, Trina would be the one to give it. Katie was a nurturer. Only Trina tossed knives and slashed at polits.

Katie wasn't in the front room when Trina reached home. Forcing away her frown, Trina dug out the purse and pulled her scarf free as she stepped into her mother's room.

"Is that pouch as full as it sounds?" Whatever else her sister would have asked, she stopped at the sight of Trina's face. Her head tilted to one side. "What's wrong?"

Trina tried again to smile but from Katie's frown, she failed. She forced energy into her voice instead. "I had a grand adventure today. One worthy of the fairy tales Mother used to read us." She dropped her gaze to her mother, seeing from the slack features that she slept, for now.

"What do you mean?"

"First, let me introduce you to the fair maidens." With the same finesse marking her skills as a thief, she launched into the tale, vanishing the threadbare hems and replacing the polits with ogres drawn from those old books.

Katie laughed as the story unfolded, especially when Trina described sauntering up to the towering ogres and threatening them with a matchstick. Trina had her absorbed until the "ogre" grabbed the woman's dress and the knife flew.

Katie's fist jammed tight against her lips. "You cut someone? Oh Trina." Tears welled up in her sister's eyes.

Trina crossed the room in quick strides, pulling her twin into her arms. "It's all right. I got away. How would they ever find out who I am?"

"Promise me. Promise me you'll never thieve there again." Even muffled against Trina's chest, the adamant words came through.

"I promise. I won't thieve there for a while. Not through the whole Festival. And I mostly keep to the houses anyway. You needn't worry. The polit was very drunk. He probably doesn't remember, or he's sure to forget over the week." Trina rubbed Katie's back.

Her twin pulled free. "He'll remember all right. He has a scar to show for it. Polits don't forget. And their children are worse."

"Not all of them."

The voice coming from the bed shocked the twins to silence. They stared at their mother, who hadn't spoken in weeks.

"My polit wasn't like most. He had heart and spirit. He wanted to make something of himself. Not like most of his kind who just lounge around and pretend to be pure of soul while others do their labors for them."

They'd heard the tale many times, but never interrupted. The story told them everything they knew about their father. To hear it in their mother's voice when both had thought her lost, no matter what they said aloud, made it all the more poignant.

"His hair flashed with the sun's brilliant light and his muscular form showed strength and determination. No weakling, my love." She sighed and her eyes closed.

Trina thought Mother didn't have the strength to continue, but then some more words trickled out.

"The Festival had just begun when we found each other. I'd escaped after weeks of testing and wandered, too dazed to find my way off the surface. He caught me when I stumbled, pressing his length against mine and sending warmth surging through both of us." A smile crossed her lips and the thoughts brought some color back to her wasted face.

"Four months. That's all we ever had. He'd already decided how to prove himself despite his family's position here. He chose to go to the stars."

Trina jerked as her mother's bony fingers brushed against hers. She'd thought her mother unaware.

Feeling guilty, Trina wrapped both hands around her mother's, trying to share some of her warmth. Her skin twitched where it met the rough dryness of her mother's flesh, a bare covering over the brittle sticks of her bones.

"I never had the chance to tell him of you, but he'll send for all of us when he learns. He will. I promise!"

The fierce whisper set off a rattle in her chest and silence fell, broken only by Trina's heavy heartbeats.

"He took care of us, even not knowing," their mother began again. "First giving me this place then with the coins passed by his man into my eager hands. I sent word of you through the courier. We've waited so long." Tears dripped from her eyes, but she shook her head when Katie reached up to brush them away.

They waited in silence for a while, waited for another faint sentence, hoping against hope their mother had broken through the disease and would start back on the path to health as she had many times before. Instead, her skin became even more translucent and a fever clouded her half-open eyes.

UNABLE TO STAND SENTINEL OVER their mother any longer, Trina followed Katie into the kitchen.

Katie picked up their makeshift mortar and pestle, and began grinding cheese and breadcrumbs together with the inner pulp of an orange slice into a sodden mess for Mother.

Trina lit the crumpled paper beneath the grill after checking how many matchsticks remained. The flame caught on the first try. She blew gently to help the fire spread, frowning when she recognized the picture of an ogre only seconds before it crisped. Like her mother's dreams, the stories their father had given them turned into just so much smoke when faced with reality. He would never come for them.

Katie put the stone vessel onto the fire, adding water from the top of their filter to avoid the silt. "Do you think our father did set up a way to support us?"

Trina started when Katie broke the silence, but the question had bothered her as well, ever since her mother revealed this new facet. "If he did, I wish she'd told us before. It would've made your life easier. I wonder if he kept coming for a while after Mother couldn't."

"Not my life." Katie shook her head. "Yours. You wouldn't have to risk yourself up there if we had something like that. The polit won't forget. You know that as well as I do. You're just trying to make me worry less, but it's not working. The stars you crave to be under are what took our father. If not for them, you could have had everything you ever wanted." She glared at the ceiling as though she could look through it to the sky beyond.

A quick step took Trina around the grill to her sister's side. "I know you fear the open sky, but there's so much up there that you'd love." She waved at the second pot Katie added once she moved their mother's broth off the fire to cool. "Like berry juice. It's tart and sweet all at once. Safe too. No need to sift or boil out the copper and poisons."

Katie laughed. "I'll drink my water hot and be grateful for the fire to warm it. Mother's medicine may be worth the risk, but we don't need any surface luxuries. We live well enough down here."

"If you could only see the polit houses. They're marvelous. You'd love the paintings and carpets. So much more interesting than the posters on our walls, even if we hadn't torn them up to feed the fire. We're half polit. Don't you ever think about that?"

Katie wrapped a scrap of cloth around the pot and carried it to their mother's room. "Sure, I think of it, but our father didn't even know the results of his seed. You're as much of a fool as Mother to hope for more. Who's to say he didn't tire of her and use the ship as an excuse?"

Trina slammed a fist against the doorframe. "Better to believe Mother than accept this as our real life." She kicked the coin purse still lying where she'd dropped it during the tale. Bright bits of metal scattered across the floor.

"Those polits you want to join are the same ones who did this to Mother." Katie half turned toward their mother's bed then glanced back. "Better a clean shafter life."

Burning pressure weighed on Trina's chest, threatening to choke her. "If she weren't a shafter to start, they'd have done nothing. She wouldn't be dying." Trina glared until Katie looked away, but that didn't make her feel any better. She needed to get out of here, to be where walls didn't surround her and press close. "I'll watch the fire until the water's hot. Then, I'm gone."

CHAPTER 5

The square didn't look much different the next day when Trina passed through it as she headed for other hunting grounds after visiting the apothecary. The purse had yielded enough to repay her debt and more, giving them a bit of safety but not enough to keep Trina at home. Still, she'd promised Katie, and she kept her promises even when they argued. She'd chosen the square because all traffic came through here, meaning Trina had to as well, but she would not remain.

Her footsteps slowed when the bench came in view. In the dim light, she couldn't see any evidence of the fight, but she knew it had to be there. Blood had dripped from his hand to color the stones.

She forced herself past, knowing she couldn't afford to linger in case the polit had gone crying for help after all, not so much for the hand, but because of his lost purse. The enforcers could be looking for her, or at the very least patrolling the area, but Festival meant the chance to secret coins away in their apartment's many hiding places. She couldn't ignore that any more than she could keep down in the shafts where the sunlight never came.

No matter what she told herself over Festival week though, Trina knew the excuses for what they were. She returned to the square with every trip to the surface, coming here as often as she lingered at the spaceport fence. One held her dreams, the other her nightmares. Neither seemed quite real for all they drew her to them.

CHAPTER 6

S amuel thumped his fist down on the pile of papers decorating his oak desk. "Stupid tradition," he muttered under his breath, not really meaning it.

Bags of papers still waited his perusal. Only during Festival, one week of the year, could the other classes have a say in how polits ran each cities. And Samuel, as grand polit, had to read all those from First City. It made the other classes feel part of the family and kept them happy. As if Menthak had enough money for even half of these requests.

Samuel picked up a heavily wrinkled paper from another stack and laughed. Since Jared slipped past him, the colony requests seemed more frequent—or maybe Samuel noticed them more. Had he been a better father to both his sons, he'd have a strong partner for running the city, and a heavier purse without the constant drain from Paul.

He rose, stretched, then crossed to the study window. The bright sunlight made him blink before he could see the ornate statue of his ancestor and namesake in the courtyard below.

The first Samuel brought hard workers and true followers determined to make their mark on this planet. Adventurers like Jared.

When they suffered dual setbacks between the cryo disaster and disease striking the technology workers, Old Samuel had stepped in to keep the colony going. He'd solved disputes, quieted dissention, and even put his own back to the stones quarried to make their roads and homes so long ago. So the histories told. From his efforts came the very first doctrine—to work with your hands is sacred and blessed. Old Samuel believed God took away the distractions of technology to remind them of this truth.

It must have been simpler then.

Now, everyone clamored on about petty needs and no one cared about work. From his own son down to the lowest laborer in the Menthak family, they just wanted to spend what little remained in the family coffers with no thought to replenishing it.

The Samuel of long ago didn't have whining from his people when rain weakened a stretch of cobblestones or a baker charged more to laborers than polits. In the beginning, people worked together to survive. Now, the first doctrine, purity maintained by the work of your own hands, had little influence, while later ones driving cooperation were so neglected even Samuel had a hard time remembering their texts.

His remaining son crossed the courtyard below. Nothing backed Paul's swaggering stride but his illustrious birth. That boy had never done a speck of work in his life, no matter how much Samuel tried.

Jared had been different. Samuel's older son wanted to live life to the fullest almost from his first breath. Like the Samuel of old, he thought nothing of dirtying his hands in the fields, or fraternizing with the laborers. He'd brought back ideas, good and bad, all year long, instead of waiting for Festival week.

Samuel had discouraged the boy then. He'd thought it wasn't suitable for a polit to be so free with others. One week a year was enough to treat them as equals.

Now, much too late, he realized his mistake.

Samuel had kept Jared trapped in the social conventions of modern polits when the boy had the adventurous spirit of their ancestors. He'd driven his son to found a new colony with his well-meaning lessons. It had taken Samuel almost sixteen years to understand, sixteen years of regret and questions.

He turned away from the window. The painting of his lovely second wife and their two boys, one tow-headed, the other dark, drew his attention. Only a couple of years separated them, but the two could not have been more different.

Samuel never expected Jared to be the serious one when they were young. Jared laughed his way through everything, even when he hurt himself on one of his wild adventures. In contrast, Paul's petulance came as no surprise, and Samuel would have to face more of it if the pounding footsteps on his stairs were any sign. Paul couldn't walk lightly if his life depended on it.

Samuel's gaze flew back to the image of his first son, the one he'd thought nothing but trouble. He wondered how Jared's little girls fared. Were they as hard for their shafter mother to handle as Jared had been for him? His son never discovered that Samuel set a tail on him, leading the father to learn what the son left too soon to know.

For years, the same man who'd followed Jared exchanged coins for snippets of the girls' lives, pretending their father hired him before leaving for the stars. The pain of losing Jared struck harder when the shafter woman stopped coming. Despite everything he'd tried, no matter how many contacts he'd approached, Samuel found no way to uncover her identity or claim his grandchildren for his own.

PAUL BURST INTO THE STUDY without the courtesy of a knock, jerking Samuel into the present. He scowled at his younger son.

"Dad, I need more money. My last allowance is gone and my friends can't support me forever. You wouldn't want word to get round that the grand polit is running short." Paul wasted no time in making his demands.

"And why would anyone think that? Could it be they see his wastrel son throwing money to the winds?" Samuel glared at the demanding intruder. "What was it this time? Did drink and tavern girls suck up so deep a purse? I should've known better than to give it to you all at once just to quiet your whines." Samuel crossed to his desk and sank into the chair. He rested his palms against the wood grain if only to keep them from leaping up around his son's neck. Even Jared at his worst had the courtesy to call him 'Father.' The new term grated on Samuel's nerves.

Without waiting for an invitation, Paul slumped onto the armchair across from Samuel's desk, swinging his legs up so he lounged rather than sat. "Does it matter? Whatever happened, I know you won't approve." His son failed to meet his eyes, looking instead at the long nails he'd adopted as part of the latest fad, their garish orange paint making Samuel flinch.

Straightening the pile of requests, he took a steadying breath and then another one. It didn't work. All he did was bring the sickly sweet perfume decorating Paul's coat to his nose. It made him sneeze. "Must you wear that in here? The smell stays for hours."

Paul smiled, only half of his face moving. "The sooner I'm gone, the sooner the scent will be. Your choice."

"I'm a businessman, a leader. Why should I keep throwing bad money after good? You think the rumors you spread about my pockets force me to pay you off. No longer. They have more than a comfortable measure of truth." Samuel kept still with difficulty but he felt a muscle in his cheek begin to twitch.

The arrogance fell away from Paul's face as if he dropped a cloak. Samuel leaned back in surprise, the squeak of his chair loud in the sudden silence.

Paul mumbled something Samuel couldn't hear.

"What was that?" Curiosity eased through him. Maybe this son had something of interest too. Maybe he'd misjudged him. Maybe by focusing on the one who'd gotten away, he'd failed to see the maturity growing in Paul. After all, for once he hadn't asked why when Paul requested more than his normal allotment. Maybe the money went to building something to save them all.

So lost in his own thoughts, Samuel failed to hear when Paul repeated his words, but he heard them the third time with Paul standing up to shout at him.

"I was robbed. Yes, robbed. Are you happy now? First day of Festival."

Hope died as quickly as it had risen. "Robbed? You carried the whole purse to walk Festival streets? Are you sure one of your friends didn't snitch it when you went for your fifth drink?" Now Samuel stood as well, his fingers gripping the edge of his desk hard enough to turn his knuckles white.

A frown bit into his son's face. "My friends are good and loyal. They wouldn't take my money. How do you think I've survived this long without asking for more? My friends. They're not like you standing here over a wealth greater than any other on this worthless planet and yet making your only son beg for little more than a scrap." Paul paced back and forth, his jerky steps reminding Samuel of his first wife, a woman of little grace who died before they could have any children, not that his second wife had lived much longer.

He'd done his best since the boys' mother had died, just after Jared turned twelve, but looking at his younger son, he knew he'd failed. "You are not my only son and never will be. It's good you have friends to stand by you. A man such as you've become needs friends." Samuel put up a hand in apology before Paul could respond. "How much do you need?"

Paul straightened, the smile on his face announcing a return of arrogance. "Forty silvers should do me fine."

Samuel jerked his hand back from the locked drawer where he kept some coins for quick access. "That much! It's more than you lost."

"I didn't lose it. I told you. I was robbed. And I have to pay my friends back, don't I? You wouldn't want your son in debt. It wouldn't be seemly." He thrust his chest forward to seem imposing, but Paul looked more like an unbalanced bird about to topple in the breeze.

"Ah, your goodly friends? So nice to charge rates for their assistance." Samuel crossed his arms over his chest.

"They have tight-fisted parents just as I do," Paul muttered, probably not expecting Samuel to hear. "They saved my life. Why shouldn't I help ease their way?" This Paul said loud enough.

"Saved your life? How so? I feed and clothe you. You have no real need for anything else. Being without money only stunts your pleasures." Samuel's head began to ache. "I tried. God knows how I tried to find a proper role for you. The teachers laughed when I sought a place for you among them, and I have to say they saw you more truly than I did. Even the laborers wouldn't have you as an apprentice. You're worthless, Paul. You and your pretty friends. What proper labor could you manage with those long, garish nails? You mock what made this colony, our city, possible." He blew out the rest of his breath, trying to disperse thick, flowery perfume.

Paul threw himself back into the chair, his trembling hands clasped in his lap. "They saved me from the thief who threatened us. The one who took my purse."

Samuel almost dismissed Paul's declaration, even as he'd ignored the first claim of threat, but his gaze fell on Paul's hands, still quivering as if he couldn't control them. "You were threatened? That seems odd with the penalties for striking a polit."

Paul surged forward until he leaned against his father's desk, shoving some of the careful piles over the edge where they fell into a jumbled mess. "You think I'd lie? About something like this?"

Backing up so he could focus on the hand thrust into his face, Samuel saw a red line of recently healed flesh across the back of Paul's wrist.

"You were attacked?" Doubts flew away in the face of such evidence. "How many? And why didn't you tell me immediately? The enforcers must find them. An attack against a polit is no simple thing, Paul. Surely you must understand this is larger than the loss of a heavy purse." He gripped his son's shoulders and stared at him, trying to find some sense buried in the boy's pleasure-ridden head. If the laborers rose up, no one would be safe.

Paul pulled away, his jerk almost sending Samuel across the desk. "No enforcers. It was just a purse."

"And an attack. That's a knife cut if ever I saw one. I might have questioned bruises or blunt injuries, but even you aren't foolish enough to play around with blades."

The look on Paul's face made Samuel wonder if he'd been wrong, if Paul made it up after all, but his son's next words banished the thought.

"There was only one. A girl."

Samuel laughed, unable to stop himself. "A girl? You and your stalwart companions were robbed and scared into silence by a girl?"

Paul scowled. "She had knives. And knew how to use them." He waved his injured wrist again.

"That much is obvious. Though you say she attacked you? You weren't struck while wrestling over the purse, were you?"

"No chance. I didn't even see my coin bag fall. I realized what had happened afterwards. As fast and strong as she was, in looking back, she must have been a shafter." Paul looked like a beaten dog waiting for the next blow.

Samuel sighed at how his son gave in to the foolish notion that shafters were any different than the surface folk. They had all come on the same ship. "It doesn't make sense. Why chance death over any purse, no matter how heavy, or how foolish the owner?"

"I'll prove it to you. I'll show you where it happened. Some drops of my blood probably still stain the pavement." Paul grabbed Samuel's arm and pulled him to the door.

Shrugging, Samuel let his son lead him out of the room. Anything was better than fixing the mess Paul had made of his careful piles. If he were a stronger father, he'd make Paul go through the letters, but he'd given up involving his younger son many years before. If anything, Paul was more frivolous than the Festival requests and couldn't see a true need if it bit him, or cut him across the wrist, as it were.

Part of Samuel wanted to leave the event unreported. He'd seen shafters before when so many were caught for the medical testing. They'd made a pitiful sight stumbling along the streets until they found a way back into their shadow realms. The lucky ones escaped underground before enforcers took them in on disturbance charges. But he couldn't chance showing weakness before them, so he followed through the busy streets.

He kept pace with Paul, his firm steps slowed to match his son's wandering gait. The boy said nothing, but his lips moved every once in a while as if trying to remember the path. Again, Samuel wondered if his son told the truth.

Paul suddenly accelerated, crossing into a square graced with a tall fountain aerating water from the treatment machines still pumping away under the surface, one of the few mechanical systems that still functioned. Their cities might resemble the beauty of ancient Earth, but trade with the spaceport, along with the few surviving original machines, meant Ceric didn't suffer the filth.

Samuel glanced around, seeing the elaborate facades that were added to the first buildings on Ceric once basic survival had been achieved. Now they formed many hiding places between carved pillars and thick facings. He'd grown up in one of those buildings toward the city center. When he'd married, the choice to live in a plainer, more functional home seemed like a moment of freedom.

"Over here! We stood here."

Samuel strolled over, taking time to notice the bench and how open the space Paul indicated was. If his son had been even remotely aware, no sneak thief could have reached him. Samuel wondered what Paul left out of the tale.

"We stood here and the thief appeared before us."

"Appeared?" Samuel raised one eyebrow.

"Well, came from over there." He waved in the direction of the most ornate building.

"And you and your friends just stopped here for what? To enjoy the beauty of this fountain?" Samuel waved at the fountain, which had little aesthetic value to draw observers despite its height. The cascading water had smoothed any fine carvings generations before.

Paul looked confused for a moment, confirming Samuel's suspicions.

"Well, we talked to some ladies?" Paul's sentence curled up as if he expected his father to write this fiction.

Samuel smiled as understanding dawned. "So, some of your tavern doxies lounged on this bench, distracting you from the thief? Probably working together."

"Oh, no they weren't. I mean…"

"How do you know they weren't working together?" Curiosity rose again.

"What I mean is they weren't tavern girls. Not polits, but high-class laborers. Not inviting, if you catch my meaning."

Paul winked in a lecherous expression Samuel found about as appealing as these apparent ladies must have.

"So you talked to some real ladies on the first day of Festival, and a thief snuck up on you, struck your wrist, and stole your purse?" The facts still didn't add up, but a clearer picture had begun to emerge.

"Not exactly. See, the ladies didn't—" Paul stopped as if aware he'd been about to say something he didn't want to reveal.

Samuel nodded. "The ladies objected to your already drunken advances?"

Paul looked away, mumbling his agreement.

"And while you tried to convince them otherwise, the sneak thief approached you."

Still looking at the cobblestones, Paul agreed.

"Then what happened? Surely, she didn't attack. With you distracted, your purse would be easy pickings on your belt." He waited to see if Paul would claim the purse was carefully inside his tunic but his son had no objections to the statement.

Samuel asked again, "Why attack? The penalty should have made your purse too risky a target."

Paul spun to face him. "She objected to our attentions toward the ladies. A scrap of a shafter daring to object! She probably wanted some attention for herself."

"Yes," Samuel said with a straight face. "The cut across your wrist shows her wants clearly."

Humor dissipated rapidly as he realized what Paul hinted. "You forced yourself on some laborers just enjoying the first day of Festival? You were lucky an enforcer didn't come by. Equality, boy! Equality means the right to say no and not be harassed by the likes of you. You disgust me." He turned his face away, no longer caring about the thief even if she'd broken the highest of laws. If he'd been there, the punishment would have been more severe. And Paul the target.

CHAPTER 7

Festival had drawn to a close, that first purse still the best of all her nabs. Despite what she told Katie, her hand seemed less steady, and her eye less focused.

Now, Trina would return to the slow process of choosing a polit house to strike. Fence would be happy to see her business after so long, and she'd find her catches in the quiet of corridors instead of out where she could be seen.

She could have chosen a different route, but went through the square again. Like that last look when leaving the dead for the death cart, she couldn't change her path.

The enforcers wouldn't be looking for her there after all this time. They had little enough to go on and didn't waste resources for so long. This time, the square would be like all others of its kind, the bloodstain washed off by the spray from the fountain and the memory of what occurred dimming into nothing more than a fairy tale to make Katie shiver.

Trina approached the square from a new direction as always, varying her entrance so she wouldn't be marked. From this side, though, she couldn't see the bench.

"Here! See. My blood on the pavement. Whatever came before, a shafter struck me."

Trina almost slipped on the water-slicked cobblestones as she jerked in surprise. Glancing both ways, she found no nearby hiding place. Katie would never forgive the risk.

"So? Your blood's on the stones. With what you've told me, the ladies should have taken your manhood instead."

The second voice stilled her. The man seemed bored despite his words, and yet who would the polit bring if not an enforcer?

Trina slipped closer, using the fountain for what little cover it provided despite the soaking she got as wind played in the water.

"It wasn't like that." Paul's whine made her jaw clench.

She could see the other man now, another polit from his clothes, the badge on his shoulder a match to some clothing she'd taken from a roof laundry line. He heaved a sigh, his broad shoulders shrugging with the force of it while his slightly rounded belly jiggled.

"And just what was it like? I have work to do. If you must walk me through your play, be quick about it," the older man said.

"She came up and threatened me, brandishing a long knife. Easily the length of my forearm."

"This girl held a knife so large? A shafter child? Paul, with the shafters I've seen, such a knife would knock her over." Sun glinted in the man's black hair as he laughed.

Paul paced back and forth from the bench to the dark red stain even Trina could see from her position behind the fountain. If only the wind had changed, water would have washed it away long ago, but wind on Ceric rarely switched direction. Nothing seemed to change here.

"She wasn't that little either. Her head easily came to…"

He put a hand just above his waist, raised it to his shoulder, and finally settled at his ear, a good bit higher than the four and a half feet Trina could claim. A giggle escaped her lips but the fountain covered her small sound. The older man was right. This polit gave them a play as entertaining as any in the shafter halls.

"Hmm. And I suppose she had big arms and a thicker neck? Something like the plowmen among the laborers."

Clearly unaware of the trap, Paul nodded. "Exactly. No small child this. She out-muscled all three of us even if she didn't have throwing knives."

The older polit smiled. "And this amazing specimen of a shafter leapt to the defense of two laborers being harassed by three drunken polit boys too full of themselves." His biting tone even made Trina flinch. "You aren't safe to set on the streets. Go to the enforcers with your tale. You can send them searching the city and even the shafts for this giant of a girl and her swords. Don't forget to warn them she has no compunction about using force against fools. She poses such a threat maybe I'll report her myself."

He strode quickly in Trina's direction, and she backed up, frantic, but all the good hiding spots required she cross into space he could easily observe. Her heart pounded loud enough she thought they would hear it over the fountain.

Trina watched the older polit with almost morbid fascination. She didn't have to think for a knife to slide into her hand. She'd already cut a polit. How could one more make a difference? Her only hope was to avoid capture.

Her body pressed tight against the fountain's wall, as if it could provide some protection. She showed clearly against the yellow marble. The knife pushed against her leg, available, but not visible.

Trina tossed her hair so it masked her face and hid her interest as the man approached, his path barely an arms-length from her. She could be any young child out to play in the fountain. He could just walk by in his disgust at Paul. He had no reason to connect her—

Before she could raise the knife, a strong hand grabbed her just above the wrist and lifted her until only her toes brushed the ground. The fingers pressed into her flesh hard enough to make her grip loosen. Trina watched as her second-best knife fell to the stones, bouncing twice before settling.

"Not quite the amazon but more what I'd have expected."

She twisted against the grip, another knife appearing in her free hand and slashing up to cut herself loose.

"Not so fast, wild one." Her other hand was captured and, before she could lash out with her feet, the man placed her on the lip of the fountain, his arms long enough so his body stayed out of her reach even though her wrists were still trapped. "It seems Paul isn't the only foolish one."

"Let me go! I haven't done anything." Trina scrunched herself up as small as she could and turned wide eyes up at him, using her slender form and lack of height to seem much younger. "Please?"

He seemed stunned for a second then his features hardened. "Paul, come over here."

Trina tried to twist free again, but she failed, her wrists burning with the pressure of his grip though she kept hold of her other knife this time.

All her finesse was wasted. It hadn't kept her from being caught. Katie had been right. What would her sister do now when Trina didn't return? The purse would keep Mother and her sister for a while, but not long enough.

Tears welled up even as the arrogant polit who'd started all of her problems appeared around the end of the fountain. She blinked the moisture from her eyes and glared at him, putting every nasty emotion into her look, as if she could burn his heart out before he condemned her.

Whether from her look or the man's, Paul's steps faltered, and he glanced from one to the other.

"I can't imagine two shafter girls would haunt this place. I believe I've found your six-foot, sword-wielding amazon."

Paul cringed under the older man's contemptuous tone, the reaction giving Trina a moment of pleasure.

"Could it be three healthy, well-fed polits ran in terror from this skin-and-bones child? She certainly deserves the coin instead of you. My coin more than any other."

"She's dangerous. I have the scar to prove it." Though his words sounded strong, the whiny tone Paul used grated on Trina.

"Just go. Out of my sight. You can live off your weakling friends until your next allowance is due." The man turned his back on Paul.

Trina met a glare from Paul more vicious than her own. Pure hate poured from his eyes. She shivered, feeling as though his emotion could reach out and strangle her.

Paul nodded stiffly before he twisted on one foot and strode off, his gait somehow awkward and unbalanced. She'd have to watch for that one.

Trina strangled a laugh as she realized her thoughts. It didn't matter how many enemies she made this day. She'd been caught. The penalty for attacking a polit was death, whatever the reason or how seriously this man seemed to take the charge. Her shoulders slumped in defeat, all life and resistance flowing out of her.

CHAPTER 8

S amuel took the second knife from the girl's unresisting hand, placing it just out of her reach on the edge of the fountain. Her gaze tracked the action, but she didn't respond. "I can't have you cutting another of us. If you make a habit of it, nothing will save you."

She raised her face with a question in her eyes, revealing again those achingly familiar features.

"No, you're not lost yet. There's no point in it. That boy needs some schooling and it's clear enough I can't give it to him. Don't worry about the enforcers. My son would have to admit a mere slip of a girl with only enough flesh to hold her bones together bested him. Paul's the one you have to be concerned about."

She jerked, and he supposed she had every right to be surprised. If not for her feminized version of his favorite son's looks, he probably would have called the enforcers. No matter what he thought of Paul, allowing attacks made polits too vulnerable. Other planets might put guards around their officials, but Ceric had managed fine on making the costs too high, and he wasn't willing to concede that point now.

Instead, he felt compelled to confide in her. "He's my own blood, but for all that, I'd have returned him to the womb if I'd known what he'd become. He's the worst of all polits. Perhaps in you I have a second chance…or third considering my failure with Jared." He watched her closely for any reaction to the name, one of her hands still trapped within his for all he'd loosened the grip.

She remained motionless, her body humming with tension and distrust.

Samuel wondered if he could be wrong, if he could be seeing his beloved son's face where no resemblance existed. Still, better to be called a fool than let even the slimmest chance pass by him. "Which are you? Katie or Trina?"

That got a reaction. She jerked her hand free and dropped to the ground faster than he could react. If she'd run, he probably would never have found her again, but her thriftiness proved her undoing. She sent a tight glance at the knife he'd placed on the fountain, clearly calculating whether she could retrieve it.

Samuel didn't hesitate. He grabbed her, pulling the girl tight against his chest, her arms pinned under his. Life didn't offer many chances and he wasn't going to lose this one.

She writhed like a wild thing, almost reptilian as her water-slicked flesh slid against his grip. She dug her nails into his legs, the broken edges having little impact through his pants. She twisted her head and sunk surprisingly strong teeth into his hand but Samuel clenched his jaw and hung on even when her jerking sent them both tumbling to the ground. At the last second, he swiveled so his back smacked into the cobblestones, her light weight barely making an impression against his chest.

Even the fall didn't stop her. He'd struck deep with the mention of her name...or was it her sister's? Loyalty and a sense of morality ran strong in this little one if her actions were anything to go by. Rare traits in a shafter, but Jared had been the same.

Pride welled up in Samuel and his hold slackened.

The girl wasted no time. She rolled against one arm, breaking free. She managed to snatch up the knife she'd dropped then rose in a graceful jump triggered from the balls of her feet.

At the last second, Samuel reached out and snagged one ankle, regretful but determined.

She jerked to a halt, terror clouding her features as she fell almost in slow motion. Her forearms hit the ground first, absorbing some of the blow, but his hold on her ankle prevented her from twisting so she'd land on her back. He saw her chest smack into her arms, which crumpled. A hard thump followed after, and her body went slack, all the fight gone.

Samuel rolled into a seated position, groaning as his own bruises made themselves known. He eased his way over to her, worried. She'd had a knife in her hands. Her body seemed so frail as he rotated it. He thought he'd lost his chance after all.

Her eyes, open and blinking, stared back at him.

He jerked in surprise.

The girl tensed again, but cried out rather than trying to escape. She flinched when her frown pulled against the lump already growing on one side of her forehead.

Samuel dragged his feet under him and lifted her in his arms, knife and all. The fountain edge offered a resting place. He soaked his handkerchief in fountain water, kept cool by the aeration process, and pressed the wet fabric against her lump.

"It'll help. I promise. I regret hurting you." The words slipped out with none of his usual commanding tone. His mind drifted in a half-forgotten past where he soothed the hurts on Jared's matchstick body. Smothering a laugh, Samuel took the opportunity to rifle her pockets, even the inside ones. He'd been quite skilled once, a long time ago.

Jared stole candies from the sweets jar many a time. It wasn't until much later that Samuel learned his older son didn't have a sweet tooth. The boy gave the candies to servant children, sharing his bounty with a generous spirit.

Her squirming protest brought him back to the present as he pulled free three other knives from carefully designed sheaths strapped to her body. He even found another tiny one strapped to the ankle he had not grabbed, designed to protrude when she kicked. Had she been trying, she could have easily wounded him enough to get away.

Relief washed through Samuel. He'd judged her correctly. She didn't strike without cause. Not even desperation triggered a violent attack, though defense of the weak apparently did.

He pulled forth what must have been her money pouch but only one copper fell free when the scarf stuffing came loose. How could she survive on so little? He didn't understand why their mother had stopped taking the money when they had so little.

Samuel scowled at the thought of this never seen shafter woman who had kept him from his grandchildren.

The girl shrank from him.

"You have nothing to fear. I want to talk. Here." He pulled out his own purse, bulging slightly but not from any cloth. Holding her pouch where she could see it, he added five coppers and a ha'silver, shaking so she heard the jingle. The pouch and scarf he tucked back into her tunic. Samuel kept the knives, though, placing them on his far side with the second he'd removed. As though nothing had happened, Samuel soaked the cloth again, flinching at the deep purple bruise already visible beneath her skin.

"Do you know of Jared? I know about you and your sister, though any information I have, your mother gave many years ago."

She tensed again at mention of her mother, but curiosity shone from her eyes. The girl tried to sit up then grabbed at the cloth as it threatened to fall into the fountain. He caught his handkerchief and helped her settle next to him.

"You know Mother?" She looked him over, as if comparing him to another she'd heard about. Her head shook in a negative just as a groan issued from her mouth at the renewed pain.

"You're expecting someone a little younger, with hair your color." He reached out and touched her yellow hair, its texture brittle with poor health unlike her father's silky strands. "You look like him."

Her throat moved convulsively. "You knew my father?"

Samuel smiled. "I know him better than any other still living as I sired him. Jared was my first born."

Her eyes grew round and her mouth opened on an "oh."

"It makes me your grandfather. Do you have grandfathers in the shafts?" He tried to keep the contempt from his voice. The sooner she left those dark, disgusting places, the better. Paul would have to learn to live with her shafter blood even as he would. Somehow, he'd convince her to come with him and her sister as well.

"We don't. Polits took them when they came up to breathe." The words came out sharp and as contemptuous as any he'd have used. Bitterness reflected in her face, and once again, she tensed as if deciding to run.

"Wait. Don't go. Not all polits are bad. I swear to you."

She paused.

He'd gained a moment, but couldn't expect any longer than that. "In the shafts, aren't there those you can trust? If no one else, your mother and sister. There must be those you can't trust as well." He knew enough of the shafts to know they held some of the worst examples of humanity ever to walk Ceric. Long ago, the cities ran purges but shafters always managed to come back. Darkness drew the bad element.

She nodded, slowly this time to avoid pain. "Not all good or bad."

"Then let me prove which I am. You know from your mother that my son didn't hate shafters. Give me a chance to show the same."

"I'll listen."

Her short speech irritated him but Samuel hid his reaction. He'd teach her how to talk properly as soon as he had her out of there. He just needed to gain her trust.

"I'd like to take care of you. Take you home—"

"No! I won't go. Not abandon Mother and Katie." She shrank back from him, grimacing as her quick movement caused pain.

Samuel savored his small victory. "You won't have to. I want Katie…your whole family…to come as well. Haven't you wondered what's behind these walls?" He waved at the buildings above them. "I can give you all that."

She started to say something, stopped, then answered. "We like our home. Don't like change." Trina pushed off the fountain edge, staggering as her feet hit the ground. Her handmade slippers seemed unlikely to provide much protection for her already battered feet.

"Wait," he called again before she could leave. "Your knives. Take them." He smiled when he noticed how he'd adopted the short sentences that had irritated him before. He'd have to watch for the influence to flow only from him to her and not the reverse.

She looked stunned by the offer, but crept forward, hand outstretched, to grab them.

Samuel touched her lightly, pulling back when she flinched. "Come in two days. I haven't much on me now, but I'll bring more coins."

She started to shake her head, but he interrupted the gesture. "Your mother accepted my coin for many years. I missed hearing about you and your sister when she stopped. Won't you give me this much at least?"

Trina looked at his face for a long moment before nodding. "I'll be here." Without another word, she snatched up the knives, somehow avoiding being cut by their sharp blades.

He watched her scamper away, amazed at the agility despite her bruises. A few days. He had that long to figure out how to convince her to bring her sister and stay. He'd even take the mother. She could live with the servants, but his granddaughters deserved more than a thief's life and starvation down where they couldn't see the sun.

CHAPTER 9

Trina didn't need a reflective surface to know what her face looked like. She kept to the shadows more than usual, but nothing would hide the bruise from her sister. Her pouch didn't even have enough coin to distract.

"What happened to you?"

Bad luck put Katie at the top of the stairs when Trina came in. No time to prepare. "Do you remember the polit I cut?"

"You didn't. You went back there. What have you done now?" Even while Katie berated Trina, she guided her sister to the table to get a better look at Trina's face. "Or maybe I shouldn't ask, considering the beating you took. At least he didn't turn you over to the enforcers." Katie's face paled as she heard her own words.

"He didn't touch me. I fell."

Katie put both fists on her hips. "Sure. You expect me to believe that? You, who can dance her way through any barrier? It's worse than the tales you spin to keep me from worrying. The only way you fell is if someone pushed you. So, was it the polit? Or a shafter?"

Trina couldn't suppress a smile for all that it made her face throb. "No one pushed me, exactly. A polit grabbed me. I fell, as I told you."

The chair Katie pulled scraped hard against the floor before her sister dropped into it. "He did catch you."

"No. Our grandfather did."

The confusion that wrinkled Katie's features made Trina wince in sympathy. "Our grandfather's dead. You must have hit your head harder than I thought."

Trina laughed. "Not that grandfather. Our other one. Our father's parent."

A gasp came from Katie, what little color she'd recovered draining away. "You cut our grandfather?" Katie shoved a hand against her mouth, staring at Trina with wide eyes.

"No, I didn't cut our grandfather," Trina burst out. She hadn't expected the direction her sister's thoughts had taken. Then her annoyance faded as she muttered, "I cut our uncle."

Katie lowered her hand to the table. "So now you're telling me we have an uncle *and* a grandfather? Why wouldn't Mother have told us about them? It doesn't seem right."

Trina pushed to her feet and paced to the tunnel map. "Maybe she didn't know. Our grandfather said he knew about us. That he'd exchanged coins for information. Maybe it wasn't our father after all. Maybe he still doesn't know about us."

She turned back to face her sister. "Our grandfather is offering coins again. You don't want me thieving. He's willing to take us, all three of us. We'd be polits like Mother always wanted."

Katie's eyes narrowed. "And you believe him? What polit would want shafters in his house?"

"We're not just shafters."

"Mother is. You want the surface so much you're blinded by it. The only thing better in your eyes would be a spaceship like the one that stole our father. You think I don't notice the chain marks in the dirt on your hands when you return? They're the same as when you used to come back with stories of crossing the fence and becoming a spacer. You don't talk about it anymore, but you still go."

Trina shrugged. "There's no harm in dreams."

"Dreams are what sent Mother to the surface in the first place. Dreams of a better life got her captured by scientists, and just like her dreams, yours are nothing but traps. Polits kill shafters. They don't invite them in for a meal. Ask the instincts that keep you alive up there if any polits you know would welcome us. The coin he promises is poison in your hands."

Katie surged to her feet and marched into Mother's room without a backwards glance, leaving Trina staring after her.

"**T**HE MODERN WORLD IS NOT like those times, Dad. Even you have to admit that much."

Paul's voice ground over Samuel's already stretched nerves like a sharpening stone.

"The doctrine just doesn't apply to us. Why should we labor? It's not like there's a need. This isn't a new colony anymore. It's high time we recognized our place in this world and embraced the honors due to us."

Samuel leapt up and slammed his hands against his desk. "And just where are those 'honors' to come from? It's labor and planning that kept the Menthak family strong, that built this city and all the money you're so happy to spend. Without something new to trade with the spacers, the family coffers will soon run dry."

He felt a twinge of satisfaction when Paul flinched. At least the boy wasn't so far gone as to ignore a threat to his purse. Not that Paul had anything constructive to add.

Suddenly, Samuel felt the weight of his years pressing down on him. He sank into the seat, holding his head between both hands. "Just go. Leave me be. Haven't you made enough demands for the day?" He waved Paul away, not even looking up.

Heavy steps moved to the door then hesitated. "You had time enough for that shafter girl. I didn't hear the enforcers come for her." Paul stepped through before Samuel could respond, hitting the stairs harder than usual.

Samuel pushed back from the desk, sighing as another pile of complaints toppled off its surface to scatter across the floor. If only his son would direct that anger toward something productive.

The window drew him again and he resisted, not wanting to face the accusations of his ancestor's statue. "See what I did with so little," the statue seemed to say. "How could you fail with so much?"

It wasn't a new question. He'd asked it often enough and not just with the disappointment his son had become. Samuel felt too young to be a failure, and yet the rest of his life stretched before him as more of the same. Dropping income from both farms and mines, combined with old equipment and little support, would come crashing down soon enough, but none of the other polits wanted to listen. If something vital like the water purifiers failed, Menthak didn't have the funds to replace them. It was the founding all over again without the will to work for success.

How could he, just one man, change that? Nothing drove the younger polits who stayed, and few of the older ones felt the need to act. Such easy, controlled lives.

Samuel laughed, his thoughts turning to a tousled blond head full of life and adventure along with a need to protect the weak. Now there's a child who bred true. Trina seemed the image of her father. She'd rejected this soft luxury without a second thought, no innocent when it came to survival. Oh, to have that kind of freedom.

He'd never had a choice. Born as he was to a main bloodline, Samuel became leader of the city when his father chose to step down. Everything had been planned for him. Even if he'd wanted to found the next settlement, that honor went to cousins, not those already with a city to run. His fate was to shore up a collapsing structure long enough to dump it and its empty pockets in Paul's lap when he grew too weary to hold up appearances.

Samuel found himself staring down at the statue. "Easy enough for you. An untouched planet, a driven team, and seemingly endless resources. Don't question my actions. I do what I have to." The fierce bitterness of his last sentence startled Samuel.

"Now I'm yelling at statues. I need a distraction. Why did I give Trina two days where one would suffice?"

He sighed, crossing the room to face the picture of his first-born son. How he wished he'd gotten another portrait done after his wife died. Jared had grown into a man, a man Samuel could barely remember.

"I'll treat your daughters better than I ever did you. You'd have sent for them if you could have, wouldn't you? They may have been Festival got, but your love for their mother seemed as strong as any my man ever saw. You crossed the lines drawn between shafter and polit with no care to tradition. Not for me, but for them you would have sent word once your colony was established." Samuel frowned at the picture of Jared not much younger than the only one of his granddaughters he'd ever seen.

The truth was harsh. Samuel couldn't promise anything to his dead son. Even now, he didn't know if he should have let Jared run wild or corralled him sooner with his responsibilities as the grand polit's first born. Jared carried all their expectations while his younger brother bore none until too late to impose them.

Jared never knew, but Samuel had gone to see the colony ship lift. He'd watched the proud adventurers march into the belly of that ship despite a lifetime of distrusting technology. The cream of Ceric families, polit and laborer alike, willing to face the trials of their ancestors. They left those who remained to wallow in the wealth of the past until it crumbled between their wasted fingers.

Samuel traced the line of Jared's pudgy cheek, the rough canvas breaking any illusion of flesh. Jared had grown out of that pudge quickly to become a healthier version of Trina then finally a muscular, handsome man.

Though he'd gambled on technology and lost, Jared would never stand at a window in the lap of luxury and be disappointed in his life. He had jumped into anything to make himself happy. Whatever the risk, all that mattered was the result. Samuel saw the same philosophy in Jared's child. Not only did she protect others, but he'd bet her thievery kept her sister safe enough. She'd been thin but not weak for it. If he'd been in worse shape like most polits, she'd have escaped him easily.

He laughed aloud. Was this what he'd come to? As grand polit over First City, it seemed wrong to be delighting in the success of a thief. And yet, what better following of the doctrine? Good work of the hands did not exist in dark shafts. She'd chosen a labor and learned it well enough to stay free and somewhat healthy. Samuel had no doubts her family ate better than most others below the surface. Trina would not be healthier than those she cared for if he was any judge.

If only he could have shaped her into the next grand polit. She had become a better person among beggars than Paul had surrounded by luxury. And yet, Paul was no worse than any of them. Menthak polits followed paths so worn by tradition they required no effort at all.

Once, he might not have noticed, but Jared had opened his eyes. Now the knowledge ate at him until he could stand it no longer. This could not be the whole of his existence.

CHAPTER 10

T rina slipped out of their apartment when Katie went to tend Mother after breakfast. Her sister would never let her go, not with the bruises marking her face, but Trina didn't plan on being seen.

Though she'd dismissed it at the time, Katie's statement that no polit would want shafter-bred children caused their grandfather's offer to linger in her mind. The coin would help, but shafter life was neither easy nor safe. To live on the surface—as a polit—could change all that.

Sunlight eased in around the cracks of Trina's favorite opening, and she reached up to loosen the cover. She had to find something to convince Katie this wasn't a trap. Trina couldn't let this chance slip away.

Though she'd studied many houses and stolen from most of those she'd watched, Trina remembered each one distinctly the same way she knew which tunnels would take her where she wanted to be. She headed not for the square but toward the house where she'd gotten the clothing with his seal. What better place to learn the truth about him?

The building itself had little of the ornamentation decorating those in the center but its austerity gave it presence. Trina watched from a shadowed servant entrance across the street, studying her grandfather's home. She slipped away only to pass into another shadow and another until she could no longer see the home.

A quick sprint and she crossed the street, ducking into a sheltered alleyway between two buildings. Trina glanced in both directions, making sure no one watched, then braced her feet and reached out for tiny cracks in the opposite wall with her fingers. She leaned against her hands and placed a foot on the nearer wall, her toes grasping through the soft cloth of her shoe until she hung stretched between the two buildings.

Trina scrambled up the wall to the roof. Though some buildings had peaked roofs, these were flat and often held laundry ready for the snatching, at least from the smaller servant lines. Trina ducked through the rows, making sure no one else passed among them even as she crossed the connected surfaces toward the one where she'd gotten the clothes that held the same symbol her grandfather had worn.

Counting each bracing wall where one building ended and the next began, Trina knew when her feet touched her grandfather's home, her family home. For a moment, her courage failed. She'd never sought out a polit house in hopes of finding the polit there. She'd never acted the spy.

Her hand shook as she brushed the door handle, seeing if the route below had a lock or if she could enter easily. The handle gave way and the door swung open to reveal a steep staircase. The dark chamber seemed to beckon her.

When she'd taken the clothes from this roof, there'd been little evidence of a lady of the house. Most of her treasures came from the women polits so she hadn't come back. Could her grandfather be lonely? Paul didn't seem like he'd much company. Maybe this drove him to search out remnants of his older son even with their shafter blood.

Trina made her way down the narrow staircase, listening at every turn. Though she'd never been in Grandfather's house, she'd found the insides of polit dwellings had the same basic structure. Grandfather wouldn't be on this stair. She'd have to move into the main house. Only servants came to the roof.

She ran her hand across the walls at each small landing, seeking doors opening onto the rest of the house. The first she bypassed because it came too soon. Most likely, it opened onto the servants' rooms. The next she leaned against, listening intently. Not too far away, she could hear voices.

"I just stored all these linens and now I have to pull them out again? And for what? Who would have thought a grand polit would just walk away?"

"Why not? He's never been the same since Master Jared left. The heart went out of him. First his wife, then his heir."

"And that Paul is no help either. Serves him right to be frozen like one of us."

"Maybe the chill will teach him some manners."

Trina pulled away, smiling when she heard the laughter though their words made no sense. She walked further down the stair, her thoughts drifting to what the voices said about her grandfather. It seemed his servants thought well enough of him to sympathize, and his obsession with her father rang true. She hadn't needed their opinion on Paul. She'd formed enough of one herself.

The next door didn't feel right. She couldn't explain it, but she didn't ignore her instincts either. She hadn't come so far to be dumped in front of her grandfather as a sneak thief. Whatever he'd intended, finding her in this way would make his offer into the trap Katie feared.

Just as she reached the next landing, the door she'd avoided above her opened. The footsteps headed toward her, and she had to take the only shelter available. Twisting the knob, she pushed, surprised at how easily the door swung open, silent on well-oiled hinges.

A quick glance revealed a linen closet of sorts. Safety. She closed the door behind her and leaned against it, listening for voices.

After a tense moment in anticipation of discovery, Trina relaxed enough to explore her environment. Each surface held cloth of a different weight or color, more than any one family could use up in a lifetime. She ran a finger along a fine fabric, the weave so tight it seemed to glimmer in the half-light coming from under the outer door.

Her touch left a dark smear on the cloth, clear evidence she'd been there. Trina's mind drifted for just a moment, imagining a life where she had hands clean enough to touch the softness. She shook her head. There was no time to daydream. If Grandfather truly wanted to help them, maybe someday her hands would stay clean.

She almost laughed at the thought as she carefully flipped the cloth to hide both the evidence of her passage and her longing. Even if she lived as a polit, her hands would seek out dirty ways and smears would appear on her face. She wasn't the type to sit still and let others do for her what she could do for herself.

A noise outside the door had Trina dropping down and crouching in the shadows. She watched the small strip of light but no darkness crossed it.

Had Piper spied on her, their friendship would be destroyed, but anyone could act true when distant from natural trappings. She couldn't convince Katie, or risk their mother, until she knew her grandfather meant what he'd said. If that made him withdraw the offer, better to stay as they were than to discover his true purpose too late.

She'd once thought Fence some kind of friend until she'd seen him encourage his goons to take a pound of flesh from a shafter who'd failed a deal. From that day on, she never made deals. She brought items, and he bought them or not. She didn't promise nor accept ahead no matter how low the coins grew. She'd made the change from pickpocket to house thief rather than accept money from Fence that she hadn't already paid for with stolen items.

Katie had been right to question. Had their grandfather given coin too easily? Trina had failed to see Fence for what he was at first. Her desire for the surface could have changed how she saw Grandfather. Let her see that love and caring in his life if he truly wanted to have her family.

A trickle of hope ran through her as she remembered the servants, but she pushed it back. Loyalty didn't mean he couldn't be ruthless to those outside his household. And how he saw her family remained to be seen. Shafters weren't welcome among polits, no matter what their genetic inheritance.

She'd waited long enough, and to tarry more risked the discovery she feared. Trina eased the door opposite from where she'd come in open and blinked at the bright light from windows lining one side of the hall. The lack of decoration on the walls revealed this was a servant area still even without the linen closet. None of these doors would lead to Grandfather.

She moved quickly, uncomfortable with the length and lack of shadows. There were no good hiding places.

The hallway ended in a junction. She glanced both ways before stretching a foot out cautiously. Here, she found the decorations she'd been expecting. A short way down the hall, a landing led onto a much wider staircase with a decorated banister: the main staircase.

Trina leaned her head out over the landing. In the far distance below, she heard some voices, too quiet to make out what they said. She turned the other way, looking up the stair. Though she heard nothing, Trina remained still. The sound of Grandfather's voice rewarded her patience.

"Not as easy as you'd think."

Steps moved away from the stairs and she heard the sound of a door closing.

She didn't know who else was there, but she'd be sure to learn more if she could hear them.

Trina moved onto the landing and walked up slowly. She kept her feet to the outer edges of each step, where the stair met the wall, to avoid any weaknesses. Her efforts failed on the fifth one. Even touching only the outer edge, the wood groaned in complaint.

She froze. There was no escape from here. Either she'd have to run up where Grandfather was, or into the servants coming to see who made the noise. She prayed to the Ceric god harder than she ever had, hoping beyond hope the sound went unnoticed.

No one came. No alarm sounded. Trina let out a breath she hadn't known she held, flinching when the step groaned again as she lifted her foot off it. She went up the main staircase quickly, determined to get out of this trap before they caught her.

At the next landing, Trina glanced into the hallway. It was clear. She crossed to the first door and pressed her ear against it. Nothing. She moved to the next and the next still without result. Trina wondered if she'd heard him up one more floor but persisted because only two rooms remained.

At the next door, she found what she listened for: Grandfather's voice.

"I want you to find out exactly what each family is bringing. Everything." The familiar rumble held such a commanding tone that Trina nodded. Now she'd learn who he really was.

"There isn't much time. This isn't like you."

"Let's just say my eyes have been opened. First City is a withered husk—you know it as well as I do. A new colony offers opportunities Ceric cannot."

"Only if you head the colony, and coming in so late, you'll be the last to influence anything."

A bark of laughter and, "I don't plan to stay at the bottom for long. I'll pay for as many seekers as you need to find out what the others have. I won't start out at more of a disadvantage than I already have."

"This purse will cover me for now. I'll come for more as needed. I never thought you'd be following Jared. That was my job."

Trina pressed closer at the mention of her father, glad the latch held and she didn't tumble into the room in her urgency. She moved back as he continued on another thread.

"True enough, but times change. We'll need more than just those who put in the Festival request. We'll need the right people from all walks of life, those who show initiative and are hard workers. Collect them. I need every skill a colony could possibly require and even some of the more specialized ones. Should we find gemstones, I don't want to lose the trade value and give raw stones to someone else to polish."

"Word's gone out for a colony ship, and there's one not half a month from here in need of minor servicing and restock. That's not much time to convince so many people."

"You know the ways. Do whatever you have to."

Trina shivered at her grandfather's tone. Had she misjudged him? Was he no better than the slavers in shafter deeps? Then she remembered his offer of coin. Who wouldn't accept a new life with full pockets? Wasn't that what drew her?

A loud thumping from the staircase jolted her out of her thoughts. She raced back to the third room, grateful to find it unlocked. She slipped inside, her heart pounding. Trina prayed the heavy tread masked the snick when her door latched. The same step groaned its protest, only just audible over the thump.

Trina watched the bottom of the doorframe, her vigilance rewarded when the shadow fell across the strip. She tensed, but the footsteps passed by.

"Paul." The brusque greeting got no response that she could hear as her uncle passed the visitor who was leaving.

Not interested in Paul's grievances, Trina glanced around the room she found herself in. Unlike the meticulous cleaning that kept the halls clear, this room lay under a thick coating of dust. Careful not to touch anything, she crossed to the curtained window and pushed the cloth aside to let a little light into the abandoned room.

Bookcases lined one wall, gaping holes revealing where one book or another no longer stood. A large desk filled the back corner with a leather chair behind it. She crossed to the desk, wondering what she could learn by rifling the drawers.

Her fingers froze, outstretched, as her gaze fell on a small, framed picture on the desktop. She knew those features better than any others even in the rough sketch of a Festival painting. Trina sank into the chair, forgetting her plan to avoid disturbing the dust as much as possible. She stared at her mother's image, stunned at how much change the illness had caused.

The picture and the dust suddenly came together in her mind and she knew whose space she hid in. The abandoned pen; a small, blunt knife; and the globe of glass showing a metal tower all meant something more than their worth.

Her father's room.

She sat in his chair, touched his things. From the painting, Mother may have been right. Maybe he had loved her enough to send for her. That he hadn't must mean he could not. She picked up the picture with a trembling hand, dust falling to cover the clean space the picture had left.

"You were right, Mother. He loved you."

She put the picture back and looked around the room again, seeking an image of her father, something to make him real. There was nothing. He'd known his own features well enough and hadn't been the type to preserve his image, a trait she normally appreciated, but now it deprived her.

Her fingers hovered over the globe, a unique object she'd never seen before. Then, she moved to the knife, thinking her collection could always use another and she could sharpen its blunt edges. She wondered for a moment why her father felt it necessary to keep a weapon so close to hand in his own home.

An argument grew loud in the next room, revealing a connecting door she hadn't noticed where it stood in shadow. Trina snatched the pen, a memento of the man she'd never known, and tucked it into a pocket inside her tunic before slipping away from the desk and approaching the door. She didn't need to press her ear to the thin wood. Their shouted words passed through clearly.

"You've taken away everything I had, even Mother's legacy!"

Trina recognized Paul's voice.

Grandfather laughed. "I should never have indulged you so long. As much as I may regret how you've turned out, this family will not suffer for it."

Her grandfather continued in a more reasonable tone. "I've stolen nothing from you. Your allowance originally came from your mother's legacy, as did payments to cover your debts and keep the enforcers from dirtying the Menthak name. I didn't steal it. You've wasted a fortune already."

"You'd really leave me destitute? Your own son?"

Trina heard the shock in Paul's voice and felt it echo in her own heart. Whatever he was, family came first.

"No."

Relief flooded Trina, making her aware just how much she want-ed—needed—their grandfather to be true. Katie had been right to cau-tion.

"Only you can make that choice, Paul. I won't make it for you."

She heard a creak as if one of them sat down.

"And what other choice are you offering? To be frozen among the laborers and taken to struggle on a fresh colony? Even your servants are amazed at the thought."

Paul's voice sounded further away, as if he'd been the one to move.

Trina allowed his words to filter through her memory again. That had been what the servants were talking about. She leaned closer, trying to understand.

"If hard labor's what it takes to bring you back from your wasteful existence, then that's what I offer you. I'll be working right alongside you, shaping a new colony and crafting a world where before only wasteland stood. Just as I intend to do with you."

Paul laughed. "You're joining this colony ship late enough that you'll have no say in the shaping. You take us from the top of a prosperous colony to the very bottom. Our family will bear the grunt tasks while others do the shaping. If we're lucky, in five generations, we'll be al-lowed to form our own city on the worst of the available land."

"You never understood, did you? Everything's changeable. You only need to find the key. You think our ancestors sat complacent after their ship rose into the sky? You think those descended from royalty chose to take directions from glorified horse traders? Just as our ancestors before, I'm crafting our future even as we speak. Fate and fortune fol-low those who work hard."

"And you'll work at it? Why freeze me then? Surely as your heir—"

"What good could you do me? You are heir only in the blood that runs through your veins. Those who stay and eat into our precious re-sources must each serve a purpose in preparing for the touchdown two years later. When you pop out of your ice coffin, restored to health and life at the same age as you bear now, I will have created a dynasty. You'll have as much to do with its making as you've aided me here."

He paused and the silence seemed heavy.

"But I'll give you this chance. Once freed from hibernation, if you join in my labors, the family will look to you for its next age. If not, then maybe it's time to forget my sweet Elise and sire another to take your place."

The roar of rage from Paul almost had Trina bursting through the door to defend her grandfather, all questions forgotten. The lock kept her from foolishness even though her knife's rough hilt pressed against her free hand.

"This serves nothing, Paul. Learn to use your emotions, not waste them." Firm footsteps moved toward the hallway, dragging a weight with them. The outer door opened and she heard a thump as if Paul hit the floor.

"If you want to succeed, you'll find some maturity. Next attack and I'll set the enforcers on you. Now get out of my sight. I have much to do."

The door shut with only a little more force than necessary, as if illustrating his point about control.

Trina waited for Paul's next move, her body thrumming with tension. She felt a brush of sympathy for him, and wondered how threats and such ruthlessness aided Grandfather's plans.

Paul's heavy steps pounded down the stairs and sounded as angry as his outburst.

She listened at the door, but heard nothing else. She needed to think about what she'd learned. Looking around her father's room one last time, Trina took a deep breath, trying to find in the old scents something like the lemon her mother loved. She smelled only dust.

CHAPTER 11

S amuel smiled at the snick of the latch next door. He'd kept Jared's study exactly as his son left it. Fate must have drawn Trina there.

He'd caught a glimpse of her dirty blond head coming up the stairs when talking with his man on the landing. If Paul had been with him then, she'd have disappeared with all the skill in her little body. Instead, he'd pointedly moved the discussion to his office in the hopes she'd follow.

He barely paid attention to the conversation beyond preparations for the colony ship. He'd been listening for the step. She couldn't have known it was there, and sure enough, he'd heard the creak as she stood on it.

Waiting long enough for Trina to escape down the staircase, he noticed this time she avoided his warning step. She couldn't have been here before, and he doubted he'd get the warning if she came again.

No simple pickpocket, Trina knew enough to make her way into the homes of polits. He remembered complaints of items gone missing and smiled, wondering how many of those baubles kept his blood fed. Polits could be so complacent. Shafters seemed created by God to shake them out of their believed superiority, making them prey to a different type of predator.

He opened the door slowly, leaning into the hallway and glancing both directions before stepping out. Samuel met the startled gaze of one of the servants and gave her a cocky grin. She looked surprised at that and a little worried. He'd never wondered what his household thought of his sudden desire to found a colony. They'd come with him of course, and their families. Did they want to? Did they like him?

The odd thought disturbed Samuel, again wondering at the effect of the little sprite who haunted his dreams. Could he take the twins frozen as well? They would never forgive him even if he managed to capture them.

His hand on the outer door to Jared's study, Samuel sighed. No, they had to come of their own free will. He'd made the mistake of trying to control Jared. If he wanted a mindless follower, he'd do better to look outside his own bloodlines. When Trina came for the coins tomorrow, he'd make his new offer. Polit life might not draw Jared's children, but perhaps they shared his love for the stars.

Samuel refused to consider the possibility Jared's children would say no. Images of his branch of the Menthak family growing healthy and strong again poured through him. He had two sisters, but their children took after the fathers, lacking the essence more even than Paul did. If he stayed here, the family would wither and die. On a new world, they'd spread and grow strong again as they were in the beginning of Ceric. Menthak weren't meant to be petty administrators. They were meant to create and control.

Samuel turned the knob then hesitated. He hadn't set foot in this room since Jared's ship soared into the sky. No one else had either. The dust lay thick on top of his memories, broken only by smudged footsteps where she'd tried to mask her presence.

Always attuned to that room even after it had stood empty for so long, he'd heard the small sounds of an occupant before the argument with Paul became too loud. For a moment, he'd thought a ghost haunted him until he realized Paul's passage must have driven his sprite within. The joining door stood locked as Jared always kept it, preferring his father came from the hall instead of bursting in whenever he felt like it.

At first, the locked door had opposed Samuel, but he'd come to see it as a sign of Jared's maturity. He was forever looking for signs, for proof his heir grew ready to take the mantle. He'd been so busy searching Jared for the ability to manage the complexities of maintaining position, running the city economy, and supervising the classes, he'd missed the wistful look whenever his son stared into the sky.

Samuel crossed to the window, seeing small streaks where his granddaughter had pulled the curtain to one side, though she probably thought to let light into the room rather than doing so to look out. He looked down at Old Samuel standing so proud in the square below. Whenever he caught Jared at this window, his son's gaze pointed upward. He'd seen enough to guess Jared would choose a different path if only he'd paid attention.

After the colony ship leapt into the sky never to return, when Samuel picked through his memories, he could recognize moments and conversations that revealed Jared's hopes. Only he took too long to figure it out and waited sixteen more years to understand what had driven his heir. But he understood now. Well enough for the father to follow the son instead of the other way round.

Samuel shifted his gaze to stare up at the midday sky. "I'm taking your daughters to the stars, Jared. You would've wanted them to join you. I know you well enough now to understand that. You'd have found a way if you could."

He turned, trying to see the room with Trina's eyes. He followed the light to Jared's desk, seeing smears on the chair. She'd sat down, probably thinking about her father. He copied her path. The groan of leather surprised him. Her weight hadn't made any sound.

Samuel put his arms on the desk, lacing his fingers in his customary pose and one he'd seen Jared imitate many times. He scanned the surface. A letter opener lay next to an ancient globe of some monument back on Earth Jared had treasured. Samuel noticed a hole in the dust and smiled. Trina had taken a memento.

His smile fell away as he found the picture. They'd argued on the day Jared left. Samuel had blocked his son's way to the study in an effort to make Jared drop such a crazy idea. Like Samuel's, Jared's decision to join the ship seemed sudden. Only after careful research had he realized his son spent months planning this escape and keeping all evidence from his preoccupied father.

Samuel picked up the picture, wiping it clean with his fingers. The smiling redheaded girl looked beautiful. The artist had captured a mischievous glint in her eyes. Trina's mother, no doubt, though he couldn't see any sign of his sprite in the well-built frame or rounded features. If he hadn't blocked Jared's path, this piece of Trina's heritage would probably have been lost along with his son.

He tucked the picture into his belt, thinking to give it to Trina. No one looking at the painting would ever see a shafter. It was safe enough.

When they touched down on their new world, Trina's bloodlines would be remembered differently. Who could tell whether his tale of a redhead from one of the families back on Ceric was true or not? He had the picture to prove she wasn't some scrappy shafter after all, even if she had not aged well.

How easily he assumed they'd come, but he didn't want to consider the other option.

CHAPTER 12

T he sun sank behind the buildings even as Trina stared through the silver links at the deep black ground beyond. The ships still seemed far away.

Half a month. Of everything she'd heard in the afternoon, that piece of information stuck.

One day she'd be too slow to snatch and grab, and enforcers would take her. Katie would starve or be "adopted" by one of the shafter slavers.

If he meant his offer to save them, it seemed now he regretted the decision enough to flee Ceric to avoid them.

Wind blew hair across her face, slashing her with sharp whips as if a taste of her prospects. Ceric held no future for either twin, but even if he meant to take them with him, how could she convince Katie when her sister didn't trust Grandfather enough to go to the surface?

She sank down onto the dirt, her fingers laced through the links of the fence. The servants seemed to like him. The few she'd seen looked well fed and dressed. Not in fancy clothes, but ones less worn than Trina's. He took care of his own.

Grandfather said only those who could help would stay unfrozen. She tried to work out the tangle of his relationship with her uncle. She knew Paul's type, but she believed families should stand by their members. Grandfather pushed Paul hard. The trouble was Trina didn't know enough to tell if he pushed out of loyalty, or spite.

A spaceship's engines flared and it jumped up into the sky. Trina followed the progress with her gaze. She'd always believed life was different up there, but now she wondered how it could be if people stayed the same. Would her blood still say shafter on another world?

Trina traced her fingers through the dirt of First City until her hand reached the fence. She slipped one finger under, meeting the edge of the hard black surface coating the spaceport ground. In color and texture, the two seemed so different. How could things not change past the fence?

She drew out the pen she'd taken from her father's office and traced the lines on her palm. Any ink in it had dried long ago. Whatever wisdom her father could have offered had also been lost. She stared at the pen for a long while before thrusting it back into the hidden pocket.

"IS HE EVERYTHING YOU THOUGHT? Or will you have to spin me a tale?"

Trina flinched at the biting words the moment she stepped in the door. She choked down a protest that she'd never make up stories about this as part of her wished she could. "It's hard to tell. Their ways are different from ours."

On the couch, Katie pulled her knees to her chest in a defensive move. "What do you mean? Of course, polits are different. That's why you should stay here and not mingle with those you'll never understand."

"You know I'd do anything for you, Katie. You know that. It wouldn't matter whether we fight or anything. We're family."

Katie scowled. "You think I stop caring just because you tear my heart out every time you go up there? We are family. Nothing changes that—nothing."

Trina shook her head. "Not you. I'd never think you. It's Grandfather." She hadn't meant to start with Paul, but the words had already escaped.

Katie's head sank on her knees. "Seems like he's trying to pull his family together," she mumbled.

Trina wished she could rejoice at Katie saying anything positive, but instead she started to pace. "But is it always what it seems with them?" She stopped in front of her sister and took both of Katie's hands in hers. "He's going on a colony ship. He didn't say so when he made the offer, but surely that was part of his decision." He'd told Paul he'd sire a new heir, not that he'd claim them for that purpose. Trina shook off the memory. "I need you to agree. Even if we're not sure of Grandfather, it has to be different out there."

Katie's face looked pinched as she stared around the main room. "But, this is home."

Trina squeezed her hands. "This is just a room. Everything in it's only stuff. The ship isn't just a chance for us. It's what Mother wanted since before we were born." She swallowed hard. "And it's her only chance. The spacers might have a cure."

Katie gave a bitter laugh. "You think the spacers can do anything. You believe if we go to the stars there'll be no polits, no laborers, no shafters, just people. Look around you. This is the real world, not the fairy-tale books we both love. This *is* a colony. How could any other be different? Besides, Mother wouldn't survive the liftoff."

Trina's hands clenched. "Is that any worse than now? You tend her. How can you have missed the signs? She won't last much longer without a miracle. Spacers could be that miracle."

Katie pulled her hands free and folded her arms so Trina couldn't catch her again. "You'd chance what time she has left? You think by starting again things will be different, but they won't. We'll be nothing more than laborers to the polits and even worse to the laborers who come. We have no skills they'd need and would have to earn the right to eat by taking on the lowest tasks. You think your precious polits would listen to those who dig the sewers? The new colony will be exactly like this one, only with no shafts to escape into."

Trina smiled at that, remembering that she'd learned something from her grandfather after all. "I heard them talking. They need skilled crafters and are willing to pay well for it. You're as skilled as they come with a needle and thread. As long as fibrous crops grow or we bring wool-bearing animals, you'll be needed."

Katie stood up. "And what role do you serve? How are these skills of yours going to help any colony? What kind of colony imports sneak thieves as part of the original members?"

"I'll find something," Trina said with more confidence than she really felt. "I'm not worthless like our uncle. I can learn."

CHAPTER 13

T rina dug through a pile of clothing scavenged from polit discards for the one with Grandfather's symbol. Each piece showed enough wear that no polit would be seen in it, but servants often wore the castoffs, and she thought it would make Grandfather happy. When she found the pants, she grabbed a tunic as well.

The brush of much-patched linen seared her face as Trina changed. Her bruise had spread, a dark blue-purple stretching from her hairline down to frame one eye.

"Do you have to go now?"

The soft question hung in the air for a moment before Trina turned to see her sister standing in the kitchen doorway.

"You shouldn't have gone yesterday, looking like a victim, but at least you weren't hanging about the streets. You think they won't mark you? If you saw someone torn up the way you are, you'd ask questions even down here. That face would hang around in the back of your mind for days. It's too risky."

Trina pulled on the pants bearing Grandfather's symbol. "I promised to go to the square in two days, Katie. If he is planning to take us, we'll need passes. About two weeks is all we have."

Katie shook her head. "You can't trust him. He's a polit like the rest. There's no good reason to have shafters with him."

A glance at the clock told Trina she didn't have time for an argument, not if she planned to be in the square early enough to avoid the work crowds. "You don't have to trust him. Trust me. We can't stay here in the shafts. It's not safe."

"It's no more dangerous today than it was before you cut that polit, and safer than up there."

Trina had already started toward the door, but at Katie's words, she turned back. "Is that enough? Is survival enough? Don't you ever long for more than a few short hours in the market before you have to hide back here again?"

Katie sank onto the couch and drew her knees to her chest. "I've learned to be happy. If you don't ask for much, you don't waste your life wanting more. Accept what you're given and happiness follows."

A laugh Trina couldn't stifle burst forth, harsh and bitter. "True happiness? Or just enough so you don't bash your head in? What we have here isn't worth accepting. You let your fears trap you, but I won't. We have a real chance now. I won't waste that on clinging to so little."

She didn't wait to hear Katie's response, almost running on her way out of the apartment.

TRINA LET HER EYES ADJUST before stepping into the pool of light surrounding the first junction. Their grandfather said polits were much the same as shafters despite their better surroundings: some good, some bad. If only she could be sure he stood with the trustworthy ones. She had no proof that enforcers wouldn't be waiting to drag her off. Despite Katie's doubts, Trina wasn't stupid, but he'd had trapped her before. What did he gain from letting her go?

Finally, Trina pulled herself up through an opening into the midday sun. She had until she stepped into the square to decide whether to follow her heart or Katie's fears. If Grandfather truly meant to accept them, they'd be living the dream of every crossbred child, that the higher parent would claim them and free them from the shafts. How many times did it really happen though, even when that parent was a laborer not a polit?

Darkness swirled around Trina where before her future seemed clear enough. As a little child, she'd believed her mother and waited too. She'd dreamed not of the surface or another colony but of being in the vastness of space, becoming a spacer.

A child's rhyme ran through her head. "Nanny Nanny Nick, girl is in a snit, kick her toe or let her go, Nanny Nanny Nick." Her mind bounced between the two possibilities, leave or stay, with each part of the rhyme. Disappointment welled up as she realized where it would end.

Trina firmed her jaw. When had she let fear drive her? She slurred the last Nick, making it two syllables and choosing to go on. No matter how satisfied Katie said she was, their life could be better. Trina could make it better just by stepping forward three strides and announcing herself.

She strode into the square with a confidence she didn't truly feel and scanned the space to orient herself from this new entry point.

A man stood next to a woman perched on the fountain's lip, his dark brown hair falling forward as he leaned toward her. The bench

Trina knew all too well held one person, male or female she couldn't tell from the back. Otherwise, any number of people could be watching for her from the windows in the buildings.

She forced her shoulders straight though she wanted to shrink to make a smaller target. No one seemed to pay her any attention, but Trina felt as though they all stared, questioning her presence, questioning her bruises. Somewhere among them was a person who would alert her grandfather as soon as she was seen.

The last thought sent her forward again. She crossed to the fountain, choosing a spot to lean against it where both the lovers and the person on the bench were visible in the corners of her eyes.

Though she wanted to sit up on the edge, Trina kept both feet firmly planted on the ground as she listened. First sound of marching boots and she'd slip out another way. If he thought to trap her, he'd be disappointed.

Confidence faded as she considered what might happen if he didn't mean to trick her, if his offer stayed true. They would go and live in a fancy polit house with servants just like those she plundered, but with him gone, who would defend their right to be there. He must want them to come on the ship.

A LIGHT KNOCK, AND SAMUEL's study door swung open to reveal the messenger, escorted by his servant Bettina.

He jolted upright. Samuel had thought for sure Trina wouldn't take the risk. Another sign of Jared in the little one. How many more reminders of his lost son would he find in her?

"You wanted to know when the girl returned."

As though the man's presence would have any other meaning. "Of course. You're sure it's her?"

"I can't imagine many looking like that painting and wearing a purple bruise over half her face. You really gave her a beating."

Samuel winced. "She fell. I had no intention of hurting her, but I needed to restrain her. Trust doesn't come easy to one who's had to fight for everything in her life."

"So you say." The man shrugged. "The resemblance is uncanny. She's a feminized version of the boy you set me to track so long ago."

He'd aged as they both had since the long ago time when Samuel set him to watch over Jared, but that didn't make him any less good at what he did. A pity he'd chosen the life he knew over starting fresh. Samuel could use men like him in the shipboard struggles to come.

"True enough. Now if only she shares his dreams." The last a murmur to himself.

"You'll find out right quick if you head down there. She seemed a little skittish to me so you may not want to wait too long. In the center it feels like eyes watch from every window." The man turned to leave but Samuel walked around his desk and put out a hand to delay him.

"A present for your troubles and for your good work over the years." He placed a nicely bulging pouch in his messenger's hand, closing the man's fingers over it.

"You won't be needing more, then?"

Samuel let out a bark of laughter. "Oh, I may. I just didn't want to forget in the rush. Things are likely to become quite interesting around here." Samuel paused. "Not long at all before we'll rise off into the sky."

"Thank you for this." The messenger touched the pouch to his forehead. "And I'll wait your call for more."

This time Samuel didn't prevent his leaving, listening for the man's quiet movement down the wooden stairs until he passed the creaky fifth step.

Samuel shrugged. As the messenger said, he had his own business to be about. He'd promised Trina another purse, a sizable one.

He went back around his desk and unlocked the coin drawer. Coins of all sizes lay in careful rows. He took some silver, ha'silver and copper, then reached for a gold. At the last moment, he hesitated. What was the right amount? He wanted to give Trina just enough for a taste, a tease. If he'd read her correctly, she wouldn't bring her family into the situation until she knew a lot more about it and saw the gains clearly.

At least, he hoped she thought that way. He'd set his path in motion, and he didn't intend to miss another moment with Jared's children. He wondered whether Trina held title of thief from luck, or skill. If the later, she'd offer more to his hopes than continuing Jared's bloodline. She could work hand in hand with him to bring about their success.

Intent on his thoughts, he almost didn't hear Paul pounding up the staircase. The weakened step drew his attention when nothing else had. Samuel reached out to sweep the coins back into the drawer then paused. Maybe it was time Paul decided about the changes in his circumstances.

"I hope those coins are for me, Dad," Paul drawled as he stepped through the doorway.

"Come sit. We need to talk. Have you given some thought to what I told you?" Samuel watched Paul cross the room and lower himself into the visitor's chair, his proper posture a clear sign he felt nervous.

"First you talk to that dangerous shafter girl, and now the colony. Should I be setting a competency check in motion? You're not as young as you once were. Maybe you should hand over control of First City just like your father did." Though Paul kept his tone even, he twisted his fingers together in his lap.

"Oh, I know exactly what I'm doing…which is more than I can say for you most of the time. There'll be a new grand polit of First City soon enough. It's past time for me to get a fresh perspective."

Paul rose and crossed the room, bracing his hands on the desk. "Father, I never thought you'd do this. You spent all your time mourning Jared and dismissing me. I never realized what you've intended all along. That thing about being frozen was a test. Of course I'll take the mantle."

Samuel answered his son's wide grin with a frown. "Sit down, Paul. No matter how much you'd like me to be, I'm not incompetent. It would be criminal, or worse, to leave this city in your hands. You couldn't administrate a meal, much less a government." Samuel followed through on his first instinct and swept the money back into his drawer, making sure none stayed within Paul's grasp.

"And why not? It can't be very difficult. You have servants and laborers doing the real work. You've just never given me a chance. What am I supposed to do while you go out and kill yourself trying to start again? I don't suppose you'll be leaving the family fortune behind." Paul flopped back in the chair, his petulance come to the fore again.

"I told you. There is no fortune. What little I had left went to fund this expedition." He continued over Paul's gasp, "Don't worry. You're still welcome to fall in with the plans I have for you. I encourage it. I can't fairly inflict you on anyone else."

The change in Paul's face was almost comical. "Cryo fails. You can't freeze me!" His voice crawled higher with each word. "You can't really mean to."

"You're less critical than the laborers who will change a barren wasteland into a viable colony. Besides, I couldn't manage two years with your whining in my ear. You'll serve more of a purpose frozen than awake." Samuel smiled, enjoying his son's stunned look. The risk of system failure used to be high—the first Ceric colonists created the doctrines so no one would forget—but times change. He'd paid enough attention to the spacer reports to know that much. Whole ships vanished, but rarely did they report system failures anymore.

Paul swallowed hard. "I won't go. I don't need this new start. I'm doing fine here."

Samuel had expected Paul's rejection. Expected and planned for it. "What will you do here? You've wasted all chance to become a teacher, and you have no head for governance or administration. What laborer would accept a self-satisfied wastrel? You can stay here if you like, but you'll be starting fresh with nothing just as my grandchildren, your nieces, had to."

"You have no grandchildren, none but those Festival-got of Jared's."

Samuel couldn't quite contain his surprise. Who'd spread that information? And how could he punish the indiscretion?

His failure of a son laughed, comfortable enough now to lounge with one leg over the arm of the chair. "You thought I didn't know. I know all that you do. You weren't the only one to follow my dear brother. If I could've caught him doing something…well, you wouldn't have treated me quite so shabbily. If only he hadn't taken it into his head to get on that colony ship. Knowing your golden boy, he would have tried to bring that trollop and her half-breed kids into the family. You'd never have stood for that."

Samuel controlled his anger with effort. "That's where you'd be wrong, Paul. I welcome his children into my barren life."

Paul sat up straight, shock painted on his face. "You wouldn't dare."

"I already have. I asked them to come live with me. They'll help make up for the waste my second son turned out to be. Enough, I have places to go."

"But-but—" Paul sputtered. "You lost them years ago. Even combing the shafts for them. They probably died." He straightened. "You're just trying to get a rise out of me."

Samuel laughed. "If that were my intent, I'd have clearly succeeded, but you're wrong again. You never were the observant type. You actually brought them back to me."

His son shifted in the chair as if suddenly uncomfortable. "I did?"

"Oh, yes. You and your marauding friends. Did you really think Jared's sense of right and wrong wouldn't breed true?" Samuel savored the look of dawning comprehension on his second son's face. This seemed suitable repayment for all the grief the boy had caused him. This, and an end to his wasteful ways. The colony should offer the second if Paul wanted to survive.

"You mean the girl?"

"Your six-foot, sword-wielding amazon? Funny, Jared always loved tales of good winning out over those who harmed the lowly. It seems a form of justice that his scrap of a daughter lived up to his morality, doesn't it?" He glanced over at Paul, enjoying the stunned look. "Hard to imagine for me too, but fate plays a hand in all our lives, and God rewards those who work hard to deserve their place in the world."

He didn't bother to repeat the rest. They both knew it well enough. Finding Trina seemed Paul's punishment for wasted years. Maybe his son would choose not to risk more of fate's bounty.

Samuel pulled open the drawer again, grabbing a handful from the coins now jumbled within. He pushed them into one of the pouches kept with the coins and slammed the drawer shut, pointedly turning the key and pocketing it.

"The servants will see you out if you can't find your own path."

His veiled threat had an immediate effect on Paul, who scrambled to his feet. "I'll find a way around this, Father. You know I will. No one will suffer shafter rats in the family. Festival-got on a laborer maybe, but shafter blood is thick with criminal elements. If this is the foundation of the new colony, you'll have a revolt on your hands."

Samuel waited for Paul to precede him out of the room. "You do what you have to. It'll be good for you to work on something. You'll need those skills on our new planet."

He closed the door and brushed past his remaining son, making his way down the stairs with quiet elegance, a marked contrast to Paul's heavy steps behind him.

CHAPTER 14

Samuel reached the square, a smile of anticipation already on his face. He looked where he'd caught her the first time but a young couple shared a flask there instead. He scanned the square. His chest tightened as he thought he'd missed her, but he refused to give up. The argument with Paul couldn't have eliminated any chance. She wouldn't come twice. He paced around the fountain.

There she stood, slumped against the fountain edge, her blond hair slicked to her face with sweat from the hot sun. She looked more like her father than ever before. He savored the image for a long moment.

"Just going to stare? Thought you had coins for me."

Samuel jumped, sure she hadn't noticed him. He should have known better. She'd never have made it to…he paused to figure her age. Around fifteen years old. Almost an adult though he'd never have guessed it. "You remind me so much of your father."

Trina tossed the hair back from her face and grinned. Leaping up in a single fluid movement, she sauntered toward him.

Samuel gasped at the sight of her bruising. "I am sorry for that." He reached out to touch, and she flinched away.

"I'll heal." She stuck out a hand. "The purse?"

"I have it right here. I'll give it to you after we talk."

He could tell she didn't like the idea the moment the words left his mouth. Her jaw tensed until his own ached in sympathy.

"Never mind. You can have it now." He berated himself for treating her as he treated others he dealt with. Shafters wouldn't like being trapped. If he wanted her to stay, he'd have to make it interesting and worth her while.

She snatched the purse, and for a moment, he thought she'd disappear before he could catch her. Then she stuffed it in her tunic, turned, and jumped up on the fountain ledge.

"So talk."

His mind went blank as he watched her swing both legs back and forth, looking more like a real child than he'd ever seen her. He wanted to pick Trina up and spin her around as he'd done with his boys even though he knew she was years past that age. He wanted to teach her to play. He wanted to give her everything she'd missed in her life as a shafter.

But the real question was what Trina wanted.

Instead of asking if she'd thought about his offer, Samuel looked over her clothes. "Did you buy those clothes off the servants?"

Trina froze, her body tense with expectation.

"Don't worry. You can have them. No polit would wear them anyway. It's just, well, you're wearing my house logo—your house logo." He pointed to the stylized version of a horse. "It's a horse for our family. Only direct descendants of Samuel of Menthak use it. Before we left Earth, long before, we bred horses. The cell storage for that section failed or we'd have some of God's creatures to help us labor. Only some of the cow embryos survived, a good thing or there would be no milk or cheese."

Trina traced a small finger down the imprint, showing no surprise at his comment. "So that's what a horse looked like."

"How have you heard of them?"

"My father—Jared—gave my mother some books. I like fairy tales the most, but they don't have many pictures."

Samuel sat down next to her, his longer legs reaching the ground. "Your father liked those stories too." Suddenly, he revised his thoughts about the empty places in Jared's library. Apparently, those books had not gone on his son's journey. "I don't think he ever charged out to save fair maidens though. Not like you did."

Trina turned to look at him with Jared's serious eyes. "My mother thought he did. She never gives up hope he'll send for us."

Samuel risked a touch, resting one hand lightly on her shoulder.

She tensed, but didn't pull away.

"He would have, Trina. You should believe it. I do."

She squirmed and moved back. "Katie says we shouldn't believe. She says we should be happy with what we have."

He smiled. "She seems like a very interesting girl. I can't wait to meet her."

Again, Trina withdrew, sliding off the lip until she leaned against it just slightly. "She doesn't want to meet you."

Samuel almost cursed aloud. It took all his will to remain seated on the fountain's edge. "She doesn't know me, but there isn't much time."

"Why?" Trina inched a little closer. "Why isn't there much time?"

Some of his tension dissipated at her interest, and he wondered again just how much she'd overheard. "I'm leaving."

"Leaving First City?" She glanced down one of the roads as if able to see through to the second city they'd founded or even further.

"Not that way." He pointed at the sky. "I'm going there."

"To the stars?"

Something in her tone gave him hope.

"Yes. Taking a colony ship like your father did. Two years out then another world." Again, he found himself falling into a version of the shorter language she used. He struggled against the influence, inwardly laughing when he didn't quite succeed. "I decided to lead a First City group. We'll be one of many. You could join me and start again on the new colony as full members, not shafters."

She became so still he thought he'd pushed too far, had misread her confusion as interest.

"You don't have to. I'd like your company, and I think you both—all three—have things to learn from me." He stumbled over the addition, but she'd tensed when he left her mother out. "Whether you stay or go, you'll be safe. I've already worked out a messenger to deliver coin to you if you choose to stay in the shafts." He stopped, wondering if he should continue, or if he should have stopped long before. What kind of hold had he given her? And what pressure to join him had he wasted.

"You'd do that? Why?" She speared him with an intense stare, as if she could see through to his soul.

"We take care of our family."

"Like you took care of Paul? He's part of the family too, isn't he? He called you 'Dad,' like you're a shafter."

Samuel grimaced, pushing away from the edge to pace. "He calls me that to make me angry. I notice you name your mother properly, and you were born down there. The younger polits think the doctrine is so much talk. They don't care about work or family." He swiveled to face her, unwilling to be judged based on his failure of a son. "Would you treat him any better? He harassed those two ladies." At her start, he nodded. "He didn't say anything, but when he came up with a story of this amazing woman who overpowered him for no reason, I figured it out."

Trina grinned at the description.

"See? How would you treat him? If your sister behaved so poorly, would you pat her shoulder and hand her a full purse?" Some of his frustration leaked out and he saw her start at the harsh tone.

"Katie wouldn't act that way. She thinks we labor with what we're given to find the only happiness we're allowed."

Samuel waved her comment away. "I didn't mean she was, just if…never mind. You've said that before. 'Katie believes.' What do you believe? Do you think because you were born in filth you have to stay there? Even when other chances are offered?"

She looked uncomfortable for a moment, and her nose wrinkled in a familiar gesture.

Samuel held his breath.

"Why give us chances if we're not to accept? Half our birth is yours, and our father would have come for us if he could." She stopped, glancing up at him through her hair.

He tried for a reassuring smile even as joy welled up inside him. She may not have meant to reveal so much, but now he knew she'd been thinking on his offer. She'd been thinking of reasons to accept it.

Though he wanted to rejoice, he realized the offer she considered involved staying on Ceric. What good would it do for his granddaughters to live well here if he couldn't enjoy them?

Feeling his way as cautiously as he could, Samuel drew forth his offer of the colony ship again. "Maybe fate is trying to make up for your father's loss. Have you thought that there's another plan for you?" He came close and placed his hands on either side of her, dropping one to his thigh when her eyes widened in panic.

"Maybe your purpose is to help me begin again."

She slipped free of him, coming to rest two feet away. "My skills are those of a thief. What role would I serve on a colony ship?"

Samuel fought back a grin. "I need your skills, your speed and ability to fit in among people not your type."

She watched him closely.

He didn't want to scare her with polit battles and knew he hadn't gained her loyalty yet so tempered his excitement. Still, he chose to stay as close to the truth as he could. "I need you to sow confusion."

Her brow wrinkled. "Confusion? Why do you want confusion?"

He tried to picture her life and what she'd relate to. He had enough spies around the city to know most of the entrances to the shafts but had never tried to close them. The dregs of society served a purpose. If nothing else, they kept arrogant polits like Paul from getting more so.

The thought of Paul gave him the answer. "When you plan to take a purse, do you go to the person staring about? Or do you wait until the target's busy?"

"Busy. Too risky otherwise."

He could tell from her look that she tried to figure out his point. Samuel didn't want her to understand too much. She wanted a new life and wouldn't come just to be his personal thief, but her skills could be critical to making the next life possible once they got to their new planet. He spoke quickly, hoping to disrupt her thoughts. "When people are busy, they don't pay attention to anything but what's in front of them."

Trina gave him a hard stare. "What don't you want them to notice?"

Samuel laughed, hoping to mask his surprise. "You grew up in a difficult environment, but the shafts are much simpler in so many ways. Polits can't just survive. They fight for position, not with knives, but—" He stopped. "It's too hard to explain. You don't have enough of a frame of reference."

"You mean the way the brothers battle each other for dominance in fairy tales? It always seemed wrong to me because family should stick together."

Again, this child of Jared's surprised Samuel. She'd spoken as clearly as any polit, in full sentences and drawing together examples from very different sources. "It is something like that, yes."

"And which are you?"

The street-smart thief was back. Trina even adopted a more aggressive pose.

"Which what?"

"Which brother. The older one who has it all? The middle who stomps the youngest? Or the young one just trying to do well? Which brother are you?"

Samuel laughed again. "I'm a bit too old to be the youngest, aren't I? Yet, the other families who are coming have planned this colony for many years. I just decided."

Trina shifted her feet. "Decided when?"

He reached for her, dropping his hand at her flinch. "Since meeting you. You remind me of all the pieces of life lost, or hidden in the shafts. You, and a statue." He shook his head at her questioning look. He couldn't explain the old Samuel to anyone. "I want more from life than to watch my son admonished by a sprite from the underworld."

She laughed at that. "That's how you see me? Troublemakers, sprites are."

Samuel stepped close to her. "And that's what I need. The only way to keep the families from building support is to create so much confusion no one knows who'll be strongest on landing. I need you, Trina."

CHAPTER 15

T rina backed away, understanding Katie's questions better now. "What purpose will I serve on your grand colony then? What role am I to play after being your sprite?"

Grandfather's face grew blank for a moment before he shook his head. "Trina, you're smart, quick to learn, and beautiful. You'll find a place easy enough."

"Digging ditches?" She thrust her chin out.

Grandfather looked thoughtful for a moment. He sat on the fountain lip before replying. "Trina, none will know of your background but you, myself, and Paul. None need to know. You can stand at my side as polit and no one will question you."

Trina stood in front of him, her tension not relieved by his response. "Paul will question. And will you? Can you look beyond my shafter mother?"

He smiled. "My dear, you wear my own blood like a badge upon your face. There's no question you came from my line. Your shafter background is an inconvenience, nothing more. Just as you seek freedom from the dangers below, so the colony gives me freedom from some of the less useful parts of polit society."

She heard his reassurance but listened to more than just what he said. Her face, the one always separating her from Mother and Katie, who had looked more like twins than the sisters did, now marked her a polit. Katie didn't have the same badge no matter what her blood might carry. An inconvenience. He wouldn't accept them as they were but wanted their shafter blood hidden. Could she agree to that?

"Wouldn't you want it?"

She jerked, his question seeming to speak to her thoughts.

"Wouldn't you want freedom from the harsh life driving you to steal? Tell me truly: what binds you to dark tunnels when you obviously prefer the light? Out here, the air is fresh and you can see so far. I can give that to you."

But to get this, she had to deny her birth.

"Say you'll come. You can stay at my side. I'll control Paul. If he wants to survive, he'll have to adapt just as we all will. I'm sure there will be work enough to keep both you and your sister happy. Good work."

"And what of Mother?" The question burst out before she could swallow it.

He laughed, a startled sound holding little humor. "I'd love your mother to join us. I've been waiting, hoping, you'd bring your sister to meet me."

Trina noticed how quickly he dismissed their mother. "My mother is as fine a person as you've ever known. She deserves everything you offer and more. What hope has your colony of finding freedom with you at its head?" In that moment, Trina saw him as Katie had. Just another polit. He had no way of knowing their mother was too sick to contribute, but she lacked the all-precious polit blood and so did not deserve his consideration.

"Wait, Trina, I didn't mean—"

He sounded so frantic she paused in her path to the nearest escape, staying back far enough so he couldn't grab her. "What did you mean?"

He flinched at her tone. Whatever his motivations, his interest in the twins seemed genuine.

Her grandfather sighed, his hands dropping to his sides. "Surely you must see our lives are very different. For a child as young as you are, change comes easy. It's harder for those of us who've passed into adulthood a long time ago."

"And yet you go."

"You're right. I go. And my household thinks I'm insane to do it." He smiled, an expression Trina didn't quite trust. "I'll make sure there's another pass. We'll find some role even for a shafter."

Trina frowned. "We're all shafters."

"So you are, but there's more to you than just that. Your mother, well, she's lived among the lowest her whole life. It's different."

"You're wrong. You think my mother defined by where she made her home. I'm glad your son wasn't so quick to judge, or I wouldn't be here." Trina glared at him.

He leaned back against the fountain. "Show me then. Introduce us. Bring your mother and sister here. Your mother has been to the surface before at least."

Anger drained out of her at his capitulation and her inability to comply. "I can't."

"Why not?" He frowned.

Trina dropped her gaze to the ground, her cloth-covered toe prodding the dirt between stones. "Katie doesn't want to meet you."

He paled. After a moment, he said, "Then your mother."

She glanced up then down again. "Mother hasn't come since polits grabbed her for their experiments, and she met your son." The words seemed so bald she wanted to snatch them back, especially since Mother had come to see their father's messenger. Instead, she looked up to see his reaction. He hadn't known, and surely hadn't expected a subject to survive long enough to reproduce.

"I see. I'd thought Jared captured by a pretty face, but this makes more sense. He was one of the first to protest the practice. It's banned now."

Trina nodded. News travelled fast among those who moved between levels.

"And she had no ill effects?"

She choked down an angry answer. He'd never supply the pass if he knew why Mother had to come. "She's fine."

"Then bring them both. Surely Katie will come with her mother."

"No. I don't trust you yet." Better she bear the burden than Katie.

He laughed. "I did say you were smart. Why would you trust me? I'm a stranger brought into your life by the oddest circumstances, but I need trust in our relationship. I have to trust you."

Trina straightened her shoulders. "You have to earn my trust."

He relaxed against the fountain wall. "I suppose I do. What can I do to gain your trust, Trina? How can I win your favor and meet your sister? There's so little time."

"There will be enough time on the ship."

He started for a heartbeat then a grin lightened his stern features. "Does that mean you accept? Both…all three of you will come?"

"Yes." She'd make Katie see this as the only way.

"Well enough. You're welcome on the ship. I'll have your gate passes waiting for you the next time you come here. Be ready. You cannot miss the ship. We'll board all day and lift into the evening sky. If you're not there, even I can't hold the launch for you."

Trina nodded her understanding but waited. She knew there must be more. Even if he'd brushed over her work before, nothing came free, especially not from a polit. The silence stretched for long enough that shadows crawled across the square as the sun moved past its height. Unable to help herself, she fidgeted, her movement breaking through the moment.

Grandfather coughed. "You recall what we discussed earlier?"

She nodded again, making him state his deal clearly.

"You'll have a place in the colony at my side, I swear. But in return, I'd like you to work with me to…manage the families."

He stepped closer and she didn't move back. She thought they understood each other well enough now.

"Through confusion? But how do you want me to do that?" Trina moved to one side, so she could lean against the wall and feign relaxation.

"I'll need you to deliver and collect items from the various families, sometimes overtly, though never as yourself, and sometimes just leaving them within one section or another. I'll do the rest."

Trina thought about what he asked. "Sounds easy enough. How can that help you?"

He smiled. "If the families battle among themselves, they cannot band together against us."

"Why would they want to do that?" Trina's curiosity drove her to ask.

Her grandfather shook his head. "There's so much you need to learn. It's all about control. You want to control your destiny, don't you?"

"I suppose." Control was a luxury. In the shafts, she did what she had to so her family would survive.

"What I'm doing is the same except on a bigger scale. I want our family to make the choices instead of following others." Grandfather laughed when Trina frowned. "Don't worry. As long as you understand your tasks, I'll do the rest and our whole family will benefit."

"Even Paul?"

"Even Paul. And the laborers and other polits who choose to cast their lot with us. Even your mother."

Now Trina smiled. He did understand family.

"As fascinating as our conversations are, my dear, I have many things to get done to prepare for our trip to the stars. You can find me whenever you want, either here…or at my home. Please knock. I'd hate for one of my servants to call the enforcers on you." Her grandfather touched a hand to his forehead in farewell, turned, and strode off.

Trina watched him go, bemused. He'd known all along about her secret visit.

CHAPTER 16

After leaving the fountain, Trina tossed her hair down over her face and ducked out onto the street. She didn't decide where she wanted to go, just needed to move. There was too much to think about.

When she finally stopped, the chain-link fence stood before her, so different from anything else in the city. She'd been right. He meant to take them to the stars.

She lowered herself until she knelt on the ground, her side resting against the fence. The distant silver structures seemed sterile when compared to the buildings made of sun-warmed Ceric stone and decorated with carvings that hinted at lost legends. Trina glanced at the sky. Her gaze sought nearby stars, but the sun still blocked even the strongest.

This time, no towering ships pointed their noses to the sky but she could feel the echo of their presence. If she closed her eyes, images of ships appeared, colony ships, supply ships, and ones that just seemed to stop for a while then fly away with some unknown purpose. The sky called her as nothing else ever had. The momentary excitement of a theft or winning a good deal from Fence never lasted. The sky went on forever.

A shadow crept over her as the day ended. Darkness stretched from the Ceric buildings up to the fence but seemed to stop as if recoiling. The black substance coating the ground remained unchanged even as the sun sank.

She shivered. Was this a sign? Would she be doing her sister and mother harm by pushing for this?

A small vehicle trundled by inside the spaceport. She paused to watch, lacking the energy to turn away from its glittering metal sides. When it neared her spot, she tensed and rose onto the balls of her feet, ready to sprint back into the city where she belonged.

Just before reaching the fence, the vehicle turned and flashed her. Its metal reflected the sun peeking between buildings behind Trina. Then the light quenched as the vehicle moved past the break.

Trina gave the metal a hard stare before she realized what had happened. The shadows did cross the fence. They hid like a shafter among laborers when on the black surface. If the first had been a sign, this seemed more of one.

Trina pushed away from the fence and her hands set off a reaction. The metal links rustled along the length of fence. Already she influenced the world beyond Ceric.

A grin split her face as she skipped back to the nearest entrance. Her grandfather's coins chinked faintly, and Trina paused to readjust the scarf muffling them. He'd shared his wealth without conditions. Only her father had shown such generosity before.

Katie's concerns about their grandfather seeped in to undermine Trina's joy. He seemed a bit like Fence with his hands spread through all the happenings. No matter what he said, he held the power of a fairy tale eldest brother.

Trina shook off the echo of Katie's worries.

It didn't matter. The spacers would heal Mother and all three of them would start a new life among the stars, a life where there were no shafts and so no shafters.

Still, a tricky old polit who thought nothing of condemning his own son to her gave little reason for trust, unless he truly considered her family as he'd said. Then rather than gossip, his concerns were a shared family matter.

She slipped through an opening and felt the shafter darkness settle around her much deeper than the gathering twilight outside. If she had her wish, such darkness would never fall on her family again.

Crouching, she eased one of her smaller knives into her hand, waiting for her eyes to adjust and ready for an attack. Katie couldn't want to stay in this. And even if she did, Trina would have to convince her to go.

KATIE WAS WAITING AS TRINA unlocked the door and stepped inside. One look at her sister with arms across her chest, and Trina knew Katie had made up her mind.

"So what did your precious grandfather say?"

Trina lowered the hand that had been about to dig out the purse, knowing coin wouldn't sway her sister. "He's your grandfather too. He wants us to come on the ship."

Katie laughed. "As what? Maybe he means to catch us out as proof he'll keep the other polits safe."

Shouldering her sister aside, Trina went into Mother's room, but Katie followed.

"There's no place for shafters on a colony ship, Trina. I told you that. If he wants us, it's for his own reasons, not ours."

Mother showed no signs of awareness, this talk of polits not drawing her out of the sleep that seemed to grow ever deeper and more fitful each day. "You have skills any colony would want."

Katie didn't argue that point. She cut right through it. "And what about you? Every colony is dying for a sneak thief? Each will bring enough extra that they don't mind what your quick fingers take? And what about Mother? What grand work does he offer her? No colony has room for the already sick."

Trina put her hand on Mother's hot forehead. "He wants me to help him. With setting things up."

A scoffing noise came from Katie, but Trina didn't turn to see.

"And Mother?"

Trina sighed. "I didn't tell him. It was enough for him to agree to take Mother at all."

Katie caught Trina's arms and turned her. "How are you going to hide it? You think he can't change his mind. We go up there and we're under his control. There's no one who will listen to a shafter on the surface, no matter what he does to us, to Mother. There's no place for shafters in a polit world."

Trina pulled away, but not to argue. She sank to the floor and stared at her hands. "We can't stay here." Her voice held all the hopelessness she felt at stating the truth aloud.

Katie slid down next to her with a deep sigh as the fight drained out of her. "I've been thinking about what you said since last night. Mother isn't getting better. She's getting worse. If there's any chance the spacers can help her, we have to take it."

Trina twisted to face her sister. "Are you sure?" She'd expected to work harder to convince Katie.

Her sister nodded then shook her head. "Yes, I'm sure. Get the passes and we'll get Mother to the ship. But—" Trina held her breath waiting for what would come next. "We can't go up now. We can't pretend we belong where we don't. And we can't hide Mother's illness."

This time it was Trina's turn to agree. "We'll stay down here until it's time to board the ship. In that confusion, surely we can get Mother aboard where we can ask for help."

They exchanged a smile, for once sharing a vision—and a hope—for the future.

CHAPTER 17

T rina rushed home from another trade with Fence, eager to share her success with her sister. He'd wanted most of what they'd have to leave behind, thinking them from polit houses. They'd have a lot more to put into supplies than she'd expected.

"Katie? Katie, where are you?" She twisted to lock the door, then froze when a scuffling sound came from her mother's room. Knives appeared in both hands, and Trina dropped into a defensive pose, scared even here in her home. The door had been locked, but shafters could have found another way in.

Movement from the back made her hands twitch around the knives.

Katie came from the bedroom, her face blotched, and eyes red and swollen.

Trina gasped. "What did they do to you?" Her knives disappeared as quickly as she'd freed them from their hidden sheaths. She stepped forward to pull her sister into her arms, easing them over to the couch. Trina sat down with Katie beside her and rocked her body back and forth, humming in an attempt to soothe away her sister's fears.

Her efforts seemed to help as Katie slumped against her.

"Mother's in so much pain," Katie muttered.

Trina pulled away, staring at her sister. "You weren't attacked?"

"No, I wasn't attacked. The door was locked. How would anyone get in?" This time Katie hugged Trina, holding her close. "I'm fine. But Mother…she's been screaming all day." As if to punctuate her words, a rasping moan came from the other room, Mother too worn out for a true cry.

Trina pushed her sister away. She stumbled to their mother's room with none of her usual grace. Her knees hit the ground next to the bed, and she reached for a trembling hand. "Mother, we're so close. Hold on. You have to stay strong. The spacers will cure you. I swear they will." Salty water dripped into her mouth before Trina realized she was crying.

She knelt, the tiles seeming warmer than the frail hand in hers. Rubbing it between her own, Trina tried to ignore how shriveled Mother appeared, each moan sinking her deeper under the blankets.

She shivered. Nothing could have prepared them for this.

"She's been like this since you left," Katie said. "I thought she wouldn't be here when you got back."

Trina looked from the frail husk on the bed to her sister in the doorway. "I'm sorry I wasn't here. I won't go again. We'll nurse her together, and she'll get stronger." She glanced back at her Mother. "She has to."

CHAPTER 18

D ays passed in a blur. Trina didn't leave the apartment, barely left her mother's side. They lived off the supplies they'd been gathering for their voyage. Trina only slept when Katie forced her to, unwilling to miss a moment of what time their mother had left.

The medicine bottles emptied, first one and then the next, with little sign that the potion had any effect. Trina remembered how Katie thought Mother wanted release. "Hold on," she whispered, more of a mantra than actual words. She refused to accept what she knew to be true.

Mother wouldn't survive long enough for them to escape.

Trina rose from where she knelt by the bed. The cold had seeped into her from the tile floor, making her bones ache. She wiped her face clean with her sleeve as she walked from room, wondering if Katie had done the same before she came out to face Trina when the latest decline had started.

Her sister had fallen into an exhausted sleep on the couch.

Leaving Katie to slumber uninterrupted, Trina headed for the kitchen. There she found two meals gone cold.

Trina picked up a block of cheese and raised it to her mouth, but her stomach roiled. She forced two sips of water down before replacing the cup. Then she relit the fire, using up precious wood. At least Katie would have hot water when she woke.

Katie came in as the water reached a safe temperature.

"Here, this will help." Trina shoved a cup into her sister's hands, knowing she'd be just as chilled as Trina had been without blankets to keep them warm.

"Thanks," Katie mumbled. She sat on one of the stools, pushing the plate in front of her away as if the sight of food turned her stomach.

"You need to eat." Trina pushed the plate back.

"You haven't touched yours either and I don't want to. It seems wrong."

Trina abandoned the fire to hug her sister, squeezing hard. "I know how you feel, but Mother wouldn't want that for either of us. We have to eat. We have to survive."

Katie pressed her face into Trina's shoulder. "I know. It's just hard. Why now?"

They walked back to Mother's room, neither surprised to see the blanket still. Mother hadn't cried out in hours, and only death could have brought her that ease. "No spacer cure can help her now." Katie murmured.

Trina dragged her gaze away from the peaceful look on her mother's face. "She wouldn't have wanted us to stay."

Katie rewarded her effort with a weak smile. "No, she wouldn't, but she was a shafter. She deserved a shafter death."

Unsure how to react to that statement, Trina just turned to the doorway. "I'll wrap Mother's body. There's a place I can take her."

While their mother had dreamed of leaving the shafts, she'd been born and lived her whole life here. Trina could have asked Grandfather to give Mother a polit burial, but this seemed more appropriate.

They lifted their mother's head and slipped the shroud Katie had made her over the frail body. Trina whispered one last goodbye before pulling the shroud down over her mother's face and hiding her from view. The body seemed too light to have ever carried a soul, especial one as vibrant as their mother's once had been. Trina tied the foot shut with a braided cord she'd helped Katie make many days before, her only contribution to their mother's death dress.

When she raised the stiff body into her arms, Trina staggered under the awkward weight. She'd lifted her mother before but it was different without a steadying arm wrapped around her neck and a smile on her mother's face. Trina would never see that face again except in memories.

Katie put her hands under Mother's legs, easing the burden. "I'm coming with you."

Trina nodded. Bad enough they'd have to take their mother's body to where the poorest left their kin. Better to have a proper procession of loved ones.

She moved over until they shared the body evenly, her shorter height making her mother's head hang lower than Katie carried the feet. Flames took all shafter bodies so disease and rot couldn't spread. She wondered if, in the place that souls went, her mother could still feel what happened to her body. Trina hoped not.

Her sister said nothing as they made their way to the cave where the dead were left. Trina had only been there once, on an errand to find a grieving shafter for Fence. The smell overwhelmed her then, and the sorrow from those still living seemed to have a life of its own.

When they went through the final twist and found only a few bodies, Trina sighed with relief. The death cart must have cleared the room recently. Those were probably as fresh as Mother's. Scented candles masked the worst of the smell as the sisters stepped toward the attendant and met his smile with their sorrow.

He took the body, hefting it to judge the weight. "Sister or brother?"

"Mom," Trina answered, using the shafter term for the first time. He didn't know who they were and wouldn't care. She'd have the proper saying over her mother's body even if they risked discovery.

Hands now freed, she hunched to mask reaching for her purse and shuffled through the coins by touch. Two coppers should buy Mother a good burning with fresh fuel. The worn symbol pressed against her finger as she found first one and then the other.

"Treat her well." She handed the coins to him, letting the copper flash in the cold red light.

He raised them to his mouth, tasting the bite of metal before tapping both coins against his forehead in acknowledgement. "As you wish. She'll be treated right proper." He placed their mother on top of two bodies already stacked on the floor behind him.

Katie whimpered and Trina pulled her close. The man returned and eyed the two of them.

"Many more at home?"

Trina didn't like his intent look. Just as she'd feared, without parents, they were vulnerable.

Bringing tears to her eyes with too much ease for her own comfort, she sniffled like the child she should still have been. "Dad works. Bro' too. We had to bring Mom."

He nodded, a tightening of his jaw the only sign of his disappointment. He wouldn't want to chance the wrath of an unknown adult. "Stay here 'til they come, or go now. No matter to me."

Trina pulled Katie away. The longer they stayed, the more likely someone would recognize her.

"I want to stay. Mother shouldn't be alone."

"Shush," Trina hissed, glancing around and seeing the stares at Katie for using the surface term. "We can't. It's not safe."

Katie pulled against her for a moment longer then slumped as she gave in. Trina ushered her back onto the familiar routes without any response from her sister.

Shadows crept through the red light behind them.

Trina cursed her inattention. Whether someone recognized her or heard them say no one else was home, shafter rats now followed them.

At the next junction, she turned away from their apartment, pulling a protesting Katie along. "We're being followed." Her whisper sounded overly loud in the dark tunnel.

Katie tried to glance back but Trina jerked her forward. "Don't look. If they know we've caught sight of them, they'll become bolder. Nothing to lose."

She regretted the impulse to ease her mother's trip. What shafter had two full coppers to throw away on a body already gone? Mother wouldn't have wanted that. She wouldn't have wanted her passing to risk their lives.

Trina took first one turn and then another in rapid succession. Katie stumbled after her as she tried to keep up.

Focusing on her memory of the map, Trina thought about how to lose their tails this high in the shafter system. There just weren't that many tunnels so close to the surface. Shafters had added the lower ones years after the system once using these tunnels had shut down.

She hesitated when they reached the bend after the last junction. She leaned out slightly and listened hard.

There, a whisper of sound and the shadows came through the junction. The rats still followed and were getting closer.

Had Trina been alone, she would have taken the path up to the surface with the next turn, but Katie's breath came out in quick pants, and her sister didn't know how to blend in above, especially not in their shafter clothing. There was no time to consider or plan. She had to go toward home.

Trina grabbed Katie's arm and pulled them into a run. If they could just get a little space, she could lose them.

Katie stumbled and went down hard, clutching the stitch in her side. "I can't run anymore."

"You have to. We can't let them catch us."

Her sister pulled on energy reserves Trina didn't know she had and put on another burst of speed, but Trina could tell it wouldn't last.

Trina wanted to check to see if they'd lost the pursuers, but couldn't chance stopping. They ran through darkened tunnels, avoiding even more shafter rats by pure luck rather than skill. Her mind narrowed in focus to the one route they could use. The lock would have to be strong enough, the thick window the same.

When the faint light showed around the curtains they'd started using to block the window since Mother became too ill to care, Trina accelerated, no longer able to hear whether footsteps pounded behind them over her heartbeat. She fumbled with the key, and jammed it twice before it slid home into the lock.

"Hurry, Trina, hurry."

She blocked out her sister's urgency, blocked out everything as she steadied her hand enough to turn the key, but it had stuck. The roar of blood through her ears deafened her while she had to blink sweat from her eyes. Her fingers felt slick against the metal key as she tried again, twisting hard enough that she thought the length would snap off in her hand.

It turned.

Katie's hands closed over hers as they grabbed the handle together and pulled, but nothing happened.

The key slipped from her trembling fingers.

Katie caught it, thrusting the end into the lock a second time and turning it a bit more.

The snick as the lock gave way seemed overly loud despite Trina's thrumming blood, but this time they were able to push the door open and jump inside.

Katie collapsed on the first step while Trina slammed the door shut and used the key to lock it once again. She leaned against its surface, straining to hear anything from the other side. Her hands twitched enough to send her knife-tips to her wrists before they retreated again.

After a moment, she brushed sweat-slicked hair from her forehead with a trembling hand, the salty liquid tasting like tears.

"Did we lose them?"

Trina jumped at the sound of Katie's voice then pressed a hand over her sister's mouth to quiet her.

Into the silence came words.

"In here. It's powered. See the light?"

The door shuddered with the impact of first one body then another, but the lock held.

Trina pulled Katie into her arms, and they huddled there, staring at the only thing between them and shafters out for whatever they could get.

"Damn. What kind of lock is this?"

They seemed so close.

Trina thrust her feet against the door as though her feeble weight would make a difference when they tried again to break in.

No more words came through, but she could hear scrabbling sounds and vibrations from the lock. Again her knives descended, and she shifted away from Katie so she wouldn't cut her sister. If they broke through, they'd find this win harder than they'd hoped.

"I can't get it. Try pushing."

Again, bodies slammed against the door.

Katie stifled her cries with a fist jammed into her mouth, but Trina just glared at the door.

More slams then what sounded like a fist.

"Can't get it open. Won't budge."

"What'd ya want to do?"

"Can you pry it?"

"No. Edge's recessed."

"Window's too high to reach even if we could break it."

"Is this some big man's space?"

Trina couldn't tell how many from the words coming through the door, but the last gave her hope. If they thought the apartment belonged to some shafter big man, fear would send them running.

"Can't be. What big man hides down an unused tunnel? Where're the guards? It's just squatters."

"If squatters, probably nothing worth taking anyway."

"But the power?"

"You want to live out here? Power ain't portable."

"Worth watching though. Power might mean more."

"For how long? Not likely many come this way, and those girls ain't coming out any time soon."

Trina itched to do something, but there was nothing she could without making the situation worse. Listening to the rats discuss their fate felt like torture.

"You're right. Sure you're right. Might as well go back. Check here later. They can't stay holed up there forever."

Trina pressed her forehead against the door as the voices grew fainter. She released a breath she hadn't known she held. Her heart still raced, each beat pounding against a fierce headache.

Katie reached out a hand to touch her leg, and Trina could feel how her sister's fingers trembled. "Are we safe now?"

The rats would come back. They'd never be safe again.

"Yes," Trina told her sister. "We're safe for now. Just keep the door secured."

CHAPTER 19

T rina glanced over at her sister from where she stood in the kitchen doorway. It would have seemed a normal day with Katie surrounded by mending, but Trina could see how her sister's hand trembled, and the stitches looked more like her work than Katie's. "Are you going to be all right?"

Katie didn't look up, but her hands fisted in the material, only luck keeping her from a needle prick. "Of course. Why wouldn't I be?"

"I need to get the passes. We go up without them, and we're nothing but shafters. With them, we can march to the fence and they have to let us through." Trina crossed the room and knelt by her sister.

"I know," Katie said, leaning against Trina's side. "And we can't stay here. Not now. It's just I don't want to be here alone, and I don't want you taking chances with that polit."

Trina smoothed a hand over her sister's curls. "He's not any polit. He's our grandfather. He wants us there."

The curls moved beneath Trina's hand. "I know that too. It's hard to trust him though. Even if our father was as Mother said…" She paused for a shuddering breath. "Why'd he leave his family if his father is so wonderful?"

They looked at each other for a moment and laughed as the same word came from their lips: "Paul."

Trina shook her head this time though. "That couldn't have been it. Grandfather says the stars called to him."

Katie snorted. "Like they call to you."

"I would never abandon my family. You know that. You have to come with me as Mother would have."

They turned to look toward the room they'd avoided since taking their mother to the dead place then both turned away again.

"You wouldn't abandon us on purpose," Katie said, drawing them back into the conversation, "but I don't trust him not to make that choice for you."

"Katie, if you could have heard him, you'd know he wants you too. Mother not as much, but you were always part of his plan."

The shirt Katie had been mending flew across the room as Katie jerked to her feet. "I guess he gets his wish then. Both of us, and no pure shafter to complicate his pretty picture. He'll dance in the streets when you tell him."

Trina rose to join her sister. "He won't."

"Of course he will. He has no reason to grieve and every to celebrate."

"He won't because I won't tell him. You don't want to meet him yet. Let him think you two are settling in together. If he knows you're alone except for me, he might try and pressure you to join him. I don't plan to give him that much control over us." Trina laughed, hearing the contradiction in her words. After all, he wanted her to give him control of the colony. "You could come with me. If you do want to meet him. And then you wouldn't be here alone."

Katie started shaking her head before Trina finished. "I don't want to meet him. I don't want to see him. If he didn't want Mother, I don't want him."

Trina stared at the curtain blocking their window. "I could get Piper." The words came slowly, but the idea grew on her. "He could stay with you, guard the place while I go up and get the passes."

A weird look crossed Katie's face and she laughed. "I guess it doesn't matter anymore. You never brought him home in all the time you've been friends. I wouldn't recognize Piper if I passed him in the market, though I know a lot about him. But now that strangers know where we live…"

Trina turned to face her sister, reminded again of the different lives they'd led. "I should have brought you two together before this. It was easier to let fear rule us. But I trust him in this."

Katie waved a hand toward the door. "Go then. Get Piper, get the passes. I'll stay here and hold our home."

Without waiting another moment, Trina swept up the key and pressed it into her sister's hand. "Lock the door after me. Don't let anyone in unless I'm with them. I won't send Piper on alone."

"I know. Don't worry. I'll be safe until you find him. And safe after if what you've told me of Piper is true.

THE SHAFTS SEEMED NO DIFFERENT as Trina slipped from their sheltered space to the more populated areas. She saw no sign of watchers, but that didn't mean they wouldn't come. Though the rats who'd followed them might not find value in such an out of the way place, they could talk to others who thought differently.

That reminder made Trina increase her pace. She wouldn't have Katie alone when some big man came knocking. As long as the door held, her sister would be safe, but that didn't mean she'd feel safe.

Trina checked down where the pickpockets and skillsmen gathered. Piper wasn't there. She searched the passageways heading for Fence as well, but found no sign of her friend. After waiting a bit in case he was making a trade, Trina started to wonder if she'd be gone a shorter time by making a run to the surface. She could go straight to Grandfather's house to get the passes.

The timekeeper in their apartment followed the movement of hours, but told nothing of days. She wondered if, in her preoccupation with Mother, she'd let the launch day slip by. If so, they'd need Piper more than ever, and the request to watch her sister would have to become permanent.

That fear built in her until it seemed to gain the weight of truth, especially when she couldn't find Piper in either of the places they often used to catch each other. If she went to the surface and Grandfather had launched, who would be left to find her in the square? She told him to get the passes. Why would he have arranged for the coins if he assumed they'd be with him? More likely all she'd catch in the square would be the attention of enforcers, and worse at his house. Either it would be abandoned, or Paul would have claimed it.

A final attempt drove her to the marketplace. Even Piper had to eat.

By the time she reached the space that had been more Katie's domain than hers, worry and fear made her neck sore with tension and her knives quick to slide into her hands. She scanned the busy stalls, overwhelmed by the number of people here, both shopping and using the light for their chores. How would she find Piper among them?

"Trina. There you are."

She spun to face this threat as though she stood in the darkest section of the shafts, not here where shafters gathered in peace.

Piper jerked back from her knife tip, scowling at her. "This is how you greet a friend? Looking for you for days."

The relief she'd felt at the sight of him soured. "Looking for me? Why? We had no meet planned."

His scowl lightened into a cocky grin. "Got something for you. Burning a hole in my side."

Trina watched him as Piper pulled out a paper folded around something thick. From the look of it, the package had not come from any shafter hand. "You? A spy, Piper?" She could not keep the betrayal from her voice. Trina had known he passed information among shafters, knew enough to keep him from learning the way to their home before this, but to cross over to the polits?

Piper pulled the package back and tilted his head to one side. "You know me better. Word is you've trafficked some."

Trina couldn't stop the blush from rising to color her face. She hadn't shared others' secrets, but she had no right to question ties to polits. Shaking off her embarrassment, Trina returned her focus to the package. "That's no shafter weave," she said as though she'd never questioned him. "What's in it?"

"For you to know, and me to pester 'til you tell. Said I couldn't look. Only for you. Otherwise no payment." Piper smiled again, and she could see the curiosity threatening to strangle him.

"Give it over, then. Who gave it to you?" She said the last with her hand already outstretched.

Piper handed the package over, but shook his head at the question. "You know better than that. It came from one of us. No more I'll say. He knew me as a source to you from Fence."

Trina froze then, her fingers already prying at the seal. Could Fence have learned about her grandfather? Had he found a way to gain from it?

"So? You going to open it? Can't find a safer spot than here…well, maybe your home, but it must be far."

His words reminded Trina of her purpose in searching for him, and that she had little time. He had no way of knowing how unsafe their home had become.

Trina slipped into the shadow between two stalls, away from prying eyes. What this contained would determine whether she could trust Piper with her sister's safety. She slid her knife forward again, this time using its flat side to crack the wax seal. The flap popped open as if the contents wanted to escape. Official scrip blurred before her eyes as she realized Grandfather had not left their presence on the ship to chance.

Piper whistled through his teeth as he peered over her shoulder. "That what I think?

She nodded. He'd teased her about the spaceport often enough to know about her dreams.

"What did you steal to earn that?"

She wished the passes spoke of anything so simple. "We're hopping a colony ship."

A startled laugh burst from his lips. "A colony ship? No shafters allowed."

Trina waved a hand for him to keep his voice down. The papers contained all three passes, a carter token, and their ship designation. A glance to the calendar beneath the market clock, which tracked surface times because of vegetable trades, told her launch was set for the very next day. "There'll be shafters on this one."

"Guess you won't be backing me up with Fence then."

Trina glanced at Piper, hearing the unspoken emotion in his voice and sharing it. Her fingers tightened on the passes, all three of them. "Hey, Piper. Why don't you come?"

He stared at her as though she'd sprouted a crawler shell. "Me? On a ship? Just imagine that."

For a heartbeat, Trina thought he would agree, that she could take a piece of her life with her the way Katie had packed up Mother's blankets.

But he shook his head. "I'll take the pass, sure, but not to use that way. No business on a ship." He stomped his feet. "This here's my space."

Trina accepted his choice with a sharp nod. Though she had only to hand over the pass and return to Katie, no longer needing the trip to the surface, still she hesitated. "I'd offer you our home, though for all I know yours is better."

"Mine isn't. I'd take that offer if I knew the cost."

"Ours comes with issues."

"And power?"

"Sure enough."

"The cost?"

"Help us defend and shift to the surface. Then it's yours."

He spat on his hand and thrust it forward for Trina to do the same.

"Can you come now? We have to make final arrangements." She waved the notice at him and pointed to the calendar.

"Nothing more pressing."

CHAPTER 20

K atie. We're back."

Trina waited for what felt like only a second before Katie jerked the door open, her eyes wide.

"You were gone so long."

After stepping through the doorway, Trina waved Piper past. "Katie, this is Piper. He's going to help us, already has."

Her sister looked confused at the last, but Trina held up the passes. "We have everything we need, and only the rest of today to get ready."

Katie gave a tight nod. "I've been packing. What we can't carry, we'll have to leave behind."

Trina grinned at Piper. "Hear that? You'll get the space and extras."

He glanced around what would soon be his new home and gave a quiet whistle. "Any help needed is paid well."

Katie pulled Trina aside as they moved into the living room. "What is he talking about?"

Trina shrugged. "We need his help to guard the place and pace us up to the surface. What better reward than to offer the apartment? We won't need it anymore."

Though her sister looked about to protest, Katie swallowed it in favor of, "Are you hungry? There's provisions left, if not much. We can't bring enough to feed ourselves for a journey that will last years, so the ship must have something to eat. I packed only for the first few meals while we get settled."

As if they'd been friends a lifetime rather than minutes, Katie and Piper headed off to the kitchen in search of a meal, leaving Trina to look around the space where she'd spent her whole life.

Katie had pulled down Mother's quilts until the walls stood bare—barren. Only the map and the tattered remains of posters still decorated the walls. Trina stroked her fingers along the guide that had taught her ways most had forgotten. She would miss this place. Miss this life.

CHAPTER 21

When morning dawned on their last day, noises from the kitchen told her Katie had already risen and was preparing a final meal. Whatever they didn't eat became Piper's once he helped them to the surface, but she could tell he enjoyed Katie's cooking. He'd never eaten so well, or so he'd said over stew the night before.

A small tunic hit her face, and she reached for her blade to fend off attack even as she heard Piper say, "Breakfast's chilling. Come now."

Trina laughed at his eager expression. "You'll have to cook proper now that you have a kitchen. Or do you plan to bring someone else?" She hadn't meant to ask, but he could answer or not.

Piper waved her to the kitchen. "Already know who. Needs more than just me to hold the place. And there's room enough."

She pushed herself to her feet. "It's meant for more, but we have only the one key."

Piper shrugged. "There are ways around that."

Trina imagined Piper here with other friends, enjoying the life she knew, and felt a twinge of longing. Her future stretched out before her, full of unknowns. She shoved the worries away. She'd wanted the stars for her whole life, wanted something different, and that she'd won.

"Hurry and dress. Katie's got a treat for us." Trina pulled her shirt off and tugged on the first polit tunic in the pile she'd left out the night before, tossing one to Piper as well since he'd left his surface clothing in his old home.

She felt bare without her knives but pass or not, she couldn't go through the fence layered in blades. She did strap on both her arm sheaths before adding four more layers.

"Better not be too warm today," Piper teased. "Maybe you should leave more for me."

Trina laughed as she tucked her main knives into their sheathes. "You're getting enough already." When they reached the gate, she'd put these in a bundle with the rest.

Excitement rushed through her at the thought. Today, she'd cross the fence. She'd feel the press of black ground against her feet and know herself on the way to the stars.

"Pure happiness. That's on your face."

Trina turned to face Piper. He'd watched her dress with far more interest than she'd expected but he knew well enough not to approach.

"Not every day you can touch your dream."

"Stars may be your dream, but you've given me mine. Power. A comfortable rest with a secure door. Nothing more for me. I'll see you off with the same happiness. You've been a good friend. Your absence will be noticed."

Trina nodded. "Yours too. Strange faces all of them. For yours never to be seen again will pain those who travel."

He reached out and pulled her into a hug, careful to keep his hands away from her sheaths. Shafters never put emotions on a person but they understood well enough. They'd miss each other and the assistance they'd provided over the years.

"Are you two ever coming? Pity to spoil a feast by lack of care." Katie waved them to the kitchen, some of Trina's excitement reflected on her face.

"Eggs?" Piper's delight was all they could have expected in seeing the planned meal.

"We thought we'd need strong sustenance for the journey. Katie made a good bargain and there's enough for three easy. They don't keep." Trina slid into her spot and dug in, feeling the scramble crumble under the assault of her teeth. It filled her mouth with a sharp, bittersweet flavor. She drank deeply from her cup and polished off the last before handing the plate back so her sister could serve Piper.

Katie had already eaten, only one cup and plate remaining behind—Mother's dishes. Piper took his time savoring the meal, reminding Trina he only picked pockets. These luxuries came rarely for her friend. She regretted keeping him so far from them. He had taught her the ways of the surface in the beginning. She should have shared her bounty once she moved from the street to houses.

"Piper will help carry to the surface, then we'll get a cart." Trina smiled her thanks to Piper who shrugged. As much as he might have wanted some of those items, he was a true friend.

They left him to enjoy the meal while they took one last walk through their home, rechecking all the secret spots with Piper occupied. The last spot held their pouches. Trina tucked two into pockets sewn by Katie on the inside of her tunic and gave the last to her sister.

Piper joined them, and Trina took him quickly through the secrets of their apartment: how the power worked, where hidden pockets existed to hide his better belongings, and finally, she handed him the key. "It's your home now. May happiness fill it."

Even as she said the words, memories rose of all the good times they'd had. Times when they played, read, or learned together as well as times spent with Katie alone once Mother no longer had the strength. Though Katie had been the one reluctant to leave at first, now, Trina wished for more time.

She sighed, turning her back on Mother's room and going to the pile of belongings. It seemed both so small to encompass their whole lives and so large to consider the three of them managing to bring it up to the surface in one load. If they were attacked, their ability to defend would be hindered, but only a large group would attack three. Faced with so many, they wouldn't be able to do more than drop everything and run even without the burdens.

CHAPTER 22

They set off through the tunnels, barely recognizable as human under their burdens. Trina took the lead with Katie in the middle and Piper bringing up the end.

Trina stopped on the edge of the pool of light that marked the last major junction. Her bundles hampered the effort to check every direction before moving forward. She depended more on their numbers than on her ability to see as she squinted into the darkness beyond.

No movement caught her attention, so she stepped through. Katie's footsteps sounded behind her, and Piper's came from further back. Relief washed over her as dark gathered around once again. Numbers or not, they'd been too exposed under the junction light.

A thud followed by a second and third gave her warning. She spun, her bundles already settling around her feet.

Katie clung to her load, pale face visible in the diffuse light from the junction.

Piper fought silently, his metal bar hitting more often than not, but too many remained around him.

Made clumsy by her layered clothing, Trina finally freed her blades and ducked around Katie. The fight stayed within the lit area, making it hard to tell how many opposed Piper but also concealing her return. They'd expected the girls to run.

Her first knife slashed a leg, disabling one man. Even in pain, he muffled his yelp. Neither group wanted to attract the attention of others. Without pausing, she cut into another's arm, making her way toward Piper.

When she reached him, Piper lashed out, almost striking her. She ducked under the blow even as he pulled it.

"You should have gone," he grunted, bracing himself against her back and striking out again.

"Couldn't," she replied. "You had the best."

She felt his head move in a nod, accepting her lie. They both knew he'd carried only the extras they'd planned to live without before he offered to carry some.

The fight seemed to last forever with neither side gaining. Then Trina realized fewer opposed them until only three remained. She grinned, recognizing the attackers had given up, seeking easier prey.

The last to leave grabbed at one of Piper's bundles, but dropped it when a hard length of metal slapped onto his hand.

Piper shared her grin for a heartbeat before they picked up his bundles and went to rejoin Katie.

"No, you can't have it!"

The tight-voiced statement sent Trina scrambling forward. She stumbled over a package in the tunnel, her eyes not yet adjusted to the dark.

A foot connected with her shoulder, the force of the blow dampened by her layers.

"Oh," Katie said, pulling at Trina's arm. "I thought you were another of them."

Blinking, Trina could make out the scene now. Katie sat on top of a pile holding both her bundles and the ones Trina had carried. She held the food package in her arms, the loosened ties showing she'd fought for it.

"Good work, that," Piper said, laughing. "Never would have expected it."

Katie retied the food bundle and pushed to her feet before turning to gather her other packages. "I couldn't let them take our things. We have so little now."

Trina picked up hers silently, unsure whether to scold or compliment. She'd never have thought Katie had it in her to defend and yet her sister's life was worth more even than the last of Mother's blankets. She said nothing.

Though it didn't take much longer, by the time they reached the opening, they all looked exhausted. They'd used what energy the eggs offered in the fight, and Trina, at least, regretted not being more selective in choosing what to bring. If they'd been carrying less, maybe the group wouldn't have attacked.

They made a chain to the surface, Katie waiting at the top, Piper taking the quick scramble back and forth with one or two bundles at a time, and Trina guarding the tunnel until their pile had disappeared below and appeared above.

The sun had only just started to crest the horizon and, even in the summer months, the early hours carried with them the night's chill. Trina shivered when she climbed out as the sweat on her face and arms dried in the wind.

Katie stared at the sky, its immensity revealed moment by moment as the darkness rolled back in front of the sun.

"I'm finding us a cart. Stay here." Trina didn't wait for an answer, adopting her purposeful stride as she left them.

Like most other openings, this one came up in a short alleyway between two buildings and only two streets over from a main throughway. Even this early, she should find a hire cart easily.

Trina pulled out the paper folder with their tickets and freed the cart voucher beneath them, sending a grateful thought to Grandfather for his clever preparation. She waved the distinctive scarlet paper toward the nearest cart, but he shook his head. Only as he passed did she see the packages already filling his space.

She waved to another with more success. He followed her back to where she'd left Piper and Katie. She felt a twinge as she led him to a shafter entrance no matter how well hidden. Her fears were resolved though when she turned the second corner. Piper must have realized the problem as well. He and Katie had moved the bundles out of the alleyway and in front of one of the bigger buildings, as though they'd come from inside.

The carter gave Piper an odd look and demanded to see their tickets before taking them to the fence gate. "Voucher or no voucher, I'm not taking this load so far only to have to return it."

His obstinate expression softened when she pulled out the passes. "There's only two passes here."

Trina pointed at Piper. "He's not going." He'd stored his pass in the apartment to trade with Fence later. Adding something so rare to the big man's collection would earn him much good will.

"I don't know what you're doing with the likes of him anyhow. You're so young. You should have your parents with you."

Trina tried to think up some explanation but even as she opened her mouth, he waved her off. "None of my business anyhow. You have the passes. I expect they'll sort it out at the gate."

She noticed he didn't turn down Piper's assistance in loading the bundles. The carter also accepted their help to push the cart up to the gate, the effort revealing the way steeper than she'd noticed when walking on her own.

At the top, Trina turned to face her homeland, presenting her back to the spacer guarding the gate while she slipped her knives free. She could only see the surface of First City, but knew a complete world rested below it. Tears welled up unexpectedly. Here she stood at the fence about to go through as she'd always wanted. She hadn't expected to feel sad.

"You'll see different things soon enough."

Piper's voice, gruff with emotion, broke through her thoughts.

Trina turned a watery smile on him. "I'll miss you." She'd spoken directly, breaking all shafter code. In this last moment, she wanted him to know. Even as she held his gaze, she slipped the knives, sheaths and all, into a bundle.

Piper ducked his head, mumbling some response she couldn't hear. When he raised it again, a brilliant smile crossed his lips even if his eyes seemed wet. "I'll tell the tale of your adventures. One of us climbing to the stars. Make it worth your while."

Before she could reply beyond a startled laugh, he raised a hand to his forehead and turned, starting back down the slight hill in full shafter swagger.

"I'll miss him too."

Katie pulled Trina's attention away from Piper's disappearing figure. Trina looked at her sister and saw the same sorrow. Though Katie stood tall against the expansive sky, signs of strain showed in the lines on her face and how she clenched her hands against the edge of the cart as if afraid she'd be blown away.

"Hey you. You're blocking the gate. Show me your passes or shove on."

Trina looked from the empty street to the man dressed in some kind of single-cloth suit clinging tight to his flesh. She quirked an eyebrow, wondering how he carried anything inside the sheer cloth.

"Just come on," was his only response.

Both Katie and the carter looked to her. Trina shrugged, reaching into her tunic to pull the packet free. She handed both passes over, expecting some formal statement of welcome to mark the occasion.

He snatched the papers from her hand and glanced over the script before waving them through a small metal frame. When Trina's turn came, he pushed the passes back at her.

The frame beeped at her, and Trina jumped, but the spacer said nothing. All her dreams of joining the Spacer Guild seemed foolish in the face of such rude behavior. Why would she want a life so lacking in joy as to create a person like him?

She helped the carter push their belongings through the gate, feeling the spacer's eyes on her as she went. When Trina glanced back, he was looking down at a thin sheet of metal in his hand and she couldn't tell if he'd been watching at all.

Her preoccupation with the spacer stole the first moments past the fence.

"This dirt's so different. Look, I can bounce on it." Katie reminded Trina of what she missed.

She turned to find her sister jumping up and down on the black surface. Trina bounced a little too, finding the sensation unnerving even while she grinned. She reached out to take her sister's hands and they bounced together, their thin, cloth shoes unmarred by the resilient surface.

"Oh," Katie gasped, laughing. "Our stuff. He's almost out of sight."

Trina stared after the carter, dumbfounded. She'd forgotten everything in a rare moment of fun.

"Come on. We'll have lots of chances to enjoy ourselves now." Grabbing Katie's hand again, she ran after the cart, determined to savor every step she took on the bouncy surface. The carter turned around a building, moving toward their ship. Trina and Katie followed soon after only to stop as the ships came into view.

Not one, but three gigantic, towering metal objects graced the sky. Their sheer size struck Trina speechless, and beside her, she felt Katie shrink a little.

"They're so large." Katie's whisper barely reached Trina's ears.

She forced confidence into her voice. "Of course they're large. They have to carry everything necessary to start a colony. Think of all the people, animals, equipment, everything." Trina fell silent as, in following her own suggestion, she realized just how many joined them on this venture. Each ship must hold more than she'd ever seen, more than the most crowded Festival streets or the shafter market.

"We're going in one of those?"

Trina thought she heard a little wonder in Katie's tone but didn't know if it was just wistful thinking. She looked around, trying to find the carter.

Unlike the main gate, this area bustled with activity. She saw more people wearing the all-body suits of spacers along with a few in normal

Ceric dress. Trina looked at a couple of laborers, wondering if they'd be frozen or not and which family they belonged to. Two children caught her attention next. Smaller than Katie, they did the same bounce game, as if they'd never seen anything as wonderful as this flexible ground before and perhaps they hadn't. Her eyes strained to take in not just the people but also the ships and buildings and everything so different from her normal life.

"Over there. Come on," Katie said.

Trina saw the carter's impatient wave as her sister spoke. Together, they ran for where he stood with other carters and Ceric folks, surprised by the sharp clang as their feet met the changed surface.

"It's about time you two caught up. You're acting like you've never seen a spaceport before."

Trina smiled into his dour face, her excitement breaking through. "We haven't. At least not from this side of the fence."

The man's wrinkled face broke into some semblance of a smile. "I suppose you missed the prospective colonist tour. They try to give all of you some grounding, but I'd heard the last group had a few unable to come. We'll be in your ship soon. Once you settle, you might have some time to wander…though don't take too long about it or you'll be left behind."

Trina opened her mouth to respond, fascinated by the imprint of good humor on this man's sour face.

Katie grabbed her arm, pulling hard. "We're rising." Sheer panic filled her sister's voice.

"Don't you worry, girl. You have to take the lift. There's nothing but the cargo loading bays down at the bottom. We'll be at the top in no time."

Trina put her hand over Katie's and nudged her sister. "Look at the bundles. I didn't even know we moved until you showed me." She waited until Katie followed her suggestion before staring out in wonder. They rose higher than the nearby buildings, until she could see down on their metal sides. Soon, all of First City lay before her, more like the tunnel map than a place large enough to hold real people.

Katie's grip and the firm metal beneath her feet helped ground Trina, but she felt a touch of her sister's fear. If all those people below disappeared at this height, what would happen to the two of them if they should slip? She glanced at the carter, and though his face had fallen back into its somber lines, he winked, reassuring her.

Looking around the platform, she realized they were not alone in their discomfort. Some of the children leaned as far over the edge as their parents' grips would allow while others held on tight. Katie wasn't the only person, young or old, to cower away from the drop. The center was crowded while few stood on the outer edges. From the number of people and the lack of other carts, they must have had their belongings delivered earlier.

Another jerk and all movement stopped. Katie gasped but said nothing. The carter stood patiently, and Trina copied his example, wanting to appear knowledgeable even if she couldn't stop her gaze from its restless wandering.

The others moved off the platform until only the three of them remained. The carter pushed against his cart, and Trina assisted, rolling onto another broad platform that faced a gaping hole into what could only be their ship.

"Papers, please."

Trina stopped in front of the green-suited man who stood at the entrance with a metal sheet in his hand like the man at the gate had held.

"Can I have your papers?" He smiled down at her as if aware just how overwhelming this experience was for them.

She looked back for a moment before fumbling for the packet. She laughed at her uncoordinated movements. No one would ever suspect her background if she kept being so clumsy.

"Hmm, two passengers. Menthak family. Aren't you two a little young to be on your own?"

Trina bristled but calmed when she saw mild curiosity in his eyes rather than the expected condescension.

"We're older than we look." She kept her answer short, waiting for his response.

"I suppose you'd have to be. And you're not frozen either. Someone paid a nice penny to have you on this ship." He gave her a lopsided grin before looking at Katie as well. "Welcome aboard the Starshiner. I'm Patty."

Katie smiled back at him and even Trina felt her lips curve.

"Let's get you settled. You'll want to keep this." He handed the packet back to Trina. "More instructions are in your quarters' computer. Don't worry. I know much of this is new to you, but it'll make sense soon enough."

He waved to a green-suited woman. "Susan, can you lead them down to Colony Section Five? They're in Cabin 5-412d. No more for this load, and I wouldn't want such young ones lost on board."

He waved goodbye as they followed behind the woman, helping the carter push their belongings.

CHAPTER 23

A cavernous room towered above them, bigger even than the shafter market. Many carts just like theirs waited, but those were empty.

Trina stared at everything, her back tense as she took in the unfamiliar environment. In contrast, her sister seemed to grow taller as soon as the sky no longer hung above her. Trina wondered how Katie would adapt to the new planet, but she had two full years to get her sister accustomed to an open sky, though how she'd do that on a ship, she had no idea.

"You'll be using an antigrav sheet from now on. Not much call for carts on board. Though I know such things are common on Ceric, I've never been to the city myself. Do you really walk everywhere?"

Trina looked at Susan, seeing polite interest. "It's the doctrine. Machine failure on landing meant not much tech and few large animals. We had to learn."

"Hmm. That was a long time ago. You'd better get used to tech now, even once you're back on a planet." Laughter sparked in the woman's eyes. "The kind of failure you're talking about, and the isolation after, doesn't happen anymore."

She didn't wait for a response. Susan walked up to a panel and pushed a colored button. Seemingly from nowhere, a piece of metal floated up to them. The crewwoman nudged it over to the cart.

A look of revulsion crossed the carter's face even as he reached to place the first bundle on the platform.

"Now that I'll never understand," Susan commented, apparently to herself. "How is a cart with wheels any different than an antigrav panel?"

Trina rushed to help him and gestured Katie over as well. Soon, they'd transferred their whole life from the last part of their old one onto a small floating platform, only the first of what was to come.

"Your help will be remembered," Trina told the carter, meeting his surprised glance.

"May the stars hold you gently, girl." The carter didn't look at them a moment longer before pushing his cart over to wait with the others.

"Come on through here. You have to nudge the platform or it won't know where to go. It just floats the goods, unlike some of the better models."

Trina nodded her understanding and pushed the platform as if it were the cart. They didn't seem so different to her either, but if the tech failed, they'd be back to carrying everything by hand.

Susan caught the platform, wincing at the force. "Gently. There's no friction to push against except air."

Trina ducked her head. Suddenly, the cart and this platform seemed worlds apart.

"Don't worry. No one gets it right on the first try. You just need to nudge it."

Trina felt better when Susan smiled. If the error had happened on the streets of First City or in the shafts, she'd have been lucky to escape a beating. The green spacers seemed a happy enough group. She wondered which division they came from. Her interest in joining the Spacer Guild rose again, but she pushed it back. She'd have to be happy with this voyage to another world.

Susan led them into a small room with no obvious exit. "We keep artificial gravity on the ship or the crew's orientation would be destroyed. This chamber will equalize us."

Katie met Trina's gaze with a shared lack of understanding as the door they'd stepped through closed. Moments later, the world started spinning.

Trina cried out and reached for Katie, falling toward what she thought was a wall but now seemed to be the floor. Their belongings tilted until the platform hung over the new floor.

"I'm sorry about that. No warning seems to make sense when it's all new to you. You just have to go through the experience."

Another door opened and they followed the woman through endless corridors, each wide enough to fit at least six adults across and with ceilings above most adult reaches. They seemed eerily familiar, as if the shafts would look much like this when seen in full light.

Trina did her best to memorize the way as they rode more of what Susan called "lifts" to move between levels and areas, but soon lost any confidence in her location.

As if aware of Trina's efforts, Susan paused at each junction, pointing out the designations. Trina tried to understand, but she had no system to match them to, nothing to give meaning.

"Don't worry. I know it's probably much larger than what you're used to, but you'll only need to know a small section, Section Five. Everything you need will be there…here actually." She pointed to a sign labeling the corridor they'd entered as *Colony Section Five, Level B*.

"This is where your colony group, umm family, will be. There are four levels to each of the colony sections. You're on D. Cafeteria and gathering sections are all on B, this level. You won't have to go to the cafeteria. Level D has inclusive cabins. You'll have privacy when you want it but can go to the main areas of your section as you please. Once we lift off, you are not allowed beyond your colony section without an escort, but we'll have some gatherings." She laughed. "You heard all this in the training, right? Just humoring me?"

Trina shook her head, remembering the carter's comment. "We missed the training."

Susan had continued walking while she spoke, but now she stopped. "Coming from where you are, and without even the training, you'll have a lot to catch up on. Watch the orientation program in your cabin first thing so you aren't completely lost."

They'd already shown too much ignorance so Trina didn't ask. She would have to figure it out once they arrived.

After a short walk, they entered another lift. The sign on the wall as the lift door opened announced this as Level D, the level Susan had said held their cabin. They followed her down the hallway until she stopped in front of a door.

"I'll key the door to you two. If you've paid for privacy, you might as well get it." The spacer pressed her palm against a dark square in the wall that stood just higher than Trina's head height then pushed several buttons above it.

She waved Katie toward the square. "Okay, now you put your palm here."

The square seemed warm for a moment when Trina's turn came and her palm tingled afterwards.

"Touch it again, and your door will open."

Trina scrubbed at her palm, letting Katie touch the panel again. When Katie laid her hand against the square this time, a door panel opened with a swish, revealing a room with a large table and four chairs. Trina took a step forward and realized the room was much bigger than it looked from the door.

Susan put a hand to her ear, and her eyes lost focus for a moment. "You can figure out the rest, can't you? They need me back at entry. I'll send someone for the antigrav later. Just stick it outside the door." She didn't give them the chance to reply as she shoved the floating platform forward so it blocked the doorway and trapped them inside. With a quick wave goodbye, Susan strode off.

They unloaded the platform onto the table and nudged the machine outside with a gentle push. The door panel closed behind it.

"So this is our home now?" Katie asked.

Trina took in the two beds on one side and a third surrounded by a large collection of drawers and shelves across the room. "There's enough space for all our things, though the kitchen's quite small."

Katie traced a hand along the blanket covering one of the beds. "I guess we won't need our bedding until we get there."

Recognizing how her sister felt lost because she did too, Trina reached for a large bundle on the table and untied it. She spread the contents across the surface.

"Just because we don't need our blankets, doesn't mean we have to hide them away." Trina took the blanket that had been holding the bundle together and spread it over the bed Katie had touched. It was one their mother had stitched together and already seemed to make the small room more like home.

Trina smothered a yawn, the long night packing coupled with the excitement of the morning overwhelming her. She reached for another bundle only to have Katie take it from her hand.

"There's no rush to unpack, is there? Lie down and get some rest. Who knows what remains to be done by the time everyone's arrived?"

"I thought we were going to explore the spaceport." As if to deny her words, another yawn split Trina's face.

Katie shrugged. "You think we could find our way back to the entrance? Besides, why explore here. We're leaving."

"I suppose you're right." She slipped out of her shoes, pulled off three spare tunics and threw them on one bed, then climbed under the covers of the other one. They had made it. She was going to the stars.

have a message for Trina of Menthak."

The strange voice jolted Trina awake, and she lay still, trying to place herself.

"How do you know her?" Katie said from next to the door.

"I have a message for Trina of Menthak."

The voice repeated as if she hadn't spoken. When the words came a fourth time with an exasperated tone, Trina half-rose to help, but then the voice came again, this time with a hint of laughter. "Push the comm, the yellow button!"

Trina held her breath, not wanting to interrupt. Katie had to adapt to this place as home, at least for the journey. With her promises to Grandfather, Trina wouldn't always be here.

"Come on. Just press the button." The voice came again, some of the humor lost.

"I did press the button, see," Katie said, jabbing the button a second time.

"See? See what?"

"You heard me." Katie laughed, but there was no response. Then Trina saw her push the button again. "How do you know Trina?"

"You're not Trina?"

"I'm her sister."

"Well, I've got a message for her."

"Oh."

Katie must have expected their grandfather. "She's sleeping."

"Well, I've got a packet for her. Can I leave it?"

"So I guess you're here then."

"Where else would I be? You're going to have to open the door."

Trina watched her sister stare at the panel and the buttons beneath, but she didn't know the answer either.

"I really do have a package. You know they scan everyone before coming on board. I'm safe enough."

Trina smiled into the covers. If he thought himself safe, he wasn't a shafter.

"What color?" The words burst out of Katie in the sharp tone of shafter speak she used so rarely, though she must have in the shafter market.

"I'm a Menthak, like you. I don't have a color. Only the spacers have colors."

Katie let out a startled laugh and Trina warmed to the sound. A real family, not just the two of them. The whole colony section could claim ties. As quickly as the concept warmed, though, Trina grew chilled. What would the cost be to protect so many? No wonder Grandfather needed her help.

"So, are you going to open the door?"

"I can't."

"Why not?"

"Cause I don't know which color button to push."

Trina almost leapt to her feet at the frustration in her sister's voice, but something in the visitor's "Oh" kept her still.

Katie laughed again, an open, happy sound Trina couldn't remember coming so easily before.

"You could tell me…or you could take your package and leave me to call out into the corridor for the next passerby," she teased.

"Hmm, come see the Menthak girls. Trapped in their own room. A silver a piece but you can only talk if the sister remembers to push the yellow button." He chuckled. "Do I have to keep calling you that?"

"Calling me what?"

"The sister."

"Oh. Well, I don't know your name either."

"True enough. Trina of Menthak's sister, I'd like to introduce…myself. Aaron of Menthak at your service."

Trina imagined him sweeping into a deep bow and looking like an enchanting prince from her father's books with Katie the princess in the tower.

"I'm Katie." Her sister's voice went soft as she pressed close to the metal panel.

"Katie. Now that's a beautiful name. Katie, my dear, would you please press the green button. I'd love to see your face."

Katie flushed bright red, and Trina wondered if she'd have to defend her sister's honor.

"Are you going to send me away disappointed? Must I always wonder about the woman behind the door?"

Katie pushed the green, and the door slid open to reveal their visitor. He looked much like his voice sounded. Healthy, tall, and muscular with dark brown curls framing an angular face. Trina guessed he was older than they were, but not by much.

He bent his head so he could meet Katie's eyes. "As beautiful as your voice."

Her face flooded pink again, and Trina squirmed, uncomfortable all of a sudden as the hidden witness. She'd seen enough in the polit houses and shafts to understand such teasing, but this was her sister.

"I think it will be interesting with you around here. You'll come to the common areas soon, won't you?"

Katie ducked the question by asking, "The package? It's the reason you're here after all, isn't it?"

He held a thick bundle of paper just above his shoulder. She reached up for it, and he pulled it away.

"Your promise to come to the commons first."

Though Katie put her hands on her hips, Trina could tell she wasn't really annoyed. "It's your task to deliver the package, not mine. If you don't want to give it to me, I'll just close the door." She reached for the button panel.

He dropped to one knee, handing over the package. For a second, he didn't let go. "I'd like to see you there."

Katie pulled hard and tucked the paper-wrapped bundle under one arm when she succeeded. "We'll see." She waved him back and pushed the green again. The door slid closed while Katie stood there, a smile on her lips.

Before he could walk away, she pushed the yellow button and called, "We were well met, Aaron of Menthak."

"Making friends?" Trina stretched, giving up the pretense of sleep.

Katie started, and her blush returned. "He was bringing you a package. From Grandfather, I guess."

Trina tried to read her sister's expression and failed. "Are you sure you don't want to meet Grandfather?"

Katie shook her head, the blush fading. "Not until we have people who know us. If he's not what you believe, we can't just run home. We need to be strong here before I'll chance him trying to take that away. You should try too. Don't spend all your time with him, whatever your tasks."

Trina laughed though she heard the truth in her sister's words. "I should find myself a prince like that Aaron, you mean?"

Katie's blush returned with force, but she stood her ground. "That would be a good start. You know better than most the importance of having friends at your back."

Trina's thoughts flashed to Piper, wondering if he'd made it safely home. "True enough. Friends make good sense."

"Why don't you go shower? We can each use the cleanser once a day."

"A cleanser?" Trina laughed at her sister's almost worshipful tone.

"I found it while unpacking."

Stripping quickly, Trina stepped inside then wished she'd asked more questions as she faced an array of buttons. One with a spray of water looked promising.

Second use. Accessing...Cabin 412 allocation acknowledged. Two showers five-minute duration per rotation. Begin now.

She almost slammed the door open at the voice then realized it told her the length of the shower. The way it knew Mother was not here unnerved her. She shrugged. One more thing to get used to.

Trina emerged clean to find the room much brighter and Katie setting up their kitchen.

"I couldn't find any other water source than that. It doesn't give much even for washing hands so we'll have to be careful."

Trina swung a chair around and leaned her arms along its back, wondering if they could find stools anywhere. "Seems like you're settling in well."

The blush rising along her sister's neck made Trina laugh as her sister focused her full attention on coaxing the fire to light. Trina wondered where they'd be able to find or buy more wood.

"I'll show you the buttons at the door. They do the lights, speech, open and close it..."

"So I saw."

The flame caught, offering Katie a welcome distraction. A moment later, she sat up and pushed something along the table toward Trina. "Here's your package."

Before Trina could reach for the paper bundle, white foam poured down from the ceiling, dousing their fire until only dark smoke rose from it.

"Hey!" Katie glared up at the ceiling.

They both jerked when one of the walls lit up and a glowering face appeared over a body encased in a red suit. "An open flame? Are you nuts?"

Trina glared back, liking neither the criticism nor the intrusion. "And how else are we supposed to cook?"

"Check your orientation. I thought you all were supposed to know the basics. Do you need spacers to hold your hands for everything?" He turned toward someone they couldn't see. "Bloody barbarians, they are. And by choice. No wonder we never get any candidates who pass."

This time Katie glared at him. "You know we can still hear you, right? Or didn't your family teach you any manners? I hadn't realized spacers lost the ability to communicate properly when they took to the stars."

Again, he looked away, but this time someone must have been talking to him. He shrugged but turned back with a bland expression. "Your computer terminal is the second screen to your right from where I am. Press the circle to start it and your orientation program will launch. Please review all ship procedures before making any more assumptions." He looked at each of them sternly then disappeared.

Trina glanced at Katie and they both burst out laughing.

"Guess we have to push the buttons after all," Trina said when she regained control.

Katie grinned. "There's more to pushing buttons than you think."

Trina laughed at the reminder of Katie's adventure with the messenger. Katie joined in and again, her sister's happiness struck Trina. Piper had been her friend. Katie never had anyone outside the three of them.

A thread of worry snuck in but Trina brushed it aside. They'd joined the colony to start again. She had to give up her shafter instincts. Here, they were simply colonists, part of the Menthak family.

"Shall we push the circle?"

Katie's question broke through her thoughts and she shrugged. "You've done all the pushing so far and we haven't been sent off the ship yet." She sent a teasing glance toward their ceiling where some of the liquid still clung and a small gray mark showed where the smoke had been pulled into a vent above them.

As Katie went to push the button, Trina noticed the forgotten package. She pulled it toward her, masking the motion by standing. "I need to use the cleanser," she said.

Once the door slid closed behind her, Trina pushed another button to bring out a seat. She turned the package in her hands, checking it from every side, but no sign of the sender marked it. Who else could it be but Grandfather, though? That he'd sent it just to her reminded Trina of promises she'd made to secure her place.

"Okay, it should start now."

At Katie's call, Trina opened the door a little, so she could see the kitchen area. The third panel sprang to life with an image of their room.

Standard Cabin Three Orientation. This cabin is made of one room separated into a dining/sitting area and a sleeping area. It comes complete with cleanser, replicator, time readout, and library…

Trina watched, fascinated, as the screen showed where they could find everything. Some of the terms were strange, but the orientation went on to explain them.

…replicator rationed based on payment. The same limits apply to all public replicators. At the end of this program, your allocations will be explained. To exceed these rations for need, you must apply to the ship council who will decide what, if any, additional allocations are allowed. All public facilities are palm-keyed to track resource usage. Staying within allocation is critical for the journey's success. Any attempt to undermine the allocation system will be handled by security.

An image of a green-suited crewmember appeared for a moment and Trina winced. She had no plans to take up thieving here, but now she knew who the enforcers were.

Trina hoped the work she did for her grandfather wouldn't provoke security. She didn't think spreading confusion should bother the crew, but as Katie had said, here they had no place to hide.

She watched through the rest of the orientation as it told them how to find the common areas and what the different crew uniform colors meant. Trina absorbed the information, knowing she'd find it useful, but maybe not as useful as the packet of papers in her hand. She couldn't avoid them forever.

Trina snuck a glance at the papers, but forced her gaze back to the screen. This orientation should teach them the basic necessities and how to be like all the others. Little things like not knowing about the replicator when the red suit, pilot she now knew, thought she should, made them stand out. How much did those on the surface know about this that she'd never seen? Missing the training had proved more critical than they could have guessed, but what choice had they had.

Cabin 412d. Allocation two persons as per cleared passes. Authorized two meals four times a rotation. Liquid nourishment available ten times. Water ration sixty-seven percent with two showers five-minute duration every full rotation.

Katie rose as the program ended, but Trina hadn't missed her sister's wince at the allocation eliminating their mother's portion. The screen blinked three times then went blank again.

"I'd like to go to the common area. You coming?" Katie started toward the door without waiting for an answer.

Trina tucked the package between the bed and the wall of cabinets after she left the privacy of the cleanser. "Shouldn't we figure out everything here before showing ourselves as fools there?" Trina thought again about how much they didn't know. She'd seen more of polit life than Katie had, but she wondered how long they could use the different environment as an excuse when they failed to recognize things like the library.

Katie thought for a moment then nodded. "You're right. Aaron shook it off easily enough, but I wouldn't want to be a fool in front of everyone."

"I know you want this chance, and so do I, but you have to remember for all we came from Ceric, we're from different worlds. If we truly want to succeed, we have to move carefully and learn by watching, not asking."

Trina jumped when Katie slammed her hand onto the table.

"I don't want to be careful. I don't want to worry about being tracked or where we'll get enough to eat. I want to meet people, talk about normal things. You said this would be different, but if I listen to you, it'll be exactly the same."

Trina just stared at her sister. Katie never complained about herself...at least not before. This new person, giggling at strange men, demanding a better life, made her uncomfortable. "That's just it, Katie. We don't know their normal things. How can you have 'normal' conversations? Think about it."

Katie sank back into her chair, the energy draining from her face. "You're right. I know you're right. I just want...I just want it to be simple for once. I want to meet someone who makes me laugh and be able to talk without worrying about what I say. Even with Piper, you couldn't tell him where you lived. He never came to visit except at the end, and then we couldn't let him leave until we were gone. What kind of friend is that?"

Trina ignored the question to soothe her sister. "I know. And it will change. Just go slowly. Give us time to fit in here. I don't mean you can't ever. Just don't rush out there. It's more than being foolish. How can we be part of the colony if they see us as separate now?"

Pulling her hand away, Katie walked over to the replicator, tension radiating from her stiff back. "Might as well go about learning all these things then."

Knowing nothing she said would make a difference, Trina went back into the sleeping area and retrieved the package. In the back of her mind, she heard Katie mutter about squares, circles and various colors, but she focused on the thick paper from the packet. The odd voice murmured again, presumably in response to her sister's efforts.

She smoothed out the creases in the parchment and stared at the sheet. Lines crossed its surface with no clear pattern. She pulled out the note as well and saw Grandfather had sent the packet as she suspected. Was Aaron mixed up in Grandfather's plans, or just a willing body?

Even as the question crossed her mind, Trina dismissed it. Katie had made her first friend. She wouldn't do anything to interfere. How could she judge Aaron when she was no better?

Glancing up to see her sister still involved with the wall, Trina turned back to the letter. Grandfather wanted her to meet with him this evening. He made no mention of Katie. The heavy paper turned out to be a map of the ship, according to the letter.

She traced one line with her finger, seeing how it intersected with others. Open spaces had letter and number designations she remembered but couldn't place. She focused on everything she'd experienced since entering the ship and the answer came to her. The woman who'd taken them to this cabin. She'd shown the markings on the wall.

With that much to guide her, Trina quickly placed them on the map, noticing their cabin seemed to touch the yellow lines connecting various sections.

"There!"

Katie's exclamation surprised Trina but the smells emanating from the wall drew her attention even more. She carefully folded up the map for later and tucked the letter inside it, pushing both back under the covers.

When Katie put a plate of aromatic food in front of her, Trina settled into her place, making no mention of the package.

"The circle means an explanation. If you remember that, you should do fine with any. It means we can see the orientation again if we need to. I'm not quite sure what this is, but there were four choices. We can pick another next time if you don't like it or have one for each meal."

Some of Katie's enthusiasm had returned, and Trina smiled in response. "Smells wonderful. You figured it out quickly."

"Thanks. It's simple, I think. You just follow the pattern. Not like the door buttons. Those you have to know or push them to find out. There's no circle button over there." Katie sat down and took a bite from her own plate, cutlery and everything having appeared from a recess in the wall. She seemed to have forgotten the package altogether.

Something about the recess triggered a memory or thought. Trina filed it away to explore later, focusing instead on her sister's words. "I suppose everyone knows what the colors mean from the training so don't need an explanation."

"That or they got one when they're dropped off. The woman, Susan, might have told us if she hadn't been called off. She probably forgot we didn't know anything." Katie smiled. "We could have been trapped if not for Aaron."

Trina took a close look at her sister, wondering whether she should warn her sister about moving too quickly. Then she realized Katie gave her the perfect opening, and a way to see their grandfather without worrying her sister. "You know, you've figured out those things so quickly. Maybe you are ready to go see more of the ship."

"This is all so strange. At home, I wouldn't trust any meal I didn't make with my own hands, but here, I have to."

Trina shrugged. "Ceric tech may have always been faulty, but the spacers trust their machines. And without tech, none of this would be possible. The doctrine served us well and will likely serve us in the future. It's just here our labors are different."

"And if we try to ignore that," Katie added, "the spacers will scold us."

Trina joined in her sister's laughter. Her only other choice would be to freeze.

She shook off the thought and relaxed. "Our path took us to the stars. We have to learn how to survive here. If we cannot cook our food, we must use the replicator machine, but that doesn't mean what we know has no purpose."

Katie nodded toward the beds. "You're right. All those years of looking for ways to match patterns and create blankets as beautiful as they were useful helps me remember the buttons now."

"You're ready for this, I know you are. What you can't see now, you'll figure out. Go ahead. Find your Aaron. Enjoy yourself." Trina waved Katie to the door.

Her sister turned back with a worried look. "Aren't you coming? They're to be your neighbors as much as mine. You can meet Aaron."

"Maybe later. I still have to figure this out. You enjoy yourself. Just remember to watch and learn before you act." It seemed strange to send Katie out to experience the new while she stayed cooped up in their room, but then she wouldn't be here for much longer.

"If you're sure." Katie finally went through the door when Trina waved her on, and the door slid closed just as Katie had said.

The green button controlled the door. Trina secured the information in her mind along with how long the door stayed open after Katie pressed the button.

She wouldn't be staying here, but Katie had to think so. If her sister wanted a normal life, the best thing Trina could do was to keep Katie separate from the polit games. When she'd met her obligation would be soon enough to reveal whatever Grandfather had wanted her for. And maybe she shouldn't encourage Katie to meet their grandfather until then either.

CHAPTER 25

rina pulled the packet out from under the blanket and sighed. She crossed to the table and pushed the dishes out of the way. If only she'd asked Katie how to get rid of them before she sent her sister to the common area.

The map made more sense this time. She found the letters and numbers easily and checked the note again. Grandfather had cabin 281a. Trina had assumed the fancy cabins were up there at the top, though she realized it wouldn't necessarily have been true anymore. Polits no longer lived on the surface above her. Instead, they surrounded her, as did the laborers ready to make a new start.

She wondered how many of those unfrozen were laborers responsible for learning how to form a colony. Were most polits rich enough to buy a cabin? Had Grandfather brought his servants to care for him? Trina laughed at the thought of bumping into someone she'd ducked as she scampered away, polit jewels in one hand.

Trina traced the lines that indicated cabins with one finger. If they were all full, many of First City's rich had come. Some she might know more about than their own families did.

That thought sobered her. She wasn't a thief anymore to skulk around watching polit movements. She needed to leave that life behind her if she was ever to become a member of the colony. Though if Grandfather was to be believed, there'd be need for her skills, just not as a thief.

She traced the path to his cabin, noticing the same yellow line along its back wall as she saw on her own cabin. Only those cabins on the outer edges had the mark. She skipped from mark to mark, following them across the levels. It appeared at several points in the large spaces that she assumed were common areas and repeated on each of the colony sections. What did it mean?

Trina rose, orienting herself in the cabin just as the map was. She walked until her hand touched the back wall and then trailed along until she reached just beyond the end of the bed she'd claimed. As expected, her fingers felt a change in the wall. She traced the new edge, looking for a way to open the panel. The yellow mark meant an entry point to something beyond.

She couldn't find any buttons or a way to get through the panel, but knew it must be possible. Grandfather wouldn't have marked them on the map with no purpose. She'd just have to ask him.

Trina returned to the map, tracing a route to his cabin that kept her out of the busy areas. She waited until she had the route firmly in her mind. Possession of a detailed ship map would be unlikely to earn her any favors. Trina shoved it under her mattress before heading for the door.

When she pressed the green button, though, her current situation finally became real. She'd made it aboard a ship, if not as crew, then at least here.

The pilot's comment came back to her about how no one from Ceric was found worthy of the Guild. Trina wished she'd have the chance to prove that pilot wrong, but she'd committed to the colony.

Trina focused on the path she followed instead, dismissing all thought but what she needed to do to fulfill her promise. The lift near the common areas sounded busy, so Trina turned in the other direction, having already found an alternate route on the map. She followed the corridor until it curved, noticing how the cabin numbers marking each recessed door showed a lower number. She turned once, walked to the end, ignored two side corridors, and entered a small lift, far from the main traffic areas.

Remembering how the security crewmember triggered the lifts took a moment, but soon she rose directly to Level A without picking up any passengers on the other levels. She preferred it that way. Trina wanted nothing else than to be on even ground with the other colonists. Whether singled out as a shafter, or the grand polit's relative, neither would tell her how people saw her.

The lift slid open just like the room doors, almost silent except for a high-pitched hum most people probably wouldn't notice. The Level A corridor stood quiet without even the echo of footsteps she'd heard on her level. Trina stepped out, her feet sinking into the soft floor.

A smile crossed her face. This level's luxuries spoke strongly of its polit occupants. She wondered if the servants shared this splendor or had to trek down to the lower floors before resting their heads.

She avoided the few people walking in the corridor by ducking into doorways. The faint lighting kept her identity hidden while it prevented her from learning who else walked this floor.

Finally, the number on the panel matched the one from the letter. Trina stared at it, having come so far only to be stopped at the last moment. She didn't know how to open this door. Her palm keyed her door open and she'd tried no other. There had to be a way to announce herself, but she couldn't see the yellow button Katie had mentioned.

Even as she glared at the panel, the door opened. She flattened herself against the wall, clearly visible if someone cared to look. Two people, servants from their clothes, came out and turned the other way without noticing her.

Trina counted from the moment the door opened and knew, if his door matched hers, she had two seconds to get through. A quick dash into the recessed doorway and she jumped through the door just as it swished closed.

Rolling across the entryway to curl against a wall, Trina struggled to slow the frantic beating of her heart. She didn't want to be caught like the platform had been when they first arrived.

Trina glanced around the room. No one had seen her come in. Unlike their cabin, this one had separate spaces with both walls and doors. She'd have to search to find him with no way of knowing how many servants remained within.

For a moment, Trina wished herself back in First City where she knew how to explore a polit house. Here, everything seemed different. She felt the same pounding excitement of her very first attempt on a house when the rituals and architecture were still new enough to pose endless dangers.

CHAPTER 26

Samuel paced the length of his tiny study, wondering how long it would take to get used to the space. His servants had finally left, believing him settled in enough to survive the night.

Paul had taken his trip to the cold chamber well, after a quick briefing on what to do if someone revived him early. No other family took the same precaution despite the jockeying that had already begun, a fact that only proved Menthak to be the one capable of leading.

Samuel pulled open a drawer he'd unpacked himself. Trina's mother smiled back at him as if happy at his efforts to save her daughters. Someday he would meet her for real, but he could leave that unpleasant duty for once his plans had come to fruition. No matter how beautiful she might be, he worried that she'd hamper her daughters' transition from shafter to polit even on a remote colony. A picture would have been easier to pass off than the reality, but he'd had no choice. If only she'd been one of the tickets that went unused, but those most likely went to polits or laborers who'd changed their minds and delayed until it was too late rather than admitting it. He hoped they hadn't lost anyone critical.

He laughed at that. Both granddaughters were on board. Aaron would have said otherwise. They would not have left their mother behind. He hoped the very loyalty that trapped him with their mother would serve him well once they accepted him as family.

Samuel sat down and reached into his desk for a piece of paper, unsure what to work on but unable to sleep. His invitation must have arrived hours ago and yet Trina had not requested an escort. He'd been so sure she would serve his needs both with her thieving skills and as an alternate heir. Had he misjudged the strength of her ties? Or had his feelings for his lost son blinded him to the fact that she'd never accept Samuel as family? Had she used him to get aboard?

A vision of Jared as a young boy appeared before him, so real it brought tears to his eyes. Samuel blinked, wondering if Paul had been right after all. As old as he was and with all he'd done for the family, he'd fail this time if his ghosts started haunting him.

"You sent a message."

Samuel jerked upright as the apparition spoke, only then realizing his tired mind had missed the clues. "How'd you get in here?"

"I followed your map."

"You can't just enter a cabin. And you need a tool for the panels." While part of him admired her abilities, the rest of him struggled with the shock of seeing her before him unannounced. Still, it proved she had skills beyond even his hopes. With her on his side, he could accomplish so much. He felt almost sorry for those other families who came to the battle less prepared.

She tilted her head to one side and looked at him, saying nothing.

"How did you get in here?" he repeated.

Trina smiled. "You asked me to come, and here I am. Why do my ways matter?"

He laughed. "I suppose they matter only to you." Samuel hesitated, wanting to ask her about her transition into a new life. He'd meant to include the twins in the basic training given those going on board, but they had not come to him since agreeing to go, and he didn't want to chance angering her now with his probing.

Instead, he rose and walked to one of the bookshelves his servants had erected. He had no right to those answers just yet. "That map isn't the sole tool I have for you. Only the first."

He felt her gaze on him as he moved a book out of the way to reveal a small box, about the size of Trina's palm. His larger hand engulfed it before he spread his fingers in front of her. "This will open the hatches to the ducts."

She reached out to touch the device, a small sound passing her lips.

He smiled. So, the markings hadn't escaped her notice. Her continued freedom despite wide reports of theft seemed more plausible now with this second demonstration of her skill. Though he'd known when she came to his house, it was only because he set traps. Other polits were not so cautious.

Before she could close her fingers around the box, he pulled his hand back. "It's not so easy. This tool gets you in and out, but you need to know a bit about the ducts before you enter them."

He waved her to a seat and leaned on the edge of his desk, facing her. "Robots, moving machines, patrol the ducts. Some make repairs. Those should ignore you as long as you don't block their way. The cleaning robots are more of a concern. They'll clean anything in the ducts without an authorization code. If you're caught, they'll push you out into space without a thought, because they can't."

"Soulless." The exclamation slipped out.

Samuel winced at the reminder of her shafter background, knowing the curse had been leveled against polits more than any other. But the thought had never been truer.

"Soulless as nothing else can be. These labor without any human hand from the time they're built to when they need repair. They may move, some even talk, but they're just metal fastened together well enough to serve a purpose. They lack the ability to think or react to any situation differently than they've been designed."

"And these robots roam the tunnels behind the walls? Why?" Her nose crinkled up as she tried to picture it, reminding him again of his son.

For just a moment, he wanted to put the tool away and send her back to her sister. Why risk the last bit of Jared on this?

He shook his head, and the moment passed. What he could give to her now measured as nothing against what he'd have with her help. "These systems are maintained through the tunnels. When we're in space, anything could happen and the robots have to have the way clear to fix it."

Trina nodded. "Anything more? What must I do?"

"Take the time to learn the ship. It's larger than First City because no space is wasted. I'll need you familiar with the ways to get around, as familiar as any of the crew would be. When you've found many paths to every location, come back for your next task." He rose, handed her the tool, and moved behind the desk, pretending to fiddle with a book. He waited for her to ask to be let out, forgetting for a moment just who he spoke to.

As the silence grew, he turned. Trina had left, the only sign of her visit a slight indent in the chair.

Sighing, Samuel lowered himself into his seat. One day, he'd stop underestimating the girl. No matter how much she resembled his son, her life had been much different.

CHAPTER 27

I'm home."

Trina jerked, trying to keep the guilt out of her smile as she tucked the panel tool away in a pocket. "How was it? Did you do okay? Did anyone suspect anything?"

Katie waved a hand to stem the flow of questions and walked over to the replicator.

"No one said anything, Trina. It's safe. Safer than we've ever been."

Trina accepted the cup her sister pushed across the table. The drink tasted like the tea Fence gave them when he was feeling generous, only much stronger.

Katie laughed. "Aaron says you have to be careful. Too much and your hands shake."

"I've had tea before." Trina's eyes closed as the complex flavor hit her tongue.

"Not like this I'd guess."

"It's good. Where'd you learn how to get it out of the machine?"

"Aaron showed me," Katie said with a contented smile.

"What else did he show you? You can't let them see your ignorance. You saw that spacer. Polits know these things. If we're not polits and we're not laborers, there's only two classes left and we don't know anything about machines. Which do you want your precious Aaron to think you're from?" The tea forgotten, Trina leaned over the table in her urgency. A moment too late, she remembered her silent promise not to interfere.

"Don't worry." Katie pushed Trina back down. "He thinks we skipped the training, which we did. If I'd known what we missed..."

"Mother wouldn't have been welcomed up there. If we'd gone, her last days would have been even worse." Trina waved off the guilt. "So how does he explain all your differences?"

Katie pushed her tea away and went to sit cross-legged on the blanket that decorated her bed. "You think I'm an idiot, don't you? You're worse than Aaron. He believes I'm some sheltered polit girl who knows nothing about her world. He enjoys his role as teacher no matter how much I wish he'd see me as something else."

A flash of jealousy surprised Trina. She should be happy for her sister, but while Katie had found a place to be center stage, she'd been studying ways to slip through the cracks.

"And," Katie continued, "you need to see beyond the shafts and the surface. There aren't any places like that here. There's only cabins. Different sizes, sure, but we've got a good space for two people from what Aaron said." She glanced toward Mother's bed then back. "You wanted to change our place in the world. You have succeeded. Isn't it time you accept the results?"

Trina flinched. "You think the shafts are gone because you can't see them anymore." She downed the tea in one gulp and shoved the empty cup away.

"At tonight's training, polits and laborers sat together as we learned how to survive on the colony. If ever the class divisions vanished, they were gone in the common areas then."

Katie rose and put her arms around Trina. "You were right all along. It's different here. We're different here. Come with me tomorrow. See for yourself. And you can meet Aaron."

Trina tensed at the mention of Aaron, even knowing her sister could feel it. If only things were so simple.

Katie pulled a chair up to Trina's and sat down. "They did a pageant. With wigs and funny costumes. They told the story of Ceric's colonization when the machines still worked, and even a bright paper tube to be the people mover that ran in the shafts at first. I got to see it all fall apart. Then, they showed how we rebuilt with the doctrine and the labor of our own hands. It was fantastic, Trina."

Her sister's attempts to convince only made Trina sense the gulf between them more. "I saw lots of pageants. They all tell that story. Even now when you say everything has changed, we're repeating the same stories."

Katie sighed. "Does it mean nothing for them to ask me to act in a play as well? Does that show how things haven't changed?"

"Only because they don't know what you really are."

Katie pushed her chair back, the metal legs scraping hard against the floor. "And who am I?" She paced to the beds then back to the table. "Am I a polit's daughter, a shafter, or a Festival got? How do you see yourself? Are you always going to be the thief even when there's no need to steal? You're throwing away this chance. You've been given another try at a normal life. Why don't you want to take it?"

Trina met her sister's glare for only a moment before looking away. How could she tell Katie and still keep her sister free of polit machinations? The more she joined the colony, the harder it would be to explain her absences.

"Hold onto your grudges if you want. I won't let you ruin my chances. I'm going to become friend and neighbor to these people in truth, not just in location. When you're ready, you can come and meet them. Until then, I'll say I have a hermit sister who doesn't know a good thing when she sees it."

Trina regretted the tears in her sister's eyes as Katie stomped off to bed, but could do nothing to soothe them. She followed, sinking onto her own mattress.

Warning. We will be leaving Ceric momentarily. Secure all personnel.

Katie rolled so her back was to Trina even after they were both on the beds with straps holding them secure. Trina wished that security could extend to all aspects of their new life.

CHAPTER 28

Trina only had herself to blame for their awkward breakfast the next morning. The polit shadow weighed heavily on her, and she wouldn't feel ready until she'd paid back her debt. Katie only knew that she was helping Grandfather, not how she was. Trina planned to keep it that way.

Her sister wanted to start their lives from a position of control. Trina felt much the same. Only their methods differed.

Why shouldn't Katie make friends and learn how to act? She didn't have a reason to stay away.

Trina forced her mouth into the semblance of a smile. "What are you planning to do today?"

Katie glared at her over the hot cereal they'd chosen. "Why? So you can question me properly? Wouldn't want you to have to work at finding excuses, now would I?"

Trina shook her head and turned back to her cereal. It should have been delicious, but sat in her stomach like a lump of dirt. Even the tea her sister had grudgingly provided tasted too bitter against her tongue. Would they always fight? Was that what they'd gained in this new life?

Katie picked up her dishes and reinserted them into the slot with a little more force than necessary. "I'm going out to the common area. That is if you don't object."

The look on her sister's face was clear enough. Even if Trina had objected, whatever she said wouldn't have mattered. Instead, she nodded, avoiding words altogether. She needed Katie to go before she could see what the ducts were anyway. In this world Katie found so different, she'd still be sneaking around dark tunnels and into people's houses, with only the reason changed.

She took another sip of her tea, turning to watch as Katie dressed and walked out the door without even a goodbye. With a grimace, she downed the last of the drink and returned most of her cereal to the slot, pressing the triangle button to signal the dishes to go. She wondered if more machines picked them up from the ducts behind then shook her head. The ducts didn't touch every cabin, just those on the outer edge. Some other mechanism managed the delivery and return of their dishes.

With no reason to delay now that Katie had gone, Trina slipped the map out from under her mattress. She'd do better to memorize it so she could hide it away permanently, but that took time. Somehow, posting it on the wall didn't seem a reliable way to keep Katie unaware of her activities. Someday, Katie might even invite this Aaron to visit them. Trina hadn't missed the palm scanner next to the replicator, apparently so guests could use their allocation wherever they were.

So many differences and yet so much stayed the same. Katie went to the equivalent of the market while she hid in the shadows.

Trina pulled on a tunic and pants before grabbing the tool she'd studied the night before. It seemed simple enough but she hadn't had the chance to try it. She pointed at the section of wall where she'd found a seam and pushed the tool's green button hoping it followed the same color patterns as a door.

Even though she'd been expecting it, Trina jumped when the top of the panel sank into the wall with a hiss, revealing a pitch-black space beyond. She crept forward, unable to see anything. Clunking sounds echoed in the far distance.

Sliding down the ramp made by the panel, she entered the tunnel. She waited for the panel to close on its own, but it remained down. Trina found the green button again by touch but the panel still didn't close. She pushed the button next to it, a blue one, hoping it wouldn't trigger something dangerous.

She released a sigh when the panel rose back into place, leaving her in complete darkness. Trina kept still while her eyes adjusted, not moving until she could make out the faint light rimming each opening along the corridor.

Soon, her shafter-trained eyes had enough light to follow the tunnel. Though its height seemed shorter and the walls closer than the shafts, part of Trina felt more comfortable in these ducts than she'd been since entering the ship.

She walked at a slow pace, remembering Grandfather's warnings about the robots. Ladders led up and down along the wall every once in a while but she ignored them in favor of continuing forward. An odd light glowed before her.

Distances seemed longer in the duct. She counted off occasional side tunnels so she could get back, determined to discover what the glow meant no matter how far it took her.

By the time she reached the light source, she felt as though she'd walked the length of the ship but it appeared she had not. The light turned out to be illuminated markers indicating the section and level, just like the signs in the corridors. Trina paused under the markers, realizing this meant other humans passed through the tunnels as well. She'd have to listen for more than just mechanical wanderers, another way these ducts reminded her of home.

She turned at the junction, exploring a little way down even though she planned to turn back. Trina didn't want to get lost on her first venture here.

The tunnel continued as hers had, a distant glimmer and the shadowy impressions of the panels the only break in the darkness. A quiet hissing sound caught her attention and she paused to figure out where it came from. By the time she realized the sound echoed from behind her, a piercing red light flickered over her face as if looking for contrasts.

Trina pressed herself against the wall, willing her eyes to recover at the same time as she prayed whatever it was wouldn't reach her. She blinked rapidly and could see, among the multicolored spots, a grasping tool jutting out in front as the headlamp swept the tunnel again.

She stood, mesmerized, as the robot approached, scanned over her, and seemed about to pass her by. Trina released her breath slowly. It must have been a maintenance robot.

Even as the thought crossed her mind, something tugged at her side. While she'd been watching the grasping tool, the robot had pushed a shredder type thing against her and started munching her tunic. Trina pulled hard as the cloth strained and began to press into her neck. The robot didn't give way or even notice her efforts. The shredder just kept munching the fabric, coming closer to her skin with every pull.

She jerked with all her strength but the machine kept coming. The tunic pulled too tight against her and there wasn't enough room to duck out of it. She had to do something. Though her mind screamed in panic, her shafter instincts still worked. She hadn't remembered strapping them on but habit saved her. The tip of her long knife pushed against her wrist, slicing into flesh. She dropped her grip on the cloth, losing precious inches, but allowing her to free the knife with her movement. The hilt slid into her palm and Trina began slashing the fabric, sparing little thought for her skin beneath.

If the robot had been seconds faster, she'd be fragments tossed into its gullet, but she managed to slice through the last strand binding her before the robot found flesh. She ran, too terrified even to pause and catch her breath. The echoes made it seem like the robot stayed close on her tail, seeking the escaping trash. Trina couldn't stop and look. She had to get away. Blood pounded in her chest and ears, making it hard to think.

A wall appeared in front of her, and she stumbled, fear giving way to exhaustion. Her legs collapsed, throwing her against the floor of the duct with a thump.

She could only hear her panting.

Trina took a deep breath, held it, then released it slowly, repeating the sequence until the blood no longer pounded against her ears.

Still nothing.

She glanced around, seeing the hints of panels but no glow. She was lost and had no idea how to get home. She looked back the way she'd come but shuddered, sure the robot still moved through that tunnel, seeking her.

Grimacing, she pushed herself up, checking her pockets for the map and tool. Without them, she was trapped and the robot would find her eventually. She sighed with relief when she felt both the solid box and crinkly paper. Closing her eyes to block out the outer darkness, she drew on her memory of the map, trying to trace her path on it. The only image she could recall was too vague to be trusted.

Trina straightened and glanced from one direction to the other. Without light, she couldn't use the map and without the map, she had no way of knowing where the panels led. She looked down one of the tunnels, paced a few steps, and stopped again. Something seemed different but she couldn't tell what.

No strange light called to her, and the panels seemed much the same. Even as that thought crossed her mind, she realized it wasn't true. Though the panels were evenly spaced, they stood much larger and a greater distance spanned between them as well. Trina knelt down, the chill of cold metal easing its way into her knees and face as she pressed her ear against a panel to listen.

None of the sounds reaching her seemed close but she had no way of knowing what lay behind the wall. Trina weighed her options and realized she had none. To find her way back, she'd have to open a panel. What made this one any different than the others? Firming her jaw, she reached for the tool, knowing she could be dropped into a meeting of the security team. With the map and tool, not even considering her presence in the ducts, they'd have questions she didn't want to answer.

She listened once more, taking what reassurance she could from the silence on the other side. Trina moved off slightly, ready to catch the edge so she could peer out before opening a gaping hole in the wall.

She pressed the button.

The panel dropped faster than she'd expected. It hit her hand and bouncing off instead of stopping. She slipped, pushed down by the heavy weight. The panel clanged as it slammed against the floor, and she made another grab, this time from half underneath. Her leg cushioned the second bounce, muffling the sound even as she groaned. Pain washed through her as she scrambled to get the panel off her leg.

Only after she'd freed herself did Trina realize how much noise she'd made. She turned to the opening, half expecting a band of green-suited security to be staring back at her. Instead, she saw a blank wall.

Trina ran her hand along it and pushed gently. The wall gave, sliding forward. She pushed again before realizing whatever she pushed actually moved in the next room. She stopped and listened, but couldn't hear any reaction to the movement. She tried to see anything in the space she'd made, but all she saw was another wall on each side.

She looked down at the heavy panel, wondering how she could get it back in place before she remembered the button. Her fingers fumbled at first and she worried about the other buttons on the device, but the only movement she noticed was the panel. It lifted and slotted back into the wall as if it hadn't dropped at all.

She moved four panels down and decided to try again, this time without interfering. When she pushed the green button, the panel dropped quickly into place, resting against the floor with only a faint thump. This time the panel didn't open onto a wall. She could see a large, dimly lit open space.

Trina scrambled up the ramp and slipped through the opening. A push of the blue button and the panel moved back into place, all without seeming to notify anyone.

Turning around, she scanned the room. The ceiling hung a shadowy distance above her and boxes covered most of the walls. She realized where she had to be even before pulling out the map. Other than the bridge, cargo spaces lined the whole length of the ship.

She ran a hand along the edge of the nearest box, wondering what lay hidden within. Trina moved further into the room, looking at the stacks of items brought by each family. The scene tweaked her memory, and she laughed when she placed the image. This storage area looked like a polit child's room with blocks stacked in every open space. Only the straps securing piles of storage boxes looked different. And the boxes lacked gaily-painted letters and numbers on their sides.

Stepping closer, she realized the boxes did have numbers, just not large ones. Somewhere, someone had a list of everything in each box. Trina wondered just how many sheets of paper such a list would take.

A deep sound rumbled through the chamber. The box trembled under her hand. Trina tensed. The sound shifted again, returning to the underlying throb she hadn't noticed until it changed. The engines must be close. Trina couldn't think of anything else capable of making a sound large enough to disturb the cargo.

She spread out her map and traced where she thought she'd gone, finding the engines nearby. Trina knew she should slip back into the ducts. The robot must have finished with her section long ago. She could be back in the cabin in a short while if she started now.

Her gaze swept the room, noting interesting shadows in the distance. She looked at the panel she'd come through. Katie could be back any moment. She should return.

Unable to restrain herself, Trina tucked the map and panel tool away and turned, not toward the panel but toward an odd shadow cast against the ceiling, a darker line in a dark patch. Curiosity rushed through her. She couldn't leave with the shadow unknown and unidentified.

Trina looked around carefully, but her ears already told her no one shared this cargo bay with her. The boxes buried almost all the floor space and so most likely would be undisturbed until they reached their destination. She scrambled up one side of the nearest tower, her bruised leg and cut wrist aching at the activity. Her wrist had stopped bleeding at some point in her run, after staining her sleeve brick red in places.

Pushing aside the pain, Trina let herself do something for pure enjoyment, her first moment of freedom since coming on the ship.

She saw the shadow, and she wanted to know what it was. The knowledge wouldn't help Grandfather. It wouldn't further any plans or plot. Knowing served one purpose only. Knowing made her happy.

She didn't even bother climbing down to use the tight path she saw weaving between the stacks. Instead, Trina raced along the top of one row then jumped across to the next. The box under her wavered, and she threw out her hands to regain her balance, her heart pounding with a mix of excitement and the pure adrenaline rush of fear.

The shadow became clearer with each jump and resolved into a series of shapes. At first, she didn't recognize the hulking machines, but then she remembered one of her father's books about the beginning of their colony. Sitting down on the top of the last row of boxes, Trina waved her feet back and forth as she identified the objects, all critical for producing food to support the colony or to build it. These were the machines that they needed so their new home could grow and support them.

After sliding down to the floor, she touched the shovel in front of a tractor. She danced over to a small plow, brushed the side of a machine she couldn't identify, and stopped to stare up at a crane. Something about the small, glassed-in box at the top of the huge machine called to her. Trina scrambled up a ladder on its side and perched on the small black stool before the controls. So many controls stood there. She wanted to touch them, move them and see what would happen. Only caution held her back. She could have this place as her own until touchdown if she didn't draw attention to it.

Trina abandoned the little glass chamber and climbed up the neck of the crane, pausing to make sure it didn't bend under her weight. At last, she achieved her goal, crawling into the claw. It shuddered, but held. She curled into the deepest part then leaned out to see the expanse of cargo extending far into the distance on all sides.

A blanket and snacks would make this the perfect place to go when she needed space. She couldn't very well go to the spaceport fence now that she'd come through it.

The thought sobered her for a moment. She'd wanted to go to space, and she had her wish—for two years at least. Trina leaned her cheek against a cold metal tooth and wished the trip would never end.

She turned to look at what she knew was the outer hull, imagining the immense darkness just behind it. To travel around the planets, meeting all sorts of people and doing wonderful things. She'd give up a lot for that to happen, but she couldn't abandon Katie even if, by some miracle, she got the chance.

Trina forced the melancholy thoughts away. If she became a spacer, she'd never get to see these machines bring forth food and buildings where only wilderness existed. And through her work with Grandfather, she could make sure this colony would have no need for shafts. She could make a real difference.

Sighing, she climbed back down to the floor. Katie would return soon enough, full of new stories about the colony training and of her friends, especially Aaron. Trina had to mend their rift and maybe absorb some of Katie's enthusiasm.

Finding the strength to encourage her sister's blossoming seemed easier now that she had a place to go. She thought the crane wouldn't mind if sometimes she talked…or even if she cried. Here, she didn't have to pretend. No one would care if she didn't watch every move or keep a happy smile when she worried. She doubted other humans would come here at all.

WHEN KATIE OPENED THE DOOR to return to their cabin at the end of the day, Trina greeted her with a meal already prepared. She'd left the torn tunic behind at the ship's wall where it would never trouble her sister.

Though cautious at first, Katie soon answered Trina's questions with grace, only giving her the occasional odd look.

Whenever Katie's openness made her tense, Trina focused on her special place. She refrained from making any negative comments, determined to repair the tension between them.

Over the next week, Trina visited the crane many times, bringing small comforts to make it her own. The spacers had provided so much, not even Katie missed what Trina took.

While Trina learned how to get to each colony section, she came to the crane to restore her balance. The hum of the engines soothed her, and she imagined the cold of space just beyond, feeling connected to the ship in ways she couldn't describe.

CHAPTER 29

S amuel stepped into his study, the pleasant mask he'd worn for the last two hours dropping away as he scowled. Only four weeks into a two-year trip and already he could feel the strain on his heart. Could he lose so many years of his life to starting over considering the time it would take to establish their new land? Maybe he should have left Paul to wade through this mess while he traveled frozen to preserve a little of his lifetime.

His bark of laughter echoed in the tiny room. The grand polit frozen. The outcry when the family found out Paul would hibernate for the voyage had been loud enough.

He slipped into his chair with a sigh. Had he really thought this colony idea through? How much weight had he put on the skill of a tiny girl, and the strength of his hold over her?

Fingers clenched on the edge of his desk, Samuel remembered the Farnwark representative's insult in the meeting he'd just left. A condescending offer to let him read over plans they'd already finalized.

"I have ten times the experience of any of them. How dare she ignore the worth of my counsel?" His shout made some glass ornaments on his shelf rattle and brought running footsteps to his door.

"Is everything all right?" Nancy asked, poking her head around the corner.

Samuel waved her off. "Fine. I'm fine." He couldn't summon up a smile for her or soften his gruff voice as he struggled to hide the sharp pain in his chest. Just stress. He knew his body well enough to tell, but she'd be worried. "Have you any tea?"

The lines in her forehead relaxed as she accepted his request with a nod. "Ready in a minute," she said, already heading back to the kitchen.

If only Trina would return.

Those dry meetings, as frustrating as they were, had provided him with a wealth of information garnered from side comments and observing the posturing between representatives. The crew also provided valuable information about the workings of this ship in response to casual questions, his own and some from his operatives, believing no colonist could make use of it.

Until his granddaughter mastered the duct system, they were right. He'd learned of the ducts through just such a conversation disguised as curiosity about the ship. It had taken some of his precious trade goods to get the control box though.

Green-suited security controlled all paths between sections. Only participants in the formal meetings approved by the captain could pass the checkpoints, though there were planned events for each family to mingle with the crew. Gatherings were initially high level but soon to be open to everyone. He planned to make full use of those opportunities when they came.

For now though, Samuel thought being able to do nothing while the other families "welcomed" him as their newest, and weakest, member would give him a heart attack long before they reached touchdown. Did his experience as Grand Polit of First City mean nothing?

He twisted his scowl into the semblance of a smile as Nancy placed a tray with tea and small sandwiches on his desk.

"Anything else I can get you? Are you warm enough?"

Samuel's cheeks relaxed under her persistent care. "No, I'm fine. Thank you for these. The food they serve at those meetings would turn the strongest stomach. Farnwark fare. They joined the colony early enough to get special meals programmed into the system."

Nancy patted his hand, the movement oddly maternal despite her comparative youth. "Well then, eat up and you'll feel much better. All that fancy politicking never did help you settle for the night, even back on Ceric."

For just a moment, an image of the luxurious study and house he'd left behind rose before his eyes and homesickness followed after. Even with the state of his coffers, the effects wouldn't have been felt until long after he lay in the ground.

Samuel shook the past away. "Challenges make you strong, Nancy. Menthak will rise to the top of this pile. You can count on that."

"Of course it will," she replied, her gaze firm and clear of doubts. "With you to guide us, how can we go wrong?"

He watched her leave, his strength restored by her confidence. Ignoring the food, he took a quick sip of tea before moving to his bookshelf. Somewhere he had a dissertation on using confusion to great effect. His plan would work. He just needed to put the right pieces in place.

Then he froze, instinct telling him he was being watched. Samuel turned slowly, tension tightening his muscles, but somehow, he felt no surprise to find his granddaughter perched on the edge of the chair she'd sat in so long ago.

"Welcome. I see you had no trouble returning."

She smiled. "It's easy enough. You're lucky I gave up my other calling."

"Your calling?" Samuel shook his head, still absorbing her presence. He'd waited for so long he'd even checked to make sure she hadn't disappeared, shoved out by a robot. Trina had more control than any of his other tools. It made her stronger and him weak. He needed to be more creative in assigning her tasks. Next time, he'd set a time limit or at least require updates. He didn't take waiting well.

Trina looked at him oddly. She must have spoken while he was daydreaming. He thought back over what he'd heard and laughed. "Thieving, of course. You'd like to take my precious things now would you? Wise to have left that calling behind for all that everything I have is part yours by blood. There are no shafts here to hide in, and security is more determined than the enforcers ever were."

Again she smiled with only half her face, contradicting him without a word. She should have been born a polit. She probably knew more about self-control than any of those fools who thought they would run this colony.

"So." He dragged his mind back to the girl in front of him. "You've learned your way around this ship? You think you can take on a little task?"

"Tell me what you want." Her expression gave nothing away, but her alert position showed her confidence.

Samuel walked around his desk, pulling open the drawer with her mother's painting. As his gaze brushed over it, he kept his face still, giving nothing away. He reached past the painting to select a necklace of true rubies, an heirloom passed down from generation to generation since the first colonists arrived on Ceric from Earth.

Trina whistled quietly as he raised it to the light. "They're real, aren't they? Dug from the New Andes mines?"

He smiled, placing the necklace into her hands so she could admire the dark red. They didn't shine as much as paste. Instead, their color ran deeper. "You certainly know your gems. I should've known. I suppose I have you to thank for my cousin's loss. She never was one to take care of her things."

"I only took from the foolish." Her lips closed suddenly. Either she regretted the insult or had planned to maintain the fiction that she'd been a pickpocket and nothing more.

Samuel waved her comment away. "These came from much further than the New Andes. These are from Earth."

Her breath whooshed out as she placed the necklace back on the desk. "Earth? You should keep them more secure."

He laughed. "Oh, they're not mine. Let's say I obtained them through difficult channels."

Trina gave him a tight stare. "You stole the jewels."

"More like borrowed. I need them placed."

"You're returning them now? How will that help?" Trina leaned forward as though determined to understand.

Samuel smiled, caught again by her resemblance to his son. Jared would always move to the edge of the chair and lean just before asking an uncomfortable question as if ready to trap Samuel if he tried to avoid an answer.

"Not returning them exactly. The necklace is Tasrien, a bridal gift to the first Tasrien matron if I remember correctly."

Trina shifted in her chair. "They're in section two."

"Hmm. So you did as I asked. Well, Tasrien's in section two, but that's not where I want you to put them."

"Not returning them? Where do you want the jewels?"

Samuel smiled. She didn't try to change his mind. She wouldn't care one way or another. As long as she stayed true to Menthak, her disinterest in the needs of others would work in his favor. "I think Farnwark's where they should be found."

"Why?"

His smiled died. She questioned him after all. "You don't need to know that."

Trina fixed him with a sharp stare. "You said I'd be spreading confusion. I gave up thieving. I'll understand my purpose before risking being caught with that." She gestured at the dark red jewels spread on the desk.

Samuel returned her stare, delighting in her conviction and strength despite his discomfort. He'd hoped to keep her separate, an unwitting tool in his efforts. Again, he'd have to walk carefully. Would she renege on their deal if she discovered he'd fudged the truth now that he had no way of sending her home? And would she reveal his plans, bringing about failure?

"Well enough." He sighed, putting a tinge of annoyance into his tone to let her think the battle hard won. "How can alliances form where there is no trust? If you found something precious to you in your supposed ally's keeping, would you want to keep working with them?"

He waited for her to shake her head before continuing. "If Farnwark has a sacred object belonging to Tasrien, how can trust build between them?" He smiled, happy with his answer. It rang true because it contained the truth, though not all of it. She needn't know he planned to be the only one in a position of strength when they reached touchdown. She'd see that part herself long after her role had completed.

Trina nodded, her forehead still creased as she puzzled through his answer. "If I found this necklace, why would I tell Tasrien I had it, knowing our accord would falter? That's like finding an object I knew belonged to Fence and dangling it in front of his face as if I'd snagged it from his pocket."

Samuel laughed, delighted and chagrined at how well her mind worked. "That's why a Tasrien must find it."

"A Tasrien? But passage between sections is controlled." The crease was back.

"Trina, passage for the likes of you might not be allowed yet, but we're planning a colony here. Two years may seem like a reasonable time, but there are maps to study, decisions to make. A Tasrien will be in the Farnwark section tomorrow. I just need you to put this in sight but not obvious. Then it will be found, and by the right person. Even though they're sure to claim it's a trap, doubts will linger."

He pulled out a copy of the map he'd given her and gestured her closer. They leaned over the map together, Samuel pointing to the cabin and describing it based on what he remembered from the last time he'd been to the meeting at Farnwark.

"This is in the center. No panels." Trina nodded toward the cabin.

Samuel tensed. Would she give up so easily? "You'll have to cross through their section. You managed well enough in First City."

She froze as if debating whether to mention something or not. He couldn't tell if she wanted to hide her ignorance or if she'd learned something that she thought he didn't know. The silence dragged at him.

"It seems a lot to risk just opening a panel in an unknown room."

He frowned. "I'd have thought taking risks was your specialty. You made a living of entering undetected."

She nodded, accepting the burden without comment. He had nothing else to offer her.

Following her example, he bent back to the map. They discussed possible entry points that would take her through areas where an unfamiliar face wouldn't stand out. Then, he showed her exactly what he'd planned.

While part of him focused on telling her which shelf to suspend the necklace from so it would glint in the eyes of whoever sat across from the bookshelf, the rest of him seemed to stand outside, marveling at their heads bent so close. Why couldn't Paul be trusted, not with these tasks, but with the planning? Maybe in time, Trina would join Samuel in designing the delicate twisting of events that would further the family. He'd gotten old and tired of doing everything himself. A fleeting thought of Jared crossed his mind. That's who should have been at his side, making Trina's entry into that role somehow poetic.

CHAPTER 30

Trina slipped back through the panel in Grandfather's bedroom after making sure he hadn't followed her. His apartment stretched so far along the wall that she'd seen markings for five different panels, but this one seemed the least likely to have people inside.

The plans turned over in her mind. She understood the meeting would be in that room and no other. Trina wondered if they'd chosen the room because it had no connection to the tunnels. If Grandfather knew about the ducts, why wouldn't the other families?

She paused as the panel snapped back into place, listening. Spacerat. That's what she'd become. Creeping around between the walls, sneaking pretty baubles.

Trina grinned. Only now, she put the shiny things in place. She tapped the pocket containing the necklace and trotted along the duct, listening for any robots, or other rats who took upright form. Two cross tunnels passed before she turned and made her way up the ladder to the final junction, seeing no need to delay her task.

Farnwark sat two sections above and the room she needed was on Level B. Trina counted off the openings as she passed them, hanging from a bent elbow every couple of levels to rest. Her panting breaths echoed down the crawlspace and would have revealed her, but she'd yet to see another human and the robots only cared about keeping the way clear.

Katie had asked about the tunic she'd hidden in the crane, but Trina pretended she'd left it behind for Piper. Just one more lie. Trina longed for the time when she'd be free of secrets, free to act like any other colonist and make friends while assembling the kits they'd need on the new planet as Katie had.

She couldn't talk about what she did with Katie or anyone. Trina hadn't realized just how much of a difference being able to discuss her marks with Katie and Piper had made even if she had to keep the details private. Now, she could only talk to deep space, but it never answered.

Her breathing even, she climbed the last half level and checked the illuminated markings to confirm she'd reached Colony Section One,

Level B. She swung over to the platform, wondering if robots used the ladders or if they were meant for taller humans. Her agility allowed her to reach the platform from the ladder where another of her size might have failed.

Trina felt tension creep up her back, starting at her hips and gathering in the base of her neck. Adrenaline flooded her and her heart pounded louder than before. She listened for any sound and moved forward when she heard none over those from her body. She reached the first panel easily, pressing her ear to it by instinct. No sound carried through the thick metal. Could she do it? Could she risk everything for Grandfather? He'd offered her no guarantees.

She stared at the device, her finger hovering over the green button. The light leaking out around the panel illuminated other buttons. One glowed a faint yellow, just like the talk button on the door. She'd been so careful to avoid the rest of the buttons because she didn't know what they could do, but what could be worse than opening a panel into an occupied room? Holding her breath, she pressed the yellow button, blood pounding in her ears.

Voices filtered through, startling her enough to fumble the device. Hands shaking, she pressed the yellow again and tucked the device in her pocket. So close. She'd almost lost everything.

But she hadn't. Her confidence reasserted itself as she realized she'd proved herself capable even in this alien environment. Concentrating, she thought through her three other possible routes.

On this floor, no cabin had more than one entry and most led to the public rooms. She just had to find an unused space. It seemed simple enough, but Trina knew these things rarely were.

She listened a little longer at the second panel to make sure, but though she could hear voices in the far distance, none sounded nearby. Wiping nervous sweat from her forehead with her sleeve, Trina triggered the panel. It swung open slowly enough for her view of the room to grow in bits and pieces as the metal moved toward the floor of the tunnel. She could see a series of tables and chairs but no people. Her heart leapt into her throat as a flash of colorful fabric appeared but she released her breath when it turned out to be a coat left on the back of a chair. The room was empty.

She slipped through, fingering the blue coat as she passed. Fine fabric the owner would miss soon enough. She pulled her hand back before the coat graced her shoulders. Trina needed to concentrate. Though thievery might sow confusion for a little while, it would make her obvious, something neither she nor her grandfather wanted.

Sauntering up to the door, she stopped, surprised to find it closed. Without thinking, her hand slipped to the panel device, the green button sinking as she pressed it. Trina laughed, but even as she glanced around to find a button panel, the door slid open. She ducked back, expecting someone to enter, but no one did. The device must open doors as well, making it easy for the crew—and her—to pass anywhere.

Trina stepped into the corridor, hoped anyone watching would dismiss her as a polit child. She paused for a heartbeat when she entered the open area, the space almost as large as the cargo section she'd made her special spot. Despite Katie's efforts, she'd avoided their common area.

The ceiling rose two levels, with balconies looking out over the open area from the Level A rooms. Trina let her gaze wander until she noticed several people sitting at tables in the open space. They faced a woman dressed in teacher garb, possibly a training session. Katie had wanted her to come to one, but Trina still stayed away. The desire to join them, to learn something useful to their new life, threatened to overwhelm her. She forced herself to turn away and entered the short corridor on her left. Trina walked past two doorways, checking for watchers before moving back to the second.

A closed door faced her. She'd hoped it would be open so she wouldn't have to chance leaving her palm print, if a Farnwark door would even open to a Menthak. She reached up, her hand shaking, then pulled back at the last moment. The panel tool. It should open the door and leave no trace.

Taking another quick look, Trina pulled out the device and pointed it at the palm scanner. She pressed the green button while praying under her breath. Each beat of her heart counted off the seconds as the door stayed closed.

Trina stared, unsure what to do now. She couldn't place the necklace without getting in. They must have a way to check the palm prints and would when they found the jewels. She couldn't fail on her first task.

Looking back, Trina willed the door to open. Nothing happened. "One more try," she muttered under her breath, bringing the tool up again. This time she held it longer, taking the chance of someone noticing both the device and her odd behavior. It had to open.

A high-pitched sound emanated from the door, making Trina clench her teeth, but the door finally slid open so she could enter. It closed quietly behind her, trapping Trina where she had no excuse to be. Chills traveled up her back and her nerves tightened.

She ran across the room. Acting like she belonged wouldn't serve her if they found her here. She pulled the necklace free, all the time driven faster by her surging blood and pounding heart.

Grandfather's directions seemed sound. She used the edge of her shirt to pull the necklace free. Spacers had tech well beyond Ceric. She wouldn't be surprised if they could trace the sweat on her palms. She jammed the jewelry between two books with just enough dangling to twinkle in the light.

Trina crossed to the opposite side of the table and crouched down to the height of a seated adult though her blood pounded out a warning to run. Her efforts would be wasted if it didn't work.

Relief rushed through her as the red gems sparkled in the lit room. She triggered the door and stepped through, remembering the sound sensor too late. Holding her breath, Trina pressed against the wall in an attempt to stay hidden. No shout or comment reached her as the door closed behind her.

Almost safe, Trina thought, turning toward the room she'd used to come in.

A young woman appeared around the corner. Trina switched directions in what she hoped looked like a smooth movement. She wondered if the woman could hear her rapid pulse.

Her alternate route was only three doors down, but a group had occupied the space when she'd checked before. She paced to the door, trying her best to look like she had business down there. The door gaped open. Trina stepped into the entryway, hiding her from anyone in the corridor while not thrusting her into the room blindly. She peered around the door, relieved to find the space empty.

Trina wondered if she should shut the door, but worried they had it keyed and she'd trigger an alarm. Somehow, the excitement and rush she'd experienced in the known territories of First City hadn't translated to the ship. Instead, she felt as jumpy as the first time she'd entered a polit's house.

Trina checked the room to make sure the panel wasn't blocked. Even as she pulled the device out of her pocket, her gaze fell on a scrap of black fur in the corner. She thought it was an animal hiding and moved forward cautiously, wondering whether it would attack when the panel lowered. She hadn't thought any animals were allowed unfrozen, but if a polit brought the creature, rules could be bent.

The animal didn't move or even react to her presence as she inched forward. She checked the room again to make sure the pet's owner wasn't sitting out of view then looked at the creature, waiting for it to react. Though nobody else shared the room, a pile of bright clothes lay scattered over one of the tables. Another creature draped across the top of the bundle, a posture that made no sense.

A laugh escaped her as she crossed the room to pick up the black wig. She walked over to the pile, looking at the other costumes with interest. Apparently, Menthak wasn't the only family to celebrate the start of their journey with a pageant.

Trina tucked the wig over her head. She pranced around, relief making her giddy now that the animal threat had vanished.

A noise in the corridor sobered her, reminding Trina why she'd come to be here and the cost if she were discovered. She pressed the button on her device, still clutched in one hand, and vaulted into the opening before the panel reached the bottom of its swing. She jerked her foot over the edge, rolling as she smacked into the duct floor, her finger already pressed to the blue button to close it.

She huddled where she fell as she tried to calm down. Finally triggering the listening function, Trina heard only normal conversation. They hadn't noticed the panel closing as they entered.

She smiled and reached for the button to turn off the sound.

"Get the costumes. We're going to practice the first play again."

"Got them. Have you seen the other wig?"

Trina pressed a hand to the false hair still covering her own. She'd forgotten to throw it down in her effort to escape. After avoiding the temptation, now she'd stolen by accident.

"It must still be out there somewhere. We keep losing the costumes."

She heard a laugh.

"The kids love to play around with the pieces. We can do without. Let them have some fun. It's so hard on them. I mean, will they even remember the sun when we finally get there?"

Trina turned off the listening device, slumping against the wall. Children had saved her. It didn't even sound like they'd go looking very far. The wig slid down over her face, dangling from one comb still caught in her hair.

She pulled it off, running her fingers through the strands. They might be leaving. Should she wait and drop the wig back? The strands tangled around her fingers as if not wanting to return.

Trina shrugged and pushed herself upright. They'd already come up with an explanation. Why confuse things? She headed back to the Menthak section, satisfied she'd successfully completed her task even with the barriers in her way.

She did wonder if the Farnwark speakers were right though. Maybe Katie wouldn't be the only one flinching at the sky. Two years was a long time without seeing the sun.

CHAPTER 31

Trina had performed many tasks for her grandfather by the time a quarter of the journey had been completed. None of the tasks seemed significant on its own. Only when taken together could she see how they pulled the other families one direction and then the next.

The latest in a string of requests had gone smoothly, but still Trina felt out of sorts as she slipped past the Menthak common area on her way back from another drop in Tasrien. She could hear snippets of laughter even though she hadn't pushed the listening button. Then she recognized Katie's voice and tracked it down.

A panel had failed to close properly, and the robots had chewed a hole through the metal at its base.

Trina laid on the floor and peered into the room beyond, unable to walk away.

Katie sat at a table with a young man who must be Aaron and two others Trina didn't know.

Aaron laughed, fingering a medallion strung around his neck. "Can you believe I won this," he said in a tone that meant it wasn't for the first time.

Katie gave an absentminded smile as she dropped a stiffened paper with a silver bird painted on it. "You were right about organizing the pieces so the assembly went faster. I just wish Trina had come. She needs to know this too. And it's not just that. I want her to see how nice everyone is. To meet you. We'll get to touchdown, and she won't know anyone."

Trina winced at the strain in her sister's voice. Katie wasted time worrying about her when Trina thought her sister had been enjoying herself.

"She's old enough to make her own decisions, Katie. If she doesn't want to be here, nothing you can do will change that."

Her sister pushed back from the table. "I'm sorry. I guess I'm not in the mood for games today. You'll have to find another to be the fourth."

Aaron said something in protest, but Trina didn't wait to hear. She scrambled up and ran for their room. If she didn't get there first, how could she explain the Tasrien shirt she wore, one of many her grandfather had supplied so she could blend in safely?

As it was, she made it with only enough time to duck under the covers as the door slid open. Trina had to wait until Katie went into the cleanser to change, pretending she'd just woken.

Katie scowled at the sight of Trina making a meal. She said nothing.

If Trina hadn't overheard her sister's comment in the commons, she'd never have guessed Katie worried at all.

CHAPTER 32

S amuel fingered the painting before pushing his drawer shut. The last organizational meeting really showed the results of Trina's work. The Farnwark representative glowered at Chelrien then Tasrien condescended not to him but to the Jeletark man. He leaned back in the chair.

The first break in their cohesive leadership didn't affect much, but it hadn't needed to. With each small discovery and bit of information slipped to the wrong family, pressure built up until something gave. And Samuel was ready to step into the breach.

Briniak hadn't bothered sending a representative. Samuel didn't know whether they were still smarting over the last blowup or abstained because of the document Trina shuffled into the papers on their grand polit's desk, as though he'd accidentally picked it up in the last meeting. The only part still bothering him was Tasrien. They seemed to stay on the upper side no matter what. He'd figured on being at the head of the table by now. Even with the confusion, some of the other polits had started to notice what his efforts had accomplished, though they had not discovered the cause.

He wasn't the only one who'd expected results faster. The drawer seemed to come open again by itself. Trina's mother stared back at him as if begging him to free her daughter, a stronger pressure when Trina had let slip that she'd died before she could join them here. This shafter woman owned more of them than he ever would, a fact that still kept Katie from meeting him. He knew the risks Trina took, both in the ducts and outside of them. Her loss would burn heavy on him. He wanted to release her from her debt, to bring her into society, but she succeeded where others failed.

"Grandfather."

Trina appeared before him as if coming out of thin air. In the first two months, she'd enjoyed startling him, her eyes twinkling with delight, but he'd grown accustomed to her voice emerging unexpectedly as if she were a ghost determined to haunt him.

He pushed the drawer shut once again and leaned on the desk, bracing his head on steepled fingers. "Trina. A pleasant surprise as always."

She nodded, leaving him to fill the silence. He didn't know if she'd been that way with others, but he found it disconcerting to have one of his techniques used against him. Some of the anticipation vanished when he knew his opponent would always out wait him.

Unwilling to give in so quickly, though, he quirked an eyebrow, hoping to draw her into speech first. His hands dropped to the desk and he forced them to be still while he looked at his granddaughter. The silence grew and his fingers twitched. She sat motionless, looking at him with a mild inquiry on her face.

Samuel sighed, knowing he'd failed again, as always. "No troubles?"

"Katie worries because I stay away. I overheard her say so the day before, but I can't be recognized, for you or for me."

"It's only been six months. There's time yet for you to become familiar." Even as he said the words, his mind wandered. Katie, the mythical sister. He'd heard enough to know where Trina kept separate, Katie had joined in with the rest of the family. Apparently, she'd even formed an attachment with a young laborer. Samuel had kept true to his promise to wait though he spent enough time overlooking the commons to have seen her from a distance.

"I'd like to meet her." The words hung on the air for a moment before he realized he'd spoken them aloud.

"When will we be done?"

Her question should have been discordant but he'd learned a bit about his young relative in the time they'd spent planning and plotting. "I don't know. The balance is shifting, but how it settles?" He shrugged, still keeping the ultimate goal from her.

"When my obligation is complete, I'll work to convince her."

"Haven't you come to know me well enough yet? Your mother's death seems to weigh lightly on your sister's shoulders. How can knowing me harm her?"

Trina jerked when he spoke of her sister, her face growing angry. "Don't imagine you can understand her grief, or why she chooses not to speak of it. And now you've broken our deal."

Samuel put out a hand to calm his sprite. "I haven't approached her. I wouldn't even know if I'd seen her unless you look alike. I just ask questions of people who spend more time in the commons, and they'd have mentioned someone in mourning."

Trina settled back into her chair, her tension easing as she accepted his word. "Katie doesn't trust you, and our deal makes me lie to her. How am I to tell her about you without explaining everything?"

Samuel felt an overwhelming desire to meet Katie. If something happened to Trina, he'd lose all connection to his favorite son.

His fingers crept to the drawer again, and he realized he had something to bribe her with. "I'll offer you a trade. Convince Katie to meet with me and I'll give you this." He pulled the picture out and pushed it toward Trina. He'd meant to save it for a reward, but maybe now was the right time.

She snagged the picture and pulled it closer. He could tell from her lack of surprise that she'd seen it before. In his mind's eye, he saw her picking it up out of the dust covering her father's desk and running her little fingers across her mother's features. He'd cleaned the picture until the face showed through even clearer, a face so different from her own.

He saw her eyes widen as she looked down at the cleaned picture.

"She looks better with the frame cleaned, don't you think? I never actually saw her in person, but I can guess what drew Jared."

Trina said nothing, sliding one finger lightly down the image.

"You could take it back with you. You could show your sister and display the painting in your cabin." He tried to sound matter-of-fact but knew he'd failed when she gave him a tight look.

"Why do you want to know her?"

Samuel sighed. "Why can't anything be simple with you? I know your cabin. I could walk down there and introduce myself whenever I wanted to. The only reason I hesitate—why I try to make bargains—is because you want me to give her time. Isn't that proof enough of my good intentions?"

Trina stood and carefully placed the picture flat on his desk, giving it one last lingering look before meeting his eyes. "You don't go talk to my sister because you know the deal would end. You bargain with things that aren't yours all to get your 'prize' before it's due. When I can tell the truth to my sister and no longer risk myself for you, then I'll convince her. I won't have her pulled into the games you play with the other polits." She pushed away from the desk and turned toward his door.

"Wait." He tucked the picture back into his drawer, face down. "Aren't you the least bit interested in your next task? I'm just as eager for our deal to end as you seem to be, while maybe not for the same reasons."

She paused at his "wait" but a nerve-wracking moment passed before she turned. He thought again how much easier his other tools were, when money and gifts held sway. For all this girl came from the bottom of society, money couldn't buy her willingness.

Samuel had felt both frustration and pride when she'd refused his offer of instant elevation to polit status at their first meeting. Those feelings continued to plague him. As much as she'd be easier to manage if she weren't so touchy and suspicious, those same traits made her the one able to do what he needed. Along with her size and experience with sneaking in and out of tight spaces.

Ever so slowly, she walked back to her chair, leaning against it rather than sitting down. "What do you have for me this time?"

He wanted so much to ask the simple questions: Have you been to any of the training sessions? How are you adapting to our new life? Have you made any friends?

Instead, he swallowed them as he had through the course of their deal. His time to be a grandparent would come.

"A document. I have a scrap of information from one source to pass to another." His network of spies might not have her agility, but the crew mingled with all sections and Ceric's trade goods were valuable. The crew brought him stray comments and sometimes full text from foolish polits who recorded their thoughts in the library machine. He mentally scoffed at them. They were so quick to let a machine handle the difficult work of putting words down on paper. Each written sentence needed fine crafting. All the machine did was transcribe their words, and it took the soul from their missives.

He glanced up, aware his thoughts had wandered. She stared at him, giving no more sign of impatience than she ever did. Mention her sister and defensiveness rose faster than he could blink. The deal carried none of that loyalty as much as he'd hoped it would. "I'm doing this for you. For all of us."

Her nod showed acknowledgement rather than agreement, and certainly not gratitude.

Samuel pushed the paper toward her, holding back his sigh. "Briniak. They must find this in their common area today. They hosted the meeting this morning. Make it seem like one of the delegates dropped it. You know the path they take."

She stepped forward to take the paper between gloved fingers. He'd given her the protective covering after hearing about a technology to track by more than just palm scans. Up to now, she'd done her job so well no one raised an alarm and the results were subtle. If she failed, he wanted as much chance that she'd escape free as possible. Losing her would hurt, and enough could see the mark of Jared on her face to tie them no matter what denials he came up with.

"Which delegate?"

He jerked his gaze to her, frustrated at his inability to remain focused. He had too many strands spread out in a web across this ship, too many things to keep track of and for much longer than anything he'd ever tried before. The First City polits had required quiet reminders and nothing more to stay in line.

"Tasrien." He could tell she noticed the time it took for him to respond. Weakness. He couldn't afford to show it in front of anyone, especially not Trina. She'd become his most important tool for all he wanted her to be so much more.

She flipped the paper over and scanned the words, something she'd never done before in his presence.

He'd assumed she couldn't read, had marked the map with symbols for that reason. Now he realized just how much she could know. He usually sealed the documents, but sometimes what she delivered had to look like it slipped out from between many sheets of paper.

"They give to Farnwark and take from Briniak. No effort to balance."

Samuel shook his head. "They're not trying for balance. They're trying for power."

Trina fixed him with a firm stare. "But you. You're trying for balance?"

He only smiled, letting her think what she wanted. Samuel hoped she couldn't see the truth or that when she did she'd understand. He'd do anything to secure the future of Menthak—anything. His family wouldn't be a footnote on the histories, not if he could influence what would happen on the new planet.

She nodded again, in recognition of his non-answer. The document disappeared so quickly that he only heard a crinkle of paper. She raised a hand to her forehead, her farewell almost mocking. Between one blink and the next, she'd left the room.

Samuel spread his fingers on the desk, seeing their lengths as his extensions into the different parts of this world. If all went well, he'd be leading the meetings soon enough rather than bowing to others' visions. Even if the other families tried to regain their standing, maintaining power came easy to him. He just had to choose the right time to make his move.

Tasrien held him back. He'd undermined their relationship with each of the other families and yet they managed to repair the damage so quickly that little harm resulted. That document would raise more questions than Trina ever supposed. Not more than two months ago, Briniak received a similar assurance with Farnwark as the loser.

Samuel sighed. He only hoped it would be enough. Though Tasrien seemed unaware of who fought the battle against them, they knew they fought in a battle for power. Their countermoves seemed too aware and too pointed for them not to see a hand behind the shifts among the council. Of all the families, Tasrien posed a real threat.

His thoughts turned to the secret in his arsenal, one he never wanted to use. Only a fool came unprepared.

CHAPTER 33

T rina fumed as she slipped into the ducts again and made her way along the passage to the Briniak section. How dare he try to bribe his way to Katie? The picture was no more his than she could lay claim to it. She pushed aside the memory of her plan to steal it, a plan foiled by his quicker hand.

She realized now, well too late, in her speed to take Katie away from the threats of their former life, she hadn't set any limits. Grandfather could string her along for the whole voyage or even further. She might never get to join the life Katie now enjoyed. She might never be freed of these lies.

Katie might worry that Trina made ties to spacers instead of colonists, the latest explanation her sister had crafted in the face of Trina's silence, but the quiet happiness emanating from her sister at other times made all this worth it. In the shafts, Katie had no one beyond Trina and Mother. Now she had a wealth of friends—and Aaron.

Someday Trina would be able to claim the family, but not yet. Katie showed little interest in her grandfather, and Trina wouldn't change that as long as he held her trapped. When the debt ended was soon enough.

A fragment of the conversation with Grandfather traced through her mind and she realized he wanted the deal to end as well. If only they could reach the point he sought. She'd long suspected confusion was only part of his plan, but she couldn't see what Grandfather would gain in this. Something about how he spoke of Tasrien bothered her though.

Trina forced herself to concentrate. She might be able to walk these paths in her sleep, but so could the cleaning robots. They ran on no schedule she'd been able to determine and she'd almost bumped into crewmembers in the ducts as well. Better they didn't know one of the colony wandered their paths. She'd seen no sign of another from Ceric so it seemed no other family had one like her, able to take advantage of the ducts.

The distant echo of the engines and faint clinks of metal on metal reassured her. None of the noises sounded nearby and she'd almost reached her destination. At least she didn't have to run back to the crane to change. The clothing of her home city was close enough to that of Briniak to pass a casual look.

The sections held around eighty people from each family. As the months passed, the presence of an unknown child became more noticeable whatever efforts she took to blend in. Though she stayed slender, and she'd never have her sister's height, soon no one would mistake her for a child.

Trina hesitated, wondering if she should grab the wig from her hiding place anyway to cover her bright hair, but then decided she didn't have time. Though they'd scheduled her visit, it seemed she'd come later than Grandfather had expected. She had little leeway before the evening gathering made slipping in and out difficult. Briniak ran weekly contests as did Menthak, and everyone attended who could. All around her, the colonists prepared for their new lives, learning necessary skills and constructing tools. Only Trina remained trapped in her old existence.

Pushing back her morose thoughts, Trina focused on the task. Wandering around rather than joining in would make her stand out. She had to drop the paper and leave before the contest gathering began.

Trina paused outside a panel, triggering the listening feature only to hear the distinct sound of a replicator delivering a meal. She moved on to the next small room on Level B, tracing in her mind all the easy routes to where she had to leave the paper.

They must have planned something special for the evening because the next two rooms also held people, much earlier than usual. Though she could see no timepiece from within the tunnels, she could feel the minutes drifting away as she kept changing plans. She'd started with so many options her task had seemed easy. Now, she could feel sweat gathering on her forehead, and her shoulders ached with tension.

Trina put the tool up to the second-to-last room she could use, despair welling inside her. How could she press her grandfather if she couldn't complete her tasks? He'd said once her efforts showed results he'd let her go. She had to succeed.

She listened again, hope rising as no sounds echoed back to her. Not waiting another second, Trina triggered the panel, slipping over it before the metal came to rest just above the duct floor.

After landing on her hands and feet, she quickly straightened before pressing the button to close the panel. She could smell the bitter taint of sweat, but hoped no one would come close enough to sense her fear.

The panel clicked shut just as approaching footsteps dashed her hopes.

"Hi there. You eating? The other rooms are full. No one wants to miss the runoff."

Trina mumbled a response, knowing she couldn't imitate the strong accent of a true Briniak. She kept her head low as she brushed past the older woman and entered the corridor to their common area.

"Probably one of the losers."

Trina smiled at the woman's response. If she only knew the truth.

Her smile vanished as Trina looked out over the common area. It swarmed with people of all ages, setting up chairs to form an audience and laughing, talking, playing games. While the adults might not recognize her as unknown, the children would. None of the colony sections had enough children. She stood still, trying to figure out how to reach where the paper had to fall without them catching her.

A hand landed on her shoulder, making Trina jump in surprise.

"Don't be shy now. They want as many playmates as they can find. Whatever happened, it'll all work out. I promise."

She turned to face an older gentleman, his features covered in wrinkles that moved to bracket his mouth and eyes when he smiled. It took her a moment to hear what he'd said because of how he stretched the words out as if he had all the time in the world. From his clothes, she placed him as a laborer, but tried to remember none of that mattered any longer. The others had been together long enough that those habits were fading from what she'd seen and Katie said.

He pushed her shoulder, his touch gentle. "Go on. There won't be much time for play tonight, and if you don't wear your energy down, you'll squirm through the challenges. At least if you're anything like my granddaughters that is." He laughed, a surprisingly deep sound coming from his slender frame.

Trina smiled back, driven to respond by his kindness but knowing her voice would give her away. She nodded, pretending to be the shy child he thought she was, and took a few hesitant steps toward the children. Why couldn't her grandfather act this way?

She heard him follow and then watched as he joined a group of adults, apparently considering his work done. Her breath rushed out on a sigh of relief, but the task remained. Trina wandered out as if looking for someone, moving closer and closer to her goal.

The common area rang with laughter and she didn't hear a single raised voice even while some worked hard to assemble the room for the evening. It reminded her of watching Festival gatherings, only better. Here, true equality had grown, or at least a close semblance of it.

She glanced back at the corridor she'd come from and then across to the archway marking the connection to the main paths between sections. She stood near enough to where the procession of visitors must have passed.

Trina imitated one of the children playing and spun in a slow circle as if dancing to her own music. She used the movement to scan the room. No one watched her. She bent over, hiding her actions as dance movements while she worked the paper from beneath her shirt and let it fall to the floor.

Straightening up again, she spun another circle. She noticed a group of workers had moved closer than she found comfortable, but she'd completed her task. She only had to get out safely.

Skipping as she'd seen other children do, Trina couldn't help noticing the only time she played was a mockery. Her gaze drifted to the children. She'd never had the chance to join in the Menthak games. Sometimes it seemed she never would.

Trina stumbled, the thought so overwhelming she couldn't maintain her pretense of playing. Her hands hit the floor, catching her weight, and she sprang back up, using skills no child should have.

"Hey, girl!"

Trina sent a frantic glance back and realized a man looked directly at her. Her heart surged into her throat. She wanted to run, but could not think over the blood pounding in her ears. What would crew security do to her? Would Katie be okay?

"You dropped something." He swept up the incriminating paper and sweat burst out on her palms, held trapped by the nearly invisible gloves. The scent of terror rose around her.

Trina bit into the side of her cheek, determined to try something to escape. The pain brought with it a moment of sanity. He wasn't accusing her. The man thought he was helping.

She scrunched up her face into a childish look and shook her head as he approached.

"Here. You dropped this." He pushed the paper at her, bent in half so the writing was obscured.

"Not mine." She dragged the words out in a poor imitation of the older man before.

This Briniak gave her an odd look but he understood well enough. "Are you sure? I put up that row of chairs. I didn't see it before."

Trina just shook her head again, shrugged and brushed past him, concentrating all her energy on maintaining what should look like a careless skip. She kept her shoulders up with sheer force of will, expecting a hand clamped on them any moment as the man read the text.

Instead, a corridor appeared in front of her. She ducked inside, unsure where she was, but she couldn't choose her shelter, not with that paper already in Briniak hands.

Once hidden by shadow, she turned, closing her eyes for a moment and praying no one would be in front of her when she looked. She opened them and blinked twice, unsure whether what she saw was an illusion. The man hadn't followed her. He'd disappeared.

Trina took a deep breath and looked again. People didn't disappear. She needed to know where he was before she tried to get back into the ducts. She scanned the room, finally seeing him over by the stage they assembled. From the distance, she couldn't be sure, but the paper seemed to be hanging from an exterior pocket on his pants.

Pickpockets in Sixth City where Briniak held sway must have had an easy time if folks tucked their pouches in those pockets. It took a moment later before she realized what it meant.

If he'd read it, he'd have called together a meeting. She knew the words written there. He wouldn't keep the information to himself whether or not he understood the implications. She just hoped when he finally read the paper, all memory of the little girl would have faded from his mind.

CHAPTER 34

T rina slipped into her darkened room using the door rather than the panel, grateful for the play they had scheduled for this evening. Katie always stayed in the common area for them.

"Trina?"

She jumped, landing into a defensive pose long before she recognized Katie's voice. Knife tips protruded at both wrists. Her hands shook as she slid them back before Katie could notice.

"Where have you been?" The tone held accusation.

"Around." As Trina stripped off her tunic, she fought a gag at the stench of sweat and fear rising from it.

"What have you been doing? You smell like you just got back from the surface and another narrow escape. What have those spacers gotten you into?"

Trina ducked her head, but Katie pushed in front of her.

"I'm not going to let this go. I've waited almost half a year. You think this is easy for me?" She stood up, pacing around the bed just as Trina tried to hide the panel device.

"What was that?"

"What?"

"Whatever you just hid from me. What was it?"

Trina moved to block her view. "Nothing."

"It didn't look like nothing." Katie groped under the mattress and pulled the device free.

Trina reached for it but Katie jerked away, scrambling over Trina's bed and back onto hers.

When Katie tried to figure it out, though, Trina snatched the device from her hands and tucked it into a pocket so her sister couldn't grab it again.

"How'd you get something like that? Is it from the spacers? "

Trina couldn't lie to her sister's face, nor did she want to tell the truth, not when her last task almost got her captured. She couldn't bear to see her sister's happiness turn sour.

"Oh no!" Katie's hands dropped into her lap and she stared at her twisting fingers rather than looking at Trina. "You're thieving again. I knew you looked wrong somehow when you came in the door. You've been stealing."

"I have not." The protest came even when silence would have served better.

Katie jerked her head up to stare. "Then tell me what that thing is. And how you got it."

Trina looked away, tracing her fingers along a line of stitching in her blanket. "I can't," she muttered. She raised her head and met Katie's eyes squarely. "I'm not stealing though."

Katie stood up and walked to the replicator as though she couldn't stay still. When she punched in a request for tea, she set it for one cup. "You go somewhere but won't say where you are. You have strange objects clearly not from Ceric. There's guilt in your eyes." She slammed the cup on the table, jerking her hand away as hot liquid splashed onto her skin. "You expect me to take your word but this is just what you did on Ceric, down to the stink of sweat and fear. You think I'm happily buzzing around ignorant of what goes around me. You think I'm blind."

She sank into a chair, her head dropping onto the table as frustration overwhelmed her. "You always did." Her voice came out muffled.

Trina brushed a hand through Katie's hair before sitting down in the opposite seat. "Drink your tea. You'll feel better."

Katie took a small sip but her lips pinched at the bitter flavor. Pushing it away, she stared at Trina.

"I don't think you're blind. I just can't talk about it." Trina wished she could claim spacer games.

"Will you talk about it when the green-suits take you? Or when we're thrown out of the family and revealed as shafters? How about when Aaron says he can't associate with thieves? When everything we've gained is lost and there's no place to go or hide, will you talk about it then?" Katie jumped to her feet, her voice loud enough to bounce off the walls.

Trina folded both arms across her chest and kept her tone low and steady. "I'm not thieving. I promised I wouldn't and I haven't. I've found places where I go. You go where you're happy. I go where I want to."

Katie thumped back into her seat, glowering at Trina. She took a big swallow of the tea then choked when the hot liquid hit the back of her throat.

Trina sighed. "I can't explain more, but believe this much: I'm not thieving and what I'm doing won't touch you. I've made sure of that."

Katie stared at her in shock. "What do you mean? You are doing something. How'd you get the box?"

With an awkward jerk, Trina pushed back from the table and rose. "I told you, I can't tell you anything. If you can't believe me, at least pretend you do. It's hard enough without…"

Trina stomped over to the shelves to pull down a new tunic and jerk it over her head.

"Without what? Without a concerned sister trying to stop you from spoiling everything? You were the one who convinced me to come here, convinced me this was our great chance. How can you throw it away? Do you really miss the terror so much you have to recreate it here?" Katie pushed Trina hard. "That smell's not healthy sweat from hard work. It's got a bitter tinge. You need the rush so badly you'll wreck everything."

Trina didn't respond. She just walked around Katie, heading for their door.

"Do what you have to, but if you take Aaron away from me, I'll never forgive you. Never." The words came out as an angry hiss that burned Trina as she pushed the button and stepped through the door.

CHAPTER 35

T he crane creaked when Trina shifted around, too restless to settle. Three days had passed since Katie confronted her but they
still weren't speaking. And why should Katie trust her word?

She swung out of the scoop and climbed down the arm. Dropping
to the floor, Trina felt full of nervous energy. Something had to break.
She raced between the rows, feeling like a trapped crawler. Why
couldn't Grandfather release her? Why couldn't it be over? If anything
happened, she knew Katie would just walk away. That's what she wanted her sister to do, but she didn't want to lose Katie.

She collapsed, bracing her back against a box while she caught her
breath. If she hadn't already lost her sister. The heat of Katie's glares
could have cooked an egg.

Trina had delivered another package, this time without any trouble,
but she knew her mind wasn't focused. If ever she had been at risk of
being captured, it was now.

Thoughts of what could happen, to her, to Katie, even to Grandfather, haunted her. Every moment she left the colony section, her back
ached and her heart pounded. Even the robots could probably hear her
coming.

She slammed a hand against the box behind her then shoved the
abused fist into her mouth. The process of pulling splinters out calmed
her a little, but only firmed her desire for freedom. She'd go to Grandfather now and demand an end. No more tasks, no more deal. She'd
done everything he asked since the voyage began. It was enough. It had
to be.

SAMUEL PUT DOWN HIS MUG of coffee, missing the taste of fresh
beans even though the crewman he'd asked about it said there was no
way to tell the difference. If he'd had time, he would've arranged to
bring a good supply. Samuel grimaced. After another year of this, maybe he wouldn't remember what the real thing tasted like either.

He pushed the synthetic food around on his plate, wondering if
they had a hydroponics section on this ship. Maybe they could start
some of the plants now and eat real food for at least part of the trip.

The seeds from the plants could restore their supplies, and he wouldn't have to suffer another almost-right meal. The crew should appreciate a share as well.

"Bettina, I'm done out here." Might as well let her clean up. He wasn't going to finish.

Samuel rose with a sigh. His feet turned in the direction of his study but he really didn't want to go in there anymore. No matter what he did, Tasrien seemed ahead of him. He wanted this to be over with, but not enough to give in. Tasrien would not lead the colony. Menthak would.

The thought had just enough strength behind it to revitalize him. He squared his shoulders and marched into his study, knowing the impression he gave those around him was as important in some ways as anything he did. If they saw him as a tired old man, he'd lack the support to bring this colony around. Paul needed years of reshaping before he could lead the family, and the same would be true of the twins even if they were valid candidates. He wouldn't risk the colony on anyone discovering their background. He'd do right by his granddaughters, but Paul would have to fail drastically before he'd let Jared's girls head the Menthak family.

Samuel stepped through the doorway into his haven and stopped short. Perched on his desk was the subject of his thoughts—Trina.

He moved around her to sit in his chair, forcing her to twist or get off his desk. She chose to shift to her usual spot rather than craning to meet his eyes.

"You took a chance coming in here with me gone. Any of my servants could have caught you. We're not ready to explain our relationship, must less how you got in."

Trina smiled and folded her arms across her chest, leaning back in the chair. "Nancy already came through and Bettina won't come to check her work for some hours yet. Besides, she doesn't come through your study because you're always here and don't want to be disturbed."

He started to laugh at her assessment but something in her eyes made him stop. "I almost didn't come in myself." Whether he spoke to test her or just because the words escaped before he could think, he didn't know.

Trina laughed at that but the sound held little humor. "You'd have come. This room is as much your hideaway as—" She clamped her mouth shut so quickly he imagined he could hear her jaw snap.

"So you know me well. What purpose that serves I can only guess." He let some of his general irritation strike at her though he knew he shouldn't.

She leaned forward to fix him with one of her intense stares, and he tried not to squirm. "I know you well enough to know you've been stewing. You sit here every day, unhappy with what's happening. If you were happy, I'd be free."

Samuel wanted to protest, seeing in his mind's eye the image of a beaten old man, but he couldn't disagree with her assessment. There was no point. "So, with all your knowledge, how can you change the situation? You've done everything I've asked you to and it works to a point. We can keep on this way for as long as it takes, all twenty-four months if necessary. Or, you could suggest something."

He watched her closely. He hadn't planned on asking her for help, hadn't wanted to involve her so deeply, but he didn't know what else to do. If Tasrien succeeded, they'd all lose, whether she admitted that or not.

A wrinkle appeared on Trina's forehead and her teeth sank into her lower lip. She took a deep breath, closed her eyes for a moment, then nodded. "If I do this—find you this way—you'll release me from the debt? I'll be free to join the colony and be like all the others?"

"You were always able to join the colony. The only one holding you back was yourself."

"Will you free me from the debt?"

She didn't acknowledge his words, too focused on her goal.

Samuel respected her concentration despite his annoyance at being unable to distract her.

Unmoving, she kept silent, waiting for his answer.

He rose and walked to the bookcase, wanting to break her stare. Samuel pretended to read the spines, running his fingers along them. Still no sound.

The silence battered him, demanding a response until he could handle the tension no longer. Samuel spun back to face Trina, returning to his chair. She may have blinked but otherwise she didn't seem to have moved at all. He sighed.

"All right. If you can come up with a solution, something I can use to make this family—to prevent Tasrien from taking over, you're done."

Trina let out her breath, and he wondered what had crossed her mind in those long moments. "If you knew what they talked about, couldn't you make their deals known in the right ways?"

He laughed, startled while at the same time knowing he shouldn't be. She'd used the time to think about what she could offer.

"Of course. Knowing everything would help immensely but that's not possible. Even if I had enough people, putting them into place now when everyone knows everyone else would only risk them for no purpose."

A smile crossed her face and for a second he allowed hope to dance along his nerves. Maybe...but no, he knew of no way. How could this little slip of a girl know more?

"The crew can."

He frowned, frustrated at her cryptic speech and at how badly he wanted to believe her. "Can what?"

"Listen. They can listen anywhere. I'd guess they're even listening here, now."

Unable to help himself, Samuel jerked his gaze around the room and to the doorway, relaxing only when they showed no one else, even though he knew they were alone. "There's no one here, Trina. No one to listen."

She smiled again, propping her chin up with one hand and letting the dreaded silence grow.

His fingers started caressing the surface of his desk as he failed to contain his energy. "Okay, how?" The words burst from him as if pushed by an unseen force. He saw from the slight shift in her expression that she knew she'd won.

"The device does it. For panels."

Impatience rushed through him followed quickly by annoyance. He didn't like being toyed with. If anyone would play with another, it should be him.

"How can a device listen? I know you want out, but fairy tales are not what I asked for or what you offered. Take some time and bring me something I can use. I have nothing for you today." He rose, hoping to push her out by sheer force of personality before he said something he'd regret.

She tilted her head to look up at him. "How do you think the panels never open when someone's in the room? Don't you think, with all the times you've sent me out, I'd have missed at least once? When you gave me the Briniak document, they'd already started their evening gather."

Out of the dregs of his patience, Samuel summoned a smile. Feeling more in control of the situation, he fixed her with a bemused look. "We both know, my dear, you're adept at listening at doors from your visit to my house. Why should this be any different?"

"If I'm skilled at such, I didn't inherit it from my mother. She's not the part of my family who seems to know what he should not."

Samuel raised a hand to his forehead in recognition of her parry. "The streetrat's gained back some of her bite, I see. True enough."

"Spacerat."

He laughed at that. "I suppose you're right. Spacerat. And adapting to it so well I think you'd be able to survive without even a cabin to call your own."

"Well enough, Grandfather." She stressed his title as if to emphasize the relationship. "But I have a cabin. I'm more than the spacerat you force me to be. I'm a full member of your colony and soon I'll be able to act like one as well."

"Soon as you come up with a real way for me to continue on without your help. I look forward to the day we can share a meal together rather than feast on our wits."

Trina looked surprised for a moment as if he hadn't figured in her plans once she paid her debt. He'd change that impression soon enough after the end to their bargain. For all he found her talents valuable now, she was his granddaughter, she and her sister both.

"You think the spacers limited, don't you?"

Now Samuel took a turn at surprise. He tried to figure out where her comment came from but failed.

"They'll never know the beauty of life on planet and so they lose touch with the truth. Yes, limited may be the right word for them. How does that matter to us? You skirt the edges of the doctrine and understand when our own labor does not suffice we must use the right tool. But dependency on tech makes us weak."

She shifted in her chair, the first sign of discomfort he'd seen in her this visit. He waited, knowing whatever came next, he'd be unlikely to like it.

"The crew makes devices for convenience but also for things they can't do. We lost that when our machinery failed, and refusing to use tech now makes us fools. Grandfather, I can no more hear through the panels than you can listen in on your servants' conversations by leaning an ear against that wall." She pointed toward his bookcase. "These aren't simple wood. They're built of the same metal as the rest of the ship."

"Then I guess you're unnaturally lucky. Festival got. God watches over your shoulder and aids us in our cause."

Trina laughed but the sound had a bitter tone. "Not God, Grandfather. The spacers aid me. Their device can listen between these walls. It's no fairy tale. And if this device can, why not one to listen always? If you get more listeners and a way to hear them, I'll place them in any room you'd like. You'll know as fast as they do what they're planning. Would that be enough? Would my debt be clear?"

Samuel stayed silent as he tried to understand what she suggested. Listening without being there. An ingenious creation if it truly existed. He felt a twinge of concern as he thought about the implications.

If the crew had this device, they would know all he and the other leaders did. They had no stake in the colony's squabbles. Unless he did something to interfere with the delivery of the colonists, maybe they didn't care enough to act.

He straightened in the chair, donning the look of a grand polit to hide his worries.

Her eyes twinkled when he looked at her, as if she saw through his disguise. This time, she didn't repeat her question. She gave him the space to think about her offer, space he desperately needed.

"This listening. You know it's true?"

She frowned, some of her confidence slipping for a second before her mask fell back into place, reminding Samuel that his son's seed bred close to the Menthak line. If he'd had her from birth, what a polit she would have made.

"I only know what the device you gave me can do, and only part of its features, but look around you. Between what I know and what I see, if such a listening device is possible, they'll have it. You need only exercise the same abilities you used in getting this." She waved the box he'd given her, already more familiar with its strengths than he'd ever be.

Samuel sighed. This seemed a slender rope to hang all his hopes on but he had no better path. "I'll see what I can learn. If this device exists, if I can get enough of them along with a way to hear from a distance, and if you can place them where I need to listen, then your debt will be paid."

She nodded, her face serious, but he caught the edge of a smile as she rose and turned toward the door.

"I'll send word when I know," he called after her disappearing form. Samuel looked down at the papers on his desk and wondered who had come out the victor in this encounter. Or was it possible they'd both gotten what they needed?

"Did you want anything, Master? I heard you call out."

Samuel looked up as Nancy popped her head around the door. "No, Nancy. I'm well." He smiled at her but didn't miss the shake of her head as she turned. How many times had she heard him talking when she knew no one else was there? As far as he knew, no one had ever seen Trina. He'd have to be more careful or rumors of senility might begin. Never on purpose—his people were loyal—but a stray comment matched to another comment and a picture builds fast enough.

CHAPTER 36

Are you going to eat that cereal or just play with it?"

Trina glanced up at Katie, forcing a smile onto her face. "I'm trying." She'd agreed to go to the commons the previous night to make up for her mood swings over the last five days, but it had proved more difficult than she'd expected.

Her sister shoved back from the table, abandoning her half-full bowl. "Are you? Are you really trying anything? Last night you just stood there, hiding in the shadows. Why bother to come if you're not going to talk to people? And you left before Aaron finished his work. It's like you don't want to meet him." Katie stomped over to the entrance, her hand ringing against the metal as she slammed the button to open the door. "I'm going now. You can follow if you feel up to participating for once."

Sighing, Trina put her spoon down. Waiting for Grandfather to send word had left her tense and edgy. She should have known just coming wouldn't be enough. She'd stayed as long as she could before escaping.

The transition to being a member of the colony wasn't easy, but soon it wouldn't matter if all the colonists saw her face. She had to become accustomed to so many people in the same space where none were targets or dangers.

They'd finally resolved their last argument and now this. Watching Katie laugh and dance with her new friends only made Trina envious of her sister's ease. Trina felt isolated even when out of the shadows and standing in plain sight—a stranger among those who should have been her friends.

She pushed back from the table and paced toward her bed. Collapsing face down, Trina pillowed her head on her crossed arms. She wanted—no, needed—to go to the crane, but what if Grandfather sent word while she was gone? She hadn't left the room in days except for following Katie to the commons. She felt trapped. Maybe half the reason she'd been so uncomfortable at the dance was worrying that she'd miss the message.

Trina slipped the panel device out from her new hiding spot and fingered the green button, debating whether to push it. A quick run in the ducts would go a long way toward releasing some of her energy. She pressed and the panel lowered as if the ducts called to her.

Looking into the darkness, Trina wanted nothing more than to swing up through the opening. Something held her back. Why had she allowed Grandfather to set the time? She could go and check on him. Had he even tried yet, or had he decided to keep her bound for longer? Did she really want an answer?

Her finger slipped to the blue button and the panel rose back into place. She thrust the panel tool into a pocket and slumped onto her bed, crumpling the blanket with her hands. Even the hope she'd be free seemed better than knowing her idea wouldn't work, but at the same time, the need for patience strangled her.

The door chimed.

Trina jerked, the sound so unexpected her defensive instincts sprang into play. She triggered her sheaths, forgetting she'd put the knives aside in preparation for her change in circumstances, all except the one she kept strapped to her ankle in case something proved her wrong. Without her knives, she would have been chewed up and spat out on her first trip into the ducts.

The chime sounded again, and Trina released a shaky laugh as she walked to the door. They hadn't had any visitors since the first time Aaron came. For all Katie wanted her sister to meet him, she had enough respect, or caution, not to force him on Trina, just as Trina didn't push her twin to meet their grandfather.

She tapped the yellow button and waited, but no sounds came out. Confused, she struggled to remember what Katie had said. This did not function like the panel tool despite the colors.

"Is anyone there? I have a message."

She jerked back as the voice poured from the panel. Reaching out, she touched the yellow button again. Nothing happened.

"Hello?"

"Are you Aaron?" Trina spoke half to herself, still trying to figure out the buttons and frustrated at her clumsiness.

"No, but I have a message."

She smiled, realizing she'd forgotten this yellow button let her speak. He had to push another on the outside for her to hear him. She held the button down as she spoke into the panel. "What message?"

"It's for Trina. Not one I want to shout through the door."

Adrenaline soared through her, making her heart jump into a rapid rhythm. Her palms felt clammy. In the confusion of figuring out the door, she'd forgotten that the message must be from Grandfather.

Since the very first time, Trina had always gone to him, checking in frequently enough he'd never seen fit to send her another message.

She pushed the door button and stared at the young man on the other side. He stood not much taller than she was. She'd expected an adult from his cultured voice.

"I'm Trina."

"Hello. I'm Marcus. I've met your sister before but never seen you around."

Curiosity gleamed in his eyes but Trina ignored his look, reaching out for the packet she'd expected.

He looked down at her hand and shrugged. "I don't have anything for you."

Trina frowned. "Where's my message then?"

"I'm afraid you'll be disappointed," he said, laughing. "It's nothing so complicated as to require a written message. Samuel, the grand polit, wanted to see you. I don't know why. He asked me if I could fetch you."

"Oh." Trina felt lost for a moment, unsure what to do. She'd never been fetched. She hadn't even gone through Grandfather's front door except for the first time. "Why couldn't you tell me that through the door?"

He shrugged. "I couldn't very well fetch you from out there. Are you ready? Or do you need something?" He looked her over and smiled with his head tilted to one side. "You look fine to me."

A blush swam up to heat her cheeks. Trina ducked as she stepped through the door, unwilling to meet his eyes. She wondered if this was what it felt like to be just another girl. Was Grandfather giving her a taste?

Hope swept over her at the thought. If he wanted her to feel normal, surely he had good news. She raised her head and walked faster, keeping pace with Marcus.

The lift door closed behind them and Trina moved to the opposite wall with relief, able to watch him without being obvious.

When the lift glided to a stop at Level A, Marcus turned his intense smile on her again. "I've got plans that don't include another long 'discussion' with Samuel. Do you know the rest of the way?"

She nodded, still feeling prickly from his attention.

"I'll see you, then, in the commons. Good luck. Samuel isn't as gruff as he seems."

Trina muttered something noncommittal to his suggestion but smothered a laugh at the thought of Grandfather intimidating her. They'd matched wits too many times for her to feel the least bit daunted, but Marcus had no way of knowing that. Someday soon, though, everyone would know about their relationship if not what they'd been up to for the first six months.

She finished walking down the corridor, reminding herself to act like she belonged. As she faced Grandfather's door, Trina remembered her first time and how she'd ducked through just after his servants left.

Her hand shook only slightly as she raised it to the yellow button next to the palm reader. She pressed, unsure what to say.

Before she could say anything, the door swished open, revealing the older of the two women servants, Bettina. "Come in, come in. Trina, right? Master's expecting you. He said to show you to his study."

Trina felt awkward as the woman ushered her forward, taking her through the cabin toward his study in a path, though familiar, she'd never walked with another. She kept expecting someone to point her out as a spacerat.

By the time Bettina deposited her in front of Grandfather's study, tension knotted the muscles on her shoulders and an ache had started at her temples.

"Ah, there you are. Come in and sit down. Thank you, Bettina. That will be all."

"Do you wish refreshments for your guest, Master?"

Grandfather smiled at Bettina over Trina's shoulder. "No, I think we'll be fine. You go along. I'll call you when you're needed."

Trina couldn't help measuring the calm, affable tone with the way she'd heard other polits interact with their servants. At least in front of guests, he presented a pleasant face to his staff. Though his servants liked him as well, indicating his behavior rang true.

Slipping into what she'd come to think of as her chair, Trina folded her legs on the seat as she waited for him to sit down once again.

He smiled, and she thought she saw a spark of excitement in his features, but she let him speak when he felt ready. The silence settled and Trina relaxed. She didn't sense any tension from him.

"You have a sharp mind. It'll serve you well. And has served me." He laughed. "You guessed correctly. They do have a listening device. It may take a while, but once you've placed the last one, you can consider yourself free of debt."

Though she refused to let it show, inside she hugged herself. "How will I know?"

As she spoke, he pulled his map out, pointing to small red marks along several rooms. Though not all rooms had access to the duct system, almost all of them shared at least one wall with the tunnels.

"I think it's best if you place them in the ducts themselves where you can but you'll have to be careful. If they protrude at all, the cleaning robots will sweep them up and you'll have to start again."

Trina rose, leaning over the desk to see where his marks were, trying to memorize them.

Samuel laughed again. "Don't worry. You can borrow my map for now. I'll move the marks when we have both maps together. I've no doubt you didn't collect yours when Marcus showed up at your door." He handed her the paper, folding it as he went. "So, did you enjoy strolling up here with a young man at your side?"

Trina looked at him. So it had been deliberate. "No," she replied. "I felt awkward and exposed."

He nodded as if he'd expected her response. "I suppose you will at first. It'll get easier. Just look at how well your sister has done." He waved off her objection before she could say anything. "I know Aaron's mother well, as I know Marcus's family. Not that there are many I don't know after more than six months. You could have as well."

"I want to meet Aaron." The words slipped free before she made a conscious decision to say anything, a continuation of her aborted argument with Katie. He didn't seem surprised.

"I can only partially understand your reasons for keeping so separate but I can't imagine it's been easy. Back on Ceric you lived on the edges of other lives as all shafters do. This was supposed to be different. Soon, it will be."

Trina nodded but forced herself to focus on the map in her hand. "Where will I get the devices?" None of this would happen if she didn't complete her task. She'd had enough of dreaming and pretending. She wanted a real life. It hovered so close in front of her that she could almost touch it.

Her grandfather smiled and pulled a small bag out of one of his desk drawers. His gaze lingered on the other contents for a moment before he closed it. "I have them here. They're small, but costly. Mind you take care not to lose them."

She reached out and plucked the bag from his fingers, feeling the devices shifting within. They weighed almost nothing and she should be able to hide them easily. Her freedom seemed closer than ever before.

Trina tucked both map and the bag into her tunic, finding her hidden pockets by habit. "I'll keep them safe as I have all of the things you've given me, Grandfather. They'll be in place sooner than you can ask about them."

She turned to go but he brushed her hand to restrain her. Trina looked a question to him, fretting at the delay.

"Plant the first few then tell me. I'd like to make sure they work before all are spread out and need to be returned."

Trina nodded, leaving that as her reply, once again heading for the door.

"Don't forget to go out the real door. I wouldn't want Bettina wondering what I did with my young guest. She gives me enough strange looks when she hears voices in here. They all do."

Trina laughed. "I'll remember. Though no guarantees for how long I'll stay in the corridor."

"Fair enough."

She heard his words echoing out from behind her and wondered how often his servants had listened to her talking with him. She might be the only Menthak still unknown to them. They'd have to wonder what their master wanted with her. She only hoped they'd rethink whatever they came up with when Grandfather revealed her as his granddaughter, though perhaps they suspected already if she resembled her father as much as her grandfather said she did.

Trina nodded to Bettina as she left. This time the servant wouldn't think her a ghost, no matter how often she'd been a phantom voice. Trina walked to the lift before triggering the device and slipped into the duct system through the access panel instead of sending the elevator down to Level D.

The outer cargo area took only a short while to reach and then she scrambled up to her nest in the crane's cabin. Trina tucked the bag full of listening devices away and spread the map out in front of her. Though Tasrien held her grandfather's strongest interest, she planned to test the system on a less suspicious family first.

"THEY'RE IN PLACE." TRINA WATCHED her grandfather tense at the statement, though whether in reaction to her sudden appearance or anticipation, she couldn't tell.

He didn't even look up as he reached for a piece of paper and typed the code out on the surface of his desk. He'd been waiting for her.

"Now we'll see if the spacers can do what you believe they can." He waved a hand toward a console on the wall much like the one in Trina's cabin. Only where their lights and buttons seemed fixed, his were changing.

First one then another light appeared along the bottom of the console.

She turned to him, unsure what they meant.

"I've activated the devices. A light for each."

He'd never been one to explain his workings, but relief appeared to make him generous.

Trina glanced back to see three lights, one for each device she'd hidden.

"Have you made plans for after?"

She dropped into her chair to delay answering. Until he'd set her free, planning seemed too much like tempting fate. "Aren't you going to listen?"

Her grandfather stared down at his desk for a moment as though disappointed in her avoidance. Then he tapped the surface again, and voices poured out. He jerked back so quickly his chair smacked against the shelving behind him.

Trina stifled a laugh, remembering her own reaction to pushing the wrong button. Instead, she rose. "You can hear them, as I, and the spacers, promised. When the other devices are in place, our deal is complete."

He recovered quickly and leaned down to read something on his desk.

She waited long enough for him to mutter agreement before heading out again. Trina did not intend to waste any time in getting her freedom. Then, she'd be able to make all the plans she could think of.

CHAPTER 37

T rina pulled the wig off her head and tossed it into the crane cabin. She'd emptied the bag.

It took a bit of doing to find the right place for each one, and she had to reseat a couple when the voices came out distorted, but she had finished. Only one day past a full week later and every possible device rested in a niche behind the wall of an important room or tucked into the back of shelves or on floorboards.

With more energy than she'd felt in the last year, she headed up to Grandfather's cabin. As she left the storage area, Trina paused long enough to jam the corner of one of the boxes into her panel. He'd have to release her now. She'd given him what he needed and more, but Trina didn't feel ready to lose the ducts even if he took back the tool. She had to have a way in if colony life grew overwhelming.

Trina decided she'd come to him like any other colony member as she climbed up the ladder to Level A. She paused next to the lift and checked if it held steady on this level. Then she engaged the panel and slipped into the lift. Once the panel swung shut, she triggered the door to open.

A sense of freedom washed over her as she marched down the center of Grandfather's corridor, looking to neither side, nor ducking into shadows.

"Trina?"

Her name rocketed down the walkway. She tensed, all confidence and freedom vanishing for a moment. Then Trina gathered her courage and turned to face the voice, relaxing only once she saw Marcus.

"I thought I recognized that hair. I haven't seen you in the commons yet."

"I've been busy." Trina returned his smile, wishing for half the assurance she'd felt around Piper.

"Visiting the grand polit again? What did he trick you into doing?"

Trina started. Did he have everyone off on a plot of some sort?

Marcus laughed. "He got me to arrange the plays when we first came on board, guessing correctly that we'd need some entertainment after the training sessions. Mother's off doing some sort of basic needlework class. Organizing it, not sewing anything. She doesn't know which end to push the thread through." He laughed. "Neither do I come to think of it. Samuel is quick to find work for any idle hands."

Trina smiled again, feeling awkward but relieved. Somehow, even with her own misgivings, she didn't want her grandfather to be some controlling big man, pushing everyone around like Fence had done.

"I'll see you in the commons later. I've really got to go," she said, gesturing toward her grandfather's cabin.

Despite her words, she stood watching as Marcus strode away. She could get used to this. He glanced back just as he reached the corner, smiling when he saw her. Trina raised a hand in a halfhearted wave before continuing.

She wished she had a way to warn Samuel this time. Her choice to act like any other colonist meant she couldn't check if he was there or if someone else already claimed his attention. She stood before his door, unable to remember any time she'd dropped by to see someone. Nobody showed up unexpectedly in the shafts. Even here, when she'd appeared without warning, her intentions hadn't been to visit.

The door swished open in front of her. Trina jerked back in surprise as the older servant stepped through.

"Oh! I didn't hear the chime. Trina, right?"

Trina stared at Bettina for a moment before gathering her wits. "Is he in? I came by to see him. He doesn't know I'm coming but I'd hoped..." Her voice trailed off as she met Bettina's sympathetic look.

"He's in his study. I'm sure he'd love to see you. He enjoys visitors." She triggered the door again and waved Trina to enter. "You know the way, just go on back. It'll be fine."

Trina paused, strangely nervous, but the knowledge that the door would close soon forced her to step forward. The door swished shut behind her, reminding her of the very first time she'd ducked through when the servants left. The cabin seemed empty, quiet lying thick in the rooms.

She made her way to her grandfather's study feeling awkward as an uninvited guest in a way she'd never felt as a spy. Trina glanced into the rooms as she passed them, admiring the handicrafts decorating the walls, some even mimicking her mother's blankets. Never before had she had the luxury of exploring his space.

When she reached the back corridor and walked toward his study, Trina noticed the door next to it stood open. Unable to restrain herself, she peeked in, seeing what was obviously a spare bedroom. Disappointment filled her. However irrationally, she'd expected her father's room brought back to life.

"Trina?" Her grandfather stepped out from his study into the corridor. "I'd say I didn't hear you come in, but I never do. Join me."

He didn't mention her snooping and neither did she, maintaining the illusion of a casual visit.

"Bettina let me in as she left. She said it would be all right." Trina felt awkward and unsure, ridiculous emotions but ones she couldn't control.

He looked at her for a moment before nodding. "So, you came by the door then. Trying out your new life?"

Trina pushed past Grandfather to fold into her chair. "I'm done. Your listening devices are planted, you've checked all but the last few and I know they work. I tested with my panel tool." The words rushed out, but Trina didn't care. He'd set her free today.

"Yes, I triggered them myself. You said you'd have them done, and I trust your word. So, what are you going to do now?" He walked around the desk and settled into his chair, for once letting his hands rest along the sides.

Trina leaned forward, one foot slipping down to touch the floor. "You mean it? You're satisfied?"

Lines she'd never noticed before crinkled around his eyes. "Yes, you've helped me more than any other. You deserve a rest. As of now, you are only my granddaughter. My granddaughter who's about to make her debut into Menthak society."

She met his smile with a wide grin. She'd done it. Even Grandfather looked happier than he'd seemed for a while. No more lying to Katie, no more hiding. A new life for real.

"And your plans?"

She shook her head lightly at the question. "I don't know. I didn't really make any. It's just, well, I wasn't sure I'd ever—" She stopped, realizing what she meant was that she hadn't been sure she could trust him. Trina shrugged. "I'd like to go to the commons."

Her grandfather nodded. "Sounds like a good plan. Start small and give yourself a chance. Your sister didn't conquer the world in just one day either."

Trina laughed. "She did. She went from a recluse to a social butterfly all because of Aaron. I'd like to meet Aaron." The last she said to herself.

"He's a good boy. You can trust Katie with him. And you'll like him too."

He looked so earnest and so much like the grandparents she'd seen when checking out polit houses.

Opening the top drawer of his desk, he ran his finger across something out of her sight. She realized what he'd touched when the picture frame came into view. "This really should be yours. Your mother tells me so often enough." He waved aside her odd look. "Just a fancy of mine. I was wrong to keep it." He pushed the painting across the desk, its frame making a scraping sound against the surface.

Trina reached for the picture, only glancing at it once before she pressed her mother's image against her chest. "Thank you. We'll be happier with this. She'll seem more with us."

"I am sorry for your loss. She must have been an amazing woman." He paused, and Trina could almost see his mind moving to his next purpose. "And Katie? Can you both join me for a meal? I'd like to meet her."

She glanced down at the painting.

Grandfather cleared his throat. "I suppose this is a bit much all at once. I won't rush you. Go be a colonist for a while. I'll send you a message in a bit to find out how you're doing. Marcus is always willing to help."

Trina felt a blush rising on her face. She hardly knew Marcus, but he seemed special, maybe because he'd talked to her like any other person—the only one to do so since she'd come aboard.

"You like him, don't you? A good boy. Only a year older than you are. He turned seventeen a few months past."

Trina glanced up at him in surprise. "He seemed nice, but I don't know him."

Grandfather rose and walked around the desk, laying a gentle hand on her shoulder. "Then you shall. Seek him out in the commons. You two should deal well together."

She shrugged off his touch, part for her unsure if he still manipulated her like Fence used to. She slipped the painting into a pocket and stood as well. "I'll go now."

"The device?"

Trina tensed. Suddenly she realized she had no way into the ducts without the tool even though she'd made an opening to get to the crane.

Her tension must have been obvious because Grandfather slowly shook his head. "Never mind. I have little enough use for it. Just be careful. A colonist has no business in the walls."

She smiled her thanks. How long before she thought of herself in those terms? Somehow, she'd expected freedom and feeling like a colonist to happen all at once. Her instinctive protection of her haven showed she wasn't as ready as she'd wanted to be.

"Maybe I'll see you in the commons." Grandfather raised a hand to his forehead, and she returned the farewell.

A quick step and she entered the corridor, moving beyond his vision. She turned first to the small storage room she often used to slip into the ducts then stopped. Shaking her head, Trina went the other way. She was a colonist now. She'd go as she'd come—through the front door.

'll come with you tonight and actually join in." Trina laughed at the stunned look on Katie's face before taking another sip of tea.

"You'll try this time?" Katie pushed the dinner plate away, her face a muddle of excitement and wariness. "They won't understand if you snub them again."

"I didn't mean to. It was just overwhelming. I'll do better." Trina's words rang with conviction. She'd walked back from Grandfather's cabin never once ducking into the tunnels, though her hand slipped to the panel tool a couple of times.

The colonists she'd passed looked surprised when they didn't recognize her, but no one stopped Trina after she smiled. Everything seemed different. She'd kept her back straight and only tensed in fear with the first few encounters.

"You think it's time? Why the sudden change?"

Her sister's voice held sarcasm built in months of useless pleading. Trina couldn't blame her.

Trina shrugged. "I want to meet Aaron."

Katie gave a tight laugh. "As if I haven't been begging you to all these months." She shrugged. "I suppose I'm just glad you've decided. Do you want to go now?"

Trina waved to Katie's full plate. "Let's finish our dinners first."

Katie gobbled her food and rushed Trina to hurry as if worried she'd change her mind, standing over Trina as she ate her last few bites.

Waving her sister to sit down, Trina reached in her pocket for the painting. "I have something to show you first."

"Can't it wait? You'll change your mind. I'm sure you will. Let's just go now."

Trina laughed at her sister's impatience. "I'm not going to change my mind. I just think you should see this. Grandfather gave it to me."

She pushed the frame across the table, watching her sister. She hadn't told Katie about the painting or her failed attempt to steal it. She didn't know how Katie would react. Now that the painting lay on the table between them, she wished she'd kept it for later.

Katie had been looking at Trina, but her eyes tracked the movement and finally glanced down when it proved too much of a lure.

Trina watched as Katie's face went still. Water pooled in her own eyes as tears started down her sister's face.

"It's Mother, Trina. It's Mother."

"I know."

"But how? How'd Grandfather have a picture of Mother? If he knew all along, why didn't he come for us?"

Trina wished she had a simple answer but knew nothing about their birth had ever been simple. "Even if he'd tried, do you think Mother would have let him? She wanted our father, not his family. She was content to wait for a message from Jared, a gate pass of her own."

Katie dragged a sleeve across her eyes and sniffled.

Trina picked up the frame, looking at it for a moment. "We can't change the past, but now it's like she's a part of our future. Just as Grandfather wants to be. Where should we put the picture?" She let her statement about Grandfather pass without comment, giving Katie time to adjust.

"I think we should put it in the center of our table. It'll be like she shares meals with us." Katie paused. "That's where you've been? With Grandfather so much of the time? I'd thought spacers were trying to steal you away."

Trina nodded, relieved to offer a version of the truth. "He wants to meet you. Always has, but he'll wait until you're ready. I made sure of that."

Before Katie could respond, Trina remembered something else she'd kept hidden. "It's not a picture but…" She went to her shelf and dug deep through it to find what she'd taken from Grandfather's house. "It's our father's pen. It needs cleaning if we ever want to write with it, but for now, it's a piece of him to be with Mother." She realized how strange it sounded, but Katie just nodded and held out her hands.

Passing over the pen, Trina watched her sister carefully arrange both items on the table. "Welcome to our home, Mother and Father," she whispered under her breath.

Katie adjusted the frame one last time before stepping back to look at them. "And now, we'll introduce you to your new life so you'll have something to tell our parents about."

CHAPTER 39

T rina tried to let it wash over her, but by the time they reached the commons, she felt tense and uncomfortable. She didn't know how to act like a colonist. She didn't know what to say or what to talk about. And how was she going to explain the months since they'd come on board? No matter what she said, she'd stand out.

They stepped into the open and she cringed, remembering the vulnerability she'd felt when first trying to place an item for Grandfather.

"Don't worry. They'll like you. Just give them a chance," Katie whispered.

Trina reached for her shafter swagger to hide her true reaction, but stopped when she realized it would make her stand out as much as her fear. She had no masks to help fit in.

"Aaron!"

Trina jerked at her sister's call. She watched the young man approach, feeling as if she already knew him from watching Katie. Despite herself, she cataloged his confident step, the way his broad shoulders stayed back and how he moved his hips. She felt her muscles adjusting in imitation.

For a moment, she let her body mimic him then shifted back to her normal stance. No masks. She wanted to be a real colonist, not pretend to be one. She'd have to learn.

"Trina? I've waited a long while to meet you."

She mumbled something in response, her determination not to wear a mask leaving her awkward.

"Go slow, Aaron. It's only her second time. In the beginning, this is overwhelming."

Trina threw a grateful glance to her sister and trailed after Katie as they approached a collection of tables.

"You missed the evening training. We're taking a break before the first geography class. The scouts sent us new information about our planet."

Katie murmured something about a delay, her hand slipping into Aaron's for a moment before she turned and pulled Trina forward.

Trina tried to stay focused through a bewildering number of introductions. Names, faces, clothing, all blurred together, giving her a headache. When her sister joined a strange game, she slipped back against a wall, finding a chair mostly in shadow. She'd promised, and she hadn't held back, but she needed some space.

Watching them, Trina forced herself to think of the people as individuals, as colonists rather than marks carrying their money pouches well hidden or within easy reach. Her fingers itched for the feel of dice as she watched them play with the decorated papers she'd seen before but never understood.

Everything around her emphasized how much she had to learn, and Katie's ease stunned her. Trina shrank back against the wall as if the shadows could mask her difference. No matter how much she'd hoped to suddenly become a colonist, she still felt like a shafter hiding on the edges of surface life, hoping an enforcer wouldn't notice her.

A hand descended on her shoulder, and Trina jumped out of the chair, the clatter of its fall bringing everyone's attention to her.

Marcus laughed. "Sorry." He pulled the chair upright and shrugged toward the watchers. "I didn't mean to startle you."

Trina glanced at the other colonists, but they'd turned back to their games. Relieved to see a familiar face, she shrugged. "It's just a little…" She waved a hand at the gathering.

Marcus pulled another chair over. "I guess it can be overwhelming. I've never found it that way, but my mother had me at gatherings like this since I was old enough to stand on my own, maybe sooner but I don't remember back that far."

Trina laughed with him, imagining a small, black-haired boy with little ringlets bouncing whenever he moved. "I've never been at a gather like this. It's very strange."

"You know, we've all been wondering about you. From what Aaron got from Katie, your mother kept you pretty isolated. You've been the subject of a lot of gossip, hiding out the way you did." He smiled, then puffed up his chest and tucked in his chin, looking a lot like the polit statues in squares on Ceric. "I've become a bit of a celebrity. I'm the only one who'd seen you before now. Well, of the younger generation at least."

Trina laughed again, feeling tension drain out of her. "I wouldn't have considered you a kid at all, Marcus. When we first met, I thought you were all grown up."

He tipped his head in a mock bow. "Thank you for that, but only someone as tiny as you are would think so. I know my height's hiding in here somewhere." He thumped his chest. "But who knows when I'll be able to look my friends in the eye without standing on a stool."

He looked so glum that Trina reached out a hand to gently brush his cheek. Before she could touch him, he straightened his shoulders and shot her a cocky grin.

"Maybe my height…or lack of it…serves a purpose after all. I only noticed you over here in the shadows because I couldn't see over Phillip's back." He shrugged. "You're much more interesting than watching them play the same old card games. It's going to be a long voyage."

Trina nodded but didn't really agree. She liked talking with Marcus. He reminded her of Piper, not in looks or even build, but they shared an attitude. The way he didn't let things like his height depress him strengthened her impression. She'd be glad to spend the journey with him.

Before the silence between them had a chance to get uncomfortable, Marcus launched into a funny story about his childhood. Trina carefully filed away details. Even though she was a colonist now, she still needed to know, and understand, how polits and laborers lived. She could leave her shafter background behind her, but she needed something to fill the void of fifteen years before the ship.

A commotion drew her attention to the common area entrance. Five spacers stood there, some in security green.

"They've been coming to the evening gathers for a while now."

Trina glanced at Marcus, having forgotten he was there.

He raised a hand as though to brush hers, but let it fall. "You don't have to be worried. They won't bother you. They only talk to people who approach them."

Trina rose, the need to talk to them replacing her fear of discovery. Spacers. Grandfather had mentioned the spacer visits, but she'd never been there to see them.

Marcus laughed as he rose as well. "Come on. I'll introduce you. Most colonists don't care. Figures the one to share my interest has kept herself hidden."

Another shock came when the nearest woman turned to greet them and Trina recognized her. From the spacer's grimace, the shock was mutual.

"I was hoping I'd see you here one of these times," the woman said in contrast to her initial expression. "I'm Susan. I was your guide on the very first day."

Trina nodded, giving no sign that she'd already known. Why would security be looking for her? Marcus had said this was routine, but had she been discovered.

The spacer thrust a hand through her hair and sighed. "Way too late, I know, but I wanted to apologize."

Marcus shot Trina a curious look, but she had no answers for him.

Susan smiled, a rueful tilt of her lips. "You've got a reputation, Trina of Menthak, among the crew. You and your sister both. I should have told you how to access the orientation. I forget how so many of you have little tech beyond the supporting machinery. Not enough to figure this out on your own. And I knew not everyone had been able to attend the preparations, especially in your group. If I recall correctly, you told me as much."

At first, her words made no sense, but then months of sneaking about and ducking crew for fear of capture faded back to their arrival and the furious pilot.

"Yes. Firebugs. That's what the crew calls you," Susan said, clearly reading Trina's expression.

This time Trina laughed, and if relief colored her humor, the others had no way to tell. "I dreamed of joining the Spacer Guild once. At least my name has a place among them." And for something no one could hold against her.

Talk turned more general after that, and Trina listened with fascination as one of the pilots explained how they went below the fold of space to turn a journey of lifetimes into two short years. She'd never given the distance much thought before, but considering how long it took to walk from one end of the shafts to another, it had to be much further between stars.

CHAPTER 40

S amuel used the code his contacts had given him in exchange for trade promises. Some of the crew didn't mind aiding him in gaining control of the colony as long as he promised them priority as the colony began trading. These ships had to support themselves somehow, he supposed.

The auditory selections scrolled past, separated out by colony section and cabin. He keyed up the Tasrien ones, his back tensing as he listened to the voices from his console. Someone there had a sophisticated grasp of shifting politics and policies. Once this all settled, he'd have to figure out who. Those kinds of loose ends could be dangerous, though he'd see first if the person was willing to change families before doing anything drastic.

A trickle of a thought crossed his mind, and Samuel laughed. What a pairing that would make. The Tasrien conniver with his own spacerat. Together, they'd keep the whole colony thrumming.

He pushed a button to pause the conversation, angry at himself. He'd promised her freedom, the chance to be nothing but his granddaughter. Her spacerat past had to be buried as deeply as her shafter roots. He missed their small battles and the echoes of Jared in her manner. How he longed to teach her everything he'd taught her father so many years before.

Samuel sighed, resting his palms against his desk. If not for Marcus's mother, he wouldn't know anything. He'd done quite well to introduce the two of them. Deborah couldn't stop talking about the nice polit girl her son had found.

"And he's had so much more confidence since meeting her. You'd think she didn't notice, well, he's much shorter than the other boys. A little quiet and she hid away for so long one can't help but wonder if something's wrong with her. Marcus likes her though and that's all I care about. They've been meeting practically every night. Any other boy and I'd wonder what they were up to. I'd be scandalized, but Marcus?"

He couldn't remember much more than that. She'd gone on for over an hour on the topic. She had a kind heart and helped in so many ways but her main fault was her love of hearing herself talk. Sometimes, he wondered how Marcus turned out so well. Every third sentence out of his mother's mouth belittled the boy.

Smiling, Samuel tried to imagine what she'd say if she knew Trina's true background. Shy didn't quite describe the quick wit and interesting abilities his granddaughter had cultivated. His smile vanished. No, he didn't really want to see her stunned look or the rejection from the other colonists.

As much as he missed her, Trina deserved to become a colonist like any other. He'd reveal their relationship later. For now, he'd stand back and watch both of them from a distance. He hadn't found the right moment to invite Katie to meet him. The activities of Tasrien kept him so busy that he couldn't spare the concentration necessary, but surely she no longer saw the need to deny him.

With a grimace, he keyed the audio back on, listening intently not just for words but also nuances. If only he could learn something critical, something he could use to tip the balance. So far the information, while invaluable, had failed to put Menthak at the head of the colony any more than Trina's confusion had.

His strongest weapon lay heavy in the back of his thoughts, but he refused to consider it just yet. There had to be another way.

The tension never lightened as he listened to conversation after conversation. His mind worked furiously to find ways around, through, and above the Tasrien tangles. He wanted to keep Trina free. He wanted Menthak to conquer and control. Never before in his life had his desires pulled him so strongly in different directions, and in the darkest moments, he feared he'd fail at both.

CHAPTER 41

T he common area rang with music, but Trina stood with her back to the dance floor. "What happened then?"

"Repairs," the pilot said with a laugh. "That's what always follows fun adventures."

Marcus shared her grin, their fascination with the spacers cementing the friendship over the last two months. According to him, the spacers came more frequently now, at least two at gathers several times a week, a fact Katie found just as appealing as Trina's gravitation toward them.

Thought of her sister made Trina glance across the room only to find Katie staring back. "I'd better go."

The pilot nodded toward the dancing couples. "You both should. I'd be out there if I wouldn't put the rest of the dancers at risk."

Marcus turned from the pilot to offer his raised hand to Trina instead, sweeping her into the mass of spinning couples. Terror turned to laughter as he proved a solid leader while she adapted to the steps much faster than she would have thought possible.

It took a bit longer than Trina had expected to get to her sister's side, but when the song ended, Marcus stepped back and grinned. "I'll go find us something to drink. See you over there." He nodded toward where Katie stood with Aaron.

Trina waited until he'd left for the drink bar, special gathers one of the few times the allocations didn't apply, then crossed to join her twin. "Have you got enough of that juice left to share?" Watching Katie take a long swallow of chilled fruit juice made Trina aware of how parched the dancing had made her.

"Why doesn't Marcus get you some?" Katie glanced around as though looking for him, but gave Trina the drink anyway.

"Oh, he is. I can't wait that long." She handed back the empty cup. "I'll share mine."

Aaron took the cup before Katie could and shook his own. "I'll get us both some more. We should take advantage of the extra when we have the chance."

Katie met his gaze for a moment before ducking her head. "Thanks. I would like another before we dance."

"You really like him, don't you?" Trina asked when her sister continued to stare after him.

Katie's expression when she turned was uncomfortably private. "I more than like him. I want to spend the rest of my life with him."

Trina frowned for all she tried to hide her worries. "Is that wise?"

When she'd expected an argument, instead Katie laughed. "We're going to be part of the colony. Did you think we'd hang on the outskirts and pretend? What about you and Marcus?"

Trina dismissed the idea with a wave of her hand. "We're just friends. He helps me adapt and never asks the difficult questions. Sometimes I wonder what he knows. Marcus has such stories. You'd be amazed at the speed gossip travels through the polits and colonists. Even the spacers."

"You spent too much time with them."

The low-voiced comment startled Trina. "What do you mean?"

"You come to the gathers but spend half of them over by the crew. You are committed to the colony, aren't you? The spacers don't want us. We're not in their guild. They just come out of courtesy."

As much as Trina wanted to protest, she heard the underlying fear. "Yes. I'm committed to the colony. As you said, there isn't any option. Besides, we're sisters. We stick together."

If anything, the assertion Trina had meant as a reassurance made Katie uncomfortable. "Yes, of course we stick together. But we're not alone anymore. We have a huge family, or at least we will once we reveal that much."

"Reveal what?" Marcus appeared at Trina's side with a suddenness that surprised both of them.

Trina laughed. "Now why would we reveal anything to a gossip like you?" She shot a worried glance at Katie though. If her sister truly loved Aaron, would she keep the secret of their past? Trina couldn't guess at Aaron's reaction, but knew from Katie's expression that a rejection would devastate her.

"So I could tell everyone else right quick," Marcus said, his cheeks a little flushed.

As Trina scrambled to bring her mind back to the conversation, Katie said, "I doubt everyone would be interested in the state of our clothing. I'm a fair hand at sewing, but lack the fabric to do anything about it."

"Really? Samuel has my mother running some kind of sewing gather if you're interested. He's providing cloth from his own stores because it's one of the skills we'll need after touchdown. I'm a reasonable hand now, but no one will ever want to wear my mother's work. She'll have to trade her organizational skills if she hopes to look better than a shafter."

Trina grew still at the mention of shafters, but Katie didn't seem at all disturbed. "If they'd like a hand, I'm willing."

The details washed over Trina as she glanced up at Grandfather's balcony. She couldn't see him in the shadows, an odd change in their positions, but she wondered when he would come forward and how awkward it would be for Katie. Even if her sister kept their shafter background hidden, she'd still have lots to explain. The sooner their true connection was revealed, the better.

SAMUEL WATCHED THE DANCE FROM the shadows of his balcony, the gathering area and his cabin both abutting the same section wall. His sharp gaze sought out the flash of bright yellow hair paired with a black as dark as his own. More than anything, he wanted Trina to enjoy this gather, to have this moment to remember.

He relaxed his hands with effort, the muscles aching from being clenched into fists. If only it were as simple as it seemed down there. If only it was enough just to enjoy life.

Turning away, Samuel pushed through the curtain blocking off his bedroom. He'd left the lights dim on purpose, hoping not to draw attention to his balcony, but the contrast seemed telling somehow. Out there, his granddaughter spun in the light, welcomed among, if not her peers, then her friends. She'd fought long and hard both with and against him to earn her place among them.

"I'm the one hiding in shadows now. I'm the one casting darkness over her light."

His words sounded hollow in the darkened room. Samuel pushed a button, raising the lights to simulate daytime. Even as the artificial glow chased away the shadows, it revealed just how empty his life had become. In his mind's eye, he imagined his granddaughters' room. If nothing else, at least it now displayed the painting of their mother. He'd carefully packed his paintings away, thinking somehow to preserve them better over the trip. Like the secret of his grandchildren, he'd thought they'd keep until touchdown, and he couldn't chance someone remarking on the resemblance between the young colonist and the painting of his older son before he was ready.

Though fanciful handicrafts decorated his walls, he missed the gentle gaze of his beloved wife. He wished somehow she could speak with him, could guide him in this. Samuel lowered himself to the bed, feeling old beyond his years. More than anything, he wished he'd never decided to take this step. Somehow, opportunity, challenge, even fun, seemed to pale next to security and safety, despite the knowledge that it wouldn't have lasted past his generation.

He leaned back, and the letter he'd received crinkled under him. Samuel didn't have to read it. Each word was emblazoned on his mind. Tasrien offered a compromise. Not just with him, but with everyone. That family now sought the balance he'd told Trina was his own purpose. If he accepted, Tasrien would be a hero and everyone would look to them for guidance. If he refused...

Only one way remained to ensure Menthak lead the colony, the way he'd hoped to bury deep in their new land.

Samuel would have happily died the only one aware of what he'd purchased. Polits banned shafter medical testing years ago, but some of the results remained available for a price.

With Trina's help, Menthak had a chance. Without her, his family would become nothing, but even if Jared's daughter would agree, pulling Trina into this would destroy whatever trust he'd earned. Samuel wondered if knowing Katie would've made this easier or harder.

Unable to stay still, he pushed to his feet and strode out of the room, leaving its brilliance to flood the corridor. He headed for his study, the one place where he used to feel in control. The pulsing red light, indicating another batch of recordings that would change nothing, glared at him as if asking why he hesitated.

Would the original Samuel have stayed his hand even for a moment? Everything was in place. Even if something went wrong, Paul stayed safe in cold storage. He'd automatically lead the colony as the highest-level polit remaining. His son's lack of skill wouldn't be important in those circumstances. The people needed someone in charge, and with his pack of friends, Paul had proved he could command loyalty at least. That would have to suffice until he gathered skilled advisors around him. No matter what happened, Menthak would succeed.

"That's all that matters." The words echoed hollowly in the room, lacking the conviction he'd once felt. He threw Tasrien's letter at the blinking light, but it fell before reaching the target. The open balcony doors brought music to echo through his home, reminding him of the happiness below. Happiness this decision might bring to an end.

Tomorrow. Tomorrow was soon enough to lose her.

CHAPTER 42

T he door chimed, and Trina smiled when she didn't even tense. Katie went to answer it, leaving Trina to sip her tea. Though both Aaron and Marcus had come to pick them up for various events, neither had been inside. Trina tried to see their small quarters through her friend's eyes but couldn't imagine Marcus's reaction. Part of her couldn't forget his comment about shafters. Would he recognize the style of their blankets?

"It's Marcus."

Trina pushed her tea away and started to stand before she realized Katie had let him in. Didn't her sister realize the risk? A familiar panic crept over her as Marcus looked around the room.

"Nice blanket work, Katie. You'll be cheered at mother's sewing group if any of it is yours."

Trina stood mute as Katie nodded.

"I've done quite a few, but most were my mother's."

He leaned over to touch the picture frame but Trina waved him off. Instead, he just looked at the painting. "Your mother? Katie, you look just like her."

"And I don't resemble her at all, I know. I take after my father." Even as she said the words, she wondered how true they were. Her mother said she did, and Grandfather had as well, but she'd never seen a picture. Did she resemble him enough for those who knew him to recognize her?

"It's sad that you lost both your parents so young. Did they die to-gether?"

Trina saw her sister's face close up even as she scrambled to think of an answer. "We don't talk about it." Her tone held more bite than intended, and she smiled an apology.

"I'm sorry. I didn't mean anything."

She watched his throat move up and down in a swallow.

"Anyway, that wasn't why I came." Marcus smiled. "Samuel asked for you to come see him."

Tension raced through her even though she'd expected this request. Trina relaxed her fisted hands and took a slow breath. She'd avoided Grandfather long enough. He'd given her two months to learn to be a colonist and convince her sister.

"What's he like, Marcus?"

Katie's question startled them both, but for different reasons. He probably wondered why Katie cared while Trina saw it as a sign her efforts had worked. It wasn't like Grandfather could kidnap them away from Mother as Katie had originally feared. Fate had done that for him.

She only half listened as Marcus told a story about their grandfather, completely unaware of the undertones. As usual, he told a tale where events went against planning. Trina laughed with the two of them but the message in how Samuel had brought everything under control by sheer force of will bothered her.

"Shouldn't we be going?" she interrupted. "Katie, you will come, won't you?"

Before Katie could answer, Marcus turned to Trina. "He only asked for you."

Trina didn't miss the disappointment on her sister's face as Katie sat down.

"Who knows? He might be working on some plan with my mother. She can no more keep a secret than she can sew a line. She's decided we make a good pair. If you're one of Samuel's favorites, I wouldn't put it past him to encourage the match."

The rush of heat to her face surprised Trina, but she didn't want to explain the truth. If Grandfather hadn't announced their blood ties yet, she wouldn't either. Maybe he wanted to meet Katie first. After all, he was a polit and they, all but for some blood, were born and raised in the underside of First City. But then why not ask for her sister?

"He hasn't said anything to me," she said, pushing her doubts aside.

"Well, whatever he's planning, will you tell me when you're done? Maybe I can help." His smile made the color in her cheeks deepen for all she saw him as a friend.

"If it's something you can help with, of course I'll ask you." If Grandfather did want to see Katie, she'd be free from the last piece separating her from the colonists. With their relationship no longer hidden and no other ties to shafters, maybe she could leave behind her fears and learn to enjoy her new life. Why had she fought the meeting for so long?

"If he's waiting, maybe we should go." She took Marcus's arm and practically pulled him out the door, eager to have the last barrier gone.

"With all your energy, it's hard to remember we danced so late last night," Marcus teased as they went to the lift.

"You don't have a hint of exhaustion on your face and you stayed as late or later. All that activity made for a good night's rest."

"It did at that."

The lift whooshed to Level A and they stepped free in silence.

Marcus laughed. "I was going to say I hope to see you around the commons but if I remember correctly that was how we first met and you never came. Instead, I'll call for you after dinner."

"I'll be there." Trina smiled as she returned his wave, remembering the first time as well while she watched his retreating back.

SAMUEL'S HANDS TREMBLED AS HE pushed the lockbox just a little further from him, wishing he could as easily divorce himself from what he'd set in motion. In his mind's eye, the statue still glared at him.

"Why haven't you taken over this paltry group? You think they're hard? Just imagine what I had to go through. You walked on this ship a respected grand polit. You think I didn't hear them whispering horse trader behind their hands? You think I didn't have to take hard measures to bring us to power?"

Samuel gave a bitter laugh. All this time his servants wondered why he spoke to himself and he'd smiled, superior in his knowledge of Trina's presence. They'd been right after all. He wanted to yell at the mere memory of a statue, a voice he'd heard pushing him, questioning him, ever since his father chose to step down.

Had his father felt the same when he played administrator over a dynasty formed by those who came before? Had he wondered if his hands ever created anything or if he'd lost the meaning of the doctrine as his labors only enhanced the work of others?

As much as Samuel tried to divert his gaze, the lockbox pulled him to it until his look and even his fingers touched the plain metal surface. Did he create something now? Could a new dynasty start up from the ashes? A fierce longing for someone to confide in tore through him, but there was no one. He couldn't share this burden or push the decision off on another. If he hadn't been willing to take this step, he would never have purchased the substance in the first place.

Samuel shook his head. If all went well, none of them would be at risk outside of Tasrien. To ensure that, he would send Trina. He knew he could count on her to do the task and do it well. She always did.

"Here she is, Master. Will you be wanting a snack?"

Bettina's cheerful voice raced over his raw nerves. He gripped the desk to still his hands and stretched his mouth into his best effort at a smile. "No, Bettina, thank you. Nothing right now."

"Well, then, I'll leave you to your visit. Have a nice time, dear." Bettina touched Trina's cheek before she whisked away.

"No need to look so worried. Katie asked Marcus about you today." Trina folded into the chair, her frame still flexible despite her change in circumstances. "She's found her place here and we're both ready to share it with you."

In the back of his mind, Samuel recognized the change in her speech, noticing how she used longer sentences and was more open with her thoughts than when she'd been his spacerat. The difference slashed at him, deepening his frown.

Trina laughed. "Though you probably wouldn't appreciate the tale he chose in describing you."

A reluctant smile crossed his face as he imagined the type of story Marcus had told. The colony would look to storytellers like him to keep the past alive and entertaining.

Then he sobered. Samuel spread his fingers out across the desk, wishing he'd called her there to talk about Katie.

Trina continued describing what she and Katie had been doing in a relaxed manner he wished he could ignore. Each word seemed like a knife cutting through his plans and duties, making him regret what he had to do.

As if in response to his wavering, her gaze fell on the box between them, and her words stopped. She reached out to touch it, but he put his hand in the way to prevent her.

"Don't." His sharp tone lashed out and his granddaughter shrank away. "Sorry. I'm so sorry." The deep sadness in his voice didn't help.

"It's not a gift then? I'd hoped for a picture of my father."

"As much as I wish you'd thought rightly, as much as I long to meet your sister and reunite our family, that's not why I've asked you here." He paused to take in a deep breath as he noticed her features tighten and her eyes crinkle up in thought. It wouldn't take her long to recognize his betrayal.

"Grandfather, you said..."

She knew. She'd taken less than a breath to connect his tension with an object he didn't want her to touch. The quickness he loved about her now burned against him as she raised her eyes, pleading for what she'd gained in the two months he'd stayed separate.

"I know what I said." Samuel dropped his gaze to his hands, finding them playing with a slender key, the only thing keeping his weapon hidden. "I said you were done. I said you'd done everything I asked and had repaid any debt you owed." He pushed to his feet and paced over to the bookcase.

"Then?"

He knew in that moment she'd refuse. In two months, his spacerat had vanished. She had ties to their family, to the colony, and even to the spacers he'd seen her talking with. No matter how smart she was, he had to craft a lie that would hold fast long enough to set their fates. He couldn't let her deny him this time. She'd do it for Katie's sake, for Marcus, and all the others in the Menthak family.

He heard her shift in the seat but kept his focus on the books in front of him.

"What is it?"

Even in this she'd changed. The spacerat would have fought the silence before breaking it first. And the concern in her voice threatened to bring tears to his eyes. He blinked, and in that moment the answer came to him.

"Your listening devices just revealed that another of the families has attacked Tasrien, too late to stop them."

She tipped her head, more the Trina he knew. "But they're your worst rival. Isn't that good for you?"

He swallowed hard, asking himself if he truly meant to go this far. One more word and it would be too late to back down.

The moment passed.

"Not this way. They used one of the old viruses. Like what killed your mother, only worse."

Trina rose from her seat. "They wouldn't. Not here where it will spread."

Most of him rejoiced as she took his bait, but a part mourned. It had to be this way. Any sacrifice was worth restoring Menthak to glory. For all that he'd grown to like her, Trina would never leave her past far enough behind to survive being thrust into a subservient role. She'd revert to what she'd been her whole life.

Samuel tapped the box. "I brought a cure as a precaution, but how am I to hold it back now. People are dying."

"You want me to bring it? Why? They don't know me."

He forced a sigh. "And they know me all too well. If you were a beleaguered Tasrien would you accept anything from my hand? They may not have been able to secure proof, but they'd be fools not to guess at our efforts."

Trina nodded, understanding him as she always did when he spoke of political issues. She would've been magnificent at his side if things were different. Now Paul would be his only choice in heir, unless Katie proved willing after their shared grief brought them together. Trina had kept her tasks from her sister. Katie had no reason to suspect.

"Grandfather?"

Samuel dragged his thoughts back to the spacerat in front of him. If she would not deliver the vial willingly, there was no other choice.

"I said I'd go. I can bring this cure to them wearing Farnwark clothes. No one will know it came from you."

He shook his head. "You say what it is and they'll waste time and the solution testing it. I have only one vial. Either it will cure them and stop the spread, or we're all lost. Even Katie." He thought for a moment he'd gone too far, but her expression hardened into what it had been before her glimpse of freedom.

"How then? Do I pour it into the water pipes that line the ducts?"

Again he shook his head, knowing his next words would condemn her. "It's designed to blanket a large area. To stop the infection and its spread."

Her brows lowered. "The cure is airborne?"

"Yes. Just drop the vial somewhere central. Smash it. Otherwise there's no hope."

She reached out and brushed his shoulder, her first voluntary touch. "Don't worry. I can do this. I'll make sure everyone is safe. When it's all over, you can tell them. Tell them the truth, and maybe you'll achieve that balance you've sought out of this."

He couldn't respond, not to the hope that had replaced suspicion in her eyes. Samuel triggered the lock, a hiss of chilled air declaring the box open. He lifted the vial carefully and passed it to her. "Be careful. There isn't much, so if you spill any, the cure might not work." He pulled a Tasrien tunic from a desk drawer. "Go straight there. Don't linger." After being in stasis, he didn't know how long the virus would retain potency. It was designed to die within hours once exposed to the air unless the virus found a host.

She grabbed the clothes, and as she left, Trina called over her shoulder, "I'll make this right. You'll see."

Samuel watched her until she passed the doorframe and vanished. If all went well, one extra Tasrien child would pass unnoticed among the dead. He'd go to Katie with genuine tears in his eyes to report a cleaning robot must have expelled her. Katie might not know everything, but Trina told him her sister had seen the panel tool.

He only had to wait now. The man who'd sold him this virus said it worked fast. He hoped the ship's quarantine worked faster or he wouldn't live to see Menthak take control. "See, Old Samuel? I can be just as driven as you were. Only survival of the family matters."

CHAPTER 43

T rina smiled at the colonists she passed, but inside she cursed this timing. Already the instinct to move in shadows drew her. She regretted leaving her panel tool in its hiding spot, something her grandfather hadn't anticipated in providing her the tunic. Two months and she hadn't walked the duct system for more than half of that, hadn't felt the need to find her hideaway. She'd fought against her shafter instincts and was winning. She'd started making a place for herself as a colonist.

And now her grandfather tore all that away. She understood he didn't have a choice. Even if he ignored Tasrien's suffering, the virus would spread to the whole ship if not stopped. This was why shafters isolated those who survived polit experiments.

No one else could do this. They needed her to be spacerat with fear and adrenaline pumping through her veins.

In the privacy of the lift, she pulled out his vial, staring at the clear liquid contained within. So much rested on so little. If polits had a cure, why couldn't she have learned of it in time to save Mother? Trina wondered if she should listen to her grandfather or if she should bring this to the spacers. Surely they had the ability to make more, but whether the spacers wasted it or just took too long to figure out a way to duplicate the cure, Grandfather had said unless the virus was stopped soon, it would be too late.

The lift halted and she shoved the vial back into the hidden pocket. She needed to get her panel tool and reach a safe place to change. When this was done, though, she'd hand the device to her grandfather. He could find another spacerat.

The door whooshed open to reveal her sister's eager face. She'd forgotten about Katie with all she'd learned.

"Well? What did he want?" Katie pulled Trina to the table, straddling a chair opposite her.

"I don't know what you mean." Colonist or no, she still wanted to keep Katie free of her spacerat activities.

"I finally want to meet him and he didn't ask to see me, did he?"

Trina jerked out of her preoccupation to see her sister's disappointed face. "Katie, it's not that simple. He does want to see you."

"But?"

"Just not yet. He's busy with things."

Katie fixed her with a hard look. "But he wanted to see you." Her glance dropped to the hidden pocket, only then making Trina aware that her hand kept stealing up to touch it. "Things that have you touching your pockets the way you would before meeting Fence."

Trina stared back, unwilling to answer. The truth would lead to other questions about what she'd become. She wanted to declare herself a colonist. Once again, she had no right.

"Don't do it." Katie's voice dropped to a whisper. "Whatever it is, don't do it."

"There's nothing to do. He just wanted to see me. To see how I was doing." Trina tried to brazen it out but could see she'd failed.

"And what's in the pocket? Another piece of our father's life to bind you closer to him?"

Trina jerked, remembering her own assumption upon seeing the box. She hadn't thought of the gifts as binding. When he used something in that way, he'd been upfront, but out of his influence, she could see how he'd played her to get his way. He always got his way. That this time it would help others mattered little against how he'd manipulated her.

Something of her thoughts must have shown on her face because Katie frowned. "If it's nothing important, show me. Show me what you're hiding in your pocket."

Trina pushed up, using anger as a mask. She'd spent so much energy trying to change Katie's mind, but faced with Grandfather's games, Trina didn't want Katie to see him as a hero. Let his act stay hidden just as she had to be.

"I'm tired. I don't want to talk about it anymore. We were up so late dancing, I'm exhausted." She seized the excuse Marcus had given her and curled up under the blanket, one hand pressed against the vial and the other holding the Tasrien tunic close.

Silence filled the room, though she could practically hear Katie fuming. She forced her breath out evenly, mimicking sleep in the hopes her sister would give up and go find Aaron to commiserate with. As though they were back in their underground home, Trina heard the ticking of time melt away. She had to deliver the cure before it was too late for all of them.

The door triggered then closed, the noise almost too soft to hear over her pounding heart. Trina exhaled and reached for the panel tool even as she pushed back the blanket and jerked the tunic over her head. She'd go now or it would be over. Her freedom came at too heavy a cost if she bought it with lives lost to the same type of disease that had killed her mother.

CHAPTER 44

Trina fought the sense of familiarity, of comfort, as the dark tunnel closed around her. She didn't want to be this person anymore. Not even waiting for the panel to close after she pushed the button, Trina set a fast pace. The sooner she did this, the sooner she could return to her new life.

Her footsteps sounded loud against the distant chatter of machinery.

Energy flowed through her, and Trina sped up as this world laid claim to her. A brief thought of Marcus and Aaron whispered through her mind, a reminder of the other world she shared. Would she ever be happy among them? Content she could manage, but happy? Could she lose the thrill and challenge in favor of a lifetime of mundane work? Katie had always claimed Trina loved taking risks, and it seemed she'd been right, at least in part.

Her life on Ceric had its hardships, but she'd never settled for content. Content would have meant she stayed a pickpocket and sustained her family without any luxuries or even Mother's medicine. She wouldn't have chosen that route.

Her mother's image floated before her, not the healthy, happy woman of her childhood but the withered, dying one. Dying because of polits and their experiments. Her fingers crept to the vial where it bumped her with every stride. She didn't slow down as she pulled it out of the pocket again. This could have saved Mother.

In her mind's eye, she saw the Tasrien commons. Children and adults she'd often seen playing, learning, and working instead lay curled in pain, too weak to lift their heads. Grandfather might only care about Menthak, but she had as much connection to the places she'd done his meddling in as to the Menthak commons. No matter what he thought, she did this for everyone.

Trina stopped next to one of the location markers to catch her breath, only then aware of how she'd been running without a thought for who else haunted these spaces. She pulled the vial free, worried the seal had loosened in her haste.

The liquid took on a bright glow that spread when she shifted, as if it had broken free of the stopper and wasted itself in the ducts. She checked, but the seal held.

Trina replaced vial then froze. Small sounds carried from behind her. Glancing up, she realized the marker exposed her much as lit junctions had in the shafts. She slipped out of the light's glow.

The noises didn't stop. They didn't sound like a robot, nor did they sound as if someone snuck through. She could hear footsteps even the poorest thief would have muffled.

Trina considered revealing herself to what must be a crewmember and giving up this responsibility, but nothing had changed. After the delay to escape Katie, there was even less time.

Trina turned away and set off in a quick trot, hoping to hear the sounds disappear off some other route. They didn't. She went faster and the noises behind her sped up as well. Definitely not a robot, nor a crewmember. Who else walked the tunnels?

She felt for her knives, only now realizing she didn't carry even one. She'd lost her edge in just two months of playing colonist. Trina had only wits and wiry strength to aid her, not enough especially when she had to be quick about it.

Speed remained the only choice, and Trina took advantage of her familiarity with the tunnels to lose her pursuer. The running cost her. She could no longer hear who came after, but no one caught up, so she kept going. Tasrien waited.

CHAPTER 45

The final turn reared up in front of Trina faster than she'd expected. She paused and glanced behind her, but if her pursuer still followed, the person had fallen far behind. Trina spun around the corner and triggered the panel tool, forgetting to check for occupants in the rush to hide from the one sharing the ducts.

Bright light cut into the darkness, laying a path for any coming after. At least no one rested in the room she'd chosen. Trina slipped through the opening and triggered it closed again, leaving no clue as to which she'd entered.

The common area seemed quiet as she made her way to the open space, and the few colonists about looked healthy, but Trina knew just how deceptive that could be. Her mother had appeared fine for many years after being infected, much longer than expected for someone taken by the polits.

As Trina glanced around, she realized the space had changed, or rather her perception of it had. Instead of checking the escape routes and such, she saw how it was a mirror image of the Menthak commons, noticed where dances would be held, and understood what the tables along the wall were meant for.

The commons should have been bustling with activity, one event ending or another preparing to begin. She might not see the bodies she'd expected, but she didn't see how this could be normal.

Trina strode to the center point of the room, a benefit of her acquaintance with this space in the past few months. The spacers could not work miracles. If this virus spread, many would die.

She pulled the vial out, only hoping the air system would disperse the cure through the whole section and into every cabin. With all her strength, she threw the cylinder at the floor.

It bounced twice against the metal surface then rolled over to the feet of a man she hadn't noticed, a further sign she'd lost her edge.

"Hey, kid. You dropped this." The man picked up the unbroken vial, meaning to hand it to her.

The stopper fell out, startling him so he jerked and the clear liquid splashed across his arm and down to the floor.

He snagged the stopper before it landed and put it back in, pressing hard to form the seal. "Sorry. I thought I had it. But there's still a little left."

Trina watched him stride toward her, frozen. Should she tell him what it was now that he'd released the cure? What would he do to her?

Her fingers closed around the vial by instinct, gripping tight as the slick surface threatened to make it fall. "Thanks," was all she could manage.

"Are you all right? You don't look so good."

"I'm fine," Trina pushed out between lips gone pale with fear. If she told him, there would be questions, and questions meant an end to any chance of returning to the colony as one of them. Suddenly she wanted that more than anything.

She tucked the vial away, hoping enough had spilled to stop the virus. If not, what little remained wouldn't work anyway.

He gave her an intense look, but nodded. "If you're sure. You might want to go lie down, and if you do show symptoms, get to the doctors quick. Sicknesses race through these ship sections."

The virus must not have spread far as of yet, or he'd have been more insistent. Trina didn't wait for him to change his mind. She wiped the slick hand down her tunic and headed for the nearest door, relief making her lightheaded.

The room was empty, saving her from coming up with another excuse, a task that seemed beyond her panicked mind. She triggered the panel and climbed through, exhausted by the strain she'd been under since entering Grandfather's study. This time it was finally over. No matter what he said, she would never enter the ducts again.

"THERE YOU ARE!"

Trina started at the sight of a shadowy figure striding toward her. She ducked under the blow sure to be coming, rolled into her attacker's legs, and knocked the person to the ground, slamming the side of her hand toward the neck below her.

She missed, whether because of the dark or her sudden recognition, she didn't know, but Trina was grateful as Katie grabbed her hands, yelling, "Stop, stop. It's me."

Trina sank to the ground and pulled free. "Sorry," she muttered, "but what are you doing here? How did you find me?"

Katie rubbed her shoulder where Trina's strike had landed. "I followed you. I knew something was wrong, and so hid to watch you. What is this place?"

"You shouldn't be here. It's dangerous."

Though Trina couldn't see her sister clearly, she could hear the scowl in Katie's voice as her sister said, "No more dangerous for you. Whatever brought you here, it's not worth your life. We have a chance like we always wanted. We can become whatever we fancy. No one's going to know or remember our background. No one unless you prove you haven't moved on. Sneaking around here where you do not belong, doing whatever mysterious things you think fulfill your need for excitement, only risks everything. Is that what you want? Is that what you want for both of us?"

While Katie had been speaking, Trina stood and started back toward their cabin with her sister following. Let her think Trina had given in. One less thing to explain.

"You don't want to give it up even if it means losing everything. You really think your need for adventure will be better served by spending years in a spaceport jail? Have you thought about what will happen to me if they catch you? Do you really think Aaron will be interested in the sister of a thief?"

Katie caught Trina's shoulder and jerked her around when they passed a location marker, the glow offering enough light to reveal both anger and pain in her sister's expression.

Trina laughed, not at her sister but at the realization Katie didn't know where they were going. Her attempt to silently give in had been a total failure

"Oh, laugh. Sure. You don't have anything much to lose, do you? You've made sure of that with keeping separate. People are just starting to get to know you. Is that what caused this? Are you so uncomfortable with sitting in the light? Why, Trina?" The last came out with more than a tinge of desperation.

Trina pulled her sister into a hug, not letting go even when Katie struggled. "Hush. It's all right. We're headed back to the cabin. I'm done with the ducts, I swear. I won't come into them again for anyone."

Katie moved back and this time Trina let her. Their gazes met, Trina's determined and Katie's wary. "Are you sure?"

Trina nodded.

This time Katie laughed as she hugged Trina. "I guess you didn't need my lecture then. How you keep track of where you are in this place I don't know. I was trying to follow you and was sure I'd lost you completely. It's only chance that I saw a light flash down here. I was searching for the light, hoping for some way out, when I found you again."

"I knew I should have tried to block the light. You aren't much of a tracker, Katie. You should leave this sort of thing—" Trina stopped, realizing too late what she was about to say.

Katie touched her cheek. "You mean to those we left behind, right?"

"Right. But we really should get going. It is dangerous. I wasn't lying about that part."

They started walking again, Trina leading the way.

"The biggest danger seems to be getting lost," Katie said after a moment. "I can see why you come here, though. It reminds me of home."

Silence fell between them at that comment, each lost in their thoughts, but a faint hissing intruded, a sound that made Trina shiver with sudden chills. "We have to move. Now."

She grabbed her sister's arm and took off at a run. If they were lucky, the robot would find something to clean. If not, it could move much faster than they could manage in the dark.

For once Katie didn't argue, but Trina could hear her sister's gasping breaths running a counterpoint to her own. Katie had spent her time in quiet tasks even before confined to the ship, and the mad scramble seemed to be wearing her out.

Then Trina's knees gave, and she fell to the tunnel floor, crying out as the hard surface came up to meet her.

Katie's frantic pulling got Trina back on her feet, but the fall seemed to have disoriented her. Trina shook her head in an attempt to clear it, an effort that only made her dizzier. "We have to keep going," she gasped out. "If it catches us, Katie, we'll be chewed up and spat into space. Don't stop. Don't stop for anything."

Together, they began moving again, Katie's arm wrapped around Trina to help her.

Then Katie stumbled.

They fell in a tangle of limbs that neither seemed able to sort out until Trina scrambled away on hands and knees. "What's wrong with you?" She hadn't meant it to sound so accusing, but the robot's hiss added a layer of fear to her words. It sounded closer, coming from every direction as the split in the tunnel before them bounced the sound back and forth.

Katie tried to get to her feet, but Trina had never seen her sister so clumsy. She wanted to berate her sister for spending all her time sitting around drinking tea, for letting herself become so weak, but there wasn't time.

"It's too close. It'll catch us both if we stay together. I know these tunnels. I'll draw it off. Just keep going down the one on the right. I'll come find you." She dragged Katie to her feet and shoved her sister in the direction she'd chosen.

Katie half turned back, but whatever protest her sister meant to make, the play of a red beam coming out of the darkness swallowed it.

"Run, Katie. Don't look back. Just run," Trina yelled, as much to attract the robot's attention as to get her sister moving. In all the time Trina had spent in the ducts, never once had she played so dangerous a game. She only wished her thoughts were clear, not distracted by worry for her sister.

IT TOOK ALL OF TRINA'S courage to stand there listening to the robot approach, but she had to know for sure that it followed her, not Katie. The red light played across the split, and Trina slammed into the side of her tunnel, the effort to start moving again more than she'd expected.

But it worked.

The red light came past the junction toward her and panic blanked out all other thoughts. She spun and reeled down the duct, an endless tunnel with no sign of safety.

The hissing came closer until it bounced from every direction.

Trina's feet slipped on what could only be sweat dripping from her body. She pushed off the floor with both hands and kept going. She wanted to collapse, but if she faltered, the robot would chew Trina up just as it had her tunic so long ago.

Her limbs ached then went numb until they crumpled when she tried to take another step. Her head spun, and if not for the warning sound, she'd have given up.

Trina struggled to her feet, but her legs refused to function, and she fell again. Her pocket clanked against the floor, the odd sound breaking through the cloud that seemed to have taken over her mind. She didn't remember what she had in there until her questing fingers closed around the panel tool.

A red light played in the corner of her eye, and clarity returned in a single, terrified moment.

Trina pressed the button to open a panel, any panel.

Three lowered in response to her motion and Trina didn't wait for the nearest to hit the tunnel floor. She climbed onto the surface and pushed herself through only to fall into something much softer than the floor.

"What the dusty hells!"

A hand brushed her forehead.

"Hey, you're burning up. Quick, Heather, call ahead to the infirmary. Report she came from the duct system."

A blurry face leaned in close.

"Aren't you one of the firebugs?"

Trina squinted at the dark face over a yellow crew suit, but her tongue felt heavy in her mouth, and her eyes drifted closed.

"No, don't sleep yet," the voice commanded along with a rough shake. "What's wrong with you? How long have you been sick?"

"Katie." She forced the name between her lips, suddenly remembering her sister left trapped in the ducts. "Save Katie."

CHAPTER 46

S waying back and forth, Trina dreamed she lay in the crane while it moved across their new land. She looked up and saw only an expanse of yellow. From what they'd talked about in the commons, yellow dirt rarely grew much. Grandfather must have failed after all.

Her gaze tripped over what looked like a pocket flap in the dirt.

A door swished open.

"Lenat, I've got a sick one," a deep voice said, the words rumbling from the chest against her side in clipped, almost shafter tones.

"Put them over on those beds. I'm setting up basic quarantine." This voice sounded softer, the cadence lyrical.

"I'm better now." Trina sat up.

The political officer almost dropped her. A red-suited woman moved closer to help.

"You can't be. Not with how hot you were," the pilot said.

Trina shrugged, unwilling to explain how she was never sick. Whatever happened must have been from running too long in a panic.

"She's a young one, isn't she?" The blue-suited doctor came over to join them. "How'd you end up with her, Nishan?"

"It was like the legends on my planet. She dropped from the sky. A gift from the gods to teach me humility." The spacer gave a deep laugh.

"If your gods gave you gifts like these, it's no wonder you were desperate enough to leave when we came. The colonists are supposed to tend their own sick."

"She came out of the duct system," Nishan said. "Ran right into me. I don't think this is something simple. Just look her over, will you?"

"I'm fine," Trina repeated, annoyed at how they dismissed her statement.

A familiar chime sounded and another voice started talking so rapidly Trina found it hard to keep up.

"It'll have to wait." The doctor waved both spacers over, and Trina followed. She had nowhere else to go.

"The early news on this isn't good. It's racing through the section with the Tasrien group. As far as we can tell, anyone not in an enviro suit is infected. It's 100% communicable, and we don't even know the transmission vectors yet. Only quarantine stopped it."

The woman in red frowned as she stared at a screen covered in symbols Trina couldn't read. "What about the blood work? Did that tell you anything? Any hope of a cure before this becomes fatal?"

The wall chimed again, and a male voice said, "We're on our way."

The doctor shook her head. "I haven't gotten them yet, Heather. Patty's on his way with the samples and the first load of sick to observe. Sorry, Nishan, but you need to get your gift out of here. Whatever she has, it can't be as dangerous as what's coming out of Tasrien."

Nishan closed a hand on Trina's shoulder, but she shook off the hold. "Wait. I have the cure. I delivered it to Tasrien already. I've been in there and I'm not sick. Here." She dug the vial out of her pocket, grateful now that some remained after all.

The doctor took the vial and stared at it, a mix of hope and terror on her face. Before Trina could ask why, the woman in the red suit collapsed.

"Heather! Lenat, help her."

The doctor paled. "Was she sick before? Has she complained of anything?"

Nishan shook her head, the other woman's shoulders braced across her knees. "She was fine. We were returning from a workout."

Lenat glanced at the vial then put it in a pocket. "That's what I was afraid of. You're telling the truth, girl? About being in Tasrien?"

"Yes. I brought the cure."

The doctor crossed to help Nishan lift Heather to a bench. "She's contagious. I don't know why she's better, but we've all been exposed."

"The cure?"

"Not until I know exactly what it is."

Trina shifted from foot to foot, wanting to do something, to help, but she knew nothing about this beyond what she'd already told them.

Lenat strode back to where they'd been and pressed the call button. "Patty, I'm in medical with what I believe is another case. Yes, I know you haven't sent any up yet. This one came from the ducts."

She paused to hear the other voice. "No, I don't know how she got in there. It doesn't matter. What's important is that you lock it down. The girl infected Heather in the time it took them to bring her here. Look, just do your best. We have to find everyone she came in contact with."

"Katie." Trina ran for the door as she realized if she'd made Heather sick then Katie was too.

Nishan caught her again, appearing out of nowhere with a shafter's quiet skill. "Hold it, kid. You're not leaving. Quarantine."

This time when Trina struggled, she couldn't get free. "My sister. She's trapped in the ducts. She won't be able to hide from the robots, and she might be sick like her." Trina pointed at Heather.

"We shut the robots down when you spilled out. You told us about Katie then, but Security would've told us if they'd found her inside. Where would she go?"

Trina stared at Nishan. "She has to be in there. She doesn't know how to get out. She doesn't have this." The panel tool came to her hand with an ease Trina had hoped lost in her time as a colonist.

Nishan grabbed the tool. "Where did you get this?"

"What is it?" Lenat leaned over, but Nishan pulled it away.

"A maintenance tool and access to places no colonist—heck, few crewmembers—are allowed."

Trina forced herself to stand still as the woman knelt to stare into her face.

"Where did you get this?"

Lenat pulled Nishan back. "That doesn't matter now. Where is your sister? You say she doesn't have a way out, but she's not in the ducts. Think, girl, think hard. She has to be somewhere."

Trina shook her head, sure there was no answer, but under the combined strength of their gazes, a faint memory teased her. "I jammed a panel. Back when I thought I was done. When I thought he would take the tool back, I jammed a panel to the ship's wall."

"Ship's Wall? What's that? Some colonist myth?"

The lack of comprehension on Nishan's face frustrated Trina. "The outer edge. The place where the ship meets the sky. Where you can feel the universe through the walls." How could she not understand? "She'll be hiding with the blocks, the boxes. The stuff for building our colony."

"The cargo bays. Stay right here." Nishan crossed to the communication panel and soon she barked out instructions to the security members on the other side.

Trina itched to snatch up the panel tool Nishan had left on a nearby table and run, but how could she? If the doctor was right, she'd made Heather sick. She'd made Katie sick. Trina would have no part in hurting anyone else.

Lenat stepped between Trina and the door. "Here. We'll all need to suit up. Nishan and I are already exposed, but I can't have us infecting more of my staff. I need every one of them if we're to get this under control."

Trina waited until Nishan signaled that security was off to save her sister before climbing into the bulky suit. She couldn't run, not with so much at stake.

CHAPTER 47

T rina thought Nishan would go help the doctor, but instead the political officer came to sit on the padded bench.

"Tell me everything you know about this virus." Her breath clouded the faceplate with each word, then cleared almost instantly. "The smallest detail could prove critical. We're scanning the logs, but there's too many for us to find the culprits in time."

The protest that she knew nothing died as Trina remembered how her grandfather had gotten her to agree. "I don't know who sent it, but my mother had something similar from the polit testing." In short sentences, Trina told Nishan everything she could remember.

"And there was no cure?"

Trina touched the pocket where she'd held the vial. "None that we knew about. Nor had the apothecary who was helping us heard of one."

"Nishan."

The way the doctor's voice lowered an octave made Trina tense, knowing whatever the woman had found in her research could only be bad news.

The political officer rose. "She doesn't know much of use."

Before Nishan could move, Lenat strode over to join them, a sealed container holding the vial between her gloved hands. What Trina could see of the doctor's face looked pinched.

"She knows more than she's telling you." Lenat waved the now empty vial. "This isn't some attempt at a cure. It's the virus. Alive and unchanged. She was the delivery system."

Both crewmembers turned to stare at Trina who shrank back. "It's the cure. I swear. That's what Grandfather said."

Nishan clamped a hand down hard on Trina's arm. "Records say you have no parents besides your missing sister. Falsifying those records is a crime, but nothing in comparison to what your grandfather has done. Tell us everything you know."

Though fear kept her body as frozen as Paul, Trina's mind spun with this new information. Grandfather had planned this all along. Why else put his only son with the laborers if he hadn't needed to keep one of the polit leaders safe? Katie had been right. Nothing changed.

"Tell us," Nishan demanded, giving Trina a shake. "Tell us everything you know about your grandfather and who he might be working for."

They thought her grandfather another shafter snuck aboard as she had been. Nishan thought she wouldn't know who gave the orders, and had Trina been a true shafter, that assumption would have been right. But her sister was the only other shafter on the ship.

"Where's Katie?"

Nishan pressed her helmet against the one shielding Trina. "You don't think to bargain, do you? Your sister's life is in your hands."

A commotion at the door distracted the political officer, but Trina sat still. Grandfather may have planned this, but she had delivered the virus then passed it to the crewwoman, and possibly Katie.

A familiar face, the security officer she'd first met on the platform when they entered the ship and since at gatherings, came over as two others carried someone to a different padded table.

More victims.

"We found your sister," Patty said. "In the cargo bay as you thought. She's very sick though."

Nishan's shoulders relaxed for a moment at hearing the quarantine was complete, but when she turned to stare at Trina, the tension returned. "Don't coddle her. She delivered the vial."

"Her? She's so young. "

The political officer gave a sour laugh. "How young was I when they picked me for the Guild? Besides, she's older than she looks. The life is hard, and it stunts growth. The polits on Ceric called them shafters if I remember correctly."

Trina looked at Nishan in surprise.

"Crew doesn't care what you were, only what you choose to be." Something in the words made the woman pause. "You may have delivered it, but you really thought it was the cure, didn't you?"

Trina could only nod.

"Death would be personal for shafters, like it was with my people. I should have realized."

Patty's gaze narrowed. "Then you can tell us where it came from."

Nishan frowned. "Her grandfather, a family not listed in our databanks."

"Another shafter then? But why would she be listed and him not?"

They seemed to have forgotten Trina, but their comments failed to distract her from the knowledge that her grandfather had used her to infect people just like polits had infected her mother. He couldn't have known she would fight it off either. She wanted no part of his family. He didn't understand what the word meant. Trina slid off the table. "I can bring you to him."

"You can tell me where he is," Patty countered. "You'll be staying right here. Be happy Nishan understands, or you'd be carted off to the brig along with him and everyone else involved."

Trina straightened to her full height, the suit bulky around her. "There is no one else."

Nishan laughed. "No shafter, no matter how clever, could have done this."

"Who said he was a shafter?"

The two of them tangled stares, and Trina slipped into full shafter pose without thinking. Her hands flexed to release knives she no longer carried. The political officer matched her down to the twitch in her fingers.

"What else could he be? No laborer or polit would raise his grand-daughter in the shafts."

"My father was a polit, my mother a shafter. He had no choice. We had no choice until Grandfather offered this."

Nishan's position shifted so slightly that the others might not have noticed, but Trina backed down as well. "And with this offer you would do anything for him."

"I did do anything. I even carried his poisons."

The political officer put one hand on Trina's shoulder, ignoring her flinch. "Unknowing."

Trina's lips twisted into a grimace. "The way of family outside of the shafts. A sacrifice in the name of owning the first settlement."

Before Nishan could respond, Lenat appeared and came between them. "Yes, he used you terribly, but in doing so, he might have saved everyone. Trina, you are the only one to recover."

Trina stared at the doctor as she struggled to find the words. "How many have died?" Her throat tightened around the last, knowing their blood coated her hands.

"Only two colonists so far. Heather and the others are still holding on, including your sister. I don't know how long they'll be able to hold out, and you are the key. I need a sample of your blood. I need to figure out what makes you unique."

Trina glanced at Nishan though she didn't quite understand why until the political officer solemnly nodded. As one shafter to another, though she'd gone by a different name, Nishan was confirming the truth in Lenat's intentions.

"How?" Trina didn't bother with an assent. This was no trick, and if it would help the others, she would do whatever she had to.

"I'll study why your body fights it off, and hope to build a cure from that."

"Give us your grandfather's name first. We'll get him," Patty said.

"I want to go. I deserve to confront him with what he's done. Katie's sick and I was too. He meant for me to die."

Patty reached toward her, but Nishan caught his arm. "Remember what I said. For shafters, death is personal, isn't it?"

Trina lowered her head in agreement, too frustrated to speak.

"I understand. You need to be there, only his death is not yours to take." She waited until she could see the acceptance in Trina's eyes before glancing at the doctor. "Lenat, hurry. For her to have that tool, there are more involved than just this grandfather. Whatever you might think, Trina, he could not have acted alone, nor could he without help from the crew."

Lenat raised a device to Trina's suit, and it formed a seal before jabbing into Trina's arm. "Sorry," the doctor said as the vial in her hand filled up with red fluid.

"Tell us." Patty confronted her as soon as Lenat withdrew.

This time Trina didn't hesitate, not after Nishan understood her needs.

"My grandfather is Samuel. The grand polit of the Menthak family. Though he has many contacts, he has the power to work alone. Who else would have agreed, knowing what he risked? He's determined to win for Menthak, even if it means killing all of us. That has to be the true reason he froze his son."

Both Patty and Nishan looked stunned at the news, and why shouldn't they be. No polit should have a shafter child based on Nishan's understanding, and Patty lacked a shafter's knowledge of how far the wealthy would go to keep that wealth.

Nishan recovered first. "Even I wouldn't have guessed this came from so high, but it makes sense. No other section froze a polit. The difference was enough to flag when you were loaded, but we couldn't see why."

"Now you know. Now we all know."

They exchanged a look full of shafter wisdom while Patty glanced from one to the other, clearly sensing a subtext he could not understand. "Why would a leader do this? There's a whole planet waiting for them and not enough people to work even a fraction of it."

"That's exactly what this is about," Nishan said, her voice sinking lower. "You can't just scatter people across a planet and expect them to survive. It'll take a lot of slow, hard work to make it happen. I've been in most of their meetings and it's all about control. Whoever controls the workers and the colonization plan controls who gets the best land and when. They're not going to start with six separate settlements. They'll start with one and only spread out once they have the first city established."

"So, this is all about being the owner of that first city?" Patty sounded shocked.

"Probably. It's the most important issue for all of them." Nishan waved toward the colony sections. "Remember the names on Ceric. I've travelled there enough to learn that First City knows the other settlements only by number. I can tell you, though, that Sixth City doesn't go by that name within its own limits. Only those who controlled the start of the colony want to remember the order."

"Important enough for this? If it isn't contained, the virus could spread through all the colony sections, especially with this girl and the other loose. How could that solve anything? If they all die, no one's going to win."

Trina could be silent no longer. "If we all die, Menthak wins because of Paul. There are enough laborers frozen to give a start, and they'll have no one to look to except Menthak."

Patty's hands curled into fists, but though he scowled, Trina could tell he didn't understand.

Nishan put a hand on his arm to catch his attention. "Consider how you felt waiting for your first ship placement. That moment when you'd do anything to clear the decks before you just to get the chance. Only Menthak acted on that feeling."

"Not Menthak. One man only."

Nishan glanced at Trina, her gaze filled with an apology, but Patty's features hardened as if he finally understood.

Then his eyes unfocused for a moment and he put a hand to his ear. "We need to get going. The team is assembling at the Level 5B main entrance," he said in response to a message only he'd received. "Meeting crew is easy for those on the top. Who knows how many helped him in this, knowingly or not? We can only hope the quarantine kept your grandfather from learning what we've discovered."

Patty stomped to the door, his thoughts clearly on traitors in the crew, while Nishan followed him.

Trina took the chance to snatch up her panel tool before scrambling after them. She needed the reassurance of its weight in her pocket.

CHAPTER 48

T hey headed for colony section five through crew areas that were all new to Trina. She tried to stay focused but curiosity had her looking at every room they passed, trying to figure out its purpose. She compared the main lift with the ones in the colony sections, finding it much larger.

"It carries cargo too."

She jerked at Patty's words, having become used to her silent companions, Nishan on one side, Patty the other.

"That's why it's so big. I saw you looking."

He smiled down at her, and Trina relaxed a bit but her tension returned as they stepped into the main corridor of Level B and crew in isolation suits surrounded them.

"My security squad." Patty looked like he wanted to say more then shrugged. What was there to say?

Trina had never thought to be working with the enforcers. Just like those on Ceric, they came in a big group, and a noisy one. Their footsteps rang on the flooring, and the air seemed full of small suit noises combining into a larger whole. Trina couldn't make out the swish of her own legs among the rest.

Her heartbeat accelerated when they neared the entrance to the Menthak section. As much as she'd wanted to confront Grandfather, now she wanted to hide. She hadn't thought about how she'd march back among the people she'd just started to befriend with a squad of green-suited security around her.

She put out a hand to stop Patty. "I want to go in alone. Let me talk to him first." Trina waved at the other people. "Without so many."

Patty stared at her for a moment before nodding. "Nishan and I'll come with you, but we'll hold back. You'll have to wear your suit the whole time. You're infected. We don't want the virus to spread to another colony section. These people don't deserve to suffer for what their polit did."

"I know." After all she'd done, she wouldn't compound the problem by breaking quarantine. A wry smile twisted her face. The suit was supposed to protect the person inside from what Patty had said over the comm, not everyone else.

"We'll monitor the conversation, and if anything happens, you are to leave. Understood?"

"Understood." Trina nodded at the confirmation they had the ability to watch anyone, but if they had the numbers to listen in on every conversation, the spacers still wouldn't have been able to put the pieces together in time. Thinking on all her conversations with Grandfather, never once did he hint at what he'd planned. If she hadn't guessed, even lulled by her time as a colonist and the hope they would become a true family, how could the crew have figured it out?

Patty waved the squad forward. The large doors into their commons swished open, each side pulling back into the wall. Trina followed the rest through, finding the open area eerily empty.

She noticed guards in isolation suits standing at the various entrances and wondered if they'd confined everyone to their rooms. At least she'd be spared the strange looks when her new friends recognized her in the suit. There'd be enough questions to answer once this finally ended without them knowing she'd been with the crew.

They went to the largest lift, but only five people could fit at one time. Trina listened without paying attention as Patty divided the forces and they went up.

She half expected to find Marcus waiting for her in the Level A corridor, but like in the common areas, no one else stirred as they moved to Grandfather's cabin.

Trina stopped to take a deep breath when she faced his door. She reached for the button to announce her presence but Patty pulled her back.

"Don't give him more warning than necessary. I'll override the door."

Trina nodded then reached out to stop him. "His servants are loyal. Best you take them back to their cabins."

"If you can bring them out here, we will."

"I'll try. Open the door."

Patty keyed in a command on the palm scanner. Trina tried to see what he pressed, then deliberately turned her face away. She was not that person anymore. Knowing the override for palm scanners was not her business.

The door swished open and Trina stepped through, bumping against a table in the hallway because the suit made her awkward. To delay raising an alarm, she called out. "Bettina? Nancy?" She hadn't thought about how the suit distorted her voice until too late.

She heard rapid steps approaching then Bettina entered the hallway, her hands twisting together. "Trina? Why aren't you in your room?"

Trina could tell the moment the woman saw her. Bettina stopped and stared.

"What are you wearing? Are you all right?" Instead of recoiling or calling out as Trina had expected, Bettina came closer, extending a hesitant hand to touch the suit. "He's been pacing back and forth, and he won't drink his tea. I'd prayed you would come. He needs you." Bettina cast a worried look down the corridor and tugged on Trina's arm.

"I need to get something. It's right outside. Can you help?" Trina cringed inwardly at how quickly the lie slipped out.

Bettina looked confused for a moment, as if her whole focus had been on the master. "They only let me stay when I begged them. Master doesn't want people to know, but he's an old man. This kind of excitement isn't good for him. They made Nancy go home but I convinced them."

Trina nodded, unsure what she should say. It was as if the servant looked to her for validation. She flinched as she realized the trust she'd betray the moment they stepped outside, but Samuel had betrayed them all first. Her voice a little gruff, she pushed Bettina toward the door. "Come on. I need your help."

Bettina moved with her but didn't seem completely aware of her surroundings. Had the virus spread here already? Even as the thought passed through her, Trina realized stress, not illness, caused Bettina's distraction. She was as old if not older than Grandfather. Why had he brought this woman on such a major undertaking? Again, she felt her anger rise.

One step outside and Patty took Bettina's arm. He handed her off to another security officer.

The servant protested, glancing back at Trina as if asking for help, but the guard led her away.

Trina watched them until they disappeared around the corner. Frowning, she went back into Grandfather's cabin.

The hallway seemed empty without Bettina's presence, as if no one lived here. Only Patty's measured steps behind her pierced the silence. Nishan managed to walk silently despite the suit, a feat Trina could not match.

As she paced toward her grandfather's study, Trina wondered if nature and stress had done the job for the crew.

CHAPTER 49

T he chair seemed too confining as Samuel stood over his desk, attention fixed on the console and the information it had revealed. His listening devices had allowed him to monitor Trina's success, or rather lack of it.

The other sections knew only that the spacers had called for lockdown. From Tasrien, few reports were made within his hearing, and those that were showed the spacers more effective in their quarantine than he could have dreamed, or the virus too weakened by the time out of stasis. There had been deaths, a few, but no mention of high-level polit losses.

Samuel stared at the console, at the lights showing each device, and knew he'd failed to achieve anything more momentous than removing the one who knew too much about his efforts and had little enough loyalty when he'd needed it. She claimed to have left that life behind, but her ease in delivering the vial as he'd asked showed she'd never have become a true colonist. He wouldn't have been able to control her once they reached their destination.

As an attempt to deal with her loss, his thoughts failed. "I should have gone myself," Samuel muttered, seeing the mocking stare of a statue in his mind's eye. "I should have been willing to make the sacrifice for Menthak." If he'd died among the Tasrien leaders, no one would have any reason to suspect Menthak. Paul would have been chosen to lead because no other surviving family could be trusted.

Instead, he'd wasted his most effective tools, both Trina and the vial she'd carried. Now he'd have to accept the truce, and in accepting it, he ensured Menthak would be among the clamoring masses, desperate for a chance at something decent after Tasrien laid claim to the best land, the best resources, and the best labor.

A flicker of light drew him out of his morose thoughts, but offered no relief.

Samuel blinked to clear his eyes, but the vision before him remained the same, or rather continued as one after another of his status lights for the listening devices Trina had placed went dark. He'd thought to minimize the damage, that if not success, he at least would not go down in flames.

Those deadening lights spoke a different message.

The only ones remaining who knew of the devices were the crew who'd provided them. If they thought it necessary to clean up any evidence, somehow he'd been found out. They didn't want any proof left to show who'd helped him.

His body froze in a moment of indecision. There had to be something for him to do, some way to make this all come out right.

The console's display faded to a black wall broken only by a few steady status lights as no conversations reached the four devices that were still active.

The stark surface reflected back a withered old man with slumped shoulders.

Movement showed behind him from the doorway, but he couldn't summon the energy to turn. "Just put it on the desk, Bettina. I promise to eat something," he said to quiet her urging. He had no reason left to stay healthy. His options had narrowed down to one—prison because he didn't have the strength of character for death.

"It's not Bettina."

The voice from the grave, distorted and strange, broke through his self-absorption. He turned to see Trina in the doorway, her slim body encased in a bulky suit.

She put one hand on her hip with a rustle of material. "Surprised to see me, Grandfather? You must know by now that I delivered your *cure*. You forgot to consider any gifts my mother passed on from her time in polit hands."

Her tone left no room for hope that she remained ignorant, and words tumbled over each other in his mind as relief mixed with a sickening betrayal swept over him.

Trina didn't wait for a response. "Do you even have a cure? Is that how you planned to survive?" With each word, she stepped forward until only the desktop separated them.

Samuel braced his hands on the surface. "There is no need for a cure. The spacers have confined the virus and soon it will die out on its own, taking only Tasrien. Don't you see? We've succeeded."

Her features tightened behind the shield. "You sent me there with poison. You sent me to kill people. Deliberately. Where is the balance in that?"

The shock of her appearance faded enough for him to remember the status lights, but the accusation in her voice wiped away his exhaustion. Samuel slammed his fists against the desk as he shoved away. "I did what I had to for Menthak. You're not so ignorant as to be blind to my purpose. I did what I did for you, for Katie, for every soul under my protection."

"What you had to?"

Though he'd expected an attack, instead she sank into the chair he'd come to think of as her own.

"Those old women and men, the little children who now suffer, threatened you somehow? You couldn't breathe if they did?"

Samuel laughed, shaking his head at how little she understood. "I wouldn't have been able to breathe any more than you or your precious sister. Do you want her crammed into poor quarters waiting on the Tasrien hand and foot in the hopes they'll allow her some scrap of un-inhabitable land? I wasn't going to let that happen to me...to Menthak."

Faster than he would have thought possible, she was back on her feet and charging at him. "Poor quarters?" she screamed. "What do you know of poor quarters? Katie's afraid of the sky."

Her hands thrust at him, making him stumble in surprise until his back rested against the window.

"She's afraid because of you and your kind. Shafters didn't just come to be. They were driven off the surface by you just as the sick and dying line the halls because of you. I suppose they're just random casualties in this war you've called."

Samuel shook off her hold. "You forget. They are enemies, every last one of them. You mock my war, but if you think they don't know what this is, you're more naïve than I thought."

Her voice dropped to a whisper and he found himself leaning toward her to hear, "You think I don't know my body was supposed to be among them."

He hardened himself against the hitch in her voice. "I couldn't trust you to do what had to be done. I couldn't tell you and still know you'd deliver the vial, Trina. Sacrifices had to be made for Menthak." Samuel's words came out soft, gentle even, and he fought the urge to gather her against his chest with an affection she'd never allowed him.

"Sacrifices. You think they know? You think the children knew today they'd be fighting for their lives? You think my mother gave some sort of twisted consent?"

His hands dropped as he accepted he'd never win her to his cause. "You must know I wasn't responsible for the shafter testing. We put a stop to it once we realized—"

"What? That some of your enhanced shafters might not be happy with where they ended up? Tortured by you then rejected by their own families if they were lucky enough to escape. Do you really think they didn't know they were being used?"

This time he did reach out to catch her arm. "Your upbringing as a shafter is unfortunate. I should have taken you both out of there years ago, but I had to wait to gain your mother's trust. Before I thought it was safe to ask to see you, she stopped coming."

Trina jerked away and glared at him. "She stopped coming because she was dying. Just like those people in Tasrien. You think you can pick people up and move them where you want without consequences, like this is some kind of game. But you can't."

"You're wrong. I can, and have, moved people at will. As have you. Look at where we are now. The crew does my bidding in keeping the virus confined all unknowing."

Her face hardened more than he'd ever seen it even when she'd been pure shafter, unaware of her connections.

"They know. They know because I told them."

It hurt more than he would have expected to hear her admit what she'd done. "All you had to do was keep silent. You could have reaped the rewards along with the rest and no one would have known your hands were as dirty as mine. Why?"

He thought for a moment she'd answer him, but then a bitter laugh escaped her mouth.

"What rewards are those, Grandfather? Do you want to share in what you have offered?"

Confusion swept Samuel at her words until she reached up and undid the clasps on her helmet, a helmet that should have given her away long ago had he only been thinking straight. He couldn't summon the energy to fight her. Maybe he had the strength to die after all.

CHAPTER 50

T rina, no!"

Nishan and Patty burst from the other room, having figured out her plan even though she'd kept it from her words.

They caught her arms, but the moment had passed with their intrusion, and she didn't fight them.

"It's not the way. Let him stand trial for his actions."

Trina turned her hands palm up in surrender and met Patty's stare. "You're right. He's not worth it, and I won't risk any others."

He didn't drop her gaze for a long moment, and Trina wondered if he'd ever trust her again, but he turned away to speak with his team and call them in, releasing her to take hold of Samuel.

Nishan stepped in front of her then, but the political officer's face held understanding not condemnation. "It was the hardest thing to learn when they picked me up. That justice meant not taking things into your own hands."

"He deserves to know what it's like," Trina said, sinking into the chair again and staring at the floor. "You heard him. He doesn't care. Even now with people dying, he doesn't care about what he did."

A gloved hand closed on her shoulder with a grip firm enough to be felt through the suit. "He planned for them to die, Trina. Why should he care?" Nishan didn't seem to expect any response.

"Because you do." Patty provided an answer anyway as he crouched in front of Trina once the rest of the team left with Samuel. "You can't comprehend what he did even though he used you to do it. That's what makes you different. That's what makes you help us instead of working with him to keep the truth hidden."

"Don't you understand?" Trina pushed to her feet, unable to stay still, her body itching with the words her grandfather had said. "He planned for this from the start. He put Paul in cold storage to protect Menthak and risked everyone not frozen. He must have counted on enough of the crew being isolated to keep the ship going. Everyone else, colonist or crew, could die and he'd have counted it a success."

Patty's jaw tensed at the mention of crew deaths, and his hands closed into fists. "Right now I'd be happy to see him pushed out an airlock. I heard everything. He thought you'd be happy, as if he'd handed you some kind of legacy. And maybe he's right. Maybe if you'd been brought up by him, you wouldn't have told us who let the virus loose."

Trina shuddered, coming to a halt between the desk and the window that looked out over the commons. "I never thought to be grateful for my life."

"Sometimes the gods offer a gift that you wished you never unwrapped until you see it fully." Nishan caught Trina's shoulders and turned her around, the political officer leaning across the desk. "Don't worry. He'll be punished as he deserves. It might not be shafter personal, but it'll be harsh. The Guild takes care of its own."

Patty caught Trina's arm to give her a light squeeze in support then stepped away, his expression turning grim. "Now show us everything you know he has so we can find all those involved. The crew might not have known his plans, but there are reasons colonists are kept separate, and rules with consequences of their own when not followed."

Trina looked at the desk where Grandfather had made his plans, and her gaze skated to the drawer that had once held her mother's picture. All their arguments, discussions, and moments seemed tainted now. Even that picture had been nothing but a bribe as Katie had suggested. She should have seen it. She should have known somehow that he would be willing to kill over who made big man on the colony. Fence would have done something like this, and had, but she'd thought the polits better despite all she knew, at least with surface lives. She'd thought him better.

"You're still a colonist. After what you've done to help, no one will hold you responsible for this. You didn't know, and without you, we'd never have caught him."

She glanced up to see Patty focused on her once again, but her attention switched to Nishan, knowing there she'd find more clarity.

The political officer shrugged. "He's right, you know. You couldn't control your grandfather then, and you can't change what he did now. You have to write your own path. Make your own choices."

Trina pulled away from both of them, folding her arms across her chest with her back braced against the window. "You don't understand. I have been running my own life, and look what I've done with it. I made this possible." She twisted to punch her fist into the glass. "If he hadn't had me—"

"He would have found some other way." Nishan spoke with a firm tone that allowed no room for argument. "You said it yourself. He had this all planned down to freezing his heir when all others kept theirs to train for what comes after. Even if you'd refused, he would have made it happen. He could have infected himself and gone into a meeting if it came to that. From his perspective, it would have been worth the sacrifice."

As much as the guilt wanted to hold firm, Trina couldn't help hearing the sense in Nishan's words. She gave a reluctant nod then shoved away from the window to tug open the nearest drawer. "This was his office. Anything he had would be here." The urge to look for more of her father's trinkets swept over her, and she stepped back, as though to give the two officers room, to where her expression remained hidden.

CHAPTER 51

E very place in this room held memories of Samuel, and every memory now twisted in her heart. He had never been her family. She'd been a tool for his ambition and nothing else.

A flicker from the bottom of the room console caught Trina's attention. Three lights held steady, their significance escaping her for a moment until she remembered watching her grandfather test the listening devices.

One flickered and went dark.

The murmured discussion between Nishan and Patty barely broke her concentration as Trina recalled that they'd turned off the robots when security swept the ducts for Katie. They were unlikely to have restored normal functions with all focus on containing and curing the virus.

Two lights remained, but for how long. Nothing was there to hinder the betraying crew in the effort to cover their tracks. By the time she explained the lights and Patty got security mobilized, the devices would be gone, along with all trace of who had given them to her grandfather.

Her hand crept to the pocket where she'd stowed the panel tool. The officers were distracted, and the remaining lights had been the very first to turn on, the first she'd placed. If she hurried, Trina could get to them before the crewmembers did. She had to make sure Patty had what he needed to stop this from ever happening again.

Trina slipped out of the room without either crewmember noticing, or maybe Nishan gave her this chance to rejoin her section as though she'd never been gone. Neither could suspect her true actions. If they had, they'd have tried to stop her, and those who helped her grandfather—helped her—would remain undetected. Who knew what they'd help with next?

No guards remained to block her path as she moved not toward the entrance but into Grandfather's bedroom. The panel tool came out, and before she could change her mind, Trina slipped into the darkness of the ducts.

This time she didn't question her comfort, didn't deny how it felt more like home to her than anywhere else on the ship except maybe the cargo bays. The ship didn't need her to pretend to be a colonist. She had to be a shafter if she wanted to slip in quick and get those devices.

If there wasn't some way to track these back to the crewmembers who had worked with Grandfather, they wouldn't be trying to clear the devices away.

Within seconds, she'd oriented herself on the nearest of the two devices. Like the crewmembers, she had nothing to fear in the tunnels, no cleaning robots to sweep her out into space.

She planted her feet and pushed off into a quick sprint, the thud of her footsteps the only sound in the silence.

Innate caution, or a flash of light she hadn't consciously seen, slowed her pace before Trina reached the last turn. Without that, she would have barreled head first into the huddle of crew that stood a short distance down the last section of duct.

Trina crouched to the floor, the last sounds of her passage faded unnoticed as the three people in the same bulky suits she wore argued and waved scanners along the walls. The suits showed how they knew they'd been discovered, but the scanners proved how foolish Trina had been. Only chance kept her secret so long. The crew could have discovered her work easily if they'd only thought to look.

Her mind fixated on the number of them. She was so small in comparison. The bulky suit hampered her movements, but more, she didn't have a single knife to protect herself. Some shafter she'd turned out to be. So willing to give it all up that, when she needed those skills, she had nothing to offer.

But her thoughts kept turning back to the three crewmembers until Trina stopped castigating herself long enough to listen.

Grandfather couldn't have traded with so many of the crew that the ducts were now full of them. If they were still searching for the other device, they would have split up. For three to be in one space meant they must have collected the other already. If she didn't get this device before them, they'd go free, eager to sell out the ship again for a few rarities.

The realization narrowed her paths to one. The device or nothing.

Trina rocked back on her heels as she struggled for an answer. Any second now, their scanners would pick up the device and everything would end with her having escaped into the ducts at the first opportunity, where she had no business being.

If only they hadn't shut down the ducts. At least then these crewmembers would have moved slower, slow enough for Patty to gather his forces against them.

Instinct made her glance behind into the darkness, though she would have heard something if the robots had been restored to their tasks. Maybe she'd made the situation worse.

When Nishan and Patty realized where she'd gone, they would keep the system down. They knew, no matter how skilled she might be, the cleaning robots posed a danger to anyone in the ducts, even crew.

The knowledge settled into her bones and with it came not more condemnation, but an idea. She'd been so good at mimicking voices to entertain her sister, and Mother before the fevers grew too strong. Could she sound enough like a robot to make a difference?

For the second time in less than an hour, Trina reached for the clasps holding her helmet secure. The only other people in the ducts wore suits like hers, so here she did not risk infecting anyone. The risk lay in whether they'd stayed in contact with the rest of the crew enough to know the robots were still turned off.

Trina had to take the chance.

Her first free breath in longer than she cared to consider offered a hiss too quiet to stretch along the empty space between them, or so she thought until the nearest crewmember froze.

"Did you hear that?"

The others stood up from their crouch and took a step towards her.

If they came toward her, she'd just have to run and hope all three would follow long enough for her to circle back. Hands shaking, Trina sucked in more air through her teeth, the hiss a little louder.

That time the reaction was more marked.

The nearest crewmember jerked and thrust his arm out to block the others. "I heard it that time. Are you sure the ducts are shut down?"

Trina leaned out a little to see the three, but they were focused on each other, not on a darker shadow in a shadowed corner.

"How can I be? If we turn the comms on, we'll show up exactly where we have no business being. Just give me a sec and I'll find the sensor. It's right around here."

Fear leant strength to her hiss that time. If they found the device, she'd have no proof of anything.

The first grabbed the one still on the floor and jerked him up. "There's no time. It's not worth dying over. They don't know about these yet or they wouldn't have turned the ducts back on. We'll come later when we can pick up the aversion signaler. Come on."

Trina clicked her tongue against the roof of her mouth as she remembered the sound when the robot had caught her.

The result was dramatic.

All resistance left the crouching crewmember as he leapt to his feet and tugged at the others to get them into a run.

CHAPTER 52

E xhilaration kept her going, close enough for them to think the robot had their scent but not so close as to be seen. Trina didn't realize how tired she'd become until she stumbled and fell to the ground, swallowing her groan.

Her helmet bounced twice and rolled out of sight back the way she'd come.

Trina struggled to her feet, the hiss more of painful bruises than like that of a robot, but the crewmembers didn't slow down. Soon they'd be too far ahead for her to keep driving them.

She stopped.

Wasn't that what she'd wanted? She could double back now, secure in the knowledge that the robots had not been released. She could get the listening device and have her proof.

Somehow it didn't seem enough, not when she had the crewmembers already. And she worried that she'd removed whatever traces Patty would need when she placed the devices.

Trina passed the section marker before realizing she'd started forward again. The hiss had become automatic.

Patty and Nishan would be looking for her. If not in the ducts, where would they think she'd go to hide?

Her smile distorted the next hiss, but not so much that the thumps of running before her faltered. Though she'd barely noticed it, somewhere in the back of her mind, Trina had read the marker.

Where else would they look for her but in the cargo bay? She'd all but admitted she kept a hideaway there, and likely they'd found Katie near it.

Her tongue started ticking off the steps, driving them harder, faster. She didn't slow when one tripped, forcing the other two to drag him along until he got his feet back under him.

Without these crewmembers willing to trade things that no one from Ceric should have had, Grandfather would have had no use for her. She could have joined the colony from the start, learned to be a colonist. Without them, her grandfather might not have decided to curse the Tasrien as her mother had been cursed.

They deserved to suffer for what they'd done, for the choices they'd made. They deserved to feel the agony of knowing they'd reached the end.

As though to punctuate her thought, first one and then all three crewmembers thudded against the ship's wall just as she had once done. The ducts all met this tunnel straight, no curve to gentle or provide warning.

And they'd made enough noise to send any security looking for her to this space.

Trina pulled in as much air as her small frame could carry and blew it out in as loud a hiss as she could manage. At the same time, her hand swept the panel tool in an arc, her finger firmly pressed on the green button.

CHAPTER 53

Every panel within range of the tool lowered to the tunnel floor. A sharp cry revealed one of the connivers was caught underneath the heavy metal, too distracted by what approached from behind to recognize what was happening fast enough. Cries came from outside the ducts as well, a mix of surprise and anger as they recognized the significance of crew where none should be.

The speed at which Patty's forces organized themselves around this new threat impressed Trina, but even as one after another of the troublemakers was pulled from the ducts, she held back.

She had the panel tool. She was quick and smart. Trina could stay in the ducts until they landed somewhere and slip away before anyone could stop her.

How well did she really know these people? A few conversations at gatherings did not make for a lasting trust, and however much Patty had seemed to accept her innocence, she had delivered the virus. With the crisis over, they might still choose to punish her for her part in this.

Trina slumped to the floor, the light coming in from the open panels creating a longing greater than any she'd felt before. If she ran now, she'd have to abandon Katie. She'd be all alone, a shafter rat forever.

"Come on out, Trina. I know you're in there."

Nishan's voice should have surprised her, but it didn't. The political officer knew the robots hadn't been turned on, and she was enough like a shafter to figure out what had happened from reports of a cleaning robot.

What did surprise Trina was the lack of anger in the woman's voice. It was enough to bring Trina to her feet.

She didn't want to be alone. She didn't want to be always running against that day when she didn't run fast enough.

Her whole body trembled as she realized it meant facing up to what she'd done, but Trina refused to let that stop her.

One deep breath for courage, though, froze her progress even as the sight of a figure climbing into the duct did not.

Trina put up a hand. "Don't come any nearer."

"It's me, Trina. You don't have to be afraid."

Just as she'd feared, Nishan's voice came through clearly, undistorted by the protective suit. "Wait. You don't understand. I'm not wearing my helmet. I lost it."

That stopped the woman. "You tried to infect them?"

Trina flinched at the change in Nishan's tone. "No. They were suited. We were in the ducts. It can't go anywhere. I had to take the helmet off or I couldn't have driven them away from the listening device."

"What device?"

The sharp tone offered no clue to Nishan's mood, but it didn't matter. Trina had decided to face whatever was due her. She explained about the listening devices, why her grandfather had traded for them, that she'd planted them, how she knew his connivers would be in the ducts, and where the last device remained. She kept her sentences short and asked for no pardon with her words. By the time she came to the end, Trina felt drained, as though she'd laid her whole life out before Nishan.

The political officer nodded. "We'll have to collect that one as well so no one else can use it, but I think we'll find more than enough evidence now that we know who was involved. We have you to thank for that."

She stepped forward, but Trina backed away. "It's not safe."

Nishan laughed as she kept moving. "You did more for us than this, though I wish you had waited to tell us your plan." She pulled something from a pocket, the cylindrical form visible in the light from the open panels. "Lenat was able to use your blood to synthesize a blocker. It isn't a cure—not yet at least—but it prevents infection and keeps us from getting worse."

"Us?" Something twisted inside Trina at the realization she'd infected both of the crewmembers who'd tried to help her.

Nishan shrugged. "Like yours, my system proved better able to fight it off. Unlike yours, mine offered no answers. This dose is for you. I didn't realize how tired I'd become until my body stopped having to fight the virus off. I don't know how much good it will do you."

Trina let the officer approach. Though she expected the same sharp pain as when Lenat had taken her blood, this one only sent chills down her arm as the medicine spread through her. "In my blood. If only it could have helped my mother the same way."

The firm hand on her shoulder offered more comfort than Nishan could have imagined. Unlikely as it seemed, she'd made a friend in amongst this disaster.

When Trina followed Nishan out of the ducts, she half expected the security officers to take command of her. Instead, the connivers had already been led away, and only Patty remained.

"You'll take her back to the infirmary? That's where your sister is."

Patty acted like nothing unusual had happened and nothing had changed. Trina followed his lead. "Is she okay? Katie?"

"She's not as quick at recovering as you were, but she's faster than any other. Lenat says she's been helping inoculate the crew and colonists who weren't infected. Lenat's impressed, and it takes a lot to impress our doctor."

Trina glanced at Nishan who nodded her agreement.

The political officer's reassurance counted for more because she came from a similar world. Shafters might slit each other's throats, but they didn't weave lies the way Trina's grandfather had done.

"What about the pilot, Heather? How is she doing?"

Patty grinned down at Trina, relieving that last worry. "She was the first crew to get Lenat's injection, and she's recovering well. Though it doesn't remove the virus, it stops the growth and lets the normal immune functions get to work. Heather might not be back at work like your sister, but she's stable and aware."

"Enough," Nishan broke in. "You've had a long day, and I'm sure seeing your sister, and even Heather, will do more to relieve your fears than all this talk. Besides, Patty, you have your work cut out for you in getting to the bottom of these inappropriate trades. The ship should not run like some backwater colony." She glanced at Trina with the last words, lowering one eyelid in a wink.

Trina stifled a yawn. "I would like to go." She turned to Patty. "If that's all right with you."

The security officer put his hands on Trina's shoulders. "I know it's hard to believe, but you're not to blame for this. You were an easy target at first, sure. Not now. Anyone seeing how hard you've worked to help, how willing you were to trust Lenat to take only blood and not inject you with something, well, we know you didn't want to harm anyone."

He didn't give Trina time to think of an appropriate response. With a quick squeeze to her shoulders, he released her and strode away, his thoughts clearly on the mess her grandfather had left to be untangled.

"Come with me. There's someone who is not so easy to reassure where you're concerned. Seems she's had cause to worry over the years."

CHAPTER 54

They arrived at the infirmary to find it a bustle of energy. So many people moved back and forth that they created a confusing blur of motion. Trina couldn't find her sister in the crowd.

Nishan put a firm hand at her back and gave Trina a shove, enough to get her through the door and into the mass.

"Trina!"

She pivoted in the direction of the call just in time for Katie to slam into her.

"They told me you were okay, and I tried to believe it, but…"

Trina put a finger across her sister's mouth. "Hush. I'm fine. Everything's fine now that you're not sick anymore."

Katie swallowed hard, blinking back the liquid that had gathered in her eyes. "And you're safe? They don't blame you?"

A laugh bubbled up from somewhere as Trina caught hold of Nishan's sleeve before the political officer could head off. "They understand better than I could have imagined. Katie, this is Nishan. She's as close to a shafter as anyone could be."

The look her sister gave Nishan lacked the welcome Trina had hoped for. "A shafter?"

Nishan's expression sobered out of the welcoming smile. "I was like a shafter before the Guild took me in. I've lived that life. I chose this one."

Katie put out her hand in the greeting they'd seen spacers use. "Nice to meet you, Nishan." Her solemn face showed little delight at the news Trina had found another like herself, but Nishan's explanation seemed to have reassured her sister. Katie led them both to a table where Lenat orchestrated the process.

"Make sure everyone infected gets a blue shot. The other is for those who haven't been in contact. We don't know how resilient this thing is, and I don't want it cropping up in another form. At least the symptoms show soon after infection so we've been able to track the spread." Lenat pushed a tray of labeled vials toward a blue-suited man before turning to face them.

"Trina. They found you. You'll need the treatment as well. With your special immune system, the risk of a mutated version cropping up is even higher, especially with what you said about your mother."

Trina touched a gloved hand to her unprotected head. "Nishan gave me one already."

Lenat laughed. "I should have known. Nishan is always one step ahead of everyone…except maybe for you. You gave us all a scare, disappearing like that. We didn't know what to think."

Nishan closed a hand on Trina's shoulder. "I should have known better. She went to catch the rest of the deceivers. Finishing what she'd started when she told us about her grandfather. A shafter's justice."

Katie helped Trina with the suit, and she quickly stepped out of the rest, leaving it in a puddle on the floor. The purposeful stride of one of the workers caught her eye, and she watched him move to a chart on the wall that showed the whole ship. He brushed a section to turn it blue.

"All of this is your doing," Lenat said, coming to stand at Trina's side. "The inoculation, the suppression, none of this would have happened without your information and your blood sample. I doubt I would've come up with something before half the ship, or more, died. If I didn't succumb while treating them."

Trina ducked her head to mumble, "Or none of it would have happened because he wouldn't have been able to deliver it." She'd promised herself to take responsibility, but with each accounting, it seemed harder.

A hand forced her chin up until she was staring into Nishan's bright eyes. "If you had not, he would have found another—or taken it in himself—as we told you. You played a small part, and if it had not been you, Lenat's right that none of this would be here. If not for your shafter side, we'd have no way to stop the virus."

Nishan held her gaze steady until Trina could hide from the truth no longer. She nodded into Nishan's fingers. "You're right. I know you're right. But I can't help feeling responsible still."

The political officer released her with a laugh. "You think you're the only one? How could I have missed the signs? I knew they were fighting for position. I knew accusations had been made."

Lenat stepped forward to add, "And how did I miss a vial of weaponized disease. We have bioscanners to prevent this sort of thing. You are not alone in the responsibility. We all share some measure of it, and just like the rest of us, you've chosen to work on a resolution rather than wallowing in your guilt. Don't start now."

Trina glanced to her sister, knowing she'd find the truth there more than among strangers. If Katie forgave her…

Katie caught Trina's hand and pulled her toward a table full of vials. "Come see what we've been doing while you were off catching those who had a hand in making this happen and who chose not to help. Lenat synthesized something she called an antibody that was in your blood, and mine too if in smaller measure. They have a way to replicate this on a massive scale."

The sheer amount of resources available to the spacers stunned Trina as she looked at a table full of vials like the one Grandfather had given her, with one crucial difference. These really did contain a cure, or at least they started the process.

She couldn't imagine having so much at her fingertips along with the ability to act. If only they'd been able to get her mother to the ship, Lenat would have found a cure.

Then Trina laughed as she realized what her sister had described. "It spreads confusion to slow the virus down." Her smile stripped away as she realized no one else would understand the joke. Her task for Grandfather had been to spread the very disease her replicated blood now sought to eradicate, not to spread confusion as he'd promised.

She glanced around the room, her gaze coming to rest on her sister's face. Katie's mouth had turned up at one side, willing to share in the joke if she only understood it. But that wasn't what caught Trina's attention. Katie's eyes sparkled with delight, her sister stood tall, and clearly, she'd been a real help as Nishan had said. Her sister belonged here. She fit in with the other healers in a way Trina had never fit in anywhere.

"That's Menthak."

Before Trina could consider the full meaning of her realization, an unfamiliar voice speaking a familiar name caught her attention.

Together Trina and Katie looked over to see their section of the ship turned blue as every man, woman, and child had been protected against the plague Grandfather had released on this ship.

In her mind's eye, Trina saw the commons filling up. She saw Aaron and Marcus coming to check on them and finding no one.

"Aaron's okay. They're all okay." Katie grinned at Trina. "I won't really believe it until I'm there too, but it's truly over."

Trina returned her sister's smile, but relief couldn't penetrate her growing depression. She didn't feel a connection to the people who probably swarmed the commons. Even Marcus failed to inspire the need to see him, though she certainly hoped he was safe.

A sense of distance swelled over her. She didn't belong anywhere but in the tunnels back on Ceric. Maybe the spacers would consider that punishment enough. She could go back to Piper and a life she knew. Whatever Patty said, Trina doubted the crew would be so willing to accept a space rat on their ship even if they forgave her actions.

As Trina contemplated her hollow future, the room slowly emptied. The ship on the display glowed blue across its full length and very few vials remained on the tables. Workers stumbled off to rest and no more shifts came to take their place.

Lenat stood up, stretching. "Go on, all of you," she told the remaining crew. "There's nothing left that can't wait until we've had a rest cycle." She yawned as if to emphasize her order, dark smudges under her eyes.

Katie touched Trina's arm, pulling her away from her study of Lenat. "Come on. We need to get back. They'll be worried."

Trina rose, feeling the ache of muscles tired from sitting too long. Her family stood in front of her now. No one else mattered, certainly not the man waiting for judgment.

Glancing over at Lenat, she found herself unsure what to say. "Thank you." The words failed to encompass what this tired woman had done but she could think of nothing else.

Fine lines crinkled around Lenat's eyes as she smiled. "I couldn't have done it without your help. Both of you. It took a lot of strength to come forward, and if you hadn't we'd have had nothing. Remember that."

Trina nodded, missing the frantic energy of trying to catch the others. Endless days to come stretched in front of her, making her feel the exhaustion she'd pushed away during the crisis.

"I'll remember."

Lenat barked a laugh. "If only it were that easy." She turned to face Katie, leaving Trina once more the outsider.

"You have a gift for medicine. We need more like you. Feel welcome back here anytime."

Katie blushed at the praise and stammered a thank you as well. The disease had left harsh lines in her face and her curls hung limp, but deep satisfaction radiated from Katie, an assurance of her place in the universe.

A surge of jealousy spiked Trina at the realization. She stepped toward the door to hide her expression. "We should be going now."

CHAPTER 55

N ot so fast. I wanted to talk to you before you leave."

Trina jerked at the sound of Nishan's voice. She'd thought the political officer had left long ago. Nishan seemed more energetic than any person should be considering the day's events. Though Trina couldn't read anything in the spacer's expression, her body tensed, and she glanced around the room for an escape.

Lenat caught her gaze, and Trina relaxed. "I'll remember," she repeated.

Nishan strode over with a laugh. "Whatever our doctor found to hold you, little hero, I should probably let you go rest. But I really do need to speak to you."

Remembering Nishan's background, almost by instinct, Trina shifted into her shafter pose. "You seeking the hero, or the pawn." She regretted the comment as soon as she heard Katie's gasp behind her, but kept her gaze on Nishan.

"What you're doing now is why I wanted to talk to you."

Nishan paused to take in a breath, and Trina realized why she'd come. "You're going to send me back to Ceric, aren't you? Patty said people would understand, but we both know they won't accept a shafter in their midst, hero or not."

The spacer shook her head. "None of those in the colony groups know what happened. All they know about you and Katie is that you worked tirelessly to help us end this. If you want to go back to your group and the colony, nothing stands in your way." Nishan pulled a stool away from Lenat's worktable, collapsing on it in a casual slump. The woman's hands trembled, revealing her energy a pose much like Trina's.

Trina watched Nishan as she processed what she'd been told. The words should have brought happiness, but they only made her chest ache. She didn't belong with the colony no matter what they didn't know.

"So that's what the crew has decided to do about the shafter in their midst. Push me back among the colonists whose acceptance is just another lie?" She shifted her weight again, her hands opening and closing as if the action would materialize her knives from their hiding places.

"Trina!"

Despite her sister's cry, Trina couldn't back down. She felt bare, exposed, and with nothing but words to protect her. Somehow, she had to convince them to return her to Ceric. She didn't belong in space after all.

Nishan's expression grew serious and she straightened. "Listen to me, Trina. The crew knows the truth—all of it. What you did happened because of ignorance, not intent. We've given up the option of charging you. There's no point. The colonists were told only what they needed to know to explain your absence. The rest would just confuse them."

Trina stared, the words failing to sink in.

"You're safe," Katie said, putting her arms around Trina from behind. "The crew doesn't blame you."

She shrugged out of her sister's touch, keeping her attention focused on Nishan.

The political officer returned her stare. "I know you. Better than any of these others, maybe even better than your sister does. What weapon do you normally carry?" Nishan waved at Trina's twitching hands.

"Knives." The word came out short and tense.

"It's hard to trust in anything but your blades. I still reach for my spinners even though it's been twenty years since I walked the streets. My guess is you paid for your passage with these services. Grandfather or not, you wouldn't be skulking in the ducts if he'd claimed you for family."

Trina nodded, her whole world condensing to Nishan's face. The other woman did know, knew too much for Trina's comfort.

"If you won't believe them"—she waved at Lenat—"then believe me. The crew doesn't count people on their blood or even on their background. What you do counts with the ship. What you did."

Trina stared into Nishan's eyes, searching out the lie. How could blood, how could shafter, not matter? Even without the plague she'd spread, how could they look beyond what scarred her soul so deeply she couldn't appreciate the freedom of being a colonist?

She stared long enough for her eyes to tear from dryness, but the other woman never flinched or looked away. Trina's tension eased, and her lips curved into a smile. An answering expression creased Nishan's face.

"Now that you've accepted you won't be thrown in the brig, what will you do?" The question held an intensity Trina couldn't understand.

"Return to the colony section and wait out the time until touch-down, I suppose."

"Is that what you want?"

Whether sensing trouble coming or just tired of waiting, Katie grabbed her arm, pulling Trina toward the door. "Of course it's what she wants. Have you any idea what we've suffered to get this far? Now that Grandfather's gone, nothing stands in your way." The last she said to Trina.

"Nothing but me." Trina's words hung on the air until Katie dropped her arm with a stricken look. Turning to meet Nishan's eye, Trina continued. "I want to go back to Ceric, to the shafts. Grandfather didn't have to threaten or even ask very hard to get me to throw away all I'd worked for. I knew from the start what he wanted of me, if not how far he would go."

She looked at her sister, silently begging for forgiveness. "The colony is not my place. Even when I started making friends, it wasn't enough. I have to do something."

Katie gave a choked laugh. "There's nothing much to do until touchdown except the training. You always wanted to learn. Once we get there, you'll have enough to keep you busy."

Trina wondered for a moment if her sister spoke truly, but no matter what she pictured, nothing in putting together a colony appealed. Polits owned the parts of the puzzle waiting to be solved. A former shafter like her had no business among those discussions, and after what her grandfather had become, she didn't want to be there either.

Nishan rose and moved to stand in front of her. "If Ceric is what you want, we'll make that happen. Without you, none of us would be here. It's little enough to ask." Nishan raised a hand to still Katie's gasp. "But I've come to make an offer. We're going to be refueling at one of the guild strongholds. There's a training facility there. You've demon-strated more valuable traits in this crisis than most ever do."

A wave of longing passed over Trina so strong she reached out a hand to touch Nishan.

"A guild member can sponsor anyone." Lenat rose from the work-bench where she'd been following the conversation.

Trina looked from Nishan to Lenat and back again. "And you'd be willing to sponsor me?"

"It would be a crime not to. The Guild needs people like you and me." Nishan grabbed Trina's shoulder. "How do you think these spacers understand the complexities of politics among their passengers or between trading centers? You may not have known how far your grandfather would go, but you won't make that mistake again. The Political Division needs you to sense out these situations and handle them before they explode if possible, or clean them up afterwards if not."

Pure joy ripped through Trina. "I'd get to join the Guild? Katie, the Guild!" She pulled away from Nishan to hug her sister tight.

Some of her excitement drained away as she took in Katie's expression. Though her sister smiled, it trembled weakly on Katie's lips.

"Aren't you happy?"

Katie sighed. "Of course I am. It's just I'd hoped we'd make a place for ourselves on the colony. We'd be together there."

Lenat stepped forward. "I can solve that problem. Katie, I'll sponsor you for the test as well. You don't have to be separated at least through training, and you can always request shared assignments. That is assuming you'll both pass, but I don't think you'll have too much trouble."

Trina grinned. "We'd be together and it'll be much better than the early years of a colony." She grabbed her sister's hands and spun around in a circle.

Nishan let out a bark of laughter. "Just wait until training begins. You may regret having given up something as straightforward as the privations of a new colony."

Though Lenat joined in the laughter, Trina could tell from the look the two spacers shared that there was at least a grain of truth to the comment.

"Thank you, both of you. I think there's little doubt we'll take the tests."

Katie said what Trina wanted to hear.

Lenat put a hand on each of their shoulders, pushing them toward the door. "And as your doctor, I recommend you get back home, reassure your friends, then sleep." A yawn broke through her words. "I'm going to be following my own advice as soon as I can get Nishan to rest as well."

"The test is in two days. We'll send an escort for you. For now, Lenat's right. Rest and spend time with your friends. Giving up everything for the Guild isn't a light decision. You can always change your mind until you're offloaded, but you have to want this." Nishan waved them the rest of the way to the door before turning back to say something to Lenat.

A GREEN-SUITED MAN LED Trina and Katie back to the Menthak commons, his smile making up for his silence.

At the last moment, Trina held back, unsure what she'd find on the other side of the big doors. When she'd come with Patty and Nishan, the space had stood empty, better than the bodies she'd expected in Tasrien, but still disturbing. Now, the commons would be filled with curious people. She could imagine the low rumble from many voices all talking at once, and it made her want to run back to the cargo bay.

"Open it."

Katie's demand destroyed any chance of a delay, and the next thing Trina saw was her sister squeezing through the barest of gaps, too impatient to wait for a return to her life.

Trina hesitated, unsure whether to follow.

The man gave her shoulder a quick squeeze. "They know only what we told them," he reminded. His hand rose in a salute then he turned and headed back the way they'd come.

"Hurry up," Katie called to her from the other side.

She could delay no longer. Trina ran her fingers across the door as she stepped through, drawing strength from the chilled metal.

Loud voices assaulted her ears, and she flinched before realizing the sound was a cheer. Every single Menthak member, old or young, seemed to fill the common area, and all of them looked toward her with smiles on their faces.

Trina wanted nothing more than to be curled up in her crane at the ship's wall.

"Make way, make way."

The sight of Marcus shoving a path through the crowd, Aaron in his wake, broke her paralysis, and Trina grinned.

"I guess you didn't understand when I said I'd come and get you," Marcus said as soon as they were within earshot. "Here you are in the commons all on your own."

It took a second for Trina to connect the comment with his statement so long ago when he left her with Grandfather. Her world had changed, but everyone else's might as well have stood still…at least here in Menthak.

"No need to look that way. I'm teasing. The healers told us where you were when they came round with the infusers. You'll have to tell me how you two were chosen to help out of everyone in the colonies."

Trina kept smiling, but that was a tale she didn't plan to tell anyone. Still, he gave her the perfect opening to mention the tests.

"We're really tired, aren't we, Trina?" Katie said before Trina could reply. "We wanted to see that everyone here was okay, but we need to sleep."

Trina opened her mouth to protest, but Katie's glance begged her not to and a yawn she couldn't quite stifle did the rest. "Can we tell you our story tomorrow? Unlike you, we weren't confined to quarters. We've been working so much it's hard to stay upright."

The teasing faded from Marcus's expression even as Aaron took hold of Katie's arm.

"We'll take you to your quarters," Aaron said. "Tomorrow's soon enough for anyone."

CHAPTER 56

I don't want to leave the colony."

Still muzzy from her exhausted sleep, Trina struggled to understand Katie the next morning. She dropped into the seat across from her sister. "You don't mean that. We've never been ones to stand by when a chance came. If we were, we wouldn't even be here. But we aren't the type who found colonies, either. If shafters made good colony material, polits would drag the tunnels whenever they wanted a ship to go out. It's cheaper than paying laborers."

Katie didn't seem convinced, but Trina wasn't done. "You'll be happier in the Guild. I saw how much you enjoyed working with Lenat. Just imagine. You could do that your whole life."

A slight smile pulled at Katie's lips. "I guess you're right. After all, I couldn't even handle the surface of Ceric for long. Why did I ever think I could manage being part of a new settlement?" She squared her shoulders and stood. "Only let me tell Aaron. Give me some time."

Trina should have recognized Aaron as the problem before this. "Just don't take too long. The test is tomorrow."

As Katie stepped into the cleanser, Trina prepared their breakfast with her mind focused on the future stretching in front of them. Finally, instead of peering through a chain-link fence, she'd be one of those flying from world to world, making new trade agreements and whatever else spacers did. Her sister would grow to love their new life as well. She had to.

CHAPTER 57

T he message Trina had been waiting for came from one of the security officers stationed at the main section entrance the next afternoon. Instead of confidence, though, knowing the test would be today made her unsettled. Katie still hadn't told Aaron despite spending yesterday in the commons with him. Trina wanted to share her excitement with someone and thought Marcus would understand, but Katie had asked her to wait.

"You have to tell him now. Our escort will come for us soon." Trina chose another shirt then put it back. She wanted to look the part of a guild member but all her clothes screamed of Ceric.

"Why? I don't have to tell him unless we pass the test." Katie sat on her bed, watching Trina with no sign of a similar excitement.

"You heard Lenat. She thinks we'll pass, and she should know. After all, she had to take it, too." Trina gave up, just grabbing fresh tunic and pants. It didn't matter what she wore. She only had to pass.

Katie stared at her twisted fingers. "What if I don't pass though? What then? I'll have told Aaron I'm leaving when I'm not and he'll hate me."

Trina sat down in front of her sister, taking Katie's hands in her own. "I believe in you. You're smart and as well read as you can be coming from the Ceric shafts. This test isn't designed to keep people out. It's to find those with the heart to be spacers. Lenat's already seen that in you." She patted Katie's hands then bounced up again, too unsettled to sit.

"What will you do if I don't pass? Will you stay here? Will you stay with the colony?"

Trina pulled the tunic over her head and met a sharp stare. "Of course you'll pass." She said it as much for herself as to convince her sister.

"But if I don't?"

"I'll die if I have to live trapped on a colony. You have to pass. There's no other way." Trina put all her determination into the words and saw her sister's features harden with the same emotion. They'd do this. They would stay together no matter what.

Drawn in by the sadness still shadowing Katie's eyes, Trina hugged her sister. "It'll be okay. We'll be together. That's all that matters. You'll find another Aaron where we're going."

As if in answer to Trina's prediction, the door chime sounded. Jamming her legs into the new pants, Trina went to answer it, leaving Katie still sitting on her bed. Without standing on ceremony, she pushed the green button and stood back as the door opened.

"Well, who is it?"

Katie's voice broke through her stunned silence and Trina waved the trio in.

"We're your sponsors so we thought we'd come for the two of you," Patty said, smiling.

"But you don't have a lot of time." Nishan hovered by the door, clearly expecting them to come right then.

Lenat stepped past Nishan, taking a look around. "Is this your mother?" She pointed at the picture. "She looks like Katie."

Trina forced back the instinct to hide the picture as if revealing something from her past was still dangerous. Her gaze fell on the pen from her father's desk. She'd cleaned it and asked Nishan for some ink. Reaching out, she picked up the pen and tucked it into an outside pocket, putting her hand in on top so it wouldn't get lost.

"Come on now. You wouldn't want to be late."

At Nishan's words, Katie finally stood, and they left the cabin that held their attempt at colony life. When they returned, all this would be behind them. As long as they passed the test.

Trina felt odd walking through the commons flanked by crew as they left for the testing room. Her mind matched it with the last time when she came to condemn her grandfather. She flinched from the stares even as she admired Katie for smiling and waving to her friends.

Trina wondered what they thought of this when no one had mentioned the test.

If only Katie had told Aaron, the colonists could have cheered them on their way. Though most didn't want to join the spacers, the Guild held a mystique even for shafters. And Marcus had been just as interested in what the visiting spacers had to talk about as she'd been.

She relaxed once they stepped outside of the colony section, aided by Nishan's wink. The colors seemed brighter and the air crisper as she marched along, anticipation humming through her veins.

They stopped at a large room full of desks, most of which were occupied.

"Go find an empty seat. This is the first stage but the test monitors will take you through the rest." Patty waved them on.

"Good luck," Lenat and Nishan said before the three turned and walked away.

"Feels like they've abandoned us, doesn't it?" Katie's mouth twisted into a weak smile.

"Yes, it does. But we don't need our hands held. We've always done things on our own." Trina pulled Katie into the room.

THE TEST INCLUDED RESPONSES TO situations, thoughts, random questions, and practically everything she'd ever learned or experienced. Trina felt drained when it was over and saw the same exhaustion mirrored in her sister's expression.

"Your initial results will be tallied in the next few minutes. Final results will take several days. You'll be notified," said the officer who'd watched over their testing. He'd wandered among them, muttering to himself and occasionally adjusting a paper or encouraging one of the test takers.

Whenever his shadow fell on her papers, Trina had flinched, but somehow her father's pen comforted her. Most of the questions didn't have a single answer anyway. Very little tested how to do things. Instead, the questions explored what she would have done. Nishan had told her Ceric never passed anyone, repeating what the pilot said on their first day aboard. Trina wondered if her experience was so different that her answers wouldn't make sense.

A touch on her shoulder jerked Trina out of her thoughts.

"Come with me, please."

She stared around for her sister and found Katie waiting in the group he'd selected. They must have failed so spectacularly that there was no point in evaluating their answers further. Her heart in her throat, she followed another officer, this one a woman, into a second room.

"We've completed the initial screens. Congratulations. All of you are invited to join the Guild. We'll be docking with a space station that contains a guild training facility in a few weeks. You'll start your training there."

Trina stared at the woman, unable to process what she'd said, barely aware of the students around her doing the same.

Katie raised a hand.

The officer nodded.

"The test monitor said it would be days."

"True, and for most, it takes days to determine aptitude. It's more than just what answers you put down. It's how those answers interrelate." She smiled at them. "You eight provided optimum correlations. We do have some profiles we look for as those with the best likelihood of success. For the others, we have to weigh and balance many factors. For you, there's no need. You were meant to serve in the Guild."

Again, Katie raised her hand.

Trina wanted to pull the hand down and tell her sister not to jinx their success, but she did nothing.

"Does this aptitude prove we're worthless for other pursuits?" Katie's voice rang out clearly and all of them, the officer included, turned to stare at her.

Katie's gaze never wavered.

The woman looked uncomfortable at first then smiled.

"Of course not. The same abilities the Guild seeks in you candidates can serve many purposes. For example, a person with a strong healer mentality could do just as well as a station doctor while someone gifted in the political areas could work in colony government. Having guild-preferred skills neither means you're better than those around you nor isolates you from the others."

Katie nodded, her expression satisfied.

"I'd forgotten. You're one of the colonists, aren't you? We don't often have colonists taking the test with us. There's no reason to feel any different from your colonist friends. You just have broader choices."

She said the last as if this choice was obvious, but suddenly Trina didn't feel so sure. She wanted this so much. Had she forced Katie to be here?

"Any more questions?"

The whole room swiveled to look at Katie, who shook her head.

"Good. Here are your standard guild contracts." She waved at a stack of papers in front of her. "These allow you to start training and cover the basics of your commitment to the Guild. You won't be assigned a specific division until you complete your training, but those of you with strong tendencies will take more targeted classes. None of this can begin until you've signed the contract. Feel free to read it over. You should know what you're getting into before you put your signature on that line. Once you've signed, only failure in training can break it."

Katie raised her hand. "We were told we could opt out up to when we start training."

The officer gave Katie a tight look before sighing. "Whatever you were told, once you've made a contract, it's binding. Now, you can wait to sign the contract until we stop at the port, but I wouldn't recommend it. There's a lot of planning and preparation to do. After all, you'll be leaving everything and everyone behind, though I suppose you already did most of that when we left Ceric."

Trina sent Katie a look of her own, urging her sister to get the contract. Finally, she started forward, her hand snagging Katie's arm as she went.

The paper seemed crisp, its texture more complex than she was used to. Trina fingered the pages as she walked over to where some chairs lined the far wall. Ignoring everyone, she scanned through the contract, trying to concentrate but finding it hard. A sense of finding her path fought with her growing concerns about Katie.

At last she abandoned any effort to understand the words before her and just watched her sister. As Katie read, a muscle pulsed in her cheek.

Trina walked over to the officer. "We can return these to you later, right? I think we want to read them closely."

The officer looked from her to Katie and back. "You're the other colonist, aren't you? Read it carefully. The Guild tries to choose well, and we feel each failure in training. Make sure this is the life you, and she, want."

"We want it all right," Trina murmured but even she couldn't keep her voice steady. She nodded to the officer and went to Katie.

"Trina, have you read this?"

"No, and I'm not going to yet. She says we can leave. Let's go over it at home." Trina pulled on Katie's arm again. Becoming a spacer had always been her dream. She'd needed to drag her sister every step of the way.

CHAPTER 58

This time, no security officer stood around waiting for them. Trina led the way with Katie trailing after. Though Trina wanted to wave her contract at every crewmember who passed, and did wave it when they smiled, Katie kept hers tight to her body. They headed into an explosion, and Trina worried they wouldn't make it back to their room.

As they entered the commons, receiving smiles from the security officers, Aaron ran up to meet them.

"What's going on? Not another plague, is it?" He spoke to Katie as though Trina wasn't even there.

Katie shook her head without answering.

Trina bit her tongue to prevent the words from blurting out of her mouth, her grin of moments before forgotten.

"Can you tell me? I've been worried all morning." Aaron took Katie's face between his hands and they shared an intense look.

Trina felt uncomfortable watching it.

She pushed between them, knowing somehow she had to get Katie away. "We're still working on something, Aaron. Katie can tell you all about it when we're done."

"Katie?" He ignored Trina, waiting for her sister's answer.

"We'll come back up in a little while, Aaron. It's not a plague." Where Trina's voice had been sharp, Katie's sounded soft.

Trina felt Aaron's stare boring into her as they walked away. When they turned to enter the lift, he still stood where they'd left him. He raised a hand in farewell then dropped it as though frustrated.

The walk back to their cabin was completed in a thick silence.

Trina could feel tension gathering in her neck and shoulders. When she reached up to trigger the door, she hesitated.

Katie came up behind her and pressed Trina's hand against the scanner. The door swished open, leaving her no choice but to step inside.

Trina crossed the room to stare at their mother's painting. Her hand slipped into the pocket holding her father's pen as if to find an answer, a better answer than what she suspected.

Katie sat down with her shoulders slumped. She ran her fingers along the edge of the table and cleared her throat, but said nothing.

Trina threw herself into the opposite chair, suddenly angry. "What is it? Why are you being this way?" She banged a fist down on the table hard enough to make the painting rattle.

"I'm not going." Katie's words when they came barely disturbed the space between them.

Jumping up, Trina slashed the air with her hands. "Of course you're going. You were all worried about the test and now we passed it better than we could have imagined. You heard the officer. We're perfect for the Guild."

She stopped next to Katie, leaning down to stare into her sister's face. "Don't you realize what this means? Someone wants us. Not for our usefulness, not for our shafter background, but because of who and what we are. Don't you feel it? We've achieved our dream."

Katie pressed her hands flat against the table, avoiding her sister's eyes. "I am wanted by someone. Aaron."

"There'll be other Aarons. You'll never have another chance at the Guild."

Now Katie rose, the chair crashing to the floor in her haste. She advanced on Trina who backed up until the replicator pressed against her.

"You think Aaron doesn't matter, especially when compared to your fancy guild. You're wrong. I've tried to imagine a life without him and it's empty."

Trina stared at her again, this time in shock. "But what about our dreams?"

Katie threw her hands into the air before pacing away. "Our dreams? Our dreams? Since when have I dreamed anything? Do you remember why I agree to come in the first place? It was to save our mother at first then the only other choice was to live trapped in a house until shafter rats broke in and enslaved us."

Walking up to her sister, Trina placed a hand on Katie's shoulder. "All the more reason to join the Guild. You only came because of fear. You've been worried about the open spaces. I know you have. If you become a guild member, you'll never have to step under the open sky again."

Katie shrugged away from the touch and sat down, tracing a finger along the table. "I didn't want to come, but I'm a part of this colony now. I have friends, people I don't want to leave behind. I have a purpose. They need my seamstress skills and will need a healer more than the Guild does. They respect me even without Aaron."

"And you don't think you'll get respect in the Guild? Did you see how Lenat looked at you? She sponsored you for the exams. What better sign of respect?" Trina knelt before her sister.

Taking Trina's outstretched hands, Katie shook her head. "That's just it. You're still looking for respect. You're still looking for someone who wants you for yourself. I've found that already."

Trina pulled away and paced to the door. She pressed a fist against the wall. She wanted to run, to get as far from this conversation as possible before it was too late. Instead, she turned back to face her sister. "And what about me? Do you want me to throw all this away?" She pointed at the papers on the table.

Katie shifted in her chair, turning to face her sister. "I tried to fail. I thought if I didn't pass, you wouldn't make me choose. You wouldn't go." Her soothing voice irritated Trina, but Katie wasn't done. "I was wrong to do that. And you're wrong now."

Trina pushed off the door, denying herself escape as she returned to the table. "But we're all we have left. I can't abandon you here among strangers. I have to go. I don't belong here. You adapt wherever you are. I'm not like that. I need this. You'll come to like it in the Guild."

Katie shook her head. "I'm not among strangers. I know these people better than I knew anyone in the shafts. I'm ready to stake my future on them, on Aaron. Don't take that away from me."

Staring at her sister, Trina finally recognized the same determination driving her to accept pulled Katie away. "Is he really worth it?"

Katie smiled. "He's worth it. They all are. While you were so busy working for Grandfather"—she put out a hand to still Trina's flinch—"I was becoming Menthak. They're my family, not like you are, but still my family."

"Then why'd you take the test at all?" The question haunted Trina. "Why pretend?"

Katie sighed, tracing an imaginary line on the table. "I didn't want to disappoint you. You wanted this so much for both of us."

Trina moved around the table to pull her sister into a hug. "I never wanted to force you into something you didn't want. I just wanted us to stay together, a family."

Katie leaned in close and whispered, "We are a family. We'll always be wherever each of us ends up." Pulling away, she stared into Trina's eyes. "And when you can choose your own posts, you'll have to choose a ship that stops at our new colony. I know it'll be a long while, but you'll get to see my children. I plan to have many. And they won't be afraid of the open sky. They'll have a real life, the life you and I were denied."

Trina wanted to protest, to demand her sister follow her in this as well. The confidence radiating from Katie stopped her. What she chose to do now would determine Katie's happiness, and whether her sister would come to hate her.

Sobering, she looked at her sister, seeing again the quiet serenity her sister had earned here. "You are happy with them, aren't you?"

"I am. I'm happy for you, Trina. Never doubt that. But the Guild isn't my dream. It's yours. You'll thrive there where I'd only survive. I'm done with just surviving. I want more from my life."

Trina twisted her mouth into a crooked smile. "Then I guess we should get this over with. After all, you've got an eager, confused, and frustrated man waiting for you up in the commons." Trina reached for her papers and signed them with her father's pen, feeling the connection to him surging through her. It was his blood, his longing, she'd inherited.

Katie picked up the contract. She stared at it for a moment, but regret didn't appear on her face. "As much as I'd like to see it burn, I don't want us getting in trouble with the crew again."

They both laughed, remembering their nickname.

"I can take it back with mine. They'll know when they see it's unsigned."

Katie nodded. "I suppose that's the best way." She brushed a hand over Trina's hair. "I'll miss you."

Trina smiled again. "I'm not gone yet. It'll be a while before we reach the port." She picked up the two contracts, tapping them against the table to straighten the pages. "Come on. We both have somewhere to be."

CHAPTER 59

The weeks until they reached the station were bittersweet. The twins separated out all their belongings into two piles. The painting of Mother would stay with Katie while Trina kept Father's pen. Trina joined the orientation classes where she prepared for what to expect with the other trainees. She spent much of her spare time working with Nishan and Patty. They asked her for every last detail of her time with Samuel, her grandfather no longer, in an effort to learn from his manipulations of the crew.

Katie spent as much time with Aaron, also preparing, but for a very different life.

The final day came almost as a surprise. Trina woke up as usual only to realize her time had come.

"Get up now, Trina. You don't want them leaving without you."

She opened her eyes to meet a wry smile on her sister's face. "You're going to be okay, aren't you?"

Katie laughed. "I'm a big girl. I've got my own adventures to discover just like you do."

"Not to mention Aaron at your side."

"I'd hoped Marcus—"

Trina sobered. "He was never more than a friend. We may send messages, but his path is different than mine." She laughed. "Though you'd never guess it from his excitement. I think he's almost as thrilled to know a guild member as I am to be one."

"Then I suppose you should get ready so you don't miss the transport. You'll make us all proud."

"I certainly hope so."

A FEW HOURS LATER, WASHED, DRESSED, FED, and completely packed, Trina stood in the waiting area with the other candidates. Across from her, she could see Katie standing with Aaron and Marcus. Nishan, Patty, and Lenat had also come to see the trainees off. They didn't question Katie's decision. Patty made the only comment: the Guild sought those who wanted to be there. Trina had felt her sister's relief along with her own.

The candidates gathered for a last lecture on what was to come, and Trina hadn't been able to say her goodbyes. She was not the only one to leave their cluster as she crossed to her sister.

"Katie." Whatever grand words had been floating in her head vanished. Trina stood dumb until her sister enveloped her in a hug.

"I'll miss you every day, but this is what we're meant to do."

Trina nodded a reply, her vision watery.

When Katie released her, Aaron took her sister close against his side. "I meant to tell you this earlier," he said, "but the chance never came. Katie told me everything. She's all that matters."

A startled glance to Katie revealed that when he meant everything, their shafter background and Samuel had been part of the discussion. Trina looked at how the two of them held each other, at the love in their shared expressions, and a knot of tension in her chest that she hadn't acknowledged loosened. Katie would be all right…and better than if she'd come. Her Aaron was someone special after all.

It wasn't until she stepped sideways to meet Marcus's curious stare that she realized the rest. With Grandfather gone, no one else needed to—or would—know. She hadn't told Marcus, and Paul had never seen Katie. Her sister had truly become just another Menthak.

Marcus shrugged at her continued silence, breaking Trina from her thoughts. "You should consider taking the test next time," she said to cover the moment. "I can talk to Nishan about it for you."

He laughed. "I won't deny I'm jealous. The Guild has always been a bit of a mystery on Ceric, but I have my place here."

"To spread the news everyone wants hidden?"

Marcus ducked his head, and she regretted the tease until he lifted it again to show a wide grin. "Sort of. I've been asked to join the council that will run Menthak now. We've decided a new planet means a new start, and we're not alone. With the plague, everyone has become aware of how much polit machinations almost cost us."

Aaron looked away from Katie long enough to add, "There's even laborers on that council, though we need to forget our past if we're truly going to start anew."

The statement held more significance than Marcus could know, but Trina appreciated the reassurance.

"Candidates, it's time to get into the shuttle. The transfer window won't hold forever."

Katie nudged Trina. "That's your call. Your turn to conquer whole galaxies."

Trina shook her head. "I plan to stop others from doing that." She strode to where she'd left her small bundle, swept it up, then joined the queue for the shuttle.

At the entrance, she turned back to wave to her sister and friends, realizing she wouldn't see Katie for years. Her pride and longing for the Guild deserted her. She wanted to drop the bundle and run back to her sister, keeping them together no matter what.

Before she could act, though, another trainee crossed her vision. His grin provoked hers as excitement surged through Trina. She was joining the Guild. She'd be a spacer. Flashing a glance at her sister, Trina raised a hand to wave one last time, then marched onto the shuttle, her back straight and her cheeks aching from the strength of her grin.

THANK YOU FOR READING

I hope you enjoyed *Shafter*, and Trina's struggles with making the right choices and finding her place in the universe.

I love to hear about your experiences with my characters, so drop me a line in email to:

* author@margaretmcgaffeyfisk.com

or use the contact form on:

* margaretmcgaffeyfisk.com

And while you're there, if you sign up for my monthly newsletter, I'll share a bit of my writing and publishing journey, fun events, and even snippets or pre-publication stories as a thank you for letting me into your inbox. You can also choose to receive release announcements, which are split into genre and go out only when a new title is available in that genre. Feel free to select as many options as you'd like.

Finally, can I ask a favor? If you're willing, I'd appreciate an honest review of *Shafter*. Your feedback will help Seeds Among the Stars find the right audience. If you choose to review on your website as well as retail and/or reader sites, you can also send me the link with permission to include it on that book's information page, if you're so inclined.

If you'd like to read an excerpt from *Trainee*, please turn the page.

TRAINEE

SEEDS AMONG THE STARS, BOOK II

A shafter has made it to spacer training at last, but will her background help or hinder as she attempts to prove even a backwards colonist has value.

The shuttle docked with a clang of metal against metal. Trina didn't jerk in surprise like some of the candidates. She'd chosen a seat toward the front and could just make out the pilot's screen through a gap in the panel separating the two compartments. Their shuttle had been approaching the station for a while now, weaving among many other shuttles.

She'd been watching the others connect for a short period then pull free and vanish out of view for some time. She knew exactly when their turn had come.

Trina had met the candidates with her in the orientation training on her colony ship, but she wouldn't call them friends. Everyone she had considered such would be continuing on to the colony or other spacer assignments. This shuttle was her last tie to that life.

The gate hissed open, offering a glimpse of a large room on the other side, bigger even than the cargo space where she'd spent so much of her time on the colony ship. The ceiling towered overhead, and she could not see the full width from their position. Opposite them stood an interior wall on which she could see the tops of many openings above the gathered crowd. Some of the doorways seemed sized for people while others were wider by four times or more. This must have been where they transferred all kinds of cargo, not just spacer candidates.

"Candidates, grab your things and get on out," an unfamiliar voice called from beyond, making Trina aware of how she lingered in the entrance. "The shuttle must return to its ship."

The others started talking at once, asking questions as though unwilling to step free, but Trina knew the shuttle had a short time before the next would need this spot. She twisted to pull her bundle free and strode through the open door only to stumble.

One second in the cavernous space, with what seemed like hundreds of voices echoing and pounding at her, cut Trina's confidence. She hadn't thought much about candidates from other ships. Their group of twenty seemed large enough for anyone's purpose.

Yet, who knew how many places had sent candidates? Judging from the sheer numbers, many. Without a high vantage point, she could not make a true estimate, but wherever she looked, layer upon layer of bodies stood between her and the internal doors she'd identified at first look.

"Keep together for now. It'll make things easier," said a woman in the purple suit designating an instructor as she waved them toward one side. "Another shuttle's coming in."

Trina joined the others, the woman's meaning clear without her saying they should move out of the way, but they had no further instructions. Her only relief came in seeing how none of the candidates from her colony ship seemed to know what they should be doing.

They kept walking along the outer wall, passing more shuttle hatches and stacks of cargo boxes. There never seemed to be a good place to stop.

Finally, they came to a disorganized halt when the room ended in a wall.

She moved through her group until she could brace against the metal curve. This wall stood too far from the engine to feel its beat, or so she thought until Trina remembered she lived on a station now. If it even had an engine, she doubted it would be of the same type or set off the same resonance.

Her shoulders hunched, but she forced them straight, unwilling to make her discomfort visible to any observer. Instead, she distracted herself by observing the others.

Not since coming onto the colony ship had she been in a space with so many strangers. She scanned those nearest, using an unfocused gaze so as not to draw attention.

The candidates came in many guises, skin tone ranging from pale white to a deep bluish tinge nothing like her spacer friend Nishan's dark color. Clothing resembled what she'd seen among the candidates from her ship except where it didn't, some standing out as much as her own Ceric clothes did. Hair had as many variants in colors, styles, and lengths.

The variety dizzied her at first. Trina wondered how she would figure out enough to blend in. How could this society work with so many differences?

The urge to run back to the shuttle, to the safety of a ship she knew, threatened to overwhelm her, but that shuttle had already undocked. She'd find no comfort in sneaking aboard any of those now connected to the station.

Trina sucked in a slow breath and narrowed her focus to just those gathered nearest to them.

Little variation existed in that group. All twenty-three wore uniformly tan-colored clothing that lay close to their bodies, and whether male or female, their hair hung down in dark, black sheets. Every one of them stood out in contrast to her, thanks as much to their clothes and hair as to having deep blue skin.

The next had fewer candidates than either hers or the blue-skinned ones, but these matched in both dress and overall look to those they stood beside.

She shifted to see another further into the room. This one had a greater variety than the first or second, but in comparison to the room as a whole, they still had more in common than not.

Her vision blurred then, calling up festival days on Ceric. There she'd seen the same mix of similar but not the same between laborers and polits. Even shafters wore colors and styles on par with the other classes, those shafters whose clothing wasn't stolen from polit rooftops in the first place.

With this realization, Trina could see how each collection must have held candidates from a specific ship. Every once in a while, there'd be someone like her who matched none of the others, but her group had clearly not been the only one told to stay together.

The room started to filter in her perception, becoming something like her sister's patchwork blankets. Each group made up a different fabric, but a fabric all the same. One composed of candidates.

Relief washed over her.

With so many candidates and so many differences, her own oddities would stand out less. She didn't have to understand everything about this society because no one would. No one would question her background. No one would even know she came from a colony planet and not a ship like the rest, though some of these others could be from planets as much as she was. Nishan had even come from something not so different from a shafter's life.

A disturbance rippled through the candidates, raised voices bouncing off the ceiling to travel to their corner as a jumbled mess.

Trina caught sight of purple-suited instructors moving through each section. They extracted one or two candidates at a time, who left to trail after the spacers.

"They're splitting us up."

Two others hushed the boy who spoke, but from the pinched look on the faces around her, Trina could see her shipmates all felt a twinge of what she had when the shuttle left.

They'd counted on having each other to lean on. She'd left everyone she could count on behind already.

DELUTH ADJUSTED THE UNCOMFORTABLE STRAPS on his pack. He'd never worn one before. The satchel had come from a random collection, each of The Headway's twenty-seven candidates using something different. Most were abandoned by colonists who'd hitched a ride, not that his ship did too much of that kind of commerce. They were traders.

He shook off the thought.

It didn't matter anymore. He'd chosen the Spacer Guild as they all had. Whatever they were destined to be, the Guild would assign them where they were needed, as they had the spacers who ran The Headway. Orientation hadn't covered methods of assignment, but somehow he doubted assigning candidates to their home ships was high on the list. Every spacer he'd met came from somewhere different.

"Just look at them. Scared little bots all huddled against the walls. You'd think they'd never seen a cargo bay before."

Deluth followed Redel's pointed finger to see some of the candidates had chosen a spot where the skin met the chill of space unlike his shipmates who'd marched to the very center of the room.

"At least they have something to lean on," he said, tugging on his straps. One of the group caught his eye. Smaller than the others, with dirty yellow hair and pale skin, she didn't seem all that impressive. But her very stillness drew him to her, a point of calm in the chaos all around him.

Redel slammed him on the shoulder. "Don't fool yourself. They're not in that place for comfort. Too close to the hatches. No, the instructors probably took one look at them, the tiny one especially, and arranged for them to be sent right back where they came from."

Now Deluth had a different reason to rub his shoulder thanks to his best friend and bunkmate since they left the separate dwellings of their parents at the age of six. "They don't seem all that different to me."

Redel turned to stare at Deluth with a familiar narrowed gaze, one that usually ended with a rough and tumble to wipe away whatever they'd disagreed about. He hoped Redel wouldn't try that here. He didn't want to be the one sent home, and he didn't think Redel would be foolish enough to chance it either.

Before that belief could be tested, one of the instructors came to a halt next to them, his head buried in a screen. He glanced from the screen to each of them before reaching out an arm and snagging Redel. "You're with me. A Pilot."

Deluth waited for the man to call him as well, but instead he faced a purple back as the instructor strode forth, Redel in tow.

"Wait. There must be a mistake. We're supposed to be together." Redel jerked free and moved to stand next to Deluth.

The instructor's expression had a lot in common with Redel's earlier narrowed stare. "Shipmates are divided into separate groups as much as possible. You're here to make new connections and learn how to deal with strangers. Not to hang out with those you've known your whole life. You could be assigned anywhere, with anyone."

Something oddly like relief washed over Deluth. He'd miss his friend, but they'd come here to change who they'd been. If they stayed with the same folks, it would be much more difficult to become something new.

The man waited for Redel to move, his scowl deepening. Then a whistle sounded loud enough to cut through the background murmur, and he shrugged. "We're behind schedule. Your group is too big to split up completely anyway. I suppose you two together is no different than any others of this lot." He poked the screen then waved both of them to follow.

Redel linked arms with Deluth and pulled him along with a big grin. "I knew we should be together. Isn't that right, bunkmate?"

"Right." If his response lacked enthusiasm, it was only because it had been a long trip. He was tired and cranky.

His annoyance faded as he realized the same most likely caused Redel's cutting remarks about the other candidates.

They'd taken the test together, planning all the adventures they'd have once free of the strict rules that made up their ship culture. They'd been excited about meeting new people from other places.

Pointing out those who were different in a sarcastic way didn't match with anything they'd shared before catching the shuttle.

Deluth held onto that thought as the instructor picked seven more candidates, but when they circled the edge, his focus changed to the girl. Would she be part of his group?

No sooner had he considered the possibility than they turned toward one of the station doors.

"Keep up now, and don't get mixed into the others. You're red, after all. Pilots don't get lost."

Redel pushed forward until he walked next to the man. "Does this mean we've been chosen for that section?"

Their instructor laughed. "Don't get any grand ideas, candidates," he said to the lot of them. "The designations are so you can mix and mingle, but will always know where to find your room. You have to complete all your training before you'll be assigned to a division based on your primary aptitude. And you may serve in more than one over the life of your career. This is just the first step. No one would tolerate an untrained rookie pilot. They'd rebel and throw every guild member off the ship first. Too much at stake. And they'd be right about it too."

He hadn't stopped to deliver this speech. With the last word, he stepped into a moving air stream and whisked away, leaving the rest of them to leap on after.

Deluth tilted into the current to speed his movement, as did the rest. A feat of safety engineering kept them from slamming into each other as they adjusted to riding a pressure wave.

He reached their instructor first. "Our room? We're all in the same bunk?"

The man raised an eyebrow as he shook his head. "No, you'll be in the same section, and you'll share eating and gathering areas, but each candidate has a separate room. I don't know what it's like on your ship, but things are designed to maximize your focus here. No staying up too late chatting after the lights go out."

"Our own rooms," Redel said, coming up on his side. "Just like the single adults. But don't worry. I'll take the one right next door so you don't have to be scared all by yourself."

Their instructor shoved them out of the air stream before Deluth had to answer. He fought to stay upright even as the others were pushed out almost on top of him. The man relaxed his grip on a hand-hold Deluth hadn't noticed and joined them.

"You're Pilots, remember. Red's your color. You get lost, find a red strip and follow it to the end. It'll be your rooms...or you'll have to turn around and go the other way."

Deluth scanned the colored strips marking various corridors, but one of the others found their color first. He joined the scramble to reach the section and see what would become their home for the next year at least.

TRINA TRIED NOT TO SHOW how nervous she felt as candidate after candidate was chosen and led away.

The bells chimed two more times, but she had no idea what they signified. She did notice how the instructors increased their pace as they plucked a girl here and a boy there.

A space that had seemed large when filled with students grew even greater with each group departing. She'd seen seven leave already, each numbering between ten and fifteen candidates, and she might have missed some in the crowds. There were many still waiting, but the choices had become slim.

Something caught her attention, and she turned to see a tall, dark-haired instructor staring at her.

He looked her up and down, then nodded as though he now understood something more than as a greeting.

She tensed when he strode toward her, no longer sure she wanted to be chosen, at least not by him.

"You are Trina of Family Menthak. From Ceric, correct?"

She hadn't heard any of the other instructors who'd collected from their group use names.

"Come with me."

He hadn't waited for her response when she'd hesitated, perhaps taking her lack of a protest as consent.

The name, the absence of other students, and something about his manner sent a spike of panic through her. For one horrifying second,

Trina knew it had all been a mistake. She didn't belong. She hadn't passed the test. They'd realized she wouldn't be a good fit after all.

The instructor had set off, assuming she'd follow in his wake. What else could she do? Her steps dragged, but she had no other place to go, and no good would come of finding a tunnel to hide in here.

Trina stopped dead, her indrawn breath loud enough to attract an irritated look from the instructor.

He stopped as well, one eyebrow raised in inquiry.

Nishan had told her what the test did. It wasn't her answers but how she'd answered the questions. The political officer said the Guild needed spacers like her, like Nishan, as well. People who'd grown up in the depths of a colony, who'd experienced the dark underside. There had been no reason to lie. No purpose for it when they had the option of imprisoning her for what she'd done.

"Are you coming?"

She'd used up the instructor's patience, but it didn't matter. Trina squared her shoulders and sped to his side. She wouldn't be here if they didn't think she'd be an asset. They wouldn't have waited until the station.

"Yes, I'm coming."

Instead of collecting other candidates and leaving the area as the rest of the instructors had done, he led her toward a group against the front wall. Other purple suits brought in one candidate at a time as well only to abandon them.

Her instincts twinged, but she forced the worry aside. Whatever the plan, she could survive it. She'd proved often enough she had what it took to come out on the right side in the end, and she'd never been one to shy from hard work.

"That's the last of them," her instructor said as she joined the others. "Good luck to you."

It took only a heartbeat to realize he'd been speaking to someone else. He wasn't to be her teacher after all.

She watched him stride away, a little lost despite her instinctive caution around him.

"Can I have your attention please?"

The man speaking had dark brown skin and stood a head shorter than the one who'd walked away, but he wore the same purple uniform.

She might have been cast aside, but at least it was into the care of another instructor.

"Thank you," he said as the last of their group turned to face him.

Though she appeared to be focused on their latest instructor, Trina scanned the other candidates' expressions in her peripheral vision. They seemed equally wary of this separation.

He coughed, clearly uncomfortable with the role he'd been given.

"It's not often there are so many of you, but we've shuffled some of the instructors to ensure you get the training you need."

Another candidate raised his hand when Trina would have bided her time until the information revealed itself.

"Yes?"

"Why are we here?"

"Ah." He coughed again. "All of you are from places where technological access was not universal."

She kept still, but many of the others nodded their agreement.

"Your orientation scores show you may need remedial training in technology." He held up a hand to stay the many questions brewing among the students. "Your candidacy is not at risk. It's just that you would struggle with some of the training exercises and might not get the full benefit because of your weakness in this area. To ensure there will be no problems, you'll complete a full technology assessment. Many of you will be sent into the standard rotation without any further delay once your skills are confirmed. For the rest, we have special training sessions to bring you up to the level of a standard candidate. We'll be covering the same material, just not in the same way. You'll be released once you've attained the necessary mastery."

Trina's face stayed blank thanks to the practice of keeping her emotions from Fence when trading the polit goods she'd stolen for coin, but inside, she boiled over.

Why had they not performed this assessment, and provided any extra training needed, in the orientation sessions back on the ship? Why not tell her this might happen? Why wait until now?

Once again, she'd been set apart as if they could see her shafter background written across her face. She'd worried about blending in earlier. Now she knew she wouldn't even get the chance.

Whatever questions the others had asked, she heard none of it.

Instincts had warned her, but she'd ignored them in favor of believing the spacer test infallible. No one thought to tell her because they'd never had a shafter among them. That the instructors identified her limitations, weakness as he'd called it, should have been a blessing. But Trina knew all too well how societies worked and how they treated those on the outer edges. She'd have preferred to struggle with the others than come in late but fully prepared.

Read a longer excerpt or purchase a copy of *Trainee* at your local bookstore or preferred online vendor.

ABOUT THE AUTHOR

Margaret McGaffey Fisk is a storyteller who explores tales across genres and worlds. Raised in the Foreign Service where she developed a love for anthropology, she has been a data entry clerk, veterinary tech, editor, support engineer, and programmer, among other roles. She pulls on her studies and experiences to give depth to the cultures and people that form the heart of her stories. As her website is titled, she offers tales to tide you over.

She'd love to hear from you through any of the contact points or social media accounts listed on her website, or you can subscribe to one of her newsletters for release announcements, snippets, and other news:

margaretmcgaffeyfisk.com/subscribe-to-my-newsletter/

Website
MargaretMcGaffeyFisk.com

ACKNOWLEDGEMENTS

Shafter had a long and tangled path on the road to publication, and there were many who assisted in the journey. Thank you to my beta readers, Maripat Sluyter, Valerie Comer, Dawn Hebein, Colin Fisk, Elizabeth McGaffey, and David McGaffey, some of whom went through multiple versions. I'd also like to call out Erin Hartshorn, Ed Greaves, Bonnie Schutzman, and Deirdre McGaffey Schwein for their assistance in making *Shafter* something I can be proud of.

Finally, I thank Dawn Atkins who, as a graduate student, taught the science fiction workshop that brought the very first version of this story into being.

A book has much in common with a child in that it takes a village. There are too many others to mention by name who, through their support or the opportunities their effort brought into being, had an impact on this novel and my writing in general. For all your support in enabling my writing career, I thank you.

And last, but in no way least, I thank my readers. You are what makes the journey worthwhile.

www.ingramcontent.com/pod-product-compliance
Lightning Source LLC
Chambersburg PA
CBHW020912130726
47904CB00006BA/1850